The Fred Weber Story

~

A Flyover County Novel

By

Richard Skorupski

South Dakota -- Social life and Customs

Family Life -- South Dakota

Man-Woman Relationships – South Dakota

Fiction

This book is a work of fiction. Names, characters, places
and incidents are either the author's imagination or used
fictitiously. Any resemblance to actual events, locals or
persons, living or dead, are purely coincidental.

DEDICATION

First to God, from Whom all blessings flow.

Second to my wife, who forgives my foibles and quirks.

Third to my neighbors and friends in South Dakota.

Thank you for adopting us into your community.

Table of Contents

Chapter One 7
Chapter Two 22
Chapter Three 33
Chapter Four 44
Chapter Five 57
Chapter Six 66
Chapter Seven 80
Chapter Eight 93
Chapter Nine 105
Chapter Ten 117
Chapter Eleven 129
Chapter Twelve 141
Chapter Thirteen 155
Chapter Fourteen 167
Chapter Fifteen 180
Chapter Sixteen 193
Chapter Seventeen 205
Chapter Eighteen 218
Chapter Nineteen 230
Chapter Twenty 244
Chapter Twenty One 255
Chapter Twenty Two 268
Chapter Twenty Three 281
Chapter Twenty Four 294
Chapter Twenty Five 307
Thanks For Reading 310
ACKNOWLEDGMENTS 311
ABOUT THE AUTHOR 312

Chapter One

It was a warm summer's day in June, the day with the most amount of sunlight; the summer solstice was just the day before. Bill Weber had taken the afternoon off to help June with the garden. Because of the birth of their son, they had a late start. Nonetheless, the plant beds were green and lush. In the back yard, the vegetable garden had taken off. They were looking forward to a variety of fresh garden salads later in the year. The flowers in the front beds had grown and covered the areas close to the house. Vibrant green, the lawn glistened from Bill's constant watering and feeding.

June was sitting on the front patio watching as Bill finished mowing the yard. He disappeared into the garage with the mower. She heard the screen door from the garage to the house open and a few minutes later he came out the front door with two glasses of iced tea. He set one glass down on the table near the deck chair June occupied. He pulled the other chair out a bit to catch more of the shade and sat. He took in a deep breath. "This is nice."

"I'll take it," June replied, "eighty-two degrees, low humidity, sunny and a gentle breeze."

"It was only a few months ago we were digging out from that big state basketball weekend snow storm."

"Let's not talk about that," June said. "Did you check on the baby?"

"He's sound asleep," he answered. "So is Jessie."

"Cory is with Jeffrey," June reported.

"I see your finch feeder is working." Bill pointed to three tiny bright colored yellow birds standing on perches pecking at the seeds.

"I watch them out the window when I'm in the kitchen. I'm only a few feet away, but I guess they can't see me through the glass."

Bill took in another deep breath. The air was warm and filled with the aroma of his freshly cut lawn. He could hear the birds in the nearby trees and wondered what they were talking about. Feeling a nudge on his hand, he looked down to see the family's black Labrador mix. His six year old son had named him Freckles for reasons known only to him. Without talking, he scratched behind the dog's ears.

It was about ten minutes before either of them said anything. Finally he spoke. "Do you know what day it is?"

"Tuesday."

"I know that, but what is the significance of today?"

"What?" June asked.

"One year ago today we arrived in Helen."

"It's been a year?" June said. "It seems like yesterday."

Bill stayed quiet for another minute. "Feels that way to me too, but at the same time I feel like I've been here all my life."

June smiled at Bill, reached out for his hand and gave it a gentle squeeze, "I can feel that too."

They sat silently again, each mentally recapping the past year. "Henry is really pushing me to run for County Commissioner."

"Why you, Bill? We only moved to South Dakota a year ago. There must be others who understand the culture and know the issues better than you. This is an agricultural community and you have to admit you know as much about agriculture as I do about jet engines."

"Well, I wouldn't go that far. I talk to the local farmers almost every day. I'm getting a feel for what they do."

"Really?" June's voice showed her disbelief. "You can't tell me that you know how to farm just because you sold some real estate for farmers, and you hang out at the Helen House for the morning coffee klatch."

"No, I'm not saying I'm an expert in agri-business; I am saying that I understand enough to ask the right questions. It doesn't matter though. Henry said he wanted me on the County Commission because I'm not from here. As Mayor, he told me that these small towns aren't represented on the commission."

"Why doesn't he run?" June asked.

"I don't know. I'll have to ask him."

"So, you're thinking about it?"

"Sure. Why not?"

June changed the subject. "I'm thinking about going back to work."

"So, I shouldn't run for the County Commission?"

June laughed. "I'm sorry. I switched subjects on you."

Bill chuckled. "You worried me for a second. I couldn't connect the dots. Why do you want to go back?"

"I went there with Mason the other day. The place is all wrong."

"What do mean wrong? Is it dirty?"

"Well, no," June hesitated. "It's hard to put my finger on it. It's just wrong. It's not the clinic I started last fall. The flavor is different. It's like they don't care."

"I can't imagine Carol not caring. She has the heart of an angel."

"It's not Carol; it's the new administrator they put in my place."

"He's not professional?"

"He's professional, and I'm sure he knows what he's doing or John Franklin would never have put him there. He's just not a people person."

"John has been in charge of the St. Agnes clinic system since it started," Bill replied. "I would think he knows what he's doing, June."

"That's just it. On the surface everything looks all right. The place looks clean, but it doesn't smell clean. The staff is professional, but not personal." June waved her hand as if she were backhanding a fly, "Oh, I don't know, it just *feels* wrong."

Turning to his wife, Bill put down his glass, "June, when we moved here I told you we could live on my income. You didn't have to work anymore. You chose to take the job at the clinic when it started because the hours dovetailed so well with Jessie and Cory going to school. Now you want to go back. What will you do with Mason?"

"Bonnie had her baby two weeks ago. We have been talking about it. She would take care of Mason while I'm at the clinic and I would watch little Mattie on the evenings she works at the Kent Library." June could see from the way Bill looked at her that this idea did not sit well with him. She held up her hand. "Hold on Bill. Nothing is set in stone. We were just talking. We are not even sure if the schedules will work out."

9

"How did you know I was going to protest?" Bill asked.

"I've been married to you long enough to know what your face is telling me." June went back to the original subject. "I haven't even decided if I'm going back to the clinic. I am just bothered by the way it's being run."

"Have you talked to John about it?"

"How can I point out what can't be seen? For instance, take the decline in personal care. Mabel was left sitting in the waiting room for almost twenty minutes. Okay, she was half an hour early and arrived during the lunch break. Both Carol and the new administrator were in the break room. I'm sure they heard the bell on the door. Nobody went to see who came in. It is just a lack of the personal touch. I would talk to John, but unless I can put my finger on something concrete, I have nothing to tell him. I can't just tell him the place simply feels wrong to me."

"Look, June, we came out here to raise a family in a community that still believes in the values we were taught as children. Being part of that community is part of those values. If you can work things out so Mason is properly cared for and home the majority of the time, I see no reason why you shouldn't go back to the clinic."

"I'm not sure I will," June said. "I just wanted to talk it out with you."

"Hello you two," Julie said as she walked up.

"Hi Julie," June answered for both of them.

"I was cleaning out the garage when I heard you talking."

"What's up?" Bill asked.

"Not much. I got done this morning and thought I'd take a day or two off and clean out the junk in the garage."

"Done with what?"

"My latest book."

"Your latest book?" Bill asked.

"I write romance novels."

"For publication?" June asked then realized how stupid that sounded. "I'm sorry, that was a stupid question."

"No it's not, you wouldn't know. I use a pen name. I'm a little embarrassed by it, they're a bit racy. Nobody in town knows, so please don't tell them." Julie's face was turning a bit red.

"So, why tell us?" June asked.

"Well, I was excited to get done so it kind of slipped out."

"I often wondered what you did for money," Bill said. "I didn't think it was any of my business to ask."

"I've been doing this since college."

"What pen name do you use?" June asked.

Julie looked at the ground, "I'd rather not say. You folks are more worldly than many of the people around here. You might understand, but I don't want it getting around."

Bill stood up. "Your secret is safe with us, Julie." He pointed to his chair, "Here, sit. I have to go mow the back yard. I did it last week, but it looks like a jungle again."

"The grass grows fast here in the spring and early summer." Julie agreed, glad to get off the previous subject.

Bill walked around and through the garage. The mower had cooled so he checked and filled the gas tank. Mowing the lawn was something he enjoyed doing. He could see the results right away, it was instant gratification. The back of the house was fenced in. It wasn't too big of an area, but even in this small space, he remembered getting lost during a blizzard last winter. He lost his way in the blinding white out when he had gone out to check the gate and make sure Freckles hadn't strayed. It was hard to imagine today with the warm air and bright sun, yet it was only a matter of months ago.

Bill and June had moved to Helen from a medium sized outer suburban town on the eastern seaboard. They moved to provide a better life for their children. They were attracted by the strong economy, the small school population and a strong moral culture. Both had flourished professionally. June as the resident RN and Administrator to the town's St. Agnes Clinic and Bill as the owner and senior partner at Huber Realty in Kent, the county seat.

They had been In South Dakota one year and had experienced all four seasons. They witnessed triumph and tragedy in their one year, and were far happier than at any other time in their recent past.

Henry Woodson, the mayor of Helen was pressuring Bill to get involved in county government, but Bill wasn't sure he wanted to do that. He knew what politicians were like back east and he wanted no part of the graft, kickbacks and under

11

the table perks that came with the office. He also knew things were different here, but just how different? What demands would be placed on him as a County Commissioner? Would it be a conflict of interest as a realtor in the county seat? What does it take to run? How much money and, more importantly, how much time would it take to run? That left the biggest question, did he really want to do it? He had to talk to Jake Samuelsson. Jake had held the job for four years, but, because he was battling cancer, he didn't have the physical ability or even the will to run again. Bill needed to talk out the details with someone who was doing the job. But not today. It was a beautiful Tuesday afternoon and he wanted to finish mowing.

BANG!! - Swoosh... Swoosh... Swoosh...

The mower stopped running and started smoking. Bill pushed it to the middle of the lawn away from the house and looked at it. He was watching for any fire. He didn't see any, but there was some smoke coming from the engine. He walked to the garage and got a fire extinguisher and walked back. He watched for a while more but the smoke was clearing. He bent over the mower and looked at it. He didn't see anything wrong. When he pulled the starter cord, it moved about two inches and stopped. The mower engine was not going to turn.

Pushing the mower around the outside of the house, Bill left it in the middle of the driveway. He wanted it away from anything flammable, just in case.

"You going to mow the driveway Bill?" June asked from the porch. She, like most wives enjoyed poking fun at her husband, especially when he was doing 'man things'.

"The thing just blew up."

"Blew up!" June leaned forward to get up. "Are you all right?"

Bill waved her back into her seat, "I'm fine. It just went 'boom' and stopped running. I'm going inside to call Henry."

"He sold you that mower almost a year ago, Bill. I don't think there's a warranty."

"Very funny." Bill looked over at his wife and next door neighbor. "I want to see if he has another one or if he can fix this one."

"Well, that is what he does." June smirked. For some reason she was enjoying Bill's minor crisis. She wasn't sure why. It was like looking at a child who just broke his favorite toy. Sad in a child, but funny in a full grown man.

Bill walked by the two women and into the house. He knew they were snickering. That confused him. He saw nothing funny about a broken lawnmower. He found his phone and called Henry's shop.

"This is Henry," the phone answered.

"Henry, Bill Weber. My lawn mower just quit. Can you look at it?"

"It stopped running? How?"

"With a bang."

"That's not good."

"I didn't think so."

"Bring it by. I'll look at it, but it might be a post mortem."

"It was smoking pretty bad when it blew. I have it in the middle of the driveway in case it catches fire. I think I want to wait for it to cool down before I put it in the car."

Henry chuckled. "Probably a good idea. I'll be here 'till five."

Bill walked back to the front door, "Anybody for more iced tea?"

"No thanks, Bill," June answered.

"Sure," said Julie.

Bill walked out with two iced tea glasses in one hand and a folding chair in the other. He set the chair against his leg and handed Julie one of the iced tea glasses. After putting the other on the table, he set up the chair, sat down, and picked the glass up again.

"What some people will do to avoid making two trips," June remarked with a smirk.

"I didn't need two trips." Bill took a sip of the tea and said "Ahhhhh" with extra flourish.

"What did Henry say?"

"He thinks it's dead."

"Is he going to do a mow-topsy?" June grinned.

"I'm not sure. I'll take it over after I finish this." Bill took another sip of tea. "I want to make sure it has cooled down and won't catch fire before I put it in the Escalade."

Bill's Escalade was his pride and joy. It was the only thing he had salvaged from the real estate agency he lost back

East. He had transferred the lease into his name before selling his office to a competitor. When the lease expired, he had decided to keep it.

"Did you see that Darla has the chart up for the chicken drop?" Julie asked.

"I haven't been in the Helen House for a few days," Bill replied, "I didn't see it the last time I was there."

"Well, it's there now."

"I'll have to stop in and buy a square or two."

"Why don't you buy five, Bill," June suggested. "One for each of us."

"I don't want to buy too many. We won last year. It wouldn't look right if we won again."

"Five squares out of one hundred doesn't clinch the odds Bill."

Bill smiled, "I guess you're right. I'll stop there on the way back from Henry's."

"Do you remember how confused we were last year when Darla showed us the chicken drop poster?" June asked, then turned to Julie. "Coming from suburbia back East we had never heard of it."

"I got even more confused when Bob told me they used to do a cow drop," Bill added.

"I don't understand," Julie said. "I guess because I've seen these kind of things all my life."

"Turn a chicken loose on the tennis court marked out like the card in the Café and the first place the chicken craps is the winner," Bill said. "The concept was so foreign to us that we would have never figured it out."

"Who explained it to you?" asked Julie.

"Beverly at the Post Office," Bill replied. "I was in there checking on my mail forwarding and she explained it."

"When Bill told me about it I laughed so hard I thought I was going to pee," June added.

"That's all old hat for us now. We're Helenites through and through." Bill said.

"You mean there's no culture shock for you anymore?" Julie asked.

"Well, I wouldn't say that," Bill replied. "When we went to the high school graduation ceremony last month, I was surprised by the turnout. There had to be twenty times more people in the audience that there were students graduating. I wasn't ready for that."

"It's a small town Bill," Julie responded. "Almost everyone in this town graduated from that school. They all have a piece of it in their hearts. That's why you see so many people at the ball games and other events."

"I knew that, but I didn't really *know* that until I went to the graduation." Bill stood up, "I guess I'll take that mower over to Henry's." He started picking up the empty glasses.

"Leave the tea glasses, dear," June said. "I'll get them."

"All right." Bill bent over and gave his wife the kind of kiss that meant affection, not passion. "I'll get going then." He walked to the lawn mower and pushed it to the rear of the Escalade. Once the back was opened he bent down and with a small grunt put the mower inside.

It was only a few blocks to Henry's small engine repair shop. In Helen, South Dakota everything was just a few blocks away or less.

"Well, Henry, what do you think?"

"I think you broke it," Henry answered smiling.

"That's your professional opinion?" Bill jibed.

"Without taking it apart that's about as far as I can go. By the way you described the failure, the engine is seized. I think it has destroyed itself internally. Maybe the connecting rod, maybe the crank shaft, but it is a major failure none the less."

"So, you're saying its not repairable?"

"Anything is repairable if you want to spend the money, Bill." Henry stood up from the mower. "I'm thinking it is not practical to try to repair the engine. I have a couple of choices for you. The deck is still in great shape. I can change out the mower engine or you can replace the whole thing."

"What's the cost of a new engine?"

"How high is up?"

"I don't understand."

"Small engines like this are like cars. They all get the job done but some cost more than others. You can pay fifteen hundred dollars for an engine that will fit this deck or you can get a Chinese one for about one hundred fifty."

15

"What do you think?"

"I think you should leave that one with me and try this one I reworked last winter. It's not as new as yours but it's in better condition." Henry walked to the back of the shop and pulled out another lawn mower.

"Does it run?"

"Of course," Henry said emphatically, almost insulted by the question.

"Then it's in better condition than mine," Bill said with a smile.

"Touché," Henry chuckled. "What I meant was it was in better condition than your mower before you blew it up. This one has an older Tecumseh engine. I rebuilt it last winter. Take care of it and it will last you long enough for baby Mason to inherit it."

"How much do you want for that?"

"I have a lot of time in it and I'll give you a one year guarantee." Henry said setting up the negotiation. "I think I should get about two hundred."

"For one hundred eighty five I can get a new one, Henry." Bill answered. He enjoyed the game and played along.

"A new one will have a Chinese engine and aluminum cylinder. This engine has a steel sleeve. The mower deck will rust away before the engine wears out. How about one seventy five?"

"A workman should be worthy of his hire, Henry. If you give me a one year warranty, I'll go with one hundred fifty."

"You're on," Henry said, "but I want your old one as trade in."

"Deal." Bill took Henry's hand. "Let's put it in the Escalade and I'll take it with me."

They rolled the mower to the SUV and put it in the back. Even though Henry was helping, this mower felt heavier. Bill walked around to the driver's door and got out his checkbook. ""What did we agree on? One twenty five?"

"I was born, Bill, but not yesterday," Henry chuckled. "One fifty."

"Well, I tried." Bill wrote out the check and handed it to Henry. "How are the plans for the Fourth coming along?"

"Everything is firmed up now. All that's left is the

legwork. The Legion is set for the pancake breakfast. Bob and the volunteer firemen will stripe the tennis court next weekend. All the pieces are coming into place. This year, thanks to your wife, the St. Agnes clinic will be doing wellness checks after the parade."

"All she did was make a phone call. John Franklin authorized the overtime and also is paying June to work the shift."

"So it works out for everyone."

"I suppose it does." Bill was a bit apprehensive about June working the booth on July Fourth. He wasn't sure if he wanted her back at work. He wouldn't stop her, but he would rather she be home with Mason. John Franklin said he would be in Helen for the parade and the festivities. Bill knew his real reason was to get June back into the clinic.

"Did you see the shotgun we are raffling this year?"

"No, I haven't"

"Darla has it at the café," Henry said. "It is a Benelli Model M2. It has their special soft recoil technology. I shot one when I went with Bob to buy it. The thing is as smooth as butter."

"You raffled a shotgun last year to pay for the new fire truck. What's it for this year?"

"Bob has his eye on a new water tanker."

"A water tanker?" Bill asked.

"That's right. Our current one is only fifteen hundred gallons. Bob saw a tanker trailer and presented it to the firehouse at the annual meeting. They want to build a fund to buy one. They can hook it to anyone's semi-tractor and haul seven thousand gallons to a fire. They can even use the old truck to be a shuttle between the tanker and the fire."

"How does that work?"

"The tanker we have now will go off road, at least a little. A semi-tractor with a trailer would be limited."

"How much will that cost?" Bill asked.

"Bob thinks he can find a good used one for between ten and fifteen thousand dollars."

"That's a lot of raffle tickets."

"We probably will not get it done in one year, but Bob thinks we can certainly do it in two, maybe three."

17

"Well," Bill said, "I'd better be going. I promised June I'd stop by the Café and buy some squares."

"You won the chicken drop last year, didn't you?"

"That's right, Bill nodded, "Tom got to me just in time to tell me that the winnings were normally donated back to the firehouse."

"Well, good luck again this year," Henry said as he saw a tow truck pull into the driveway.

"I wouldn't want to win two years in a row. I'm not buying a lot. One ticket for each Weber, five in all."

A man got out of the tow truck and walked up toward the other two. "Good afternoon Henry... Bill."

"Hi Mike, what's new?" Henry answered for both of them.

"I'm hoping you have a set of these." Mike held out something small and metal that Bill didn't recognize.

"Points?" Henry asked, "What do they go to?"

"They're from an old dirty water pump. It's a Tecumseh engine but an old one."

"You're stealing my business and now you want parts?" Henry jibed.

"Actually the thing is mine. I've had it around for years in the back of the shop."

"What brings you to fixing it now?" Bill jumped in, "Bored?"

"No," Mike replied, "I've got plenty to do. I'm fixing the thing up to donate it to the firehouse. Bob saw it and asked about it. He wants one for his new tanker. With this he can pull water from any river, lake or even a swimming pool."

"Boy, he doesn't miss a beat." Henry chuckled. "We haven't even started the account to buy the tanker trailer and he's soliciting accessories."

"You know Bob," Mike answered. "He never misses an opportunity."

"Let me see that point set; I might have something we can use."

"I'm heading out," Bill said. "You two have fun."

"We always do," Mike said.

Bill pulled away and drove the two blocks to the Helen House Café. Once there, he went inside and walked over to the poster board tacked to the wall. There was a pen hanging on a string and a coffee can on the table next to the poster. Several of the squares, filled in like a doughnut, were already taken. There were many names on the outer edges and a few near the center. Bill picked up the pen to start marking five squares. He held the pen, but stopped and set it back down.

"What'd you do," Darla said from the counter, "change your mind?"

"No," Bill answered. "I just decided that this is too important a decision to be made exclusively by me. I'm going home to get June and the kids."

"I suppose that's right," Darla went along. "The kids should be involved in picking their own squares."

"I'll be right back." Bill left the café and drove home. No one was outside. Walking into the house, he was about to call June when he remembered the baby might still be sleeping. Bill quietly crept back to the nursery and saw the crib was empty. He checked Jessie's room and found his thirteen year old daughter was also missing. Over to Cory's room… nothing. It was then he realized the dog was not following him either. "I'll try out back," he said to the empty house.

Once out in the back yard he looked and saw his whole family in the garden. Jessie and Cory were pulling weeds with June supervising to make sure they were, in fact, weeds. Baby Mason was in the shade under the leafy umbrella of the large oak tree that towered over the fenced in area of the yard. Bill walked through the gate and into the side yard. "Hello Webers!" he said as he walked up.

"Hi Dad," Jessie answered.

"Daddy look!" Cory ran up, "I found a caterpillar!"

"He wants to squish it but Mom won't let him," Jessie said.

"Caterpillars become butterflies," June added.

"Not all the time," Bill replied. "I was going to get the squares for the chicken drop but then I decided that this decision is much too important to make alone. It has to be carefully considered over milkshakes. Anybody with me?"

"I am!" answered Jessie

"Me!" shouted her seven year old little brother.

June looked over at Mason. "Bill the baby's sleeping; you

go ahead."

"Nonsense." Bill walked over and took June's hand. "We'll take Mason along. If he wakes up the whole café will be cooing and ooing over him."

"All right." June laughed, "We'll all go."

"Yea!" shouted Cory.

Once they were in the car June asked, "What happens if one of the kids win? They're not going to want to donate the prize."

"I know. I'll have to make it up."

"That's a lot of money," June said.

"I know, but with ninety-eight to one odds, I'm not uncomfortable."

Bill once again pulled up in front of Helen's finest and only eatery. He remembered the first time he was there. They had walked down from the Helen Motel. They had met Darla, the owner, and some of the local residents. He still remembered how surprised he was to find that everyone knew who they were and that they had been expecting them.

"I want chocolate," Cory said as they walked in the door.

"You always want chocolate," Jessie said as she passed her father holding the door.

"I think I want Chocolate too," Bill said. They migrated to their 'usual table' and took their normal seats.

Darla came out from the kitchen and looked at her latest customers. "Well, look who we have here." She walked over to the baby carrier and bent down. "Hello Mason. You bring the family in for an early supper?"

"Actually, we came in to sign up on the Chicken drop board," Bill said. "I was going to do it earlier but I thought it was too big a decision to make for the kids. They need to pick their own squares."

"Good idea," Darla agreed. "Coffee? Pop?"

"A decision like this takes more than coffee or soda Darla," Bill said dramatically. "It requires serious thought over a milk shake."

"I want chocolate," Cory once again voiced his preference.

"Please," June corrected her son.

"Please," Cory repeated.

20

"And what about the ladies?" Darla asked.

"Do you have strawberry?" Jessie asked.

"We do, in fact," Darla answered.

"I think I would like that too, please," June jumped in.

Knowing Darla was going to split the shakes Bill went with the other half of Cory's chocolate.

Once the milkshakes were served and about half consumed Bill, Jessie and Cory walked over to the Chicken Drop board. "Jessie, you're the oldest, you pick first."

Jessie looked at the board for almost a minute, then pointed, "I want this one."

"Put your name on it," Bill said handing her the pen.

Cory had waited, but now that it was his turn he spoke almost immediately, "I want that one."

"Put your name on it," Bill said, "but write small. You have to get Cory Weber to fit inside the box."

"I can do it," Cory said then wrote his name as small as he could. Bill concluded that sticking his tongue out the left side of his mouth helped him concentrate.

June walked up, "I'll take this square, Bill, and Mason wants the one next to it." She took the pen from her older son and entered the two names.

"One more and we're set," Bill said as he chose his square. "Let's finish our shakes."

Chapter Two

July Fourth in Helen, South Dakota was very much like the July Fourth celebrations in most Midwestern towns. Each unique in their own right, but all have the same general flavor. In Helen, the day started with the pancake breakfast at the American Legion Hall, then on to the parade grandstand where they held the Dolly Madison contest to pick the Grand Marshals.

This was the second Fourth of July celebration in Helen for Bill and his family. The first year they were surprised at how different a small town in middle America handled the holiday. This year they were more prepared. Bill took Jacob Johnson up on his offer to ride in the Johnson family's decorated buckboard. He had turned down the offer last year because the small town experience was new to his family and he wanted them to take the whole thing in. This year was different. They had been here for just over a year. The culture shock was almost gone. He thought riding on the antique buckboard being pulled by a team of horses would be fun for the kids.

What Bill didn't realize was how much he would enjoy the experience himself. It was like looking at piece of Americana from a new vantage point. While the kids had a great time throwing candy from the wagon, Bill enjoyed the scenery passing by on each side. He watched the town's kids chasing after the candy. He also saw the older folks wearing their patriotic outfits sitting in their lawn chairs on the sides of the parade route. He was glad to see the acknowledgments and waves from people. Tom Ogden caught his eye and pointed toward the baseball field where the lawnmower races were to be held. Bill understood and nodded. He shouted, "I'll meet you there."

"You'll meet who where?" June asked.

"I'm going to meet Tom at the lawnmower races," Bill replied.

"You know I'm going to be working the Helen Clinic booth until the chicken drop."

"You want me to take the baby?" Bill asked, hoping she

would say no.

"I'll keep Mason with me. Carol and John are setting up the booth in the Legion Hall. He'll be inside with the air conditioning." June looked at her husband, "Don't look so relieved. It's better this way. Besides, I'll have the lady's room if I need to change him."

"You know me too well," Bill smiled.

"Plus," she looked at her daughter, "Jessie will be there to help."

Jessie made a face, then shrugged.

"All right. I'll take Cory with me. We'll meet at the tennis court for the chicken drop."

The parade ended one block beyond the flatbed trailer made up as a reviewing stand. The parade route turned left just past the reviewing bleachers so the marchers could disburse out of sight. Bill carefully stepped down from the back of the wagon then turned to help June. She handed him the baby carrier then stepped down. Jessie and Cory jumped.

"All right," Bill said. "We'll meet at the chicken drop."

"Keep an eye on Cory," June cautioned.

"He'll be fine," Bill said. "We're meeting up with Tom. Cory and Joey will be together."

"I'm not sure that makes me feel any better," June smiled. "Just make sure they don't run out in front of the lawn mowers."

Bill smiled back. "I'll see you at the tennis court." Then he turned to his son, "Come on Cory, let's find Uncle Tom and Joey."

As Cory walked along with his dad, he looked ahead and saw Joey and took off running. Bill was about to call him back but he could see that he was heading straight for Tom so he let it go.

Bill took his time. He walked by the pit area where the mower racers were preparing for the first heat. Last year he only knew a couple of the racers. This year, he realized he knew almost all of them. "Life in a small town," he said to no one.

"Hey, Bill!"

Bill looked over at the man who called his name. It was Al Stillwell, Carol's husband. "Good morning Al. You ready

23

to go?"

"No, I'm not. I checked this thing over top to bottom yesterday and it was great. I rolled it off the trailer today and I discovered a linkage problem."

"You want me to find Henry or Mike?" Bill knew better than to offer his own help. His strong suit was real estate, not mechanics.

"No, I just need a third hand. I can get the parts in place but it takes two hands. Can you put the pin in when I get these two things aligned?"

"Sure, where does it go?"

"See this hole?" Al pointed, "Once I get these two pieces together, put this pin in the hole."

"I can do that."

"Great," Al said. "Here we go." Al wrestled with the two parts. It was as if they were magnetically repelling one anther but he continued to fight it. Once he got them together and aligned he said, "Now!"

Bill pushed the pin in. It got half way and stopped. "It won't go in all the way."

"There's a crescent wrench in on the seat. Tap it in with that," Al instructed.

Bill used the makeshift hammer to drive the pin the rest of the way in. "That's it."

Al relaxed his grip and took a breath. "Thanks Bill. That's a bugger of the job to do alone."

"You're all set now?"

"You bet," Al smiled, "as soon as I put the keeper on."

Bill had no idea what the two pieces did or just where the 'keeper' went. He was glad to have helped. "Great, I'll be watching for you."

"Just watch the finish line. I intend to be the first one across."

Bill started walking away from the pits when he saw Oscar. He was bent over another lawn tractor talking to someone on the other side. "Hello Oscar," Bill said. "More trouble over here?"

"What?" Oscar turned. "Oh, hi Bill. No nothing's wrong. We're just tightening the belt tension. That's the last thing before the race. We don't want any slippage. This is Nancy's first race and we want her to take it by storm."

It was only then that Bill realized that the figure on the other side of the tractor was Oscar's niece Nancy.

"Well, good luck Nancy."

"I won't need it," Nancy replied. "I have this thing tuned to a tee and I have a weight advantage. I'll be leading the others around the track."

"I'll be watching," Bill answered. "See you at the end."

"You bet. See ya."

Bill walked out of the pit area and to the portable bleachers set up for the race. He found Tom along with Frankie, Joey and Cory sitting near the top. He climbed up and sat down next to Tom. "You decided to sit at the top?"

"Frankie did," Tom replied. "He said we can see better from up here."

"Frank," Frankie said under his breath.

Tom looked out across the track, "Well, this isn't the Daytona 500, but I suppose you can enjoy the show. The principle's the same."

"I think it's better," Bill said. "We know the drivers and the teams. Did you see that Nancy Richland has an entry?"

"No, I didn't. Good for her. They don't handicap the riders with weight like they do horses. She can't weigh more than 98 pounds."

"I saw her and Oscar in the pit area on my way over. She told me her weight advantage will help her win."

"Well," Tom pointed to the mowers over his shoulder in the pit area, "if you look at some of the other drivers, she has a good point. You see Alex Beams? He's got to weigh 300 pounds."

The announcer came out to the start / finish line. It was the same announcer as last year. Bill didn't know him then. Now he did. He had been with Tom to a few auctions. Harvey Luther was a well established auctioneer. He had originally been chosen as announcer because he had his own battery operated loudspeaker. Over the years he found he liked it. He had the speaker on a strap hanging from his shoulder and brought the microphone to his lips. "The first heat is about to begin. Just to review the rules, this is an elimination stage. Four lawn tractors will start each heat. The top two move on to

25

the final heat. Each lap is one eighth mile and each elimination race is three laps. The final race for the trophy is five laps. So, let's have the first four racers at the line now."

Bill could hear the lawn mower engines start up. They sounded louder than his mower at home but he figured it was because there were four of them. They moved to the start line. Lyle Jamison, Cory and Joey's teacher from last year, was the line judge. He held up an air horn and nodded to the man with the portable loudspeaker. Harvey nodded back. Lyle dramatically held the horn high and pushed the button.

BRAAAAAT!!!!!

The mowers took off. Nancy, with her weight advantage pulled out and got on the inside for the first turn. Her lead didn't last long, by the time they reached the end of the back straightaway, Paul Carr had caught her. She held the inside and forced Paul around the long way.

Nancy had the lead coming to the line to start the second lap when suddenly she slowed. Knowing she had racers behind her she swerved into the infield. The mower stopped and she shut it off.

Paul was now in the lead. He pulled around turns one and two and kept the power on. He was pulling away from the pack. The mower engine was screaming.

"That doesn't sound right," Bill shouted to Tom.

"He's tinkered with the governor to get more revs out of it," Tom said.

"If the engine can turn over faster then it will drive the wheels faster," Frankie explained the obvious.

"Won't he blow it up?" Bill asked.

"If he doesn't, he'll win," Tom said.

"That's a gamble."

"Yup," Frankie agreed. Frankie was fourteen and trying very hard to be one of the grown men watching the race. He was all but ignoring his little brother. He mentally separated himself from his boyhood and joined with his dad and Bill in this men's club.

The race ended with Paul Carr in first and Gary Stoddard in second. "What do you think happened to Nancy?" Bill asked.

"Looks like the belt snapped," Frankie said. "See it there

on the track?"

Bill looked where Frankie was pointing and he saw the belt on the ground. It looked like a thin snake. "That's all that pushes these things?"

"The real lawnmowers, yes," Tom said. "I've read about some direct drive racers built just for racing but the rules here say it has to be a mower or more accurately has to have been a mower at one time."

"I guess that keeps out the ringers."

"Not all together," Tom said, "some of the racers push the rules."

"I talked to Oscar just before the race. Nancy was tightening the belt tension."

"Guess she went a bit too far," Tom answered.

Al Stillwell won the second elimination with Gary Hawkins, Bill's neighbor, also qualifying.

The third race was a nail biter. Joshua Orland and Glenn Stratford were neck and neck for all three laps. They ran side by side swapping the inside and the outside twice almost wrecking in the process. They were so far ahead nobody paid any attention to the other two racing mowers. As they approached the finish line on the final lap the entire crowd was on its feet half yelling and cheering for Josh and the other half for Glenn. When they came across the finish line, it looked to Bill like they were dead even.

Lyle Jamison had taken this possibility into consideration He had two high school students on each side of the finish line to take pictures as the mowers crossed. He gathered the four kids together to look at the pictures. The crowd was nearly silent as the judge made his decision. He looked carefully at the little screens on the phones. Then turned to talk to the announcer. They stood, huddled in conversation for almost a minute before the Harvey took up the microphone, "What we have is a history making event. It is a true tie. The judge has reviewed the photos and can not tell who led the final lap. Since this is an elimination race, both contestants move to the final."

"You know if that happens in the final race there'll be hell to pay," Bill observed.

Tom laughed, "They'd have to cut the trophy in half.

Neither driver would let the other guy have it."

"The spirit of competition lives on in Helen, South Dakota," Bill said. Then asked, "Is my memory faulty? Didn't they have six mowers in each race last year?"

"I think so. They adjust the number each year so they can get in three races before the final. Guess there were only twelve entries this year."

"I wonder why the participation dropped," Bill said.

"They changed the rules this year. The mower has to have been a mower and, more importantly, the engine has to have been a mower engine. That kept out the ringers with home built racers."

"How did that happen?" Bill asked.

"I guess the guys in the club who kept losing ganged up and voted them out," Tom chuckled.

"Maybe they need a separate ringer race."

Tom looked at Bill. "Now there's an idea. A race of un-mowers. Anything goes, as long as it has four wheels and weighs less the one hundred pounds."

"That could get ugly," Bill said.

"You're probably right," Tom laughed

The announcer interrupted their chatter. "All right, mowers line up for the final race. This will be a five lap race. Winner takes home the July Fourth trophy and gets to display it for one year. The mowers will line up by qualifying speed from the first race, slowest to the inside. Our tied racer's positions were decided by coin toss."

"Fifty - Fifty tickets here! Get your Fifty - Fifty tickets!" Fred Hansen was walking around with a wad of tickets. He came up the bleachers and started hawking again. "Only a few left, get 'em while they're hot!"

"What's the other fifty for?" Bill asked reaching for his wallet.

"Ball field maintenance."

"That makes sense," Bill chuckled. "I'll take two." He took one and gave the other to his son.

"Two for me as well Fred," Tom said.

The six mowers came out from the pit area behind the bleachers. They slowly moved in front of the bleachers and lined up according to their position. Lyle looked at the line up and moved one mower forward a bit and another back behind the line. He walked to the side of the make shift track and nodded to the announcer.

"Okay, we're ready to go," the announcer spoke through his bullhorn. "During a meeting before the race it was decided that this final race can not end in a tie. If two mowers are tied at the end of five laps, there will be race off. The two will continue to race until one crosses the finish line first. Racers watch the flag man at turn one. If you see the green flag, keep going!"

"Oh, this could get good," Tom said.

"Yup" Frankie agreed.

The announcer looked at the line judge and nodded. Lyle raised the horn.

BRAAAAAT!!!!!

The mowers took off. It was clear from the first that the outside racers were faster than the inside racers. By the time they got to the back of the track, the two inside mowers had fallen behind. Al Stillwell had been second from the outside when the race started. Now he was fighting to get by Gary Hawkins. Gary was keeping the inside for himself and Al couldn't quite get enough speed to pass him on the outside. Al had beat him in the elimination race by about two feet and Gary wasn't going to give him that two feet in the final race. Al was intense, he saw Paul Carr in first place about thirty feet ahead. He knew he could catch him if he could just get by Gary.

The bleachers were electric. People had been sitting down at the start of the race but by lap three they were all on their feet. The race seemed to be among three drivers. Paul Carr was leading with Gary Hawkins and Al Stillwell close behind having their own race. On lap three Al managed to get by Gary on the inside of the kidney bean turn. He raced on to try to catch Paul. They crossed the finish line with Paul about six inches ahead of Al.

As the other mowers drove behind the bleachers to the pits, Paul Carr took one extra victory lap. He pulled up to the finish line and his mower gave out a popping sound, a wheeze, a cough and quit.

"You need a fire extinguisher?" the announcer asked, then

held the microphone reporter style so the crowd could hear.

Paul laughed, "No, but I think I'm going to need a tow."

Bill laughed along with the rest of the stands. The trophy was presented and the crowd moved off the bleachers. "I'm going to check on June," Bill said.

"Sure thing, I'll see you at the chicken drop," Tom replied. As he turned to leave, Cory followed Joey.

"Cory, you're with me," Bill said. Cory turned and followed his dad. After walking away from the bleachers Bill asked, "What did you think about the races?"

"I thought they would go faster," Cory said.

"They were going pretty fast," Bill countered.

"Not like horses or cars," Cory said.

"No, you're right there, Cory. They are not as fast as cars. I'll tell you what, let's look at the schedule and you and I will go watch the stock car races in Huron. Would you like that?"

"Yeah, can we bring Joey?"

"Maybe we will, but that would be up to his dad."

"Mr. Carr has a race car too. I'll bet he wins."

Bill told Cory about the one third mile dirt track in Huron and how they raced on Saturday nights in the summer.

The conversation concluded as they approached June. "Hello boys, you have fun at the races?"

"Dad is going to take us to the car races," Cory said.

"He is?" June replied to her son while looking at her husband for amplification.

"I told Cory we would check the schedule and go to the dirt track races in Huron."

"Mr. Carr has a race car. He won the last lawnmower race," Cory added.

"You almost done here?"

"I'll be about ten more minutes. I want to help Carol and John take things back into the clinic."

"You need help?"

"No, we'll get it."

"All right," Bill said. "I'm going to take Cory over to the chicken drop. I'll see you there."

"I'm hungry," Cory announced.

"You're always hungry," Bill replied. "They'll have the lunch set up at the picnic pavilion after the chicken drop.

30

We'll eat then, but for now, don't you want to see where your square is on the tennis court?"

"Okay." Cory hesitated, "Hey! There's Joey!" Cory ran ahead.

Bill didn't mind his seven year old son bolting. He could see him and he knew where he was going.

"June, thanks for helping today," John Franklin said.

"Honestly, John, I enjoyed it."

"So you're saying its nice to be working again."

"I won't go that far, John. It was nice to see people and we did catch a couple of walking time bombs. That's always gratifying. There was a difference. I had Mason with me, I couldn't do that in a clinic setting."

"I could watch him," Jessie said.

"And what about when school starts?" June asked.

Jessie didn't answer at first. When she did, it had nothing to do with the conversation. She had seen Jeremy Finney out the window. Her mental focus now was on finding something to carry outside. She picked up a box, "I'll take this over to the clinic."

"The clinic's locked," John said, dashing Jessie's plan. "Give us about five more minutes and we can carry all this at once."

"Here, Jessie, you can put these away," June said pointing to St Agnes Medical Group brochures.

Jessie looked out the window again. Jeremy was gone. She turned to the table and started filling the box.

"Careful young lady, that's not garbage," June cautioned." We intend to use them again."

John Franklin smiled at June's use of the word 'we'. "I want to talk to you about an idea I have, but not now," John said. "Right now. we need to get this stuff put away and get to the chicken drop."

"You're going to the chicken drop?" Carol asked as she helped Jessie put the rest of the leftover handouts in the tote.

"Of course, I have four squares."

June started folding the chairs when Carol said. "I'll get that June."

John added, "Carol's right. You take care of Mason, we'll

31

finish this. I'll see you at the tennis court."

"Oh," June chuckled," you must really want something."

"I do, but not today. Go be with your family."

"All right," June said. Then she turned to her daughter, "Do you mind helping carry things to the clinic?"

Jessie was looking out the window again. She saw Jeremy and was trying to find an escape. "Well uh…."

"We'll get it," John said interrupting the thirteen year old. You go ahead with your mother and Mason."

Jessie's heart jumped in the air at the hint of freedom, then crashed to the ground just as quickly when her mother said, "Here Jessie, you carry the diaper bag and I'll take the baby."

Jessie said a barely audible. "Okay."

June walked out of the Legion Hall with her one month old's carrier crooked in her arm and the thirteen year old daughter at her side. She could see that something was bothering Jessie and could only presume it had to do with a boy.

Chapter Three

Jessie Weber was at the age when certain feelings awaken in a young girl. The horses that were so important last year, though still interesting, held a lower place in her list of priorities. Today her priority was to get the attention of Jeremy Finney. Jeremy had been on the track team last year and even as a Sophomore, he had been number three in the four man relay team. Jessie would go to the home meets whenever she could. She would cheer and call his name as he ran. Unfortunately, he hardly noticed. She *had to* find a way to get his attention. She was frustrated. There he was, only twenty feet away and she was stuck holding this diaper bag. She just *couldn't* be seen by him like that. She moved to the other side of her mother using her as a shield.

"Hey shrimp."

Jessie was brought back to reality by the voice. She turned and looked at Frank Ogden. They had been a 'couple' last year, at least Jessie thought so, until Frank asked Katie Sands to the dance. She didn't understand why she liked him last year. What she did understand was that she didn't like him now. "What do you want?" she snapped.

"I don't want anything. I just stopped to say hello."

"Well, you did. So just go."

Frank shrugged and walked away. He never did figure out why she was mad at him. They had the school play last year and during the play she snapped and started crying. She had not wanted anything to do with him since. They were friends, good friends, then one day they weren't. Frank walked away.

"Look, there's your dad and Cory," June pointed.

Jessie looked. She saw her dad and little brother standing by the fence. She also saw Mickie standing on the other side and Mickie was next to Jeremy.

"I see Mickie, can you take this?" she tried to hand off the diaper bag.

"No, you stay with us," June said.

Once again Jessie's plan to get next to Jeremy Finney had been destroyed. She paid little attention to her mother's next sentence but it sounded something like, "You have a square

33

with the family." She followed her mother and stood by the fence. She could see Jeremy talking to Mickie. Mickie looked over and waved for her to come over but she shook her head and pointed at the baby.

Bill looked at his daughter, "There's your square. Three in and two up. You see it?"

"Whatever," Jessie said.

"Jessie, watch your tongue!" June snapped.

Jessie didn't answer. She was looking at Jeremy and Mickie. They were pointing at the chicken carrier and laughing. She wanted to be part of that group and not with her parents and her two brothers watching some lame chicken thing. "Why don't adults understand?" she was thinking. She reached for her phone. Texting to Mickie she said, "watso fny"

"tl u l8r" was the reply.

Jessie looked at the phone, then across to her friend. Mickie didn't notice Jessie's stare. Jeremy had all of her attention. It looked to her that Mickie was trying to be with Jeremy. Mickie was her best friend, she knew better. Jessie stared and the longer she stared the more frustrated she got.

"All right folks, gather around. We are about to start the chicken drop." Mayor Henry Woodson had Harvey Luther's loudspeaker. "As you know, the proceeds from the chicken drop go directly to next year's fireworks display. As you can see the chart is almost full. The only square left is the center square. If the center square wins, the pot is doubled. Thanks to Bill Weber and Huber Realty for guaranteeing the double pot this year."

"I didn't know you did that," June said.

"Bob talked me into it when I stopped in for a haircut."

"Seems he's good at talking people into things. You should have seen him talking to John Franklin this morning. If he could have had his way, St. Agnes Medical Group would have fully stocked and supplied the ambulance. As it was, he got a five hundred dollar donation out of him."

"All right, it's time to auction the center square," Harvey Luther had the microphone again. "Here we go! I'll start this low so everyone can get on and ride. Who'll gimme fifty.... Who's got fifty, there's fifty now who's got seventy five, I got seventy five now one hundred, who's got one hundred, who's got one hundred.... One hundred? Okay, we'll do it the hard way. Who'll gimme eighty, I got eighty, now eighty five, now ninety, ninety five, one hundred? There's one hundred. (there was polite applause in the crowd). Now how about one ten, one ten? I got one ten, now fifteen who'll gimme fifteen? There's one fifteen."

"One hundred fifty!" Fred Houser called from the crowd. There was another polite applause.

"I have one fifty, who's got one seventy five? One seventy five? Okay one sixty. I've got one sixty, who's got one sixty five... One sixty five? One sixty five? One sixty five?... Sold! Your name sir?"

"John Franklin, Saint Agnes Medical Group."

"That's funny," Bill said quietly to his wife, "He'll do anything for a plug."

"Bill, that's not fair. John does a lot for the communities St. Agnes serves."

"You are sounding like an employee. Did he get to you?'

"Shhh," June held up her hand. "They're about to put out the chicken."

Henry had the microphone back in his hand "Remember, we have a lunch at the picnic pavilion as soon as the chicken drop is done."

"When will that be, Henry?" A boisterous voice from the crowd asked.

"Here we go," Bill said to June.

"That will be up to the chicken," Henry replied bringing on the polite laughter from the people who heard this joke every year. "This year the chicken is from the Stillwell farm. As part of the tradition, Art and Carol do not have a square." Henry looked over to the couple. "Are you ready?'

"We're ready!" answered Carol.

"Then turn her loose!" Henry commanded.

Carol tossed the chicken into the space containing the squares. The chicken flapped and moved around the grid. Around the fence all kinds of strategies were in play. Some people were calling the chicken with "Here chickie, chickie." Others were making chicken sounds trying to draw the bird near. Another strategy was to position clappers around the court to drive the chicken in the right direction.

Bill held his breath as the chicken stopped on the center square. She stood there for about three seconds and then moved off again. It took a full four minutes before the natural bodily function of the chicken left its mark on square number 27.

"That was close, Bill."

"I almost didn't get away with that."

"Square number twenty seven!" Henry announced. "Darla, who has square number twenty seven?"

"It's me!" came from the crowd.

"The winner is Natalie Miller!"

Natalie walked around the fence and onto the platform to join Henry. "I've never won anything," The eighteen year old said as she got up on the platform. "Well, you have now."

"Not really though."

Henry lifted the microphone to his mouth and said "Here's our winner! Natalie, here's your winnings."

Natalie had composed herself, "Thank you Mayor. I never won anything before but today I get to win twice," She turned to the Fire Chief who had suddenly appeared on the stage, "Mr. Houser, please take the booty and put it toward the fireworks for next year."

The crowd cheered and applauded Natalie. She looked at the crowd. In the middle she could see her father smiling. She looked for Justin, her fiancé, but didn't see him.

"All right folks, next stop is the picnic pavilion for an amazing feast!" With that Henry gave the loudspeaker back to Harvey and walked off.

"Can I go now?" Jessie said to her mother.

June didn't like the sense of irritation in her daughter's voice but she had to pick her battles. "Sure, and thanks for staying with us." June wasn't sure if Jessie had even heard the last sentence. She had turned her back and started moving at the word 'sure'.

"What's with her?" Bill asked. "She sounded a bit snippy."

"She's becoming a teenager, get used to it."

"I don't think so," Bill said emphatically. "Teenager or not, she'll show some respect."

"Good luck with that," June said remembering when she was thirteen.

Jessie looked for Jeremy. She couldn't see him. She looked for Mickie, she couldn't see her either. She kept walking toward the picnic pavilion. She saw them standing in line with some other friends. "What was so funny at the tennis court?"

"You had to be there. Jeremy was talking for the chicken," Mickie answered.

"Like what?" Jessie smiled at Jeremy who looked over her shoulder. It was as if she wasn't there at all.

"Oh, I don't know. It was funny at the time, now it would just sound stupid."

As Jessie stood there she could feel the power of Jeremy drawing on her. She wanted to move into his arms and have him hold her. It was almost as if he were a magnet drawing her closer and closer. She had to say something that would get his attention. But what? Something funny, but she couldn't think of anything.

"Hey… no cutting!"

The voice drew Jessie back to reality. She turned to her accuser, "I'm not cutting, I'm talking."

"You're talking and wheedling your way into the line. Go to the back. You think you're special?"

"No, I…" Jessie was embarrassed. Now Jeremy was looking at her. She didn't know what to say. She moved off. She didn't go to the back of the line. She didn't know what to do. It seemed every time she got close to Jeremy, something went wrong. What would Jeremy think of her if he knew, what if he didn't care? She didn't know which was worse. She decided to walk home.

"The lunch today is provided by Darla and Fred Houser at their cost. It is the finest of the Helen House cuisine." Henry had the microphone in his hand. "This year's sponsor is the Helen Elevator. There is a free will donation box at the dessert table. The proceeds will be split evenly among the Boy and Girl Scouts and the FFA. Please let the riders in line at the front, they have to eat and get ready for the horse show."

"I have this feeling of déjà vu," Bill said with a smile.

"You have done this before?" June asked.

"Yup, last year."

"Oh Bill, I thought you were serious."

"I am serious. I think those were the exact same words Henry said last year."

"Let's get in line," June said.

"Where's Cory?"

"I see him, he's with Joey," June replied.

Bill looked where June was pointing and saw his son and Jeffrey, Cory's friend from down the street. They were all with Tom and Sarah Ogden. "Looks like this year they have the herd."

"What do you mean?"

"Last year I had the three boys almost all day. The parents would come find them and take them, but they would be back with Cory in no time. This year we get the break."

"You don't mean that," June said.

"What?"

"You don't like having your son around?"

"That's not what I meant," Bill answered. "I meant I'm not watching two other boys along with my own this year."

"Well, watch this one," June handed Bill the baby carrier.

"Maybe we should have brought the stroller."

"I don't need the stroller, I have you," June said with a grin.

Bill let it go. He looked around, "I'll find a spot in the shade while you get your plate."

"Okay."

Bill found a spot for the baby at the end of a picnic table. There was plenty of shade.

Bob Houser, the Fire Chief walked up just as Bill got Mason settled. "Hey Bill, I thought I was going to get some extra money at the chicken drop today. That chicken hovered over the center square for quite a time before moving away."

"I was a bit nervous."

"Not me! With John Franklin holding the center square, I know I'd get the whole take," Bob spread his hands wide as if receiving a large gift. "I would have used that money toward a couple new Scott Packs."

"I thought the chicken drop money went to the fireworks?" Bill asked.

"It does. But the center square is ***bonus*** money! I can use that anywhere.

Bill laughed. "So, let me guess, you're here to hit me up for the center square money even though it didn't hit."

"Well….. now that you bring it up…."

"Wait a minute Bob, I was playing the odds on the chicken drop…"

"But you had to be ready to donate the money," Bob interrupted.

Bill laughed, "Bob, you're relentless."

"Only when I smell an opportunity."

"How much are these Scott packs?"

"They run about three thousand new. I can get refurbished ones for less."

"How about I donate a hundred to the Scott Pack Fund in baby Mason's name?" Bill pointed to the baby carrier.

"You're a good sport Bill." Bob looked around, "Excuse me, I see another victim."

"What did Bob want?" June asked as she sat down across from her husband.

"What do you think?" Bill chuckled. "He was trying to get me to donate the center square money."

"I think he's getting out of control," June said. "You would think this whole July Fourth celebration day was made as a fundraiser for the firehouse. You didn't give it to him, did you?"

"No, but I did promise a hundred dollars in the name of Mason."

"Bill, we bought chicken drop tickets, I know you bought raffle tickets for the shotgun, we donate to the firehouse during the annual fund drive dinner. Now you gave another hundred?"

"Bob Houser is a great Fire Chief. His knowledge of propane tanks saved your life last year when that elevator building blew up. I want him around. If donating to the firehouse can keep him and the other firemen safe and capable, then it is a small price to pay."

"Don't let Bob hear you say that," Tom Ogden said as he

stepped up. "He'll have you on the loudspeaker as he walks the crowd with his hat out."

"Hi Tom."

"I thought I'd drop off your son," Tom pointed.

"Thanks." Bill looked over at his son, "Well Cory, let's get in line and get some lunch."

"Swell," Cory said.

"Swell?" Bill stopped and looked at his seven year old son. "Where did you get that word? I haven't heard it in years."

"Brady used it," Cory answered. "I think it's dope."

Bill gave up. He had no idea who Brady was and from the context he concluded that 'dope' was a good thing.

"What do you think, should we get the chicken or the burgers?"

"I want hot dogs."

"Hot dogs it is." Bill helped Cory get his lunch and carried his own plate along with the drinks back to the table. As he sat down next to June he looked around, "Have you seen Jessie?"

"Not since the chicken drop."

"She must be with the horses. Some of her friends are riding today."

June pulled out her phone. "Let me check."

The text looked like this:

whr r u
hm
r u ok
y
wnt me hm
no

"That's not good," June said. "She's home."

"What's she doing home?"

"I don't know. I'll call her." She looked at the phone "Call Jessie"

"Hi mom"

"Jessie, what are you doing home?"

"Making mac and cheese."

"Why did you leave?"

"I just did, that's all."

"Are you all right?"

"I'm fine."

"Are you sure?"

"Mom!"

"Okay, we're going to finish lunch and head home. Mason needs a nap. Are you going to the horse show?"

"I don't know yet."

"Well, if you do we'll see you later."

"Bye mom."

"Bye dear."

Jessie hadn't thought about the horse show. She wanted to see it but not if Mickie and Jeremy were there. She had decided in her mind that Mickie had stolen Jeremy and was trying to keep him for herself. She felt betrayed by her best friend. Why did they have to move to this tiny town out in the middle of nowhere anyway? She can't get any privacy, everybody knows what everybody else is doing. She knew she could get Jeremy to like her if she could only get his attention. She wanted so much to have his affection, but the last time they were together was a disaster. She wasn't sure if she could get past it.

Normally when she had these kinds of troubles, Mickie would help her think it through. Now Mickie was part of the problem. She wasn't sure who she could turn to. She had other friends, but they weren't as close as Mickie. She had stayed in touch with her best friend from Fairview, but she would never be able to explain the small town lifestyle. It was like she moved to another planet.

Jessie sat at the kitchen table. She was pushing around the mac and cheese, not really eating it. She had to do something, but what. She decided to go to the horse show and move in on Mickie. She could get Jeremy away from Mickie. She knew she could, but she couldn't do it here in the kitchen.

The distance from the Weber house to the football field location of the horse show is only three blocks. As the Webers drove home, June saw Jessie walking back to the field. She pointed, "There's Jessie. I guess she's doing okay,"

"Well if she isn't, she's handling it," Bill said.

"I think we'll get baby Mason down for a nap," June said.

"Good idea," Bill chuckled, "maybe a very good idea."

"Not me!" Cory said from the back seat.

"What are you going to do Cory?"

"I don't know."

Bill's phone rang. It was his standard ring tone so he had to look at the screen to see who it was. It was his brother. "Fred, happy Independence Day to you!"

"Same to you. How's things going out there in East Anthill, South Dakota?"

Bill played along, "East Anthill? That's the county seat. I don't know. I haven't been there in a couple days. How about you? I thought you were out floating around somewhere."

"We got in yesterday around eighteen hundred."

"Civilian time please."

"Six o'clock yesterday evening. I have duty until midnight then I'll be on leave. Want company?"

"You want to come up?"

"Actually I ordered the plane tickets three weeks ago. Thought I would rent a car and surprise you."

"Okay."

"Well, it turns out I can't get a rental car."

"What airport are you flying into?"

"I booked the flight to Huron, South Dakota. It looked to be the closest airport. Then I got looking at Budget, Enterprise and some others and they all operate out of Sioux Falls."

"Don't worry about that, I'll pick you up."

"I would still like to have a car of my own while I'm there."

"We can do that," Bill said. "I have a friend in Watertown who has a used car lot. He has a side business as a car rental agency. We'll get one for you from him. It will cost you less than the chain outfits.

"Good enough."

"When are you coming in?"

"I fly out tomorrow morning from Regan National. I have to change planes in Denver. The flight from Denver lands at one forty seven in Huron. I'll e-mail you the flight number and the gate information."

Bill chuckled, "You do that. We'll be there."

"All right, I have to go. This ship won't run itself."

"You're running the ship?" I didn't know you had that much clout."

"I have the OOD watch. Hold on a second." Bill heard muffled voices. "I've got to go. I'll see you tomorrow."

"All right - bye," Bill ended the call.

"Who was that?" June asked.

"That was Fred. He's coming up to visit."

"I thought so when you said something about floating," June said. "When is he coming?"

"He's flying into Huron tomorrow."

"Tomorrow!" June turned to Bill. "He doesn't give much warning, does he?"

"He was going to rent a car and surprise us. But none of the chains serve Huron Regional Airport. So he called. I said we'll pick him up."

"Well I'm glad he didn't just pop in. The house is a mess."

"The house looks fine, June. At least it was fine when we left and I don't think Jessie would trash the place."

"Bill," June said in the voice she used when she was trying to explain something to her dense husband, "the house is tidy enough for us, but it's not 'company clean'."

Bill knew the tone and said nothing. He knew also that any plans he had for joining Mason in afternoon slumber were now gone.

Chapter Four

Jessie got back to the football field just as the horse show started. She looked for Jeremy and didn't see him. She saw Mickie in the bleachers and climbed up. "What happened to Jeremy?" she asked.

"He said horse shows were lame and he left," Mickie answered. Then asked, "What happened to you?"

"I went home," Jessie said, providing no further explanation.

"I saved a seat for you. I, on purpose, sat across from Jeremy so you could sit next to him."

Jessie had to quickly re-evaluate her best friend. She thought Mickie was trying to steal Jeremy and all the time she was maneuvering to get Jessie in the right place. "I couldn't stay. Not after what happened in line."

"You should have," Mickie said. "Jeremy stuck up for you. He told Bobby Stacks that he had been holding your place."

"He did?"

"I think he likes you."

"You think so?"

"Why else would he tell Bobby to back off."

"Where did he go?"

"I don't know. He said he didn't care about the horse show."

"Maybe I can find him at the fireworks later."

"Are you two going to talk all the way through the show?"

Jessie turned around, she knew the voice. "No, Mr. Sanderson, sorry."

"Good."

Jessie had to think. She had new facts to deal with. First, she thought Mickie had been trying to get Jeremy for herself when what she was doing was trying to get them together. Second, Jeremy stood up for her in the line at the picnic pavilion. She wondered if he was going to come back for the fireworks. How could she find out? Who did she know who knew Jeremy? Wait, that's not right, everybody knew Jeremy.

Who did she know that she could ask about Jeremy? She couldn't think of anyone. They were over two years apart in age. At thirteen that wasn't a gap, that was chasm. Their friends didn't cross. She wasn't friends with anyone who was friends with him. She was going to ask Mickie about it but she didn't want to hear Mr. Sanderson again. She thought about asking Mickie to step down from the bleachers but she saw Mickie was watching the show. Then she saw her friend Candy Parks was next to perform. The Jeremy problem could wait. She wanted to see Candy win this year. She came in second last year.

She had met Candy through Frank Ogden. The two of them spent a lot of time with Candy and her horses when she was going with Frank. That was before Frank dumped her to take Katie Sands to the spring dance. She had stayed friends with Candy but didn't get out to see the horses as much as she used to.

Jessie was looking across the arena, she thought she saw Jeremy from the back but when the boy turned around, she realized it wasn't him. She felt the bleachers move next to her. She looked over and saw that Frank had taken the seat next to her. "What are you doing here?" she asked.

"I'm watching the horse show," Frank answered. "What are you doing?"

"Well you don't have to watch it here. Go sit somewhere else," Jessie said as she slid away from him.

"I like it here. I can see better. Besides, we both want Candy to win."

"All right, but don't talk to me."

Jessie could feel the magnetism from Frank. It was not as strong and not tempting, but she was aware of it. She reminded herself of what he did last spring and the feeling of attraction went away. She focused on the horse show.

Candy's performance was flawless. Jessie knew the routine, she had watched as Candy had practiced with Muffin a few times in the past month. The horse knew what to do and when to do it. It was almost as if Candy was just along for the ride. When she was done, the crowd stood and clapped.

"That was fantastic!" Frank said. "She'll win this year for sure!"

"Oh, why don't you go kiss her!" Jessie barked.

Frank took a step back as if Jessie had hit him. He recovered and replied, "Maybe I will," and walked down the bleachers.

"What was that about?" Mickie asked.

"Frank was sucking up. I told him off."

"Good," Mickie agreed. Then she pointed, "Here comes Mary Bayer. She's the only one who can beat Candy."

Jessie watched intently. She was looking for any mistake, just the smallest hesitation or misstep will give the win to her friend. She watched the whole performance and didn't see anything wrong. It would be up to the judges.

Bill spent the afternoon helping June with making the house 'company clean'. They moved Mason's crib out of the nursery and set up the blow up bed for Fred to use during his stay. June also moved some of the baby's other items into their bedroom so Fred would not be interrupted. Bill was trying to figure out how to get everything in their bedroom and still maintain some space for his office work. He was failing.

June walked in. "Bill, that won't work. You have the crib so close to my side that I can't get out of bed."

"It won't fit on my side at all," Bill replied.

"Let's try this," June started pulling, "If we move it here we can both get in and out of bed."

"That's fine, but I'll have to crawl under it to get to my desk."

"You can move it to get to your desk." June was starting to get irritated. She was already irked that Fred didn't warn them, now Bill was still trying to keep his man cave rites.

"I can't move it if the baby is sleeping," Bill answered.

"If the baby is sleeping, you won't be working at your desk."

"Why not?"

"Bill..." June said with just a hint of the frustration she was feeling. "just do it this way, okay?"

Bill saw this was going to become a big argument and decided it wasn't worth it. "Let's try it this way. I'll work around it."

June wasn't done, "I think it was pretty rude of your

brother to just barge in on us."

Bill was about to say he didn't barge in but he knew what she meant. He also knew she was a lit fuse. He had to be careful as to how he answered her. "Fred is a Navy bachelor. He has spent the past twenty years on a ship. I don't think it even occurred to him to warn us."

"Then he's stupid."

Now Bill bristled. "Fred isn't stupid. He's Fred. He thought he was doing a good thing trying to surprise us. I understand that. Our uncles and aunts used to do it all the time when we were kids. He only knows that kind of family life."

"Well he should have….."

"Look June. We have plenty of time. I'm here to help. What else do we need to do?"

June thought about it. Her mind ran through the house, it was in good shape, just not clean. Can you dust the furniture and I'll get out the vacuum?"

"Sure."

"Second place again!" Jessie was upset. "Candy was way better then Mary."

"The judges don't think so," Mickie said.

"What do they know," Jessie said.

"What are you going to do now?" Mickie asked.

"I don't know, go home I guess," Jessie replied.

"We could go to the pool," Mickie said.

"I thought it was closed."

"No, they're opening it from two to five."

"Okay, I still have to go home and change," Jessie said.

"Me too," Mickie replied. "I'll text you when I'm ready and we can walk over together."

Jessie and Mickie had decided they were too old for bicycles. They were trying to attract the attention of the boys with cars, they couldn't do that sitting on a bicycle. They walked together to the corner near Mickie's house then separated. Jessie walked in to see her mother dusting. She also heard a vacuum running somewhere in the house. "What's going on?"

"Your uncle Fred is coming," June said. "Go clean your room."

47

"Is he sleeping in there?"

"Don't give me any trouble young lady, do what I said."

Jessie knew that tone. Mom was mad at something or someone. She knew better than to be nearby. She quickly departed the room.

Jessie followed the sound of what she thought was the vacuum and found her father filling a blow up bed in Mason's room. "Uncle Fred's coming?" she asked her dad.

"I'm picking him up at the airport tomorrow afternoon. Want to come?"

"Okay, can I bring Mickie?"

Bill hesitated, "Sure why not. He's flying into Huron. We'll leave here a little after twelve."

"Dad?"

Bill stopped the airbed pump. "What is it peanut?"

"Why is mom mad? Doesn't she like Uncle Fred?"

"She likes Uncle Fred just fine. She doesn't like getting company on short notice. You know how she wants everything perfect for company."

"That's why she told me to clean my room?" Jessie asked. "That's not fair."

"What's not fair?" Bill looked back toward the bed. "Your room could use some spit and polish."

"Some what?"

"It means it could use some work."

"But it's a holiday. Mickie and me…"

"Mickie and I."

"Mickie and I are going to the pool."

"You can go to the pool once your room is picked up," June had walked up behind her. "Now stop bothering your father and let him get his work done."

Jessie left the area without comment. Once she arrived in the safety of her room, she closed the door. She took out her phone and texted Mickie with the news and the delay. Once that was done, she looked around her room. She didn't see anything wrong with it. She picked up some clothes from a basket and put them away, she picked up some other things and put them in the back of the closet. She made, really made, the bed and neatly arranged the things on her night stand and dresser. She looked around once more and, satisfied, changed into her swimsuit.

"Look," Mickie said.

"Look at what?"

"There by the pool entrance. There's Jeremy."

"Oh no!" Jessie said and turned her back to the entrance. "Is he looking over here?"

"No, he's talking to Cody Croft."

"Good." Jessie swam to the side of the pool farthest from the entrance. She hopped up on the side and moved to the table where her towel was. She kept her back to the entrance.

Mickie followed her. "What are you doing?"

"I don't want him to see me. Not like this!"

"Why not?"

"Why not?! Look at this suit! Look at my hair! I've got to get to the bathhouse. Is he still by the entrance?"

"No, he's coming this way."

"Which way around the deep end or the shallow end?"

"The deep end."

Jessie started walking toward the shallow end. She had to get to her locker and her hair brush. She needed to brush the kinks out from swimming and pull her hair back before she could meet Jeremy. She had made it around the end of the pool when Mary Bayer walked up. "Looks like I beat your friend again this year."

"Candy can't help it if you have an in with the judges. She was flawless, you stole it."

I did not!" Mary said indignantly. "Just because Uncle John is on the judging panel doesn't mean I get special points."

"Sure looks like it from here?" Jessie said and turned to walk away.

"You saying I cheated?" Mary flared.

Jessie suddenly realized she was in over her head. "I'm saying it's not fair to have a family member on the panel. That's all."

"My Uncle John wouldn't cheat. If anything, I have to be better to get the same score. You're just mad your friend isn't as good as I am with Baxter."

"She is as good or better. We'll see at the State Fair when

49

the judges won't know anybody."

"You are nothing but a little....."

"There you are," Jeremy interrupted what was almost certainly going to turn into a fight. "Mickie said you were going to the locker room. I thought I missed you."

Mary's features changed from angry to cutesy in almost an instant. "Hi Jeremy. Did you see the horse show? I won."

"I don't go to horse shows," Jeremy said brushing off Mary's maneuvering.

"Well I.... oowf," Mary turned on her heel and left.

As Mary stormed off he turned again to Jessie, "I don't like her. I think she's a snob."

"She's all right. Just stuck-up." Jessie wasn't sure why she said that. She didn't like Mary either.

"You going to the park tonight?" Jeremy asked. "Some of us are going to hang out by the pavilion."

"Sure I'm going," Jessie answered, hoping to be invited to join the group.

"Can I pick you up for the fireworks tonight?"

"Pick me up?" Jessie felt as if her head was whirling. "Sure... I mean all right."

"Good we can sit in the back of the pick-up and watch the show. I'll be at your house at nine."

"Okay." Jessie was doing her best to stay cool. She wasn't sure what to say next. So she pointed to the ladies side of the pool house and said, "I've got to change. My uncle is coming into town tomorrow and I need to help my mom."

"All right, see you tonight."

Jessie walked into the locker room, she took out her phone and texted Mickie.

cm hre

wre

lckr rm

k

It was almost a full minute before Mickie got inside the locker room. To Jessie it felt like ten.

"I saw you talking to Mary, then Jeremy, what happened?"

"He stuck up for me again and then he asked me out!"

"Out? Where?"

"He's picking me up for the fireworks!"

Jessie had no more time for swimming. She had to get home and get ready for tonight. She did a quick rinse in the shower and dressed for the walk home. Then she waited anxiously while Mickie showered and changed back into her shorts and tank top. As they walked home they discussed the upcoming event.

Jessie was watching out the living room window. She didn't want to miss Jeremy when he drove up. She had taken over two hours to get ready. It was no small challenge. She had to make sure she looked good enough for Jeremy while not drawing the attention of her parents. She got through the process with only one "You're not going to wear that?" from her mother.

"What are you looking for?" Bill asked.

"I'm watching for Jeremy, he's picking me up for the fireworks."

"Jeremy who?"

"Jeremy Finney."

"So you're not going with us?"

"No." Jessie's 'dad radar' detected danger, so she didn't say anything more.

"Where will you be?" Bill asked.

"A bunch of us kids are going to sit together by the pavilion." Jessie was on the edge of the truth and she knew it.

"Who else is he picking up?"

"I don't know."

"Is he going to pick up Mickie?"

"Dad! I don't know." Jessie didn't like the way the conversation was going. She had to find a way to deflect it. She figured out what to say, it wasn't a lie… really. "I was talking to Jeremy at the pool. We were talking about the horse show. He told me that a bunch of kids were going to hang out at the fireworks and asked me if I would like to be with them. We are going to sit in the back of his pick-up truck and watch the fireworks." Jessie said it in such a way as to lead her father to believe that more than the two of them were going to be in the truck.

"I'm not sure I'm comfortable with you riding around

51

with older boys, but if a group of you are together, I suppose that's all right."

"You and mom will be there too," Jessie added.

"All right," Bill said. "But straight home afterwards. If Jeremy and the other kids want to stay longer, you can come home with us."

Jessie cringed on the inside. She could not imagine ending her evening with Jeremy by having to ride home with her parents. She would find her own way home. She would walk if she had to, but she hoped she wouldn't have to. She said what her father wanted to hear, "Okay Dad," then turned and watched out the window again.

Bill walked into the bedroom where June was dressing Mason for the night out. "Do you think the mosquitoes will be too much?"

"I don't want to use harsh chemicals to keep the bugs away," June replied.

"Are you going to use the stroller and the netting?"

"I intended to do that. I hope it's enough."

"Well, we'll keep an eye on him. If he gets bit, I'll take him to the car and run the AC," Bill said. He changed to the other subject at hand. "Do you know Jessie isn't going with us?"

"Sure I know. She's been getting ready for hours."

"Getting ready?" Bill repeated. "You mean this is a date?"

"She thinks it is," June replied.

"She didn't tell me that. She told me she was hanging out with friends." Bill thought for a moment, "I don't know that I like this."

"Get used to it Bill. Your little girl is growing up."

"She's not growing up that fast. She's only thirteen. How old is Jeremy Finney?"

"I don't know, fifteen I guess, if he's driving."

"That's too old." Bill turned to walk back to the living room.

June stopped him. "Bill, wait. You are over reacting. The kids are going to be in the same park as we are. We will be able to see them. What if this isn't a date and Jeremy is picking up a bunch of kids?"

"That's what Jessie told me," Bill said, now even more

confused. "So which is it? A date or a bunch of kids hanging out?"

"I think it's probably both."

"That doesn't help," Bill said.

"I think your daughter has a crush on Jeremy and Jeremy is being nice."

"He's too old for her," Bill said firmly.

"You mean she's too young for him."

"What's the difference?"

"If he was fourteen like Frankie, that would be all right?" June asked.

"I suppose so."

"But he's not. He's a few months older."

"He's driving!"

"So…?"

"How do I know how safe he is behind the wheel? How do I know his car, uh, truck is safe?" Bill was getting upset. The more he thought about it the more he didn't like it. "I'm going to stop this right now."

"Bill, stop!" Now it was June's turn to be firm.

Bill stopped.

"In the first place, this is Jeremy Finney, Mike Finney's boy. You know what kind of mechanic he is. That truck wouldn't dare to have even one screw half a turn loose. Mike is a good father. I'm sure Jeremy knows how to drive safely."

"But…"

"No buts, listen to me," June said forcefully. "Your getting all worked up over nothing. They will be in the park with us. They will be around other kids. I know these kids, they're not hoodlums. They're good kids. Your little girl is growing up. You have to ease off a little."

"I still don't like it."

Bill heard the sound of a high performance engine drive down the street. He looked out the window to see an old Dodge pick up truck pull into the driveway. The truck looked bright and clean. Some of the paint was worn as if it had been polished away by over waxing.

"There he is!" Jessie shouted from the living room. "I'm going!"

"Have a good time dear," June called back.

"Be home right after the fireworks," Bill barked.

If Jessie heard either one, they would never know. All they heard in reply was the front door slamming.

The first time Bill went to see the fireworks in Helen he didn't expect much. He had been to the "Fireworks on the Mall" in Washington DC and the Baltimore Inner Harbor for their show. What could a tiny town of Helen do compared to that?

He was pleasantly surprised. No, it wasn't a gala event with synchronized music, but it was a substantial display. It reminded him of his childhood, before the high tech and computerized commercial shows. Helen did it the old fashioned way. The volunteer firemen used road flares to touch off the mortars each in turn to provide a dazzling display.

He was looking forward to tonight. With baby Mason safely ensconced in his traveling seat, Bill held the passenger door of the Escalade for his wife. Cory had jumped into his spot behind dad. "Are we ready to see some fireworks?" Bill asked as he got into the driver's seat.

"Yeah!" Cory replied.

"Do you remember them from last year Cory?" Bill looked at his son in the mirror.

"They were sick. I liked the loud ones."

"I'm not sure Mason will like the loud ones," June said. "We'll have to see."

"Can Freckles come?" Cory asked just as Bill started the car.

"You remember how Freckles hides when there is a thunder storm?" June asked.

"Yes."

"Well, I don't think it's a good idea to bring him around loud fireworks, do you?"

"Okay," Cory dropped the subject. If he noticed his sister was not with them, it was not important enough for him to mention.

The Webers pulled the car up at the edge of the park. Bill walked around back and got out the stroller frame for the car seat. He unfolded it and pushed it over to June. He then walked back and got out three chairs. He handed Cory the smaller one. "Here, Cory, this one is yours."

"Okay."

He set up the other two chairs in front of the Escalade. June pushed Mason next to her chair and sat down. Cory followed suit by placing his chair next to his dad.

"Do you see Jessie?" Bill asked.

"No," June said, looking around.

"There she is," Cory pointed.

Bill followed Cory's point and saw his daughter sitting on a picnic table in the pavilion. There was a crowd of kids in the pavilion so Bill relaxed. It looked to him that Jessie was right and there would be a bunch of kids hanging out together. "Good," he told himself. "Now I can enjoy the show."

"What?" June asked.

"What?" Bill responded. "Oh," he realized what he had done. "I was just commenting to myself that Jessie was with a group of other kids."

"Where did you expect her to be?" June asked.

"Never mind, it's not important."

"Hi, Bill!" Tom Ogden and family walked up minus Frank.

"Hi Tom, Sarah. Hello Joey," Bill replied.

Tom set his chair down, "Joey, put your chair next to Cory." He set the other chair next to June.

"I didn't expect to see you," Bill said "Don't you normally watch this from home?"

"The straight line distance is only about three miles. We get a pretty good show from home. This year Frankie wanted to come in and hang out in the pavilion with the other kids. So we drove in."

"Next year he'll do that himself," Bill said.

"Don't remind me," Sarah jumped in. "I feel old enough."

June laughed. "Don't I know it. Jessie is on her first non school date."

"That's a bit scary," Sarah agreed.

"I thought you said it wasn't a date?" Bill asked.

"It isn't Bill, but she thinks it is."

"How does that work?"

The explanation would have to wait. There was a thud

and a streamer of sparks rising quickly into the sky. The world lit up with a starburst and the ground shook with the first detonation. The people in the park applauded.

Then another thud sound, Bill automatically looked up. He saw another large fluorescent pattern emerge.

Joey and Cory had been in deep conversation. "Can we go sit on the bleachers?"

"Sure," June replied, "but stay where we can see you and come right back when it's over."

Chapter Five

Jessie saw her parents drive up. She was glad to see them park a good distance away. She turned her attention back to Jeremy, who had become the center of attention. Mary Bayer kept trying to get between them. Jessie jumped up and sat on the picnic table to block her most recent approach.

"You mean he was thrown by a lawnmower?" Mary asked, shooting a frown at Jessie.

"A riding mower," Jeremy answered.

"How do you do that?" Jessie asked.

"He was mowing under a tree in the yard. When he didn't duck enough to get his head under a branch, the mower kept going, and he got swept off the back. He had to get up and chase it to get back on."

"That had to be funny!" Mary said, laughing.

"Was he hurt?" Jessie asked.

"Just his pride when he saw us at the window."

"I thought those mowers would quit if you got off. It's a safety thing." Ryan Woodson asked as a statement.

"You know my dad never leaves anything stock. He removed all the safety devices."

"Isn't that dangerous?" Mary asked, trying desperately to stay in the conversation.

"Of course, moron. That's why he fell off!" The kids laughed at Jeremy's answer and Mary moved off.

There was a thud, and everyone stayed quiet for a second. Then the area lit up followed almost instantly by the loud boom. "They're starting," Ryan said.

"We can't see anything in here," Jeremy said looking at Jessie. "Let's go to my truck."

"I'll come too," Mary said.

Jeremy didn't even turn to look at her. He said, "Three's a crowd," and kept walking.

Jessie half walked and half floated behind Jeremy. Not only was she invited, she would be the only one invited. Jeremy put one foot on the back bumper of the truck and lifted his other leg over the tailgate. Jessie repeated the action. Jessie saw that Jeremy had two sleeping bags in the bed of the truck.

He opened one and spread it out. He unrolled the other and re-rolled it. Then he laid on his back and used the second one for a pillow. "Here, lie on your back, and you can see the whole thing."

Jessie sat down and leaned back on the sleeping bag, unsure of what she wanted to do. Half of her brain said, "Try to crawl up next to him" and the other half said, "run away screaming". She compromised by sitting up in the bed of the truck leaning against the sleeping bag pillow.

"What's up with Mary Bayer?" Jeremy asked.

Jessie stayed silent. She wasn't sure where the conversation was going.

"Can't she figure out I don't really like her?" Jeremy continued.

Jessie still didn't say anything. She didn't want to talk about Mary Bayer or anyone else. The fireworks were going off one after another in the sky over her head and in her heart. She could sense the heat from his body next to her. It felt like he was ten degrees hotter then she was. The magnet was drawing her, and despite her earlier fears, she slowly slid down and was lying next to him. She thought about putting her head on his shoulder but quickly changed her mind. The world was perfect. The sides of the pick-up bed hid them from view. The sky was lit up with fireworks and they were together at their own private show, in their own private world. She felt Jeremy's arm come over her shoulder and pull her a bit closer. She knew he was trying to kiss her, but she intentionally missed the cue.

Her heart was pounding, her breath was short. She wasn't sure how long she could avoid his hints when the finale went off. The sky lit up with a thousand sparks and just as they did she felt Jeremy lean over and kiss her. The sparks moved from outside her head to inside.

Then it was over.

The world crashed in with Ryan looking over the side of the truck and saying, "That was all right. I've seen better."

Jessie would swear to Mickie later that Jeremy had looked at her and said, "I haven't."

Jessie sat up and looked over toward where her family was packing up. Then she saw Frank. He was standing in the pavilion alone, looking at her. When he realized she saw him, he turned and walked away.

"That was a great show," Tom Ogden said to Bill. "I'm going to come into town every year."

"Oh come on, Tom," Sarah said, "it was good but it's not Macy's,"

"I thought it was better. I didn't realize we could get this close." Tom replied. "The only other time I got this close was when we had that Fourth of July cruise on the Delaware. Remember?"

"That was before Frankie was born," Sarah answered.

"I love the small town fireworks," June said. "It's more genuine somehow."

"Probably because you're involved in it. You helped pay for it, and you know the people doing it," Bill said.

"You're right," Tom agreed, "it's more personal. Anyway, I intend to be in the park here next year. I've learned my lesson."

"Do you see Joey?" Sarah asked.

"No. Hold on," Sarah reached for her phone, "I'll text Frankie and get him to bring Joey."

"If he sees Cory, get him to come back, too," June said. Then she realized how silly that statement was. The two boys would be together.

Bill started putting chairs away. June took the baby carrier out of the stroller frame and set it in the Escalade. She made sure the belts were tight. Cory and Joey came running up with Joey in the lead. "I won!"

"You cheated, you started first!"

"I said on three."

"But you didn't count, you just said 'Three!' and ran."

"Sucker!"

"All right boys," Tom said in his 'Dad' voice. "That's enough. Joey, where's your brother?"

"I don't know." Joey shrugged.

"I'm right here," Frank said as he walked up. "Are we ready to go?"

"Just as soon as I put these chairs in the car," Tom said.

"Good." Frank got in the car ending any further conversation.

Once Tom had everything in the trunk, Sarah got in on the passenger side and turned to look at her son. "What's wrong Frankie?"

"To start with, my name is Frank. I'm not six, I'm almost fifteen."

"Your name will be mud if you don't watch your mouth," Tom said.

"Tom..." Sarah said reprovingly. Then she turned to the back again. "What's wrong?"

"Nothing."

"You sure?"

"I'm sure!"

"Frank!" Tom looked into the mirror.

"Sorry."

Jeremy had rolled up the sleeping bags and put them away. He looked at Jessie. "I hoped you liked that," he said.

Jessie wasn't sure if he was talking about the fireworks or the kiss. She liked one and loved the other. She chose to comment on the lesser. "The fireworks were good. I've never watched them lying down before."

"That's what makes it fun. My dad used to take all of us to the fireworks in his pick up. The whole family would lie in the bed and watch." Jeremy hopped out of the truck and walked back into the pavilion. Jessie followed. She looked around for Mary, but she was nowhere in sight. She smiled.

"You know, we could go over to the lake." Cody Croft suggested.

Jessie's radar detected danger again. This time she paid attention. "I think I need to get home."

"Suit yourself," Jeremy shrugged. "I'll take you home." He looked at the four remaining kids at the table. "My dad wants me to help him install an engine in the morning; I think I'll go too." Jeremy turned and walked to the truck, Jessie followed. She got in on his side and only slid to the middle. She wanted to feel him next to her again.

They drove home listening to a song Jeremy liked. The

song wasn't over when Jeremy pulled into Jessie's driveway. He leaned over to kiss her again, and Jessie pulled back. "My father's right there," she said as she pointed to the open garage door.

Jeremy looked over and saw Bill hanging the lawn chairs on a hook. He got out and Jessie followed. He walked Jessie to the garage door, "Good night," he said.

"Good night," Jessie replied. Then she turned and ran into the house.

Jeremy turned to walk away when he heard, "That your truck, Jeremy?"

"Yes, Sir," Jeremy always said 'Sir and Ma'am' when addressing adults. His father was retired Navy and had drilled it into him from the time he was old enough to talk. Even though the other kids abused him over it, the response was automatic. "My dad bought it out of a farmer's field and helped me restore it."

"What year is it?" Bill asked. He was more curious about the boy who brought his daughter home than he was about the truck. He asked just to keep the conversation going.

"It's a nineteen seventy-eight," Jeremy answered. He was getting uncomfortable and decided to keep his answers short so he could get out of there.

"Well, it looks very good for a truck over thirty years old."

"Thank you."

"Well… have a good night. Thanks for bringing Jessie home."

"Sure. Goodnight." Jeremy got into his truck quickly and drove off.

Bill walked in the house. He didn't see Jessie anywhere. He walked back to her bedroom, the door was closed so he knocked, "Jessie?"

"She's in the shower," June said from their bedroom. "I'm in here changing the baby."

Bill walked in to see June wrestling with fifteen pounds of wiggling flesh. "That's amazing. He slept through the fireworks, all the noise over his head never bothered him. Now when you put him in his crib, he woke up?"

"Actually he was still asleep. I wanted to change and

61

feed him before putting him down for the night," June said as she closed the fresh diaper. "What time are you going to get Fred?"

"His plane gets into Huron at about one forty five. I figure I'll leave here about noon and treat the kids to a Burger King lunch."

"You may want to wait until he gets in. He'll be hungry, too."

"I hadn't thought of that. I don't want to take him to Burger King. Not for his first meal. I'll have to think about that again. Do you want to go?"

"No, I think I'll stay home with Mason. You take the kids."

"All right."

"Mommy?"

"What is it Cory?" June answered her son.

"I have to go, and Jessie is hogging the bathroom."

"Use ours dear."

"Okay."

"Where are your slippers?"

"In my room."

"Shouldn't you be wearing them?"

"I forgot."

"What are we going to do about Jessie?" Bill asked after his son had gone back to his room.

"What about Jessie?"

"She was sitting in the middle of the truck seat when they pulled up."

June hadn't looked up from the baby, "So?"

"So..." Bill repeated. "There was nobody else in the truck."

"Sounds as if she's attracted to him," June said.

"I said it earlier. He's too old for her. She's young and naïve. He could take advantage."

"He could," June said.

Bill was surprised by his wife's answer. "That doesn't bother you?"

"Of course, it bothers me, Bill." June turned and faced her husband. "Look, we raised Jessie to have good judgment. She's more than capable of making the right decisions."

"She can, but when she's worked up over this boy, can she keep her head?"

"I would think so."

"Well I'm not going to take the chance. I'm going to stop it. She can date boys who drive when she can drive."

"Bill, now you're being unreasonable," June said. "Give this one week. I'll bet it's over, and she has another boy in her sights."

"One week," Bill agreed. "But if it isn't over by then, I'll end it."

"Okay," June agreed. "Now how about unwinding that mainspring of yours and start thinking about getting some rest?"

"All right," Bill said. "I'm going to get a shower."

"I hope your daughter left some hot water."

Bill chuckled. "A cold shower might be better for me tonight anyway."

The morning was bright and clear. The weatherman said the temperature would be about eighty-five without any chance of rain. Bill woke up to the sounds of birds singing outside his open window. Things were right in his world. Even his thoughts about Jessie were clearer today. He was still not happy with her choosing a boy so much older than she was, but he was willing to see if June was right about it being a brief passing romance.

He had decided that he would wait the week and if Jessie was still dating Jeremy, he would go talk to Mike about it. If both fathers stood firm, the whole matter could be over.

Bill walked over to his dresser, he took out his 'work' jeans. He would wash and wax the Escalade this morning so it would look good for Fred's arrival. Normally, he used the car wash near his office in Kent, but he had not been working in the office this week. He found his favorite tee shirt. It was a throwback to a younger time. It was well worn and had "Boat Chesapeake" emblazoned across the front.

Once properly dressed for the work ahead, he walked out to the kitchen. "Good morning!" he said.

"Hi Bill," June replied, "About time you got up."

Bill looked at the clock on the stove. He thought maybe

the clock in the bedroom was wrong, but it wasn't. "Eight forty-five," he said. "What's wrong with that?"

"Oh, nothing." June smiled sarcastically. "The rest of the family has been up for an hour."

"Even the kids?"

"Even the kids. They've had breakfast and gone on their own separate ways."

"Gone?"

"Gone," June repeated. "Jessie went to Mickie's and Cory is down the street with Jeffrey.

"So, we're alone?" Bill started to mentally shift his plans. Maybe washing the car would wait.

"All except Mason." June pointed at the baby carrier on the table.

Bill moved up next to his wife. "I was going to wash the Escalade, but maybe that can wait."

June leaned back into him, giving him even more encouragement. "Wait for what? Do you have something in mind?"

"Well I was thinking maybe we could walk back to our bedroom…"

"Mommy! Mommy!" Cory's voice crushed any mood that was about to start.

June pulled away from her husband and moved to meet her son at the door. "What is it?"

"I smushed my finger in the door! It hurts!"

"Let me see, which finger?"

"This one, and this one too."

June took a look at the two fingers Cory was holding up. There was no blood. "Nothing's cut," she reassured her son. "Can you move them? Can you make a fist?"

Cory slowly made a fist and released it. "Yes."

"Okay, it's not cut and it's not broken. I think you'll be fine."

"But it hurts!"

"Does it hurt as much as when it happened?" June asked.

"No."

"Then it's already getting better."

"It is?"

"Sure." June reassured her son. "Just use the other hand for a while, and it'll be okay."

"Okay," Cory said. "Can I go back to Jefferey's?"

"Go ahead."

June turned to her husband, "Another crisis averted."

"And another child left un-conceived," Bill chuckled.

"Oh, Bill. you're just a dirty old man."

"And don't you forget it."

"Well, the mood's gone now," June said. "Besides, there's no telling if Cory will stay at Jeffrey's."

"You're right," Bill reluctantly agreed. "Time for breakfast, after that, I'm going to wash the Escalade."

"You should use that shirt. It's not much more than a rag anyway."

"My lucky shirt?" Bill said dramatically, "Perish the thought, woman!"

"Lucky shirt?" June pulled on the sleeve. "You're lucky I didn't turn it into a dust rag years ago. Why don't you take your car over to the church? The youth group is doing a car wash today."

"I hadn't heard about that."

"You would have 'seen' of that" June mis-repeated, "if you had read the church bulletin."

"I don't know. The Escalade is a dark color. If they do it wrong, the streaks will be permanent. I think I'd rather do it myself."

June knew better than to get between a man and his SUV. "Suit yourself. I'm taking my Caravan over in a bit. They are only charging three dollars."

"I know. They charge three, but everybody gives them five."

Chapter Six

"All right…" Bill shouted from the kitchen, "the airport express is leaving for Huron in ten minutes. Who's ready?"

"I am!" Cory said as he ran up.

"Cory, look at that shirt!" June said. "You can't wear that?

"I wore it yesterday," Cory replied.

"Which is exactly why you will not wear it today," June said firmly. "Let's go find another shirt."

"I know how."

June started to argue that he had just demonstrated he didn't, but changed her mind. "All right. Go get another shirt, a clean one this time."

"How long do you think it will stay clean?" Bill asked.

"I don't know. If you get him right to the car…" June didn't finish the sentence. Instead she said, "I think he could get dirty playing with a bar of soap and a bucket of water."

"Soapy mud pies?"

June laughed, "Don't give him any ideas."

Bill walked back to Jessie's door. He knocked. "Jessie are you ready?"

No answer.

Bill knocked louder.

"What?"

"Are you ready to go pick up uncle Fred?"

"I'll be right there."

Bill walked back to the kitchen. "I should have just gone alone. I'd be there by now."

"And you'd be two hours early," June retorted.

"How's this?" Cory asked coming into the room.

"Much better."

"June, will you hurry up Jessie and I'll get Cory into the car."

"Sure." June walked down to Jessie's door. "Jessie, your dad is getting in the car."

"All right!"

"Mind your tongue young lady or you'll find yourself in your room all afternoon."

"I'm coming."

"Now, please."

The door opened and Jessie walked by her mother. She was looking at her phone, her thumbs moving rapidly.

June almost let her trip, but her mother's instinct got in the way. "Watch the basket."

Jessie looked up from her phone, skirted the laundry basket and continued into the kitchen. She put the phone down, got out a glass, filled it with water from the pitcher in the refrigerator, drank it then left the glass on the counter. She turned to walk out of the room.

"What do we do with the glass?" June said. Then thought to herself, "Oh no! I sound like my mother!"

Jessie stopped, put her phone down, opened the dishwasher and put the glass on the top rack. She closed the dishwasher, picked up her phone and started walking and typing again, all without comment.

With June following, Jessie walked out to the Escalade and got in the front seat. She pulled on her seatbelt and continued texting.

"Okay," Bill said, "Everybody ready?"

"Let's go!" said Cory.

"Yes," answered Jessie absentmindedly.

Bill turned to June. "I guess we're off. If Fred calls, let me know."

"Why would he call?"

"I don't know. He'll call if he misses the connection."

"I'm not going anywhere. If he calls I'll be here to get the phone." With that she moved in for the anticipated kiss.

Bill responded as expected. "See you in a few hours."

Bill backed the Escalade out of the garage, down the driveway and started the slow drive out of Helen. The speed limit inside town is twenty miles per hour and Bill did his best to keep the Escalade at or under that speed. He did it, not because there was a patrol car on every corner. On this particular day, there wasn't one within twenty miles. He did it because he lived there and agreed with the speed limit.

Once out of town, he set the cruise control at sixty nine miles per hour, exactly four miles over the speed limit. At this speed it would take them just under an hour to get to the

Huron Regional Airport. He looked at the clock on the dash, eleven fifty five. If he wasn't held up, he would be there almost an hour early. He wanted the cushion but wasn't sure what to do with the time.

Jessie solved the problem for him. "Can we stop at the Western Store while we're in Huron?"

"We will be about forty-five minutes early if we don't get delayed. We can stop for a little while. What are you looking for?"

"I don't know. I just like the place." Jessie looked at her phone again. She giggled.

"What's funny?" Bill asked.

"Nothing."

"Can we go to McDonalds?" Cory asked. "I'm hungry."

"No, Cory. Your Uncle Fred is coming to South Dakota for only the second time. I don't want his first meal to be McDonalds."

"Where are we going to eat then?"

"We are going to eat at home," Bill replied. "Your mom is making ribs with Old West dipping sauce."

"But that's going to be *hours*! I'm hungry now."

"You're always hungry. Didn't I see you eat a sandwich just before we left?"

"Only one."

"You'll live until we get home."

"But I..."

"That's enough. Maybe we'll stop for a milkshake if there's time."

"A milkshake, at McDonalds!"

Bill realized almost as soon as he said it, he had made a mistake. The milkshake would have to wait until after they met the plane. Bill didn't want to take the chance of Cory spilling the shake on his shirt.

Bill considered himself lucky. The stop at Jessie's favorite western store cost him less than two hundred dollars. They walked out with a new belt for Cory, two new button down embroidered blouses for Jessie and a pair of leather braces for himself.

Bill didn't like suspenders. He considered them the

attire of old people, but leather braces with snap hooks, that was different. He wasn't sure if June would agree. He would certainly find out.

They got to the airport terminal about ten minutes before the flight was due to arrive. They sat outside and watched the runway for an approaching aircraft. Bill could see the landing lights in the distance. Huron was not a hub of activity. Bill was fairly sure the lights he was seeing were from the only commercial carrier to serve the Huron airport. He pointed the lights out to the kids, "There…. There it is."

"Where?" asked Cory,

"Look at where I'm pointing. See the lights?"

"Okay."

"How come uncle Fred isn't married?" Jessie asked.

"I don't know. You'd have to ask him. I suppose it's because he had to spend so much time at sea."

They watched as the landing lights grew more defined and turned into an airplane. Then, at Dad's lead, they got out as the plane landed. Cory ran ahead to the fence and watched the plane roll by. "That was cool," Cory said. "I want to be a pilot when I grow up."

"You can be what ever you set your mind to be, Cory," Bill said. "Let's go inside."

Fred met them and after the hugs, handshakes and the 'Look how big you've growns', they grabbed Fred's two bags and walked out to the Escalade. Fred was carrying Cory in one hand and his smaller green canvas bag in the other. Jessie was walking beside him.

Bill had the other bag; a much larger canvas bag. "Interesting luggage, Fred."

"On a ship there isn't much space. There's almost none for personal items. I have to use luggage that folds up neatly. The one you are carrying was designed to hold four parachutes."

"Parachutes? Since when do you need parachutes on a ship."

"We don't, but we do need parachute riggers to take care of the helicopter crew's flight safety equipment." He lifted the one he was carrying slightly to call attention to it. "I had this one made for overnight and to hold my computer."

"My tax dollars at work?" Bill quipped.

"I guess you could say that," Fred laughed.

"I'm hungry!"

"Cory, you're always hungry. Mom is making a nice supper. We'll eat when we get home."

"What about the milkshake? You promised," Cory said.

"I didn't promise, I said if we had time."

"But …"

Fred interrupted, "You know, I could go for something cold and wet too, if we have the time."

"Okay," Bill relented. "I'll take you by the giant pheasant and we'll stop in the café there for a drink. Will that do Cory?"

"Can I get a milkshake?"

"Sure, if you promise to be careful," Bill said.

"I want chocolate."

Fred turned in his seat. "Jessie, what flavor of milkshake do you like?"

"I like all of them, except chocolate," Jessie answered without looking up from her phone.

As they pulled up Fred saw the statue and the sign, 'The World's Largest Pheasant'. "I've got to get a picture of that."

"That's what those platforms are for. You get on that one and I'll go on the other one and take your picture," Bill said.

The next several minutes were taken up with Bill and family changing places with Fred, finding different angles and different subjects all with the giant pheasant statue in the background. Once the photo fest was over, they walked into the café.

"So, Uncle Fred, how long are you staying?" Jessie asked.

"I have three weeks leave."

"You can stay away that long?" Bill asked.

"The ship is in for refit. It will be tied up at the pier or in dry dock for at least a year."

"You are going to be on land for a year? How will you stand it?" Bill quipped.

"I'm going to have to get used to it. My days at sea are over."

"Over?" Bill was surprised. He thought his brother loved the sea.

"The ship is in now and will not go out again with me on it," Fred said.

"Are you in some kind of trouble? Do we need to talk privately?"

"No, I'm not in trouble. I'm retiring."

"You're retiring? From the Navy?" Bill repeated.

"Well I'm not retiring from General Motors, Bill."

"What will you do?" Bill asked.

"I'm not sure. There's no civilian equivalent to what I do for the Navy," Fred explained. "Not that that would matter. I am thinking about taking the advice of a friend of mine who retired about five years ago. He got out and went in a totally different direction. He was a turbine engine mechanic in the Navy. He retired and got a job on a horse ranch. He couldn't be happier. I've seen other guys get out, move over to the civilian equivalent and be totally miserable. I think I like the idea of getting away from anything Navy for a while."

"I never thought I'd hear my big brother say that. You have lived and breathed Navy since your eighteenth birthday."

"Don't you think that's long enough?"

"I never really thought about it. You have been in the Navy all my adult life." Bill was still a bit stunned. Fred's announcement added a whole list of questions. "When does all this happen?"

"I put in my papers. My last day should be sometime in early September."

"So, you're going to be here for three weeks and then back to the ship for a month. Then what?"

"Then nothing. I'm done. They give me a quick ceremony, a flag and a pat on the ass. Then they pipe me over the side and I become a distant memory."

Bill didn't know what to say. He fell back on dad mode. "We should get going. June is looking forward to seeing you."

"I'm looking forward to seeing her too," Fred answered.

They left the café, after a discussion as to who would pay for the drinks. Bill finally let his brother win. On the way back to Helen, Fred told story after story about his adventures both on board ship and in foreign ports.

"You must have been on every continent," Jessie said.

"Every one but Antarctica."

"Why not Antarctica? No girls in those ports?" Bill quipped.

"No ports," Fred answered.

"Here's Helen," Bill said as he turned off the highway.

"That was quick," Fred replied. "It looked longer on the map."

"Time passes quickly when you start spinning your tales of adventure," Bill said.

"Uncle Fred, were you ever on a submarine?" Cory asked.

"I was once, but not underway. That takes a special kind of person, and I'm not one. I like the feel of salt air in my face. Anyway, I had a friend I met at the CPO club in Groton, Connecticut. He invited me aboard for a tour and lunch in the goat locker."

"Goat locker?" Cory laughed. "They have goats?"

Fred laughed in turn. "No, Cory. It's just an expression. The Goatlocker is the place where all the old goats hang out. I guess today you would call them old farts."

"Then that would make it the fart locker," Jessie said, bringing a laugh to everyone.

"We're here," Bill said as he pulled into the driveway.

June opened the door between the mudroom and the garage. Freckles bounded out. He ran to Cory's door first. Cory got out and got a face full of dog kisses. "Freckles! Stop it!" he giggled.

Fred opened the passenger door at the same time Jessie opened the back door. "Hi June! Good to see you again," he said.

"Fred," June replied, "welcome to Helen, South Dakota."

"I'm glad to be here."

"How about a beer?"

"Now you're talking my language," Fred smiled. "Let me just grab these bags."

"I'll get this one Uncle Fred," Cory said reaching for the larger one.

"I think that's a bit heavy for you Cory," Fred pushed the smaller one toward him, "Here, take this one."

"Okay."

"Jessie, show your Uncle Fred where to put his luggage."

"This way," Jessie pointed, "we cleared out baby Mason's room for you."

"You didn't have to do that. The couch would have been fine."

"Nonsense," June said. "You'd never get any sleep on the couch."

"I could sleep in a shaft alley."

"A what?" Bill asked.

"The part of the ship where the propeller drive shaft runs," Fred said. "It doesn't matter, what I mean is I have learned to sleep anywhere."

"Well, you'll sleep in here," June said firmly.

Fred put his larger bag on the bed and grabbed the smaller one from Cory. "I have presents for you and Jessie."

"Yea!" Cory said.

"For you, Cory, is an official Navy web belt with the logo of my ship on the buckle."

"Great!" Cory took the belt and looked at the buckle. "What's FFG?"

"It stands for Fast Frigate, Guided Missile."

"Oh," Cory said.

"Jessie, I have an official ship's cap for you."

"Thank you," Jessie said as she took the hat. She walked across the hall to her mother's mirror. She used the adjusting hole in the back for her hair, making it a pony tail holder. She walked back into Mason's room. "How's that?"

"I've never seen anyone do that before," Fred said. "It looks great."

Fred reached back into his bag and pulled out two objects each wrapped in a tee shirt. "These are for you and Bill," he said to June.

"Oh good, I could use a new tee shirt," Bill quipped.

June unwrapped the shirts and found two FFG-59 coffee mugs. "That's nice," June said.

"Look at the front."

June turned the cup around, it read "June Weber - CINC House" the other read "Bill Weber - Commander - Weber Family".

"They're great!" Bill said.

"I had them made up months ago. I thought about it too late for Christmas, so I brought them along. Now, how about that beer?"

"Step right this way," Bill said.

When they got to the kitchen, Bill handed his brother a cold bottle. "Want a glass?"

Fred held up the bottle, "I have one."

Bill took a bottle for himself and moved to sit at the kitchen table. Fred followed suit.

"Oh, no you don't," June said. "We have to get the table ready in here and we don't want the two of you in the way."

"Let's go this way," Bill led his brother to living room.

"This is a great house. You told me you paid under a hundred?"

"Fifty."

"Amazing," Fred said. "Is the fireplace real? Does it work?"

"Sure. We used it quite a bit this last winter. It warms up the house quite nicely."

"So you don't get cold?" Fred asked.

"What do you mean?"

Fred sat down in Bill's recliner, "You told me it can get below zero up here. Doesn't the house get cold?"

"Fred, I won't kid you. It gets cold. I've seen minus numbers that would scare an Eskimo, but this house stays warm. It can be minus ten outside and I'm walking around in a tee shirt."

"Must cost a fortune in heat."

"I spent less on heat last year than any of the past ten years in Fairview."

"Supper's on the table," June announced, ending the conversation.

After a bit, Fred pushed back his seat from the table. "June, that was amazing. The way you cook it's a wonder this

74

brother of mine doesn't weigh three hundred pounds."

"This time I can't take the credit," June said. "The barbeque sauce did all the work."

"The sauce? You didn't make it?"

"No, I can't match that," June said.

"The sauce is made right here in South Dakota," Bill said. "In a little town west of here called Mellette. We really like the flavor."

"It is really good," Fred said. "Now, June, you go and relax and let brother and me do the scullery duty."

"The what?" Cory said.

"Scullery duty, Cory. That means wash the dishes." Fred ruffled Cory's hair. "You can help."

"Okay."

At Fred's urging June moved out of the kitchen. Fred, with the help of the rest of the Weber family, made quick work of the kitchen. Fred even found the 'swab' and got Jessie to wash her way out of the room. Once done he turned to his brother, "Is there a place where we can talk privately?"

"We could go out to the garage," Bill said.

"How about that sports bar by the motel?"

"Sure, we could go there if you want."

"Let's do that."

"I'll tell June."

"Invite her along if you want," Fred said.

"I thought this was private?"

"Just from little ears, at least for now."

Bill was concerned. Fred had never wanted this kind of conversation. His mind went back to earlier when he said he was done with the Navy. He wondered again if he was in some sort of trouble. Bill checked with June and she chose to stay home with Mason. So, the two men climbed into the Escalade and drove the almost three blocks to The Ringneck Tavern.

The Ringneck bar was not a big place. It had about six tables on one side and a long bar on the other. The bar had swivel seats, Bill chose one and Fred took the one next to him. There was no one in sight. "Is it always this crowded?" Fred asked.

"I don't know where they are," Bill said. "Let me look

in back." Bill got up and walked through the back door. He saw the big walk in door open and two people at the door. "What's going on?"

"Charlie bashed his knee," the man said. Then he turned toward the voice, "Oh. Hi Bill. Charlie was getting a case of Bud for Lester. He slipped on the wet floor and went down on his knee. He thinks he broke something. Paul's coming over with the ambulance."

There was a knock at the back door, Bill opened it and saw Paul and Wesley Sanderson with the gurney. "Where is he?"

Bill pointed, "In the cooler."

"Well, at least you didn't have to ice it down," Paul said as he entered the walk in.

"Very funny," Charlie said.

The two first responders got Charlie's leg immobilized and got him out of the building and into the ambulance. Once it rolled away the group gathered up front at the bar again.

"Well, I guess that makes me chief bartender," Eddie Watts said. "I wasn't planning on working tonight, but I'll keep the place open for Charlie. What can I get you Bill, and who's your friend?"

"This is no friend,'" Bill smiled, "This is my brother, Fred."

"The Navy man?" Eddie asked.

"That's right," Fred answered.

"Well, thank you for your service. The first one's on the house. What can I get you? But before you order, I don't have any San Miguel."

"Actually that was before my time. They closed Subic about the time I got out of boot camp," Fred said.

"That's too bad." Eddie shook his head. "I remember the days. The place was an adult Disney Land. Anything and everything was for sale there."

"You were in the Navy?" Fred asked.

"One tour. I was a store keeper on the USS Samuel Gompers."

"The Love Boat!?!"

"I was on her long before she went coed. I served aboard from 1972 to 76. Then I got out."

"Well, thank you for your service as well."

"You bet. So what'll it be?"

"What do you have on draft?"

"Bud, Miller Lite and Coors regular."

"I'll take the Coors."

"Same for me," Bill said.

"Sure, Bill." Eddie winked at Fred, "but you landlubbers have to pay."

Eddie drew the two mugs and placed them in front of his guests and wandered down the bar to take another order.

"All right, I know you were speaking English, but I have no idea what you were talking about. What's subik?"

"Not what, where," Fred answered. "Subic Bay, The Philippines. There used to be a Naval Base there. They closed it in the early nineties I think. San Miguel was the local beer. I was told it was of dubious quality."

"That helps, but not much. I don't think I'll ever get used to your lingo. We have a guy here, I'll introduce him to you, he is the local mechanic. He's retired Navy, too."

"I'd like to meet him."

Bill decided to bring the conversation back to the original subject. "So… what did you want to talk about?"

"What would you think of me moving to Helen?"

"You? Here? I hadn't thought about it," Bill said. "Frankly, I figured this would be the last place you would want to be. It is over a thousand miles from salt water."

Fred took a swallow of his beer before he spoke, "I told you earlier I wanted to make a clean break from my Navy career"

"I know, the guy on the horse ranch," Bill said. "You want to work with horses?"

"No, I don't know the first thing about them."

"So, what then? I don't understand."

"Bill, with mom and dad gone, you're the only family I've got. I never got married, so I have no one to go home to. I want to come here."

"You want to settle in Helen?"

"I want to try it," Fred said. "I want to see if I like it."

"What are you going to do?"

"I don't know. What is there to do here?"

77

"There are a lot of jobs around. What did you do in the Navy?"

"You know I can't talk about that. Let's just say that what I did has no counterpart out here. I have an associates degree in business management, and a good deal of leadership experience. I'm not sure where that will take me but it is something."

"This is out of the blue, Fred," Bill said. "I didn't expect it. I was just getting used to you not being in the Navy when you drop this on me."

"I'm not dropping anything on you, I'm just kicking around an idea." Fred turned in his seat to face Bill, "Look, little brother, I'm not looking to move in, I'm not looking for a job, I'm not looking for anything. I'm just feeling out the possibilities. If you don't want me here, just say so."

"Wait a minute Fred," Bill held up his hand using the international stop sign, "you are more than welcome here. You're my brother, June loves you and the kids adore you." Bill took another breath. "Look, I chose the wrong words. What you want to do is a shock, I wasn't ready for it. That's all."

"All right, let's start over."

"Good," Bill nodded. "I do this all the time for my clients. I help them get here and get settled. I can certainly do it for my brother."

"Do you think I could find a house or an apartment to rent? I would need it in September."

Bill's brain went into realtor mode. His mind ran through six possibilities. "Do you want something you could buy?"

"Not right away. I want to see if I like it first. I would like to rent for now."

"I'm thinking of a place here in town," Bill said. "Stewart Godfrey is moving to De Smet this month. His son want's him nearer to him and to the hospital."

"Is he sick?"

"No, he's eighty seven. His eyes are going and he can't see well enough to drive anymore. His son is making an apartment for him out of his garage."

"Will he rent the place here?"

"He will for a time, I think, but eventually he'll want to sell it."

"What's the place like?"

"It's small, two bedrooms I think. It has a detached one car garage in the back."

"That sounds possible."

"We'll look into it in the morning, after I pick up June."

"Pick up June?"

"Sure. She'll faint when I tell her you want to move here."

Chapter Seven

June walked into the kitchen. Fred was already there. He had a copy of the Helen Times and was paging through it. "Good morning, June."

"Good morning, Fred," June replied. "I see you found the coffee."

"You made it too easy," Fred smiled, "leaving it out on the counter. I didn't wake you, did I?"

"No, Mason has me up early in the morning. He's already had a change and his breakfast," June answered. "Cory will be up soon and he'll want breakfast. I'd rather make it for him than have to clean up the mess he leaves."

"He looks to be almost a foot taller than when I was here last March. What are you feeding him?"

"Just good old fashioned country food," June explained. "We're here in the nation's breadbasket. We are surrounded by farmers. I try to stay away from processed foods if I can."

"Probably a good idea," Fred agreed.

"Can I get you something?"

"Oh no. I had breakfast at the Helen House an hour ago."

"What time did you get up?"

"I was up with the sun, about zero five thirty."

"Why? Did something wake you?"

"My internal clock," Fred said. "I walked down to get the paper and the food smelled so good inside the restaurant, I stopped for breakfast."

"I've never been there that early. It must be a different crowd."

"I met a few truck drivers and three guys who work at the Helen Elevator. They start at seven."

"We have a good friend who works over there."

"I know, I met him last winter. Tom was his name, wasn't it?"

"That's right. I didn't know Tom started that early."

There was the shuffling sound of slipper-socks and both adults turned to see Cory walk in. "Hi mommy, hi Uncle Fred."

"Good morning small fry," Fred said.

"What would you like for breakfast?"

"Cheerios."

"You always want Cheerios. How about some pancakes instead?"

"Okay."

June walked out to the mudroom and retrieved the large griddle. She knew Bill would eat pancakes too. She started mixing the batter and almost as if on cue Bill walked in as she was ready to pour. She looked up as he walked in, "Pancakes?"

"Absolutely," Bill answered. Then looked to his brother, "You save me some coffee?"

Fred pointed to the pot, "Plenty."

Bill poured a cup of coffee and helped June with getting things on the table. He and Cory got everything in place in time to sit for the first batch of pancakes. June set the platter on the table and poured the second batch. She sat with them until she had to flip them.

As she got up Bill offered to do it, but Fred stepped in, "I'm not eating. I'll take care of it."

"You on a diet?" Bill asked jokingly.

"Our world traveler has already had breakfast. He walked down to the Helen House, ate breakfast and got back before you got up."

"I get it, military time," Bill said.

"Habit, and the time zone change."

Bill looked at his brother. "You walked to the Helen House?"

"Sure, why not?"

"You could have taken my car."

"It's your car, brother."

"Next time feel free to take it."

"Shouldn't be a next time. You said something about a friend who has a car rental place?

"Marty," Bill answered. "He has a car lot over in Watertown. I'll call him and get things going."

"Watertown, that's quite a distance."

"About an hour. I'll take you over."

"That's a bit far."

81

"Not really, I'm going into the office today anyway. It's only another half hour from there. Let me call him and get things started. You got your driver's license?"

"Finish your breakfast first," Fred said.

"Knock, knock." They all heard the voice from the garage door.

"Come in Julie," June said loud enough to be heard across the mud room.

"Good morning," Julie said as she walked in the door.

"Hi Julie," Bill said. "You remember my brother Fred?"

"No, I don't think I do." She turned, "Julie Sorenson, official next door neighbor to the Weber family."

Fred continued the banter, "Fred Weber, official brother and guest. Pleasure to meet you."

"Fred was here last March for a week. You didn't meet him?"

"That must have been when I was away. I was gone for two weeks in March."

"That must be it," Fred smiled. "Frankly, there is no way I would not remember meeting you."

"Thanks." Julie turned to June. "I started to make apple pie but I realized all my pie tins are still at the church. Can I borrow one?"

"Metal or Pyrex?"

"I prefer Pyrex."

Bill slid over a bit and pointed to an empty chair. "Have a seat, coffee?"

Julie looked at Fred. She caught him looking at her left hand. He smiled and nodded. She moved to the chair, "Sure, why not?"

"Hand me the platter, these pancakes are done," Fred said.

"So, they make you cook?" Julie quipped.

"Slave labor. They told me I had to cook and clean in order to stay at Weber Castle."

"Tyrants," Julie said and continued to watch Fred. Her eyes also floated to his left hand then back to his broad shoulders. She had decided she liked what she saw and from the way Fred was acting, the feeling was mutual.

"How do you like your coffee?" Fred asked.

"Right from the pot."

"No pretenses." Fred smiled as he handed Julie the cup. "I like that."

Bill stood up. "Let me call Marty and get things going. Fred, do you have your driver's license?"

Fred reached into his pocket, pulled out his wallet and handed the card to Bill. "Here you go."

"Any preference?"

"No, just as long as it has four wheels."

"All right. I'll call Marty and Stewart and get things going."

"So," Julie said pulling Fred's attention back, "you're a Navy man?"

"I am, but not for long. In two months, I'll be a former Navy man."

"You're quitting?"

"Retiring."

"Retiring?" Julie started rethinking scenarios. "you don't look old enough to retire."

"The Navy is a young man's game. Once you hit forty, they consider you over the hill. I have just over twenty three years on active duty. It's time to step aside and let the younger folks take over."

It was a relief. Julie was starting to think this brother of Bill's might be too old. As it was the age worked out just about right. "They retire you out at forty?"

"Anytime after twenty years," Fred said. "They want the young blood, not old worn out sailors like me."

"You don't look worn out," Julie smiled.

"One of the advantages of military service is the ability to have two careers," Fred said. "I'll retire with a pension and I'll still be young enough to start a new life. It kind of makes up for all the sea time and low pay."

"Your medical expenses are paid too, aren't they Fred?" June asked. "I know Mike Finney is retired from the Navy. When he came into the clinic, St. Agnes billed TRICARE."

"I know there is medical care available after I retire. I'm not sure how it works. I may have to talk to your friend Mike about it."

Bill walked back into the room. "We're all set. We can get the car anytime today and Stewart Godfrey said he would be home and we could stop by on the way out of town."

"I'm ready as soon as you are. I want to look at the place."

Julie connected the dots. She had to make sure she had connected them right. She looked at Fred, "You are thinking about buying Stewart's place?"

"I want to see it. I'm thinking about moving here when I retire."

"That would be great!" Julie blurted out. Then she recovered. "I'm sure the kids would like their Uncle Fred nearby."

Fred picked up on the initial implication. "I want to see if this small town living my brother raves about is all it's cracked up to be. So far," his smile was directly aimed at Julie, "I like what I see."

"It doesn't much matter to me, Marty," Fred said. "I guess it should be big enough that I could have Bill's kids with me."

"All right, that leaves out the Beemer and the Miada. I got a Sebring rag top."

"I don't think I want a convertible," Fred said.

Marty turned to Bill. "Your brother is just as difficult as you are."

"More."

"Here's a nice car." Marty was looking at his picture board. "It's a 2006 Charger. Plenty of room for Bill's kids and still sporty enough for a bachelor."

"Now you're on the right track, Marty."

"I'll get it pulled around." Marty pulled out a small radio and told the person on the other end to drive around the Charger. "I can let you have this for three weeks at one fifty a week."

"One fifty a week?" Fred asked without giving away whether he thought it was too high or too low.

"That's about twenty bucks a day."

"Make it twenty a day and we'll be good." Fred said.

"You gonna keep it three weeks?"

"Maybe a day or two less."

"Done." Marty put out his hand. "Let's take a look at the car."

Bill, Fred and Marty walked around the car, Fred pointed out a couple scratches and Marty took notes. Fred opened the hood, then sat inside, started the engine and tried both forward and reverse while keeping his foot on the brake. "What would it take to buy it?"

Marty didn't miss a step. "Well, let me think," Marty said. "This is a really nice car. It's only got seventy two thousand miles on it. With these new engines, that's barely broken in. I've got the report on it and it has never been in an accident. No major repairs. I think I could let it go for ninety seven hundred."

"Marty," Fred leaned in mimicking Marty's Connecticut accent, "this ain't no RT. That's a V6, not some monster rat motor. I'm thinking about eighty two."

"I might as well burn it for eighty two." Marty looked hurt. "You want my kids to starve? Take a look at this car. She's as fresh as the day she was born."

Bill was watching. He had never seen this side of his brother. "I should record this for YouTube," he thought. "Nobody will believe it."

"Marty, don't blow smoke up my butt. Speaking of smoke, the last owner was a smoker. I know you cleaned and deodorized it, but I can still smell it. It will be months before that goes away. How about eighty five."

"You're killin' me here."

"I'm not killin' nothin'. Turn me down and I'll rent the car. We'll just forget the whole thing."

"Now wait a minute," Marty knew he was being handled and being handled by one of the best he had seen in a while. He saw the 'take away'. What Fred didn't know is that Marty only had six thousand invested in this car. "Let's ride this horse one more furlong. I'll go nine."

"Nine." Fred repeated. "Okay, here's the deal, if I decide to keep it when I'm ready to leave, I'll give you the nine. But, the rental fee is part of that nine."

"And if you don't decide to keep it?"

"You rented me a nice car while I was here."

85

"Let me get this straight, you want to rent to the car for three weeks and at the end of the deal, you want to pay me about eighty six hundred."

"No, at the end of the deal, you'll get your nine grand. Or you'll get the four hundred or so for the rent."

Marty pretended to think about it. After about ten seconds, he shrugged, "Split it and we have a deal. You pay the full twenty bucks a day for the car. That's a separate deal. If you want it at the end, you give me eighty eight hundred."

"Done." Fred put out his hand.

"Good, now let's finish the rental contract." Marty turned and walked toward the storefront office.

"How did you learn to do that?" Bill asked.

"Do what?"

"Negotiate a deal. I didn't think you did that kind of thing in the Navy. I thought you bought seven hundred dollar toilet seats. Marty is from a family of car brokers in Connecticut. He is one of the best wheeler dealers around. I have never seen him handled like that."

"Handle him? He handled me. I'll bet you lunch he's into that car for less than seven."

"He'll never tell."

Fred laughed, "You're probably right."

"If you're okay here, I'm going to head to the office. You remember how to get there?" Bill asked.

"Sure, it's only two turns."

"Good, I want to check on some things. I won't be there long."

"Famous last words. I'm going to buy a GPS while I'm in town here. I'll need it to find my way around anyway."

"Marty should have one he can loan you."

"Loan me?" Fred grinned, "You mean rent me."

Now it was Bill's turn to laugh. "See you at the office." He walked back to his Escalade and drove off.

Fred followed Marty into the office. They finished the contract and Marty shook Fred's hand. "There you go. You're all set."

"Thanks Marty, now, can you give me directions to a local Walmart or Radio Shack?"

"Sure, go back down the road you came up and turn left

onto 212 again. That's away from Kent. Both of those stores are on that road but on the other side of town."

"Thanks Marty."

"Sure thing."

Fred followed Marty's directions and found both stores. He also found a Target and several other chains. At the Radio Shack he bought a new headset for his phone. He wasn't sure of the laws in South Dakota, but he knew many states had gone to 'hands free' laws. He thought it was more comfortable to use the headset then to hold the phone anyway. He bought a windshield mounted GPS and sat in the parking lot entering Bill's home address and Huber Realty. That would be good enough for now. He let the unit find its location then asked it to find a local flower shop. The map drew a line and the male voice said "Please drive to highlighted route."

"Oh, that won't do," he said to the unit. He reached up and took it from the windshield and changed the setting to a female voice. He found the flower shop and, after looking around, bought a plant for June. He drove around the town. He wasn't looking for anything in particular. He just wanted to get the feel of the place. If he was going to live in Helen, he figured he would be over this way quite a bit. He called his brother.

"Hi Fred," Bill answered, "can you hold on a second I'm on the office phone."

"Sure," Fred answered.

"Be right back," Bill said and the line went dead.

The call was to test the Bluetooth. It worked. That was all he needed to know, but he didn't have time to tell his brother. At a traffic light he selected Huber Realty and told the GPS to find it. "Please drive to highlighted route," the unit said in a female voice.

He looked at the windshield mounted box. "That's better."

"What's better?"

Fred didn't expect an answer. It took him a split second to realize his brother was back on the phone. He recovered. "I just set my new GPS to the female voice. I'd rather have Bitchin' Betty than Bossy Bob."

"Okay," Bill chuckled. "How's the car?"

"The thing runs great. I'm probably going to keep it. That is, if I can find a place to store it for a month or so."

"I don't think that'll be a problem." Bill had already thought of that. If Fred commits to Stewart's house, he was sure Stewart would allow him to keep the car there until he returned.

"You ready for lunch?"

"Where are you?"

"Just leaving Watertown."

"I'll be ready to go home by the time you get here."

"It's only one o'clock? You quitting early?"

"With my big brother in town, I can take a Friday afternoon off."

"I wouldn't make a habit of it. The boss won't like it," Fred quipped.

"We won't tell him." Bill went along with the joke.

"I've seen your office. I'll just head home."

"Suit yourself," Bill said. "I'll be right behind you."

"I'll try not to hit the brakes hard."

"Very funny." Fred heard what sounded like an intercom speaker in the background. He couldn't tell what was said. "Look, Fred. I've got another call. I'll see you at home."

"All right.," Fred said. "How do you say it here? See ya!"

Bill chuckled. "Goodbye Fred."

When Fred pulled up he saw Julie in her front yard watering a flower bed. He walked over. "Good afternoon."

She looked up, pretending she had not noticed him. "Good afternoon Fred. I see you got a car."

"I like it," he said. "It suits me; a bit sporty, but practical."

Julie chose not to comment. "How did you like Stewart Godfrey's house?"

"We didn't get to see it. Stewart had forgotten about a doctor's appointment. Bill and I are going over there this evening."

Julie turned off the hose, "Would you like a glass of iced tea?"

"I would," Fred said, "thank you." He followed Julie

88

through her garage and into the house. He noticed the garage and house were tidy and neat but not white glove inspection ready. The kitchen was clean, but the coffee cup from earlier was still in the sink. This told him a lot about Julie. "This is nice," he said, looking around the kitchen.

"Thanks."

Julie continued talking as she took two frosted mugs from the freezer and filled them with ice cubes. "I've lived here about three years now, so I've had the chance to make over every room. Some just needed paint or wall paper, others needed the floors done."

Fred looked around. "The overall feel is homey. It's very comfortable."

"Thanks." Julie poured tea from a pitcher into the two mugs. "Sugar?" she asked.

"No thanks."

"So you think you're sweet enough?" she said with a grin.

"My mother thought so."

"We'll see." She placed the mug on the table and pointed. "Please, sit."

Fred sat.

Julie sat across from him. She took a sip from her mug. "So, what do you do in the Navy?"

"This might sound phony, I know it comes off that way. Believe me I am not trying to be." Fred took a breath. "What I do in the Navy has to do with highly classified electronic surveillance. Other than telling you my job description, I really can't talk about it."

"That's interesting," Julie said, "and yes it does sound too pat."

"I normally tell people I'm a helicopter mechanic just to avoid looking like a come on," Fred said.

Julie smiled, "So, Mr. Weber, just how do I know this is not a come on?"

"Frankly, because I don't know a thing about helicopters." Fred smiled.

Julie laughed, then asked, "How do I know that?"

"I just told you." Then they both laughed. "How about you? You work around here?"

"No, I work online." Avoiding telling Fred what she did was as real as Fred not being able to talk about his work. She chose her next sentence carefully. "In fact, I was in New York with my bosses when you were here last winter."

"That's why we didn't meet," Fred said and pushed on to his next agenda. "We can make up for that now. Are you busy tomorrow?"

"I have no plans. What do you have in mind?"

"When I was in Watertown this morning, I learned about the Terry Redlin Art Center. I'd like to go see it, but it's not as much fun alone. I'm hoping you would join me."

"I'd like that," Julie answered, "I haven't been there in a while."

"Great. It's an official date." He stood up. "I'd better get going, I have a plant in the car for June and the windows are up. I don't want it to wilt."

"All right, call me later and tell me about Stewart's house."

Fred walked to the door, and turned. "I'll do that."

"Talk to you later then."

"Sure thing." Fred turned and walked out the door.

Julie stood in the kitchen. She didn't move. She liked Fred. She thought she could like him a lot. She didn't want to consider anything more than that. It was far too soon. Tomorrow would tell her more about how the man was made up. She caught her imagination running into the future and stopped herself. She wrote romance novels, she didn't live them, she told herself. She would go out with Fred tomorrow. She tried not to let her mind go farther than that, but tried as she might, she failed. Her mind ran through a series of scenarios, some from her books and some from books not yet written. Could Fred be "the one'?" Is there really a "one"? Could the feelings she was having be the beginnings of a true fairy tale love affair? Or is it simply animal lust? After all he was buff.

Julie walked into her work room and opened her computer to her "ideas" page. She made some notes then went to her diary page and wrote the whole thing as she remembered it. A year from now she would look back on this notation. One of three things would happen then, she thought.

She would smile at the memory, she would laugh at the joke or she would regret what could have been.

Bill and Fred drove up to the Godfrey house. They had been that far earlier in the day but Stewart had to cancel at the last minute. Now he was home and available. Bill knocked on the screen door. The front main door was open to the evening breeze. "Stewart?" Bill shouted. "It's Bill Weber!"

"Come on in Bill," came the return call, "I'm in the parlor."

Bill pulled open the screen door and held it for his brother. They walked into the anteroom then turned left into the living room. Stewart was sitting in an overstuffed chair that had been placed about four feet from a forty eight inch flat screen television. He turned it off as they entered the brightly lit room. Bill knew that, at a distance, Stewart would not be able to distinguish who was who, so he walked up and said, "Good evening Stewart. This is my brother Fred."

"Nice to meet a fellow sailor," Stewart said.

"Thank you sir. What ship were you on?"

"The Saratoga. I was all over the Indian Ocean and in the South Pacific with the old girl."

"The Sleezy Sarah," Fred asked as a statement. "CV-60. I saw her, she's rusting away up in Newport."

"No, not that one, her predecessor, CV-3." Stewart corrected. "That one lies in Davy Jones' Locker. Sunk by an atomic bomb in '46."

Now it was Bill's turn. "Somebody dropped a nuclear bomb on one of our ships in 1946? I don't recall reading anything about that."

"Sure you do. We sunk her in an atom bomb test."

"So, she's a reef off Bikini Atoll," Fred said finishing the thought. "So that would put you aboard her during World War Two."

"That's right. Joined up with her right out of boot camp. Met her in San Francisco and spent Christmas day of 43 underway to Hawaii. I spent the rest of the war chipping paint, and cleaning heads in officer's country. I wanted to be gunner's mate but I never got there. Probably saved my life. I was below deck when the kamikaze hit. Those forward gunners didn't have a chance."

"Well, seaman, thank you for your service."

"Thank you for yours. You on one of those new nuclear carriers?"

"No, I'm on a Fast Frigate, at least until September. Then I'm thinking about moving here."

Bill jumped in. He wanted to get things moving. "Which is exactly why we're here, Stewart. Fred is interested in moving to Helen when he leaves the Navy. I thought with you moving to De Smet, you two should meet."

"Well, Bill, you know I'm not quite ready yet. We've got to finish the apartment, move what I want to keep and auction the rest. It'll be another month before this place is empty and clean."

"That works out about perfect for me, Mr. Godfrey," Fred said. "I'm here for about three weeks and then back to the ship for a month and then I'm done. It looks like your schedule and mine couldn't be better matched."

"Well, take a look around. If you like what you see, we'll let that brother of yours put together a deal. I kinda like the idea of a sailor having the place. It's almost like keeping it in the family."

"Thanks, Mr. Godfrey. We'll take a walk around," Fred said.

Chapter Eight

"I'm telling you it's the oil companies that are doing it. They are giving ethanol a bad rap because they want to sell more oil," Oscar Richland said.

"Look, Oscar," Jeremy Waldman chimed in, "you see a conspiracy behind every tree."

"I know what I read," Oscar said flatly.

"Did you see that the auditorium will be finished in time for the graduation?" Bob Houser forced a change in the conversation. Lively political discussion was often a part of a visit to Helen's only barber shop, but Bob would always change the subject when things got too heated. He turned off the clippers. "Alice gave her progress report to the school board yesterday and she said the work is almost complete. We can have the ceremony in our own auditorium."

"That's great news." Jeremy had taken the hint. "It's only right that our kids walk down the same steps we did."

"They got that done already?" Oscar asked. "They had to rebuild the whole stage lighting and control panel after the fire.

"You know Ephraim Green's boy, John?" Bob had traded the clippers for scissors.

"Sure," Jeremy answered. "he worked some summers for me while he was in college."

"Well, that college paid off," Bob continued. "He's an electrical engineer now. He talked the EE Department Dean at South Dakota State into allowing three of the juniors to intern with him. They redesigned and rebuilt the whole stage system. Everything is controlled from a keyboard now. The lights, the curtains, the backdrops, everything. One person can control the whole deal."

"He took the summer off to rebuild the stage control panel?" Oscar asked, wondering how he could afford to do that.

"He works from home most of the time, Oscar," Bob answered. "He was around to supervise the kids as they did the work. Jim Coleman donated his time and did the heavy electrical work."

93

"You mean the house lights, the curtains and backdrops and all will be operated by a computer?" Jeremy asked.

"This is real state of the art stuff," Bob answered. "We will have the most up to date control system in the state. One of the kids is even building in a laser light show for the graduation."

"I wonder how that's going to work," Oscar said slowly. "We have always had all the kids involved in our plays and such. By putting all the work in the hands of one person, how will we get the other the kids involved?"

"What is this, Oscar?" Bob looked over to the waiting area, "Are you saying every silver lining has its cloud?"

Jeremy laughed. "Come on, Oscar, you can't be serious."

"No, I'm not serious," Oscar retreated. "I'm looking forward to seeing the results."

The door opened and Bill Weber walked in. "Good morning," he said casting his eyes around the room.

"Good morning. Bill." Bob had answered for all of them. "How's the real estate biz?"

"We're doing just fine. In fact, I'm heading into Kent this morning. I have a house up near Groton I'm showing this afternoon."

"I hear your brother's in town," Jeremy said.

"He's here on a three week vacation," Bill said. "He's about to retire. Believe it or not he's thinking about moving here."

"What's does his wife think about that?" Oscar asked,

"Fred has never been married."

"How old is he?" Bob asked.

"Forty one."

"And he's retiring?" Bob switched back to a light trimmer.

"The way he explains it, after about twenty years, the Navy wants you out and new blood in your place. They want to keep the service young."

"So he wants to move here, get away from the salt

94

water and try something completely different," Jeremy said.

Bill was surprised. "Have you talked to him? Those are almost the exact words he used."

"No, I have a brother too. He was an aircraft mechanic for the Air Force. He retired over at Ellsworth. He packed up and moved to Jacksonville, North Carolina and started driving a logging truck. He is near the big Marine base down there but he has nothing to do with aviation. He says he'll do that until he gets the sound of jet noise out of his ears."

"When did he retire?" Bill asked.

"Seven years ago."

"That's funny," Bob said and laughed.

"You're working on a Saturday?" Oscar asked. "I thought you had a whole brokerage full of minions to do that for you."

Bill laughed, knowing the barb was meant in fun. "This one is special. I bought the house on spec, I supervised the updates and I know the couple who are interested."

"Up near Groton, you say?" Oscar continued, "That's a bit of a reach for you isn't it?"

"I was up there with Tom Ogden for an estate auction. When I saw I could get the house for a song, I bought it."

"That's quite a gamble, isn't it Bill?" Oscar asked. "You could carry that for a while."

"Oscar, when you sold me the house I live in today, you told me you couldn't understand why a city boy would want to move into a tiny town like Helen, South Dakota. Well we've been here through all four seasons, do you understand it now?"

"I know what you have told me, that people are getting fed up with the corruption and crime in the congested cities and surrounding suburbs and they're looking for nice places like Helen to raise their families."

"Exactly right," Bill nodded. "I bought that house knowing I could sell it within sixty days to a family who wanted out of the rat race. Well, that family flew into Aberdeen last night and I'm meeting them this afternoon."

"Where are they from?" Bob asked. Then with a

flourish, he swept the smock from the man in the chair and said, "You're good for another month, Jeremy."

"They're from Sunnyvale, California. He's an electrical engineer and she's a tax accountant. They've worked in Silicone Valley since college but now they want some place with a good school and no traffic."

Bob waved to Oscar and held the smock. "They'll get that in Groton. The schools are good up there. The Tigers will have a strong football team this year."

"Why here?" Oscar nodded to Bob and got up to move into position.

"That's the same thing you asked me, Oscar," Bill replied. "They have two children. Twin boys. They suspect the soccer coach has been molesting boys and recently he's turned his attention toward the twins. They can't prove it, but they want the boys out of that school."

"The school board won't do anything?" Bob asked.

"Not without proof," Bill answered. "Nonetheless, they want out, even if it is just rumors, the fact that the school board will not even look into it bothers them."

"Why don't they simply switch schools?" Jeremy asked

"California is not like here. We have an open enrollment policy here. California doesn't. The kids go to the schools that the state tells them to, or they have to go private," Bob answered.

"Okay, I can understand them wanting to move, but why here?" Oscar asked again.

"The house I have is about ten miles west and a little south of Groton. It's an upgraded late sixties house with about fifteen acres. It's about a thirty minute drive to Aberdeen. The local folks might think that's too far out of town, but it is a short enough drive for our country seeking clients. The boys will go to Groton for school and the adults expect to work in Aberdeen."

"Why would they buy fifteen acres? You can't make money with that," Jeremy said as he got near the door.

"Hobby farms are a big deal now. Especially with the 'prepper' crowd. What makes Huber Realty so good at it, is because we know that. I understand these people. I know 'where they are coming from' if you'll pardon the play on words. I lived with the dirt, the congestion, the corrupt government, high taxes and the crime. I'll bet dinner at the Helen House that I have a solid offer in my pocket before three this afternoon."

"I'm not taking that bet, Bill," Oscar said from the barber's chair.

Bob had to pull his clippers back quickly from Oscar's shaking head, "Careful Oscar, you almost won your self a divot."

"Sorry Bob," Oscar said. Then turning back to Bill, "You took Jack Huber's business and put it back on the map. I can't and won't argue with success. No bet."

"Too bad, I was going to order Prime Rib," Bill replied bringing a laugh from the room.

"How many people you got working there in Kent now, Bill?" Bob asked.

"As you know, we started out with just myself, Jack and Laura. When Jack passed away suddenly, it fell on me. Laura was planning on going to Texas for the winter so I had to build quickly, so I hired Amy Price as a part time receptionist. Once she qualified, we moved her to broker associate. Then John Gange joined the team and, of course, Serena Townsend is our office manager. We would stop cold without her."

"This spring we brought on two more agents. Phillip Cassidy is our youngest associate. He is fresh out of Augustana. What he lacks in experience he more than makes up for in energy and enthusiasm."

"You said you brought in two people," Oscar asked the question as a statement.

"That's right. I'm not sure if you know Teresa Beseler, she ran a realty office in Prairie Center. She is with us now."

"You bought her outfit?" Oscar asked.

"There wasn't much to buy. She's just a one person office. We made a deal. She will work mostly from her office and come in only occasionally. We took over her advertising and administrative overhead. In exchange, I got another broker and another office. It was a good mix."

97

"So, you're booming," Bob said.

"I'm not sure I'd put it that way," Bill nodded. "Huber Realty is simply expanding back to its original size of three Brokers and three Broker Associates."

"And an office manager," Bob finished the sentence.

"Mrs. Townsend is a licensed broker associate. She doesn't do much selling, but she can if she wants."

"You still doing rentals?" Oscar asked. Then, turning to Bob, "A little more off the sides."

"I'll give you the Marine look if you want," Bob replied.

"We don't need to go that far," Oscar chuckled.

"I have a part time property manager," Bill said. "She handles our rentals. We currently have over twenty properties."

Oscar leaned forward, forcing Bob to chase him with the clippers. "I want to talk to you about that. I have a couple houses over on the other side of Kent. It's a bit far for me to keep going over there. I'd like to see your management package."

"Sure Oscar," Bill answered. "Give me a call during the week and I'll set up an appointment with Mrs. Townsend and our rental manager."

"How's that Oscar?" Bob asked, unsnapping the smock from Oscar's neck.

"Looks good."

"Then you're done," Bob said, once again whipping the smock away like a toreador.

"Bill, if you please," Bob said, extending his hand to the chair.

Bill moved to the place indicated.

"Same as usual?"

"Works for me."

Oscar handed Bob a check. "Watch out for him Bill, he seems to want to leave hair longer today."

"Job security, Oscar," Bob said with a chuckle. "Brings you back sooner."

"That's just it," Oscar said with a smile. "We'll see ya." He turned and went out the door.

Bob placed and fastened the smock around Bill.

"You've been here about a year already haven't you?"

"A little over," Bill replied.

"You know there was talk you would move back out right after the first winter."

"We love it here, Bob. We're staying."

"And now you're bringing your brother in too?"

"Looks like it," Bill said. "We looked at Stewart Godfrey's house last night. Fred wants to rent it for a bit, with the option to buy within one year."

"Why would he do that?"

"He's basically hedging his bets. If it turns out he doesn't like it here, he's not stuck with a house."

"Makes sense, I suppose."

Bob changed the subject, "I hear Henry is talking to you about running for County Commission."

"He mentioned it. I said I would look into it. I'm not sure if I want to get involved in politics. I'm going to talk to Jake Samuelsson about how much time and energy the job entails."

"I think you would do us a great service in that position, Bill. We need someone like you on the Commission."

"Henry said the same thing," Bill chuckled. "Was he in here this morning?"

"He was here yesterday. He had been out to see Jake. We were talking and your name came up."

"I have to talk to Jake myself. With Huber Realty in expansion and a new baby, I don't know if I'll have the time."

"People around here respect you, Bill. You moved in here and became a part of the community. You and June are as much Helenites as the folks who were born here."

"That's nice of you to say, Bob…" Bill raised his hand as if to dismiss the compliment.

Bob touched his shoulder for emphasis, "I mean it, Bill. With you selling Real Estate and June running the Helen Clinic, you have both touched a lot of lives around here. We value your opinions. You have a world view that many of us don't have. I think you would make a great Commissioner."

"Henry told me I have until August to make up my mind. I'll talk to Jake and think about it."

"August will come soon enough, Bill." Bob turned the chair so Bill could see himself in the mirror, "How's that?"

"Great."

Bob whipped the smock from Bill and gave it a quick shake. He hung it on a hook and picked up a broom. "You know, I have a cousin who has been talking to me about moving back here. He has a job offer in Watertown. Do you think you can help?"

"That's what I do."

"I told him I knew a good realtor." Bob picked up a pen, "Here, I'll write down his phone number."

"So, you think you can impress me with this fancy car?" Julie quipped. Fred was holding the door. It had been a while since someone held a car door for her. She had seen Fred's brother do it for June. She thought it was cute. Now she thought differently. It made her feel special somehow.

"You mean my fancy rental?" Fred answered. "No, if I had wanted to try to impress you with a car I would have taken Marty up on the Sebring convertible. I chose this car because it was practical without being a mini-van."

"What do you drive at home?"

Fred did a mental double take. He didn't think of Norfolk as 'home'. He really didn't have a home. The ship was his home. When he was on shore duty he kept a small apartment but not when he was on the ship. He answered the question. "I have an old Chevy pickup truck."

"That'll fit right in here."

Fred chuckled, "I guess it would, I hadn't thought of that." He started the car and backed out of the driveway. "Do you want to stop at the Helen House for coffee to go?"

"I have a better idea, if you'll let me play tour guide," Julie said. "There is a place in Watertown that makes the best coffee I have ever tasted. It's delivered from the plant fresh roasted every morning. June took me there the first time. Now I try to stop in every time I'm over that way."

"This I have to try," Fred smiled. "Lead on."

"Do you know the way to Watertown?"

"Wasn't that a song?" Fred asked.

Julie laughed, "The South Dakota version."

"I drove back from Watertown yesterday. Once I'm on the highway, it's only one turn. I think I'm okay."

"So, you live on a ship?"

"That's right."

"You don't keep a house or an apartment?"

"I have had apartments when I was on shore duty, but that wasn't very often. The ship is underway so much I would hardly use an apartment. I would be away so much, it would just be a target."

"A target?" Julie asked. "I don't understand."

"I've seen it happen several times. The bad guys somehow find out who has the apartments and when the ship will be away. They can come in and clean the place out at their convenience. It could be months before anyone finds out. I think it's simpler to just stay on the ship."

"I never really thought about that." Julie was quiet for a bit. "So that means you don't have any furniture?"

"Actually, no," Fred answered. "I have a storage unit in Norfolk that I use to keep some of my personal effects but I haven't accumulated much over the years."

"What about the times you had apartments?"

"I rented them furnished."

"So, when you move out here, you'll move in with nothing?" Julie asked.

"Practically nothing," Fred answered. "I have my old component stereo I bought in Japan on my first cruise and a restored Strato-Lounger. Other than that, no. I talked to Bill about it. He said Stewart might leave the kitchen items and some of the furniture. It's older stuff, but he said I can replace it over time at the auctions. I wasn't quite sure what that meant, but I figured he knew what he was talking about."

"They have estate auctions around here," Julie said. "He's right. If you have a base, you can replace pieces with nicer things as you see them. That's the way I did it. I started out with 'early rummage sale' and replaced things as I saw better ones at auctions. I'll help you," Julie hesitated, maybe she was getting in too deep too fast, "if you would like."

"I would like," Fred said, easing the tension. "Stewart's furniture isn't very exciting, but if you and Bill say I can easily upgrade, then that's the way to go."

"That pick-up will come in handy too."

"I guess it would. I was going to sell it. I guess I could

keep it."

"Is it in good shape?"

"The thing has been passed around the pier. It's a beater. The engine runs pretty good and the rest of the running gear seems okay. I just use it around town. It's got some dents and dings, the paint is shot. It's just old and ugly, kinda like me."

"You are not either one," Julie said.

Fred's phone rang. He knew the ring tone. It was the ship. He answered. "This is Chief Weber."

Julie could only hear one side of the conversation. What she heard made no sense at all. "What was that about?"

"The promotion list just came out. One of my kids was just passed over for Chief. They called to let me know."

"Chief?" Julie asked.

"The Chief Petty officer ranks are the highest an enlisted person can go in the Navy and still be an enlisted. The Navy, unlike the other branches of service, make a definite distinction between E-6 and E-7. In the other branches, it is simply a promotion. In the Navy it is a move into leadership."

"E-6?" Julie was more confused than when she asked.

"Sailors join the Navy as an E-1, as they grow and learn they can get promoted to E-2 and E-3. After that, there is a skills test. Think of an E-4 as an apprentice, an E-5 as a journeyman and an E-6 as a foremen."

"So what is an E-7?" Julie asked.

"The Chief is the backbone of the Navy. He or she is the person that provides stability. The Navy Chief is steeped in tradition. He is normally the final authority on how things get done."

"I'm not sure I understand," Julie said. "What about the officers?"

"One of the jobs of the Chief is to train the junior officers. It's one of the ways he provides stability. He has several years of experience and can guide the kids fresh out of college. The smart ones listen. The really smart ones listen even when they've been around long enough to become senior officers."

"I'll take your word for it."

"Have you lived in Helen all your life?" Fred switched the subject.

"No I moved to Helen a few years back. My brother lives

102

in town and when our parents died, I wanted to be near family."

"That sounds familiar. That is exactly why I'm looking at Helen. Mom and Dad are gone. Bill is the only family I've got. I never got married so there's no connection there either. I love Bill's kids and June is a sweetheart."

"She's become a good friend."

"Bill always talks about how wonderful it is out here. I figure I'll try it for myself."

"What are you going to do?"

"I'm not sure yet. There's no counterpart to what I do in the Navy, not a legal one anyway. Bill says there are plenty of jobs around. I'll just have to look around and see what suits me. I have a good bit of savings built up and I'll be getting a pension. Looking at the cost of things up here, I may just look for something part time."

"What would you do with the rest of the time?"

"Oh," Fred thought for a second, "I've thought about writing mystery novels. I have a few ideas," He looked over at Julie, "Maybe I'll just date pretty girls."

"Not much money in that," Julie played along.

"No, but it sure would be fun."

"Ms. Price," Bill said as he walked into the front reception area of the Craftsman Style home that was Huber Realty, "I need a favor."

"Yes Mr. Weber," Amy answered in the formal manner used in the front of the building.

Bill handed her a folder. "Can you generate a rental agreement for me, please? My brother is going to rent Stewart Godfrey's home in Helen. I need a contract with the option to buy. That option needs to be good for one year only."

"You want it as a lease?"

"No, month to month. Fred is going to rent the place to see if he likes Helen."

"That's your brother in the Navy, right?"

"Soon to be retired from the Navy," Bill answered. "The contract should be effective immediately with an occupancy date of September first. The other details are in the folder."

"I'll get right to it."

"Do you have any appointments this morning?"

"Actually, I was going to show the McNeal house at one," Amy answered.

"That's more important. Forgive me. I'm getting tunnel vision because it's my brother. This isn't your job anymore. It can wait for Mrs. Townsend on Monday."

"I do have the Gordon documents you wanted. They're on your desk."

"Thanks," Bill answered. "The Gordon family flew into Aberdeen last night. I didn't expect them until Monday. They want to see the property today."

"Sure would have been nice to let you know in advance they were flying in early," Amy said.

"Mr. Gordon told me it was a last minute change in plans. Thanks for doing the paperwork on this."

"It was my turn to be on the phones today, so I was working at Serena's desk anyway."

"I guess I got lucky that my former secretary now turned agent was at the ready this morning," Bill said with a smile.

Chapter Nine

"Other than my Dress Blues, I don't own a suit," Fred answered Julie's question. "If I want to go to church and be respectable, I guess I'll have to get one now."

"The men don't wear suits in the summer. In fact, only the older men wear suits in the winter. Our little church doesn't hold to a dress code. It's pretty much a 'come as you are' kind of place."

"That's good to know," Fred answered. "I've been checking my phone and I don't see any real mens' stores in Watertown. J C Penny has a store and also a place called Herbergers, but not any real haberdasher."

"Haberdasher," Julie said slowly as if savoring the letters. "Now that's a word I haven't heard in a while. Most people go down to Sioux Falls."

"That's over two hours away," Fred said.

"People make a day of it."

"I would think they would have to."

Julie pointed, "Here's the Past Times."

Fred parked the car and walked around to open Julie's door. She caught what he was doing in time to not open it for herself. Old fashioned or not, she could get used to it. He led her to the front door of the restaurant and held the door again. Once inside Julie started pointing out the décor. She showed him the seamless and tasteful mix of the old tin ceilings and original hardwood floors and the new state of the art coffee brewers and small metal sign that read WiFi Zone.

"This place is great!" Fred said as he walked around.

"Good afternoon, welcome to The Past Times Café," the hostess said.

"Two please," Fred said.

"Certainly, please follow me." The hostess led them to the back of the restaurant and sat them at one of the old style wooden booths.

"This is cozy, with the high backs, it's almost like we have the place to ourselves," Julie said.

Fred took in a deep breath, "I can smell the coffee. If it's half as good as it smells, it will be amazing."

"Wait and see." Julie smiled.

Their server arrived and they decided on a light meal to go along with the coffee. She brought back the mugs and set them down with a smile.

"Go ahead, you go first. I want to see your face," Julie said.

Fred brought the mug up and made a flourish of passing it under his nose as if it was fine brandy. "It has a nice nose." He took a sip and put the mug down. "There was a small bistro in Rota Spain that served nothing but exotic coffees and high quality cigars. They even served civet coffee, if you're willing to pay for it. My friends and I would stop in the place anytime we were in port. The coffee was good and we could legally smoke a Cuban cigar. The coffee here is as good as any I had there."

"I thought you would like it," Julie said. "Civet coffee? Is that what I think it is?"

"Kopi Luwak," Fred answered. "Monkey Bean Coffee."

"Have you ever tried it?"

"I did. I was the butt of a joke."

"If you'll pardon the expression," Julie giggled.

Fred laughed, then continued his story. "I was sitting around the mess..."

"Mess?"

"Dining room on the ship for lack of a better word. It's more than that, but 'dining room' will do for the story."

"Okay."

"The other guys knew of the bistro. They started talking about the best coffee in the world. They forced the conversation toward me. They wanted to get me to admit I was a good judge of coffee. When I did, they asked me to prove it. They brought out three cups of coffee all the same and asked me to tell the difference. I couldn't but I didn't want them to know that. So I fudged. They had the set up. When we got to Rota and out on liberty they took me to this place. Since they were calling me the expert coffee taster they wanted me to pick the best coffee. The server placed three cups in front of me. Two were really good, and the third was civet coffee. It was truly the best coffee I had ever tasted. I told them so. That's when they told me it was monkey crap coffee."

106

"What did you do?"

"What could I do?" Fred smiled. "I finished the coffee and ordered another cup."

"That's gross," Julie said.

"I made my point and they didn't try any more practical jokes," Fred said.

"Would you drink it again?"

"Not hardly," Fred laughed quietly. "It's one of those things you will only do once."

"I need to talk to you more. You are a wealth of information," Julie giggled. "I could use some of your stories."

"For what?"

Julie realized she had become too relaxed, too comfortable with Fred. She had let down her guard. She wasn't sure what to do, she couldn't figure out a way to deflect the question. Could she trust him? Really, at this point she had no choice. All these thoughts ran through her mind in under a second. She decided to share her secret. She looked across the table and took Fred's hand. "Fred, I'm sorry. I let that slip. What I am about to tell you is a closely held secret. Nobody in town knows this. That is except June and your brother. You can't say anything."

"My whole Navy career has been based on keeping secrets. The government trusts me with information that would curl your hair. I can keep a secret."

"I'm a writer. I write romance novels."

"Okay...," Fred said, hoping to help Julie get to her secret.

"That's it."

"That's it?"

"Fred, you don't understand. These novels aren't rated 'G'. I write some pretty graphic stuff. I don't want the town to know about it."

"Now I understand," Fred nodded as reinforcement. "I won't tell a soul on one condition."

Julie squirmed mentally, "What?"

"That we continue to talk about it. I want to know about you and I don't want this secret to get in the way."

Julie relaxed again. "All right, but only when we're in

private."

"Deal." He reached over and took her hand again. "Your secret is safe with me."

Bill pulled up to the Groton house. He was glad the driveway was empty. "Good," he thought, "I got here first. I can go in and open some windows." The house had been repainted just before Huber Realty bought it and the carpet was new. He wanted to let some of the fumes escape. He also had not been in the house since the bathroom in the laundry room had been completed. When he bought the house the toilet and sink were free standing in the laundry room. He had a shower added and separating wall built to close it in.

The house looked great, the fresh paint in the remodeled laundry and lower kitchen added to the cleanliness. He had hired a local contractor to go through the house. He was known to flip older houses so Bill trusted him to do the job right. He was glad his trust was well founded. The house simply looked great.

Bill walked back outside. The grounds were well maintained and the out buildings looked good from the outside. He couldn't be more happy with the curb appeal.

Bill heard the crunching of gravel on the driveway in front of the house. He walked around to see a GMC Arcadia pull to a stop. He walked up and greeted the occupants. "You must be the Gordons."

"We are," the woman answered as she stood up. "You must be Bill Weber."

"I am," Bill responded in kind.

"I'm David," the man said as he got out from the other side, "this is my wife, Gail."

"It is certainly a pleasure to meet you in person," Bill responded.

One of the two boys followed his father around the SUV and joined the other. Bill shook the hands of the adults and then looked at the twin boys. "Which is Martin and which is John?"

"I'm Martin," one of the twins said, then hooked his thumb, "he's John."

"Well," Bill shook both the boys hands still trying to find

a difference, "it is certainly nice to meet you both." Bill turned back to the adults. "Any trouble finding the place?"

"Your coordinates were right on," David answered.

"What a drive," Gail said. "Everything's so open and so green."

"You were also right about the time," David added. "We zipped right down the road. I don't think I've been over fifty miles an hour in a year. The traffic in the valley is brutal. Unless it's the middle of the night, you can't even make any time on the Bayshore Freeway or even the 280."

"I told you highway twelve was fast," Bill replied. "I moved here from the east coast last year. One of the first things I realized was I was enjoying driving again."

David nodded and added, "I can see how that could happen. Before we get started, I want to apologize for moving up the timeline. The corporate jet was going to New York, so we hitched a ride. It is one of the perks of the company. We paid the company the equivalent of airline coach fare for the four of us and they landed the jet here."

"That's quite a perk," Bill answered.

"The boys loved it," Gail said. "I couldn't get Martin away from the window and John sat up front with the pilots."

David turned the conversation back to the business at hand. "So, what have you got to show us Bill. It was a nice plane ride, but that's not why we came."

Bill started his pitch, "The property surveyed out at fifteen point six acres. If you look over that way to the west you will see a fencepost painted bright orange. That's one corner. The one over this way," Bill pointed east, "is the other corner."

"That's a lot of land," Gail said. "What do people do with this much land, Bill?"

Bill was not surprised at the question. For the people who live here, sixteen acres is not considered a farm; but to people from more urban areas, it's like moving into wide open spaces. "Huber Realty has been involved with the sale of many hobby farms. Some people raise horses, others llamas or alpacas. Almost all of them have big vegetable gardens." Bill mentioned the gardens because he already knew from previous conversations that Gail liked gardening.

"Where are the other houses?" one of the boys asked.

"If you look over that way you can see the barn of your neighbor's farm. They are about a mile down the road." Bill turned. "Over that way is another neighbor. That house is about two miles. There are two more over the hill." Bill pointed again.

"You mean we won't have a next door neighbor?" the twin asked again.

Bill had figured it out. "Well, you do, Martin. It's just 'next door' is about a mile away."

"Can we go inside?" David asked.

"Surely," Bill answered and guided the way with his hand.

"You boys stay close," Gail cautioned. She turned to Bill, "How did you know he was Martin?"

"John is the shy one," Bill answered.

"Most people don't figure that out," Gail said.

"What attracted you to this property?" Bill asked as they were walking up to the front door.

"The price, for one," David said catching a sideways glare from his wife.

"We've told you about the trouble we had with the school," Gail said. "We needed to find a place for the boys to grow up without that kind of influence."

"We're not talking about the lifestyle," David added almost as if he felt he had to. "We're talking about the way they protect the teachers, regardless of what is happening."

"I understand," Bill said. And he did, more than he wanted to.

"We also liked the second kitchen," Gail said. "David's mother is getting up in years and she lives alone. If we move the boys away, it will break her heart. We're thinking about finishing the downstairs as an apartment for her."

"There are safety egress windows in the unfinished section of the basement. If you would like, we'll start our tour downstairs."

"I think I would like that," David said, then looked around. "Martin, John, where are you?"

"Picking out bedrooms," one boy answered.

"You'd better be picking one together," Gail called.

"Your grandma gets one initially, then dad gets it for an office."

Only silence came from the other end of the house.

"I guess that's the sound of a bubble bursting," Gail giggled, then turned serious again. "How do we get downstairs?"

Bill led them to the lower floor. He pointed out the features of the kitchen and laundry room. In the unfinished area they had a discussion about making an apartment for David's mother. David walked off dimensions and made notes on the listing sheet he was carrying. Bill told them about the contractor he had used to frame and finish the half bath and the laundry room.

They walked upstairs and, after another discussion about each son having his own room, the boys picked the one closest to the bathroom as the one they would share. David let Gail pick the room for their master and he took the third for his future office.

Bill watched as they walked through the house. David measured the space for the refrigerator and decided theirs would fit. He watched as the couple took on the house as their own.

"How far is the school?" Gail asked.

"About ten miles. The bus will pick the boys up right out front.

"And it's a good school?"

"You know it is Gail," David interrupted, "we did the research."

"I know, I just want to hear it from someone who lives here."

"Well, I live in Helen, South Dakota," Bill answered. "It's a little over an hour from here. I have heard that it's a good school. They have a strong athletic program."

"What was that you were telling us about schools, Bill? If we don't like one school, we can move the boys into another public school?"

"That's right. The state of South Dakota has an open enrollment policy. Say, for some reason, you would rather the boys go to school in Aberdeen near your work, you simply move them."

"If they had that in California, we might have never met," David said.

Martin came up and asked if they could go out.

"Sure, but stay close and don't go into any of the other buildings without us," Gail said.

"Speaking of other buildings," David shrugged, "I guess we should look at them."

Bill guided the couple out and through the other buildings. The heated shop held some interest for David. He thought he might take up furniture restoration as a hobby. The other buildings were the typical red hip roofed barn and the other a smaller calving or hog farrowing shed.

The boys had retrieved a soccer ball from the Arcadia and were kicking it around the yard. David pointed to them, "They can't do that at home."

"I've seen them kick the ball in the back yard," Gail challenged.

"Our back yard is only thirty feet by forty. They can't play like this," he pointed again.

"If you'll excuse me, I need to make a call." Bill stepped away from the couple, not to make a call, but to let them discuss the property. He called June.

"Hi Bill? How's it going?"

"They love the place. They are talking about appliances, measuring windows and David is thinking about starting a furniture restoration hobby in the shop. I'd say it looks very good indeed."

"So you're calling me to give them space?"

"Exactly."

"I feel so used," June quipped.

"I could have called Tom Ogden."

"I know, he was there when you bought the place. Sarah told me he thought you were crazy."

"We'll see how crazy in the next half hour."

"Break a leg."

The couple were looking at Bill. They had stayed a respectful distance but he could see they wanted to talk.

"Thanks, honey," Bill said, "I'm going to get back to work." Bill put the phone back in his pocket.

David walked up, "Did you say the furnace was new?"

"Newer," Bill answered. "It was installed three years ago when they remodeled the kitchen. The plumbing and electrical were both upgraded at the same time."

"So you don't think we would have any trouble getting a home warranty?"

"No problem at all. I can arrange it for you if you would like."

"How about a home inspection? Can you arrange that?"

"I could, but I won't."

David had been looking at the kids kicking the soccer ball. He turned his head and said "What? You won't? Is there something wrong with the house?"

"No. I don't know of anything wrong with the house or any other building on the property."

"Then why don't you want an inspection?"

"I do want you to get an inspection. Frankly, I was going to recommend it."

"Now I'm really confused," Gail said.

Bill smiled. "I'm the seller. I do not want to recommend a home inspector. It would be a conflict of interest. I have a phone book in my car that has them listed. You can also call the local Chamber and see who they recommend. I just will not suggest a name."

"Now I understand," David said.

"I get asked about it all the time. I don't think anyone should buy a house without a good going over. If the buyer doesn't have the knowledge or the time, a home inspection service is the next best thing."

David looked at Gail who looked back at her husband and some kind of non verbal communication occurred. David looked at Bill, "We like the house and the property. How firm is your asking price of one hundred fifty five thousand?"

"You know what you can get in Sunnyvale for that kind of money," Bill said.

"Sure," David nodded, "Maybe a one car garage to be used for storage, but this isn't the Silicon Valley. This is South Dakota. I've looked at other properties on the internet and this is one of the higher listings. How about one twenty?"

"This is South Dakota. That's what makes it special. Did those other listings have recent upgrades? Do they have a second kitchen and space for your mother's apartment? This is a premium property. I know I can get my asking price if I wait for the right family." Bill smiled. "But, I do have a good deal of money tied up in this. For the sake of not waiting, I'd be will willing to go down to one forty nine."

"Here's the deal, Bill." David was leaning on the Arcadia. "We can sell our house, pay off the mortgage, pay the taxes and move. Once we do, we will have about one hundred fifty thousand left over. We would like to own this property outright. I can give you one thirty five, that will leave me fifteen to finish the downstairs for Mom."

"Let's settle on one forty and we have a deal." Bill put out his hand.

David held back his handshake, "I want the right to turn the deal down if an inspector finds something drastically wrong."

"Done."

"Contingent on a sales agreement on our Sunnyvale house?"

"I'm not comfortable with that," Bill said. "I know the housing market in northern California."

"We already have a buyer, Bill," Gail said candidly. "One of my co-workers wants our place. He commutes over two hours now and wants to move nearer to work. We held him off until we came out to see this place."

"Here's what we can do. You go ahead and make that call. We'll write our contract of sale with a three day escape clause. We can sign it today but either of us has the option to back out, without penalty, for three business days. That would give you until close of business next Wednesday to wrap up the deal on your California house."

There was the awkward silence. It was the point in the negotiation when each party knew the next one to speak was the one caving in.

It was Gail who broke the silence, "Oh, do it David. You know Chad is going to take our place."

"Done," David said and put out his hand.

Bill took his hand, then Gail's. "Wonderful. I'll get the paperwork."

"You have the deal with you?" Gail asked. "How did you

know the details in advance?"

"I didn't," Bill answered. "I left the particulars blank so we could fill them in together."

"That's smart."

"It helps to keep things simple," Bill answered. "Let's go inside where we have a counter."

"We don't need an attorney?" Gail asked.

"Lawyers aren't needed for normal real estate transactions. The closing is normally done by the title company or in the office of the lender," Bill answered.

"I think I'm going to like it here," Gail said.

"Terry Redlin is nationally known for his wildlife paintings," Julie said, "I think you're going to enjoy this."

"I looked at the museum website. His work looks interesting," Fred said as he, once again, held the door for Julie.

"Wait until you see it in person," she said as they walked up to the reception desk.

"Good afternoon, welcome to the Redlin Art Center."

"Good afternoon to you," Fred answered the young lady at the counter.

"Have you been to the Art Center before?"

"I have and I love it. My friend is from out of town, he hasn't been here," answered Julie.

"Well, we hope you enjoy the experience."

Fred looked at Julie to make the double meaning obvious, "I'm sure I will." He picked up the pen and signed the guest book. Out of curiosity he glanced up at the names and locations before him. He was fairly sure he was the longest distance visitor. He was about to say so when he saw the names of a couple from Nome, Alaska. He chose instead to ask, "Where's a good place to start?"

"Let's start up top and work our way down," Julie suggested.

"Sure," Fred agreed.

"Terry Redlin did some paintings that were a series, my favorites are upstairs. I really want you to see them while this experience is fresh."

Not knowing what else to say, Fred said, "Okay."

As they walked, Julie pointed out the paintings she liked best and Fred did the same. They learned that their tastes, though different, harmonized with one another. Julie could see a print of Fred's favorite in her living room without it upsetting the décor.

Fred was moved by the American Portrait Series. Tears welled up when he saw and understood the final painting. He blinked hard, moved away and sat on a bench nearby.

"Are you all right?" Julie asked.

"I'm fine. That last one just got to me. I have had to do that twice."

"Do what?"

"Go to a parents house and tell them their son isn't coming home," Fred answered quietly.

"Oh, Fred… I'm sorry. I didn't know that."

"Its part of the job," Fred said. "A part I could have gone my entire Navy career without doing." Fred took a deep breath, then stood up. "Okay, lets keep going."

"Here's a better one. It's called the 'America the Beautiful Series'." Julie led him to the wall of paintings, we start here with 'Oh Beautiful for Spacious Skies'."

They walked together from one painting to the next, Fred realized he was holding Julie's hand. He didn't remember doing that, but it felt natural. The pain he had experienced a few moments ago was gone, replaced with a contentment he had not felt in years.

Chapter Ten

"I thought he would at least text me." Jessie was sitting on Mickie's bed.

"Did you text him?"

"I sent him a 'what's up' text," Jessie replied. "He texted back, 'nothing'."

"Then what?"

"Then silence."

"Really?"

"Really."

"What are you going to do?"

"I don't know. I know he likes me. After the fireworks he said so."

"We could walk by his dad's shop and see if he's there," Mickie suggested.

"No we can't! If he is there, then he would see us," Jessie said.

"I have an idea." Mickie stood up. "Let's go back to your house."

"How does that help?"

"Because we're going to walk back to your house by walking by Abby's place. You can see Mike's Garage from between the houses. You can see if he's there from a block away and he won't know you're looking."

"What if he does?'

"What if?" Mickie repeated. "We're a block away visiting a friend."

"Okay," Jessie hesitated, "wait. They're on vacation, they won't be home."

"Maybe Jeremy doesn't know that."

"What if he does?"

"Then we'll tell him we were checking the house." Mickie pulled her best friend to her feet. "Let's go, you can't just sit here fretting all day"

"All right." Jessie got up and followed her out the door. As they got to the front yard, she stopped again. "Did you say 'fretting'?"

Mickie giggled, "I guess I did."

"Where did you get that?"

"I was reading a romance novel by Margaret Purcey last night. The story's is set in West Virginia and is filled with words like 'fret', 'fixin', and 'y'all', I guess it leaked out."

"Be careful around Jimmy, he might think you're going southern on him."

The two girls walked by Abby's house and saw Jeremy's pick up truck in front of his dad's shop. So, they knew he was there. Now they had to find an excuse to go by there.

They got to Jessie's house just in time to see Fred and Julie walk into Julie's Garage. If they thought anything of it neither one mentioned it. They walked back to Jessie's room and started working on a reason to visit Mike's Garage. "We could let some air out of your bicycle tire," Mickie suggested.

"I can't let Jeremy see me on a bicycle!" Jessie said.

"Okay, I reckon' you're right."

"You're doing it again."

"What?"

"You said 'I reckon'."

"Oh no!" Mickie laughed.

"You've got to find another book."

"Have you ever read any of her books?" Mickie asked.

"No"

"Then you don't know what you're talking about. She really gets…"

"I didn't know you two were here," June said standing in Jessie's doorway.

"We just got here," Jessie answered.

"Do you want to go to Kent with me?" June asked. "I want to pick up a few things at the grocery store."

"Will you have to stop at Mike's Garage?" Mickie asked, seeing an opportunity.

"No, the car's running fine."

"Do the tires need air?" Mickie continued probing.

"What's this sudden interest in my car?"

"Jeremy is working with his dad today," Jessie answered bringing her mom into the web of conspiracy.

"Oh… I see…" June walked in and sat on the bed. "And you two are trying to come up with an excuse to go see him."

"Sort of," Jessie said.

118

"Yup," Mickie agreed with a giggle.

"I don't want to lie to Mike," June said.

"What if one of your tires was low?" Mickie asked.

"No," June said firmly, "not if you're thinking what I think you're thinking. That's plain dishonest and I won't have anything to do with it."

Mickie shrugged, "All right. What can we do then?"

"Go to the pool," June suggested.

"How does that help?" Jessie asked.

"Let him find you, don't chase him."

"What if he doesn't?" Jessie asked.

"If he likes you, he will," June replied.

"What if he doesn't?"

"Then why do you want to be with him?"

"Mom!" Jessie said. "You don't understand. Never mind, Mickie and I will figure this out ourselves."

"Suit yourself," June said as she stood. "I'm just trying to save you some pain."

June walked back to the crib. Mason was sleeping quietly. "Jessie, you could do me a great favor and watch Mason while I go to the store."

"But Mom…."

"You help me with my problem and I'll help you with yours. My air conditioner isn't blowing as cold as it used to. I could stop and talk to Mike about it."

"How does that help if we're here?" Mickie asked.

"Simple, I'll tell Mike, loud enough for Jeremy to hear, that I have to hurry back because you want to go to the pool."

"But what if he doesn't come to the pool?"

"Then you'll know. Won't you?"

"Know what?" asked Mickie.

"Know I have to work harder," Jessie said. "Will you be long?"

"Not too long. Just over to Kent and back."

"Okay."

"I have a bottle in the fridge for him if he wakes up. I fed him about an hour ago."

"Okay Mom."

Sunday mornings in Helen, South Dakota look much like

Sunday mornings in most Midwestern towns. The streets are quiet, not that they are really busy any other time of the week. Most business are closed. The Quick Stop on the highway is open for convenience items and fuel and the Helen House is open for the after church crowd. Cars start moving around town at nine fifteen a.m.. As if by a magnet, they gather in the parking lot of the Helen United Church. Sunday school for adults and children starts at nine thirty. At ten fifteen a second group of cars gather around the first. The occupants empty out and file into the main entrance of the building. Bill Weber and family were in the first group while his brother Fred, along with Julie Sorenson, were part of the second.

Bill was waiting in the vestibule when Fred and Julie walked in. "Fred, I'd like you to meet someone. This is Mike Finney, he's retired Navy."

"Hello Mike," Fred said to the man twenty years his senior. "Thank you for your service."

"And yours too," Mike replied. "What rate are you?"

"I'm a CT, CTTC to be exact."

"So you're a Black Shoe Chief." Mike asked as a statement, referring the tradition of aviators wearing brown shoes with khaki uniforms.

"So what were you?"

"I retired as an ASM1."

"AS... I'm not sure what that rating is."

"Avaition Ground Support. ASM is a Mechanic. H was Hydraulics and E was electrical. I don't know if they changed any since I left. I don't keep track." Mike stopped for a half second, "CT... that's a spook, right?"

"I've been called that by some."

"Yeah, I know," Mike chuckled, "any more and you'd have to kill me."

"Fred is thinking about moving to Helen when he retires in two months."

"A Black Shoe moving in?" Mike smiled "There goes the neighborhood."

Both men laughed at the inside joke. Then Fred continued, "I understand you have an auto shop?"

"Best one in Helen," Mike answered.

"I'm renting a car from a friend of Bill's. He has a lot in

120

Watertown."

"I know Marty," Mike interrupted. "He's 100% east coast, but a straight shooter."

"That's good to know," Fred answered. "I'm thinking about keeping the car for when I move here. I'd like you to give it the once over before I decide."

" I'm booked solid all next week," Mike said. I'll tell you what, let's do it this afternoon."

I wouldn't want to ruin your Sunday."

"It's not a problem. Consider it a favor for a vet. Give me call and we'll meet at the shop."

"All right, if you don't mind." Fred stood there expecting Mike to hand him a business card.

Instead Mike said, "Time to go in." and turned away.

"That's funny," Fred said to his brother.

"What's funny?"

"I asked Mike to look at the Charger and he said sure, give him a call."

"And?"

"And nothing, I expected him to give me a card."

"Why?" Now Bill was having a bit of fun at his brother's expense.

"What do you mean 'why'? I don't understand."

"Welcome to Helen, South Dakota. Mike didn't give you a card because he more than likely doesn't have one. Everyone knows where his shop is and most folks know his number. I do, it's 2910."

"2910?" Fred was still confused.

"That's right." The tempo of the music changed again. "We'd better get inside," Bill said ending the conversation.

On the way inside Julie told Fred that all the land line numbers in Helen started with 829. "That's funny, I'll have to get used to that," he said.

"Good morning!" Reverend Jim Clower said from the front of the church.

"Good morning," came the united reply.

"I'd like to welcome all of you this morning. What a beautiful day we have to worship the Lord. I'd also like to point out a few guests, Rebecca Henswirth is here with her husband Glenn and Bill Weber's brother Fred is visiting us

121

from the Navy."

"I think this morning I would like to start out with number 67 'To God Be The Glory'. As we stand, please welcome those around you."

The church service looked to Fred like many he had seen in chapels and officiated by Chaplains throughout his Navy career. He was not overly religious, but he would attend services on Sunday morning when he was at sea. During his time on shore duty he was a bit less vigilant.

The Webers took up one whole pew for the service. Julie was at the aisle, next to Fred, who was next to his brother, then June, then Cory and Jessie at the far end.

Jessie had maneuvered herself near Jeremy in Sunday school, in the hopes that he would ask her to sit with him. He didn't, so she sat with her family.

Sitting directly in front of the Weber family was the Ogden family. Before the service started, Bill had a moment to talk with Tom and make arrangements for them to meet at the Helen House after the service.

"Dad!" Jessie said as only a teenage girl could, "Everyone's going to the lake."

"Who is everyone?"

"I don't know. Jeremy and Mary Bayer and Ryan Woodson, and more I think."

"I'm not comfortable with this. If a bunch of you are going, that's one thing, but if it's just the four of you, that's another. Find out who's going."

"Dad!" Jessie pleaded, "I can't ask that. I'd look like a child." Then she added sarcastically, "My daddy wants to know how many kids are going so he can decide if I can be allowed to go along."

"Well, with that kind of attitude, I'll solve this problem for you. You're not going."

"Dad!" Jessie pleaded again, "I have to go, don't you see, Mary is going."

"What I see is you spending the rest of the day in your room if you don't drop this right now."

Bill pulled up in front of the Helen House. As he parked, Jessie asked, "Can I walk home?"

"Suit yourself," Bill answered.

Jessie got out and slammed the door. She walked away without another word.

June saw her daughter reaching for her phone as she moved away. "Maybe we should have let her go."

"I would have if I knew it wasn't just the four of them," Bill answered. "I wouldn't have liked it, but I would have allowed it."

"She's growing up, Bill."

"She's thirteen."

"What's your point? Look at her," June pointed, "she developing a shape. The rest of her is growing up too."

"It's too soon," Bill said quietly.

"You can't change it."

"I'm hungry!" Cory said. "Let's go eat."

Bill let out a breath. "Okay Cory. I'll race you to the door."

"Bring it!" Cory said and sprung open the back door of the Escalade.

Bill ran to the door just fast enough to let his son win. After the congratulatory pat on the shoulder, he pulled the door open for his son and his wife.

They took their usual spot in the back of the Helen House. The Weber family was on one side and the Ogden Family was on the other. June looked across the table, "Where's Frankie?"

"He's heading up to the lake with a bunch of friends."

"Really?" June looked at Bill.

"We didn't know that," he replied.

"Maybe we should text her and tell her she can go."

"Not after the way she mouthed off," Bill said firmly.

"Who's Frankie going with?" June asked.

"I'm not sure, Candy's older brother is driving, Frank rode home with them to change," Sarah said.

"Got room for two more?" Fred said as he walked up to the table with Julie.

"Sure," Tom replied, "pull up a chair. Good to see you again."

"Excuse me," June got up and left the table.

"Oh… this gets better and better," Darla said as she walked up with a coffee pot.

"Good morning Darla," Tom said. "What gets better?"

"The rumor mill. First I find out from Eddie Watts that Bill's brother is moving to Helen, then I find out he's buying Stewart's place, and now I see him sitting here after church with Julie Sorenson." Darla smiled, "The town's gonna' be buzzin' today!"

Fred didn't quite know what to say. He started but Julie interrupted him. "Darla, you tell that rumor mill that he's mine until I say otherwise."

"What she said," Fred smiled.

After a bit of discussion the whole table decided on the buffet, except Cory and Joey who both wanted hamburgers and french fries.

"So, Fred, what do you intend to do when you move here?"

"I'm not sure yet. There's nothing in the civilian world like what I do for the Navy. Not that I would want to do that anymore anyway. I'm looking for something simple and fun."

"The Helen Elevator has a few openings."

"I'll look at that. Are they on the web site?"

"I think so, if not I'll get a copy of the job descriptions and drop them by."

"Thanks Tom."

"You know, Fred," Bill jumped in, "the way you negotiated for that car, you should look into sales."

"Marty is making good money on the deal, I didn't beat him out of anything," Fred hesitated, "but that's a thought."

"Bill, can I see you over there?"

Fred said, "Little brother's in trouble."

June shot Fred a look, then said to the rest of the table, "We'll be just a minute."

Bill followed June to an area of the restaurant that wasn't currently occupied. June turned to her husband, "I told Jessie she could go to the lake. I also told her she owed you an apology."

Bill thought about it for a minute. At this point there was nothing he could do. He did feel better to find out that other people would be there, including Frankie. On the other hand he didn't like the idea of them not having a united front. He decided not to let it ruin their meal. "Thanks for telling me," he said and walked back to the table.

June turned and walked to the lady's room. She knew she had done the right thing. She also knew her husband was upset. They would talk about it later. He would see she was right.

June looked at her hair and makeup, made minor corrections and walked back to the table. As she approached she heard her brother in law say, "... so I said 'Well, Lieutenant, where do think I found it? In the chow line?'"

Tom, Sarah and Julie all exploded with laughter, Bill smiled and nodded. He had heard it before.

"Fred," Sarah asked, "aren't you going to miss that?"

"Of course I'm going to miss things like that. What I won't miss is the long watches in rough weather. I won't miss not being able to talk about what I do for a living."

"What about the travel?" Julie asked.

"I have been around the world at least three times. I have been across both the Atlantic and Pacific oceans more times than I can count. I have been everywhere from Algiers to Zanzibar. I've had occasion to drink warm beer in Spain watching a bull fight and cold beer San Diego watching the Padres. I have been on every continent except Antarctica. I spent the past twenty three years bobbing around the seven seas, but you know what I haven't done? I haven't owned a house, I haven't had roots. As Julie pointed out yesterday, I don't even have furniture. I think I want to stop traveling for a while and see what it's like to sit in one place."

Darla walked up with her coffee pot, "Well, you can do that in Helen. I know of some men around here that have that down to a science." The table laughed again. "Who needs a refill?"

Now it was Fred's turn, "So you think there might be a seat at the pinochle table for me, Darla?"

"I'm sure the morning coffee group would let you in, Fred." Sarah continued the banter.

After a while Fred leaned back. "Wow, that's good chow. I'll have to watch myself. I'll get too fat on leave and they won't let me out of the Navy until I get back down to the standard weight and girth."

"They do that?" Julie asked.

"They've been very strict about weight and physical condition over the past ten years or so. I was joking about not letting me out, but if you don't stay trim, you can't stay in."

Everyone's head turned as Mason let out a wail. June picked up her baby and did a quick inspection. She looked to her husband, "Bill, we'd better go. I think this young man needs a change and his lunch."

"All right, I'll settle up with Darla."

"I'll get the check, Bill," Fred said.

"You got the last one."

"So?" Fred said, "You get the next one."

Mason started crying again. Bill looked at June, then at Mason, then at Fred, "Okay. Thanks."

"See you at home," Fred said.

"Okay Fred." Bill looked at his son, "Cory? You coming with us?"

"Okay," Cory said and jumped down from his seat. "Can we go to the pool?"

"There's an idea," Bill looked over to his wife, "Maybe we should find this lake all the kids like."

June shot him a look that would melt cement. "Let's just go."

As Bill and family left the restaurant, Julie turned to Fred, "Do you have a few minutes for a ride? I want to show you something."

"Certainly, give me a minute to pay the bill." Fred got up and walked over to Darla. He took the checks for the table and paid them all. Once done, he walked back. "All right."

"Tom, Sarah, it's good to see you again," Julie said as she stood.

"Same goes for us," Tom replied.

Julie was getting used to having doors opened for her. She decided she liked it even if it was old fashioned. She slid into the passenger seat of the Charger.

Fred closed her door and walked to the other side. He got in and started the car and said, "Where to?"

"Take this road down to the end then and turn left."

Fred followed Julie's instructions. He made three more turns on gravel roads. They drove by field after field of corn, soybeans and already harvested wheat. Finally they were in a grove of trees. There was a driveway to the right and at Julie's direction, he pulled in. To call it a glade would be too much, but it was a two acre patch of mowed grass. The driveway made a big circle around the patch which, from the air, would look like a large lollypop.

On the outside of the road was a stream. It had all but encircled the clearing before it wandered off into a field. Trees had grown along side of the stream, providing a shelter from view.

"Pull up here and stop," Julie said.

Fred stopped. He got out and opened Julie's door. Once she was out of the car, he looked around, "This is beautiful."

"I love it here. Sometimes I bring a chair and folding table and set up my laptop. It's a great place to write."

"I can see that, especially if you write romance novels." Fred looked around a bit more. "Is it a park?"

"No, it's private property."

"Really. Who owns it?"

"I do."

"You do?"

"Nobody in town knows. This is another secret," Julie said. "I bought it through an arrangement I have with my publisher's attorney. He did the paperwork as a side job for me. He pays a local farmer to maintain the property."

"Doesn't the farmer get suspicious?"

"No. Ben, that's the lawyer, likes to pheasant hunt. He brings his motor home out here each fall for opening week of the season. The farmer, Lonny Ringstadt, just thinks he's another city boy with too much money."

"That's funny," Fred said. He took her hand and they walked over to the stream. The water looked to be about a foot deep and ten feet wide, It was in a gully about ten feet below the clearing. "I guess there's no threat of flooding," Fred said.

"I came out here to check when we had a really wet spring. The rivers were all bulging and devouring up the low land. The stream was a river, but it was still three feet below the bank."

"What a great place to build a house," Fred said.

"There was one here when I first bought the place. It had

been empty for at least twenty years. I had a man from Sioux Falls check it. He said it was not worth restoring, so we tore it down." They continued walking. "You see this pipe?" she pointed down. "There is an old artesian well on the property. It still runs. It dumps into the river. That spigot on the top of the pipe is for a hose. You see that small building?" Julie pointed.

"The one that looks like an outhouse?"

"I hadn't thought of that." Julie giggled, "No, that's the spot where the electricity comes in. There is also a reservoir tank and a pressure pump for the artesian well."

"I thought artesian wells were free flowing." Fred asked as a statement.

"They are. Some are better than others. This one runs about ten pounds and one half gallon a minute. Good enough for getting a drink, but not to do anything serious." Julie pointed again, "If you look over that way you can see where the dump station is. That's the white cap on the big pipe. The pipe is tied in to the original septic system."

"So... Why are you waiting? Why don't you build?"

"Honestly?"

"Honestly."

"I can't maintain it."

"Mowing doesn't take that much."

"It's not the mowing. It's the rest. The driveway maintenance, clearing the tree belts, snow removal and the like. I make a good living with what I do, but I don't make enough to hire a full time groundskeeper. Besides, this place is special. When I do build, I want to share it with someone special."

Fred stayed silent. He took her by the hand back to the center of the lollypop. He sat in the grass, then laid back. "It is beautiful here. So quiet. I can't hear a single man made noise."

Julie joined him, laying down and using his chest for a headrest. "I love it here. This is my happy place."

"I can understand why." After a while Fred shifted so they were face to face. He hesitated half a second then leaned in and kissed her.

Chapter Eleven

"Look June, I didn't like the idea in the first place. Regardless, I would have gone along if I had known that more than the four of them were going to this lake," Bill said, trying to keep his voice calm.

"So, that's what happened," June told him forcefully. "I found out that there were more kids going. Once I knew that, I told her she could go. *I did what you said to do*," June said the last sentence slowly for emphasis.

"You did not!" Bill said in frustration. "I told her she couldn't go because she was mouthing off. Now she thinks she can talk to me like that and get away with it. Well, I won't have it and I don't expect you to condone it either."

"I don't condone it," June said. "I told her she owes you an apology."

"An apology isn't good enough," Bill said. "What are we teaching her? Ten years from now if she gets drunk and kills somebody while driving, will she think she can just say 'Oh… sorry' and everything will be fine?"

"Bill, now you're being ridiculous."

"Ridiculous or not, we have to stand together. Jessie is becoming a teenager. If she can separate us and get us fighting, like we are now, she will run wild and make our lives a living hell."

"You're overreacting," June said. Her voice was softening. Bill had a point, he was mostly right, not to the degree he was talking, but he was right. "Jessie is a good kid, she's responsible. I don't think she would intentionally make our lives miserable."

"Jessie is a teen." Bill took his wife's two hands and held them. His voice became softer too. "Teens have a different way of looking at things. Don't you remember those years? I know I do. My parents, who I had idolized just a year before, had became prison guards. They were the enemy to get over on or escape from anytime I could. I was a nice responsible kid too. That all went out the window when the hormones started raging."

"Jessie won't be like that," June said firmly.

"Jessie is already starting. Look at where we are. We're standing in our living room shouting at one another while she is at some lake with her friends. She won this round."

"Bill, it's not a competition to keep score."

"No, it's not. You're right, I chose the wrong words." Bill sighed. "Look, we have to stay in harmony if all of us are to be happy. If you and I are not in agreement, we have to discuss it and hold a common position."

June bristled again, "You mean your position."

"I mean *our* position," Bill said. "You know me better then that. We have to agree to support each other."

"We do Bill," June replied. "Almost all the time we are on the same page with the kids. The rules we established years ago are still in place."

"We need to abide by our rules even more now. Jessie is thirteen. When she's twenty, Cory will be fourteen. We have to keep ourselves focused and single minded or they'll run over us like a freight train."

"Bill, you're talking about our children, not some caged animals."

"Caged is just what I mean," Bill said. "When the teen years hit they feel caged and will fight to get free. We need to continue what we've been doing. Encouraging good behavior and discouraging the bad. These are good kids, but our work gets harder now if we want to keep them that way." Bill pulled his wife over to the couch and they sat down. "Please don't get me wrong, this isn't a battle, or even a competition. I just don't want what happened today to happen on a regular basis. We're better parents than that."

"So what do you want to do now?" June asked, still with a hint of sarcasm, "Should we tell Jessie to come home? I was a teenager once, I remember. If we did that, the embarrassment would be devastating."

"No, we won't do that," Bill said. "Let her have her day. I'll talk to her about how she speaks to us after she gets home."

Julie was sitting on her bed. She had her laptop open. "I took Fred to my 'happy place' today. We kissed and stayed quiet for a almost an hour. I have not felt that kind of a kiss in a very long time. Fred wasn't pushing for anything more. He was content with what we were doing. Look, Diary, I'm no prude, but I can tell the difference in kisses for kisses sake and kisses looking for more. If this doesn't work out, my happy place might not be so happy anymore. Did I make a mistake? I've only known him for a matter of days, yet we're so comfortable, I feel like I've known him for years."

Julie closed the diary file and opened the book she was working on.

> Chapter Nine - Alonzo burst through the door, his clothes tattered from the explosion. "Rachael! Rachael! You're alive! I thought I had lost you."
>
> "Oh Alonzo," Rachael raised her bloody and bruised head from the bed. "I lived for you my love."

"Oh, that's terrible," Julie said to herself. She deleted the text and closed her laptop again. She had a thought. She wondered if her relationship with Fred was ruining her writing. She dismissed it as soon as she had it. "That's silly," she said out loud. "One doesn't have anything to do with the other."

Julie got up from the bed and started into the kitchen. She had invited Fred for supper before checking what she had to serve. She had just blurted it out when he opened the car door for her in front of her house. She didn't want to be away from him. She opened the freezer and found, thankfully, two rib eye steaks. She set them on the counter to start thawing. She looked further and saw she had the makings of a good garden salad. In the crisper drawer she found five whole potatoes. She took out two larger ones for baking.

With the plan in her head she walked out to the garage and got out her portable grill. She rolled it through the back garage door and over to the door near her kitchen. She filled it with charcoal. Back to the shelf in the garage for the charcoal lighter. It wasn't there. Then she remembered, she had used the last of it when she grilled the salmon last week. Who to call? Bill and June had a gas grill, they wouldn't have any.

She called the Quick Stop.

"Quick Stop, this is Natalie."

"Natalie, Julie Sorenson, do you have charcoal lighter?"

"I'm supposed to have it, let me go look." There was silence on the phone for about thirty seconds. "I have two bottles."

"Great!" Julie said. "I'll be right there."

"I'll have it at the counter."

"Thanks."

"See ya."

Julie drove over to the Quick Stop, got the charcoal lighter and a frozen layer cake for desert. She looked around but couldn't think of anything else. On the drive back Julie turned one corner onto her street and saw Fred's car turn the other corner. She was wondering where he was going. The thought didn't last. She had too much to do and only three hours to get it done.

"Jessie, come around this side." Jeremy called to her. There was a large grass outcropping jutting out into the lake. It was part of the base from an old railroad. The mound was still there but the tracks and trestle had been gone for years.

"What's around there?"

"You'll see, swim around the mound."

Jessie swam around to the other side. Jeremy was there all alone. Jessie didn't realize it was a set up. "It looks the same as the other side."

Jeremy swam up to her "The other side is crowded." He moved up closer to her. They kissed. The kiss wasn't as strong or as powerful as the one under fireworks but it still left her lightheaded. She returned it.

Jeremy took her hand and led her to a place where she could touch bottom. She turned to him, he reached out and pulled her close. She melted. She could feel his breath on her neck. Then she felt something bump against her hipbone. She moved, he moved and she felt the poke again and realized what it was. Jeremy had removed his suit and had started working on the knot holding her top. She jumped back, "What are you doing?"

He stepped forward again, "I'm only doing what you want

132

me to do."

"I do not! Jeremy Finney, you keep away from me!"

"But Jessie I thought you…"

"Whatever you thought, you were wrong!" She swam away. She swam around to the other side of the mound. Most of the kids had gone home and the rest were on the beach drying off. Candy was still there and so was Frank. Jessie swam to shore and walked up. "Candy can your brother take me home?"

"Sure."

"What happened to Jeremy?"

"He's a pig," Jessie said without further explanation.

Frank handed Jessie her towel. "What did he do?"

"Leave it alone Frank," Jessie snapped. "I just want to go home."

"Dad, I'm sorry." Jessie was standing in the living room in front of her father. She knew she owed her dad an apology, she also knew now he was right. There could have been real trouble if Frank and Candy hadn't been there to take her home. She knew better than to tell her dad about the incident. She wouldn't be allowed to go out until she was thirty. She chose a different path. "But I really didn't know how many kids would be there."

"How many were there?"

"About fifteen," Jessie answered. "Some from our school and some from Crandon."

"Jessie, you're growing up. I know that. I don't like it because I still think of you as my little peanut, but the facts are the facts. I have to face it.

"You have to face it too. These years are wonderful years to be alive. You will experience new things and dream new dreams. Your life will take on a whole new meaning over the next five or so years."

"I know," Jessie said.

Bill waited, but she didn't add anything. "There are going to be times when we disagree and there are going to be times when you will feel like we are holding you back. Please understand that we love you and are trying to protect you from pain."

"I know Dad." She couldn't tell her dad just how well she knew.

"While we are on the subject, I want you to rethink going out with Jeremy Finney. I think you are too far apart in ages. It could put you in a bad position."

"I won't be seeing Jeremy again, he..." Jessie quickly rephrased, "We had a fight."

Julie got out two candles, she looked at them and put them away again. "Too much," she thought. She wanted the meal to be perfect, but at the same time she didn't want it to be over the top.

Julie was excited and nervous all at the same time. This relationship was going somewhere, but she wasn't sure where yet. She had all the signs of falling in love, missing him every moment he was away. How her heart jumped when he kissed her. When she thought of him, which was almost all the time, she found herself smiling. She had written about all these things, yet had never experienced them herself.

Of course she was no prude. She had been out countless times. She knew what it was to be with a man. She had been less than proper in college. Looking back she considered it gathering material for her novels. She had also dated after college. She had man friends and boy friends over the years, but never one she wanted to marry. When she moved to Helen, she found the pool of eligible bachelors to be small. The guys were nice and each of them had things in their favor, but none of them were "The One", if there even was such a thing. She wrote about "The One". She had written in great detail about whirlwind romances. She could set a scene, have boy meet girl, date, fight, split up, grow apart, find each other again and fall in love and live happily ever after in under two hundred pages. She had loved and won and loved and lost in print thirty four times.

This was different. This wasn't some heroine in a new Margaret Purcey novel. This was *her* life, Julie Sorenson. This was Fred Weber, not some made up character. Fred matched none of her characters. He was quiet, rather than bold and brassy. He had a quiet power about him that said confidence. He didn't have to brag because he knew who he was and was perfectly happy with it. Julie had never met, or written about, a man like Fred.

So, this dinner had to be special. It had to be something he would remember when he went back to the ship. She wanted it to be domestic. She wanted him to feel married. Even if it was only for a few hours. That's why the candles were too much.

"The Charger is a good car, the aerodynamic design gives it the mileage. You say he had the report on it and it showed no accidents and no major repairs?" Mike was standing outside his auto repair garage looking at the car Fred brought in.

"That's what he told me, I haven't seen it," Fred answered.

"Marty wouldn't lie about that. Too easy to find out for yourself."

"I did," Fred replied. "I looked up the VIN number on Carfax. It was clean."

"All right, let's get it inside and take a look."

Mike it's Sunday. We don't need to do this now."

"I'm booked solid all next week. For a shipmate I can do a favor on a Sunday." Mike pointed to the bay where he wanted Fred to put the car. He walked to the back of the bay and directed Fred over the lift using military style aircraft director's signals. Fred followed the directions and got out. "Is that how you directed pilots in the Navy?"

Mike replied, "It's a habit I got into working the flight line. It works here too. You did pretty good for a black shoe."

"You know, Mike, not all CT's are on ships. Some of us have aircrew wings and brown shoes."

"You're not one of them."

"How can you tell?"

"I'm not sure, Fred, I just can. Just like I can tell a Sea Bee when I see one."

Fred thought about it. He could tag a member of the Sea Bees, too. It was a matter of attitude and the way they looked at things. Each sub branch of the Navy has its own traits and kinds of behaviors. Airedales, or people involved with Naval Aviation, had a way about them. So did the Construction Battalion folks. Black Shoes or seagoing sailors were different

135

too. The 'Bubble Heads' who served aboard submarines were a unique group as well. It takes a special kind of person to live underwater in a metal can for six months at a time. Most sailors had a way about them that they had picked up from living in their environment. If you stayed around the Navy long enough, you could see the 'tell'. Fred nodded, "I think I understand."

"You want to pull the hood release?" Mike said.

Fred pulled the release handle and got out. He walked up to the front of the car and looked under the hood. He was more adept at working on cars than his brother Bill. He had done all the maintenance on his beater pick up since he bought it six years ago. He had friends on the ship that knew their way around cars and trucks, so when he had a major job, like changing the clutch, he would ask for help. Norfolk Naval Station had a well equipped hobby shop or self help auto repair facility. He would rent a space for the time needed to do the job and take advantage of the rental tools on hand.

Fred looked into the engine compartment and mentally compared it to his truck. "They sure cram a lot of crap into there, don't they?" Fred asked rhetorically.

"This is an easy one. I've seen much worse," Mike answered. He got a box down from the shelf over the workbench and pulled out a mechanic's stethoscope. He placed it on his ears then poked the probe end in various places to listen to the running engine. "You can shut it down," he said as he put the tool away in the box and the box back up on the shelf. He pulled the dipstick for the engine oil, rubbed the oil around in his fingers, then smelled it. He did the same for the transmission and the power steering. Then he walked to his bench and got a small eye dropper. He dipped it into the brake fluid reservoir and did the same thing again. He reached down into the engine and pulled out a spark plug wire. He looked it over carefully. "These are original."

"That's not good," Fred answered thinking that car possibly had not had proper maintenance.

"It's not bad either. I see it all the time now. These newer cars don't need the kind of maintenance the old ones do. Spark plugs can last a hundred thousand miles."

"So the ignition wires are okay then," Fred asked as a

statement.

"Probably so. It runs smooth, that says a lot." Mike stepped back. He reached back up to the shelf and got out a code reader. He hooked it up to the pigtail he found under the dashboard. He turned the ignition on and after pushing several buttons he nodded and disconnected the unit and turned the ignition off again.. "No nasty codes there, let's put it in the air."

"The computer is happy?" Fred moved out of the way.

"The computer says the car is happy." Mike set the pads to lift the car by the uni-body 'frame' and pulled the lift handle. The shop got noisy as the whine of the hydraulic motor spoke to them about the heavy lifting. Once the car was in the air and the safeties were set, Mike walked under. He started in front and, with a bright flashlight that had appeared in his hand, made a cursory look around. "I don't see anything obvious. The brakes look good, plenty of meat on the front pucks. How deep do you want me to get?"

"What do you mean?" Fred asked.

"If I were to go all out, I would compression check the engine, change the oil and tear down the filter looking for foreign matter or metal. I'd do the same with the transmission. I could send both oil samples in for testing."

"I don't think I want to go that far, Mike. How about we change the oil and filter on the engine and give that a visual inspection. How did the transmission fluid look to you?"

"It wasn't overheated or burnt. From the looks and feel of it. I'd say you're in good shape."

"Okay, we'll leave that alone then,"

Mike said. "I still want to look at the rear brakes."

"Let's change the oil. While it's draining, we can look at the brakes."

"You are including yourself?" Mike smiled. "You know if you're going to help, that doubles my labor rate."

Fred held up his hand. "No.... I'm not going to get involved. This is your shop, not the hobby shop. I'll just watch if that doesn't cost too much extra."

"Well, since you're Navy... I'll have sympathy on a black shoe and let you watch for no extra charge."

Fred laughed, then changed the subject. "You know

137

where I can get a bottle of wine in town?"

"I think they have some at the Quick Stop and I know the Ringneck has some," Mike said. "But they won't be open until later. Got a hot date?"

"Now that you mention it…" Fred answered with a smile.

"These rear brake shoes are okay, they have plenty of shoe material left. Since I don't know your driving style, I would suggest looking at them again in six months or so."

As Mike continued to look over Fred's prospective purchase, they got talking about the Navy. "You weren't around for the Vietnam years. That was a tough time. Just being in the service, any service, automatically made you a baby killer and village burner."

"I've heard that. That had to be tough," Fred answered.

"The public perception was so bad, we could hardly go out into the civilian world. To get by, I had my hair cut by a professional hair stylist. It was 'high and tight' underneath but she left enough other hair to cover it."

"I could pull my hair up and smear Brylcreem all over it to hold it in place. That would expose the military clean cut around the ears. When I got home I would wash out the hair gunk and blow dry it. When it was down it would fall over my ears and hide the military styling."

"Sounds like an awful lot of trouble," Fred said.

"I had to do that just to go out on the town. If I didn't, I would get the evil eye in every club. It wasn't until Reagan became President that I could wear a uniform in town again."

"I'm glad we show respect for the troops today."

"You and me both."

"This oil looks fine. I drained it through this filter cloth. If there was any metal, it would show."

"Super. Looks like I'll buy this car. That is if I can find a place to store it until I get back." He almost added 'home' but caught himself.

"Let me put on a new filter and fill the oil and you can be on your way."

"Suits me," Fred said.

"So, what's it like to be a spook?" Mike asked.

"I'm not sure what you mean."

"For instance, you're in a bar and talking with a young

lady and she asks what you do in the Navy. You can't tell her you're a spook."

"No, I can't," Fred chuckled. "In fact if I did, it would sound phony anyway."

"So what do you do?"

"I normally tell them I'm a helicopter mechanic. It's a job that needs doing but its not too exciting. Since most people don't know anything about helicopters, they let it go."

"That's smart." Mike replied.

"Speaking of that, what is a Ground Support Mechanic?"

"When you go to the airport, you see all the ramp lice?"

"Ramp lice?" Fred repeated.

"Tow tractors, air start units, baggage carts, fuel trucks."

"I get it."

"My job in the Navy was to maintain the equipment that was used to service the aircraft. I worked on everything that had a reciprocating engine."

"You fixed the tow tractors and the like." Fred answered showing his understanding.

"A lot of my friends, when they got out, went right over to the airlines and made four times the money doing the same job. The problem with working for the airlines is assignments are by seniority. All the entry level jobs were in the big airports like Kennedy and LAX. I wanted to come home. I wanted to raise my family in Helen, where I grew up. I bought this place on contract and made it my own." Mike pushed the control handle to let the car down.

"So it was a garage before? It looks like an old style gas station."

"It is. It was born as a Gulf station around nineteen sixty two."

"It certainly is in nice shape for being over fifty years old."

"I gave it a facelift after the note was paid off. That, and a new tar roof."

"What happened to the gas pumps? You take them out?"

"They were gone before I got the place. Too bad too. Those pumps are worth some good money to collectors." Mike closed the hood. "All done but the paperwork."

They walked into the office. The old wooden swivel chair

squeaked as Mike pulled it to the matching desk. As he wrote out the invoice, he commented on what he had seen. "The car's in good shape. I don't see anything that could be trouble. Of course, to guarantee it I would have to do a complete teardown and that's just not practical."

"No, I'm sure it's not."

"Here you go."

"Forty dollars?"

"Plus tax," Mike added.

"Mike you're shortchanging yourself."

"How so? I charged you twenty five for the oil change and another fifteen for the look around. Seems reasonable."

"You spent more time than that."

"Many of the things I looked at, including your brakes, I do as part of my oil change service. The extra fifteen dollars is for the time I spent checking codes and poking around a little deeper."

"Still seems too little for what you did."

"I could charge you an extra fifteen for watching if it bothers you that much." Mike smiled.

"That's all right." Fred handed him a fifty dollar bill.

Mike opened a desk drawer that was a cash box and gave him the change. They walked out to the bay again and Mike directed Fred out using the same flight line signals he had used before. Once out, Fred waived and drove to the Quick Stop.

Chapter Twelve

At six p.m. Julie's doorbell rang. She hurried to the front of the house to let Fred in. "You certainly are punctual."

"The Navy kind of insists on it. You get in a habit," Fred said. He handed her a bottle of red wine. "There's not much selection at the Quick Stop. I chose a wine made in a South Dakota vineyard."

"Perfect," Julie said. "We'll save that for later, I think."

"Fine by me."

"Come into the kitchen, I'm working on the salad."

"Anything I can do to help?" Fred asked.

"You can light the charcoal." She pointed, "The grill is outside the door."

"Sure thing."

"Here's a lighter."

"Thanks." Fred walked out and found the grill with charcoal already placed. The lighter fluid was standing next to one of the legs. He reached down and picked it up. When he flipped open the lid and turned it upside down to squeeze some out, nothing happened. He looked and saw the seal was still in place under the cap. He unscrewed the cap and poked at the seal with no success. He walked back into the house. "I was never a boy scout."

"You can't start a fire?" Julie asked.

"I don't carry a pocket knife." He pointed to the seal.

"Oh," Julie let out a small giggle. She hadn't thought to check to see if the bottle she bought was sealed. She handed him a steak knife from the block on the counter. "This should do it."

"Thanks." Fred broke the seal and peeled it off the bottle. He looked around for a place to put it.

"I'll take it," Julie said.

Fred put the seal in Julie's open hand. "Thanks."

"Anytime, Chief," Julie said with a flare.

Fred had turned toward the door. He stopped. "Why'd you call me Chief?"

"Well you are one, aren't you?"

"Sure, but that doesn't mean here what it means on the

141

ship."

"Are you insulted?" Julie was concerned.

"No," Fred smiled. "Actually I'm complemented." He walked over to her and took her in his arms. "But I like it better when you call me Fred," and kissed her.

Julie melted into the kiss. After a few seconds she pulled away slightly. "We keep that up and we'll never get to supper."

He held her from getting too far. "And the downside of that is…?"

She pushed him off with a light laugh, "Go light the grill."

"Only with the promise of a return engagement," Fred said.

"Watch that word engagement around me, it could get you in trouble." Julie panicked. That had just blurted out. Had she gone too far? What would he do?

Fred stood still in front of her for what felt like an hour but was in reality about a half second. He smiled again, "Or it might lead to something very nice." Now it was his turn to be nervous. He turned and walked away before either one could say any more.

Fred got back outside and thought about the encounter in the kitchen. Getting married and starting a family was one goal he told no one about. He had seen too many marriages go south in his time in the Navy. The months away from home did nothing for a family. The strain on a marriage all too often led to ruin. He had spent countless nights in bars and enlisted clubs either consoling soon to be ex-husbands or listening to them a year later bashing their ex-wives.

He didn't want to be, or be the cause, of any of that. He had decided early in his career that he would not do that to another person. Now that he was about to retire, it was time to think about marriage. He thought about the idea of being married to Julie. So far, they seemed compatible. It was a pleasant thought.

Julie continued working on the salad. She was starting to think she was too comfortable around Fred. That was the second time something had slipped out. She wished her mother was still around. She wished she could ask her if this

142

was a good or a bad thing. This was going too fast. Or was it? It felt so right. That was the frightening part. She felt like she had known Fred forever, but in reality it had not even been a week. Her mind was running in overdrive. She decided she needed to slow down a bit. She took two bottles of Coors out of the refrigerator and walked out to the grill.

Fred saw her coming through the door and moved two lawn chairs together near the grill. "How about a seat?"

"Sure," she replied "how about a beer?"

"Now you're talking my language," Fred said.

They sat quietly for a full minute before either one spoke again. Fred was the one to speak first. "I am still amazed at the quiet. On the ship there is always noise. Machinery, the engines, people moving around, the 1MC going off."

"One MC?" Julie looked at Fred. "You have an MC on the ship?"

Fred laughed out loud. "I'm sorry. That was rude. I'm not laughing at you, but what you said just struck me funny. No, the 1MC is an old term for the ship wide public address system. There are speakers outside and in every compartment."

"I remember that from my dad's old war movies."

"Same thing. Just newer technology." Fred looked at the grill, "The coals are ready. What are we burning?"

"I have rib eye steaks." She leaned forward to get up.

"Sit," commanded Fred. "Tell me where they are."

"In the refrigerator, second shelf. They're already seasoned."

"You stay put, I'll drive."

"You mean he was naked?"

"That's exactly what I mean. It's a secret. I'm only telling you because you're my best friend and you're nice to him."

"I was only nice to him because you liked him," Mickie said.

"Than don't be. He's a pig."

"We should tell everyone," Mickie said.

"You CAN'T!"

"But if…"

"Mickie, this is really secret. You can't tell anybody.

143

Promise me."

Mickie shrugged, "Okay."

"Say it."

"I promise to keep your secret."

"Good."

"What did it feel like?" Mickie asked.

"What do you mean?"

"I mean what did it feel like? Was is hard?"

"You're gross."

"No I'm not. I just want to know."

"It felt like a finger or maybe a thumb."

"And he poked you with it?"

"I don't want to talk about it anymore."

"What are you going to do about it?"

"Nothing. What can I do?"

"You could tell his father."

"And he would deny it. Who's side do you think his father would take?"

"You could tell your father."

"Are you nuts!" He wouldn't let me out again until I was an old woman of twenty five!"

"How about your mother?"

Jessie shook her head, "She wouldn't understand."

"She's a nurse."

"That's right. That means you could tell her if it happened to you; but if I tell her it happened to me, she'll think I'm a slut." Jessie sighed, "No. I have to keep it a secret."

"Okay," Mickie said, "but we have to find a way to get back at him."

"He's a pig. Just leave it alone."

"He'll do it again."

"Not with me."

"That was as fine a steak as I have ever eaten." Fred said as he placed his fork down on an empty plate.

"You cooked it."

"I put it on the fire," Fred corrected. "That's the last step in a long chain of events. A chain forged by you. You chose the meat, you seasoned it, you told me when to turn it and when to take it off. No, this was all you."

Rather than argue the point, Julie simply said, "Well, then thank you." She changed the subject, "So, tell me. What do you think of our little town?"

"I think I'm going to like it. I think this is exactly what I'm looking for."

Julie realized Fred was staring into her eyes, making the double meaning obvious. She chose to take the easier path. "There's a lot to say about a small town. I think the people here are friendly, they'll help you adjust to the country life."

"That is something I know nothing about. I grew up in a city environment and joined the Navy when I was eighteen. I spent most of my time on ships, those ships have home ports. Those ports are always in or near cities. Norfolk and San Diego are two good examples. I have never been out in the country like this. I saw it the first time when I came out here last winter to see what my little brother had done to himself."

"I think he's done pretty good." Julie said.

"Don't get me wrong," Fred held up his hand, "I agree with you. This was one of the smartest moves he could make. They say the economy is turning around; I don't see it. Around Norfolk there isn't much work to be found. With the downsizing of the military and contractors, even the guys getting out with years of good experience can't find work. Years ago, it was a given. If you got out with a qualified trade, you could have a job either in the shipyard or with one of the contractors. Not the case today. These kids are looking around at the dismal job market and either staying in or leaving the area completely."

"That's good for the Navy isn't it?"

"Normally it would be. The military as a rule does better with recruitment and retention during a recession. But the climate is different. The Navy is trying to downsize. They're not encouraging anyone but the best and brightest to stick around. Problem is, the best and brightest are the ones finding jobs in town. It's a lose - lose all the way around. The average kids can't find work in, or out, of the Navy."

"I didn't know things were that bad."

"That's what is so amazing about here. Just driving through Watertown I saw 'help wanted' signs all over. I haven't seen even one of those in Norfolk in the past few years."

"Speaking of help wanted, have you figured out what you want to do?"

"Not really." Fred leaned back in his chair. In a different time and place Julie pictured him lighting a pipe. "I will have a retirement check from the Navy every month. It isn't much, it's the equivalent of holding down a part time job. Out here, with the cost of living being so low, it might be just enough."

"Just enough?"

"Enough that I wouldn't have to work if I didn't want to. I wouldn't be well off, but I wouldn't be payday to payday either."

"That's amazing. So you could actually retire at forty one years old?"

"I could, but I most likely won't. I think I'd get bored."

"You talked about writing mystery novels. Have you started any?"

"I have a few started, I can't quite get the traction. I think, once I have a place of my own, I'll try it again. I'll have my own space to work, not something shared with others. It's too crowded on the ship for any kind of real privacy. I'm looking forward to my own little house and my own personal space."

"Can I show you something?" Julie stood up.

"Sure." Fred followed suit.

Julie led her guest down a hall and to a bedroom. The door was closed. She stopped before opening it. "This is my inner sanctum. I keep this door closed, always. No one in town has ever seen this room. They would ask questions I don't want to answer." Julie opened the door. The room had bookshelves on two sides and a large desk on the third. The desk held a large computer screen and keyboard. Around the keyboard was a clutter of notes, books and printed web pages. "It's kind of a mess."

"I feel better about you." Fred said. "I thought you were a total neat nick."

"I only allow myself to get messy in here. When I'm in the middle of a story, the space around me gets filled up with research notes and material. My stories are fiction but they still need to ring true."

"I couldn't agree more."

Fred looked on the bookshelves, "Which of these are yours?"

"None of them." Julie answered. "These are research books. Tools of the trade."

"Where are yours?"

"Not yet, Chief."

"But soon?"

"Maybe."

***

I ND 2 C U
U R A PG
IMPRTNT
N
PLZ
NO
PLZ
N LV ME ALN

Jessie put her phone down. She had no interest in talking to or seeing Jeremy. He would know that, if he wasn't such a pig. She was still upset by the whole thing. Who did he think he was to try something like that. Just because they kissed didn't mean he had full rights to her body. She had to do something to make him leave her alone. But what? Mickie had some ideas, but they all involved letting the secret out.

The phone buzzed again.

IT WS A MSTK
N SHT
RLY I ND 2 TLK
N

Jessie had enough. She blocked any more texts from Jeremy. She put the phone in her pocket and went to the kitchen. The refrigerator offered the same bill of fare it had twenty minutes before. There was still nothing appealing. She found cookies in the back of the bottom shelf of the pantry.

She was sure they had been hidden there by her little brother. She took the plastic sleeve out of the box and put the box back. That should teach him.

Her phone bussed and tickled in her pocket. She got irritated for a second then she remembered she blocked Jeremy. She looked, it was Frank.

U OK
Y
SRE
Y
I KNW
KNW WT
HPND
N U DNT
YUP
MY SCRT
I KNW TLK
N
Y

Jessie's phone rang, it was Frank. "What?"

"Look, before you get all up in yourself, listen."

"Go ahead." Jessie was going to put down the phone and let him talk to the air, but what he said next stopped her.

"There's more to this than what Jeremy did."

"What do you mean more."

"There's rumor going around that you're a slut. I got it from Bobby Kline."

"What?!?"

"Really, he wanted me to get you two together. He seemed to think he's the only boy in town who hasn't hooked up with you."

"That's a LIE!" Jessie screamed at the phone.

"I know, we almost got into a fight about it before he told me who told him."

"Jessie are you all right?" Her mother's voice asked from the living room.

"I'm fine." Jessie lied. She walked back to her room and

closed the door.

"Who?" she said back to the phone.

"Mary Bayer."

"Mary Bayer!" Jessie said trying not to scream. She certainly did not want her mother involved.

"Bobby told me she has been spreading it all over town that you are a world class slut. You'll go with anybody."

"Frank, you know it's a lie."

"I know it, but how do we stop it?"

"I don't know."

"I have an idea."

"What?"

"Be my girlfriend."

"What?"

"Be my girlfriend. If you're my girlfriend, I can stick up for you. I can turn off the rumor."

"You would do that for me?"

"Of course."

"I have to think about it. You really hurt me last year when you took Katie Sands to the dance instead of me."

"I know. It was a mistake. She used me. She dumped me right after the dance."

"You deserved it."

"Look, I made a mistake. I know it now. I want to make it up to you. I can fix this if you let me. We can show Mary to be the liar she is.

"How?"

"Be my girlfriend."

Jessie decided to give him a chance to redeem himself. "Okay, what do we do now?"

"Meet me at the pool tomorrow," Frank said.

"Okay."

"Here's the deal that I want, Bill." Stewart Godfrey was on the phone. "I'll rent the house to your brother on a month to month basis for one year. After that if he doesn't want to buy it, I want you to sell it. Can you do that?"

"What if he decides to buy it after say, six months?"

"Then I'll sell it to him. I've got no more use for it once I move. No contract though, he has to find his own financing,"

Stewart answered.

"That sounds workable to me Stewart, I'll run it by Fred," Bill answered. "Fred was also wondering about some of the furniture and kitchen appliances. Would you be willing to sell them?"

"He'll have to go to the auction sale and bid like everyone else."

"When is the sale?"

"August tenth."

Bill sighed, this part wasn't going to be as easy. "Fred will be back aboard his ship the whole month of August. He won't get back here until September sometime."

"Well, I guess you'll have to bid for him already."

Bill let that go. He would work something out. He moved on to the last item on his list. "Fred is going to buy that car he is renting. He would like to store it in your garage until he gets back into town."

"That's fine, but it will have to be after the auction sale," Stewart replied.

"I'll see how that works out. Thanks Stewart, I'm sure Fred will be happy with the deal. I'll have the paperwork done and bring it by for you tomorrow evening."

"Good enough then, goodbye."

"Goodnight."

Bill put down the phone. He was sitting at the kitchen table. Mason was asleep, so he couldn't use his office space. He was getting used to conducting business at the kitchen table. He walked into the living room to see June sitting on 'her' spot on the couch reading a book. "Any idea where Fred is tonight?"

"Having dinner with Julie." June pointed toward the house next door.

"He's been seeing a lot of her this week."

"Is that a problem?" June asked.

"No, just an observation," Bill said. "I like Julie, I hope she doesn't read too much into it. Fred is not the settling down kind. He's more like the 'girl in every port' kind."

"I wouldn't be so sure. You haven't noticed how they look at one another."

Bill made a motion that could have been interpreted as a

shrug if it had been more pronounced. "I guess we'll have to wait and see."

The door bell rang a single ring. That was the garage entrance. Bill was surprised. Most people opened the door and announced their presence. "Who can that be?" June asked.

"I have no idea. It has to be someone we know. If it were a salesman he would have used the front door."

"No salesman would call at this time of the night," June replied. "It's a quarter to nine."

"I guess I'll find out." Bill walked through the kitchen and into the mud/laundry room to the garage door. He opened it to find Jeremy Finny standing there.

"Hello Mr. Weber. Can I talk to Jessie please?"

"I'll tell her you're here," Bill said and left him standing in the garage. It wasn't that he didn't like the boy, he seemed like a nice kid. He just didn't like the idea of this boy dating his daughter. He didn't want to do anything to encourage him. He walked back through the house to Jessie's room. Her door was open once again and she was playing a video game. "Jeremy Finney is here to see you."

"Tell him to go away." Jessie didn't look up from her game.

"I thought you liked him."

"I don't," Jessie answered. "Not any more. I don't want to see him. Tell him to leave me alone."

"Don't you think that's something you should tell him yourself?" Bill asked.

Jessie stopped the game. She rolled over on her bed and sat up. "Dad, I did tell him. He won't listen."

Bill could see that Jessie was getting upset. He had no idea what happened between them but he was glad to see that it was over. "I'll tell him you don't want to see him."

"Thanks, Dad," Jessie said and rolled over on her belly and picked up the game controller again.

"What happened between you two?" Bill asked.

"That's private," Jessie said and started the game again ending any serious conversation.

Bill let it go. June was better at the affairs of the heart then he was. He would ask her to talk to her. He walked back through the house and passed the message to Jeremy.

151

"Can you ask again, please? It's really important," Jeremy said.

"You heard her answer. She does not want to talk to you."

"But…"

"Okay," Bill stepped onto the garage steps, "now I'm not asking, I'm telling. Leave now."

"Yes sir." Jeremy's voice was quiet, almost too quiet to be heard. He turned and walked out of the garage.

Bill watched as Jeremy got to the street and started his truck. He continued to watch as he drove away. Once back in the living room, he sat next to June. He said quietly, "Seems there's trouble on the boyfriend front."

"What's going on?"

"Jeremy came to the door and asked to see Jessie. She refused to talk to him."

"Told you it wouldn't last," June said. Then she thought about it. Kids didn't come to the door. They either texted or phoned. They never met in person anymore. "This must be serious," she said half out loud.

"Why?" Bill asked.

June put her book down and looked over at Bill. She had not been really talking to him. She had been more talking to herself, but Bill didn't know that. She explained, "Think about it. Kids don't visit. They don't come over. They text or they talk or they send messages through the games they are playing. They almost never meet face to face. It something this generation just does not do. This must be really serious if Jeremy would drive over here to talk face to face."

"Why don't you ask her about it?"

"I will," June responded, "but not tonight. If it's important enough for a face to face conversation, then I think she is really upset by it. I'll wait for tomorrow and sneak it into a conversation. If she wants to tell me, she will."

"What if she doesn't?"

"Then she won't."

"That's not acceptable," Bill said. "If he did something wrong, I want to know about it."

"What are you going to do, Bill?" June looked at her husband. "Put her on the rack and torture it out of her?"

"Well, no, but…"

"But nothing. Bill," June interrupted. "She's entering a part of life where girls have to control the boys they're with. She has friends to talk to. She may never tell us about it, but she will do the right thing. Frankly, I'm thinking she already did."

Bill let the control line go. He remembered what he was like at fifteen and he knew what she meant.

After her father left her doorway, Jessie paused her game again. Jeremy had actually come to the door! She almost melted away totally when her dad said he was there. She had to act cool. She couldn't let her father know what happened. Her life was over. She had been tagged the town slut by a spiteful liar. She wasn't sure what to do. She texted Frank.

JRMY WS HR
WHN
NW
DID U C HM
N
GD C U @ PL TMRW

Next was Mickie.

JRMY WS HR
@ UR HSE
Y
HE HS BLS
Y
DID U C HM
N
GD LT HM SFR
WHT CN I DO
DNT KNW
MBY FRNK WL FGT HM
Y
HS MY NW BF
WHT
FRNK WNTS TO B BF
K

153

HE HS PLN
HE CN FX IT
HE SYS SO
CN HE
DNT NO MT @ PL TMRW
K

She put down the phone. Frank said he would stick up for her and fix it. She wasn't sure if it could be fixed. Maybe she should run away and hide. She wanted to get away from this tiny town where everybody knows everything about everybody and hide. But where could she go? Maybe she could move back east again to Fairview. She still had friends there. Maybe she could just move to one of the colonies. Would they take her? Probably not, not with her ruined reputation. Mary Bayer had ruined her entire life. She didn't know what to do.

Her mind went in circles until she finally fell asleep around midnight.

Chapter Thirteen

They had fallen asleep on the couch. Julie woke up to find herself resting against Fred's shoulder. She liked the feel of it. She wouldn't have moved if her leg had not gone to sleep under her. She had to get it out. She slowly pulled herself up and unfolded her leg. Then the pins and needles hit. She tried not to make any noise as she stretched her leg out straight.

"I was wondering when you would wake up," Fred said quietly.

Despite Fred's quiet voice, Julie jumped. Half a second later, when she recovered, she said, "I didn't know you were awake."

"I have been for about ten minutes."

"My leg fell asleep," Julie said. "I'm trying to get some circulation back into it."

"Would you like me to rub it?" Fred offered. "I'm a fairly good amateur masseuse."

"No, it's coming back," Julie replied. "I just need to stand up and walk on it."

"What time is it?"

Julie picked up her phone, "Two thirty."

Fred stood up, "I guess I'd better go," then he stopped. "Maybe I can't go. I wonder if the house is locked next door."

"I doubt it."

"Why would you doubt it?'

"Well," Julie stopped walking in circles and looked at him, "in the first place, you are still out. Bill would certainly not lock you out."

"Maybe."

"In the second place, I don't think that house has been locked in a year."

"He doesn't lock the house?" Fred asked.

"Nobody does. I keep the keys for this place in my jewelry box. I didn't even lock it when I went to New York last winter."

"You left it unlocked that whole time you were gone?" Fred asked for clarity.

"Sure," Julie nodded. "June was in here every other day to

water the plants and check on things. I told my neighbors I was going away so they kept an eye on things, too."

"That's just the opposite of what I would do with my apartment in San Diego," Fred said. "If I had to go away, I would leave a radio on and have lights on a timer so they would turn on and off each night. I would stop the mail and the newspaper. I wouldn't want anyone to know I wasn't there."

"Your neighbors wouldn't watch the place?"

"Sure they would. They would watch to see me leave then rob me blind," Fred said.

"That's awful."

"That's life in the big city," Fred said, then added, "I really need to get going."

They walked to the door and Julie stopped before opening it. Fred took the hint and took her in his arms. They kissed a long passionate kiss. Julie melted into Fred. She wanted to tell him to stay. She could tell it wouldn't have taken much encouragement, but she wasn't quite ready for that. She forced herself to pull away. They stood looking into each other's eyes, neither one moving more than a couple inches from the other. It was Fred that broke the spell. "I'll see you tomorrow?"

The words shook Julie back to earth. "I have some writing to do in the morning, then a teleconference with my editor. She seems to think I'm distracted."

"I hope so."

"I'll be around after dinner," Julie said. "What do you have in mind?"

"I'm going down to Sioux Falls tomorrow to look for a suit. I can't wear my uniform after I retire. I was hoping you might come along"

"Not tomorrow. If you wait for Friday, I can."

"Good. We'll go then."

Julie leaned in and kissed him again. This time it was a goodbye kiss not an 'I wish you would stay' kiss.

Fred responded in kind and opened the door. "Goodnight."

Julie giggled, "Good morning is more like it."

Fred turned and walked out the door. He felt like he was

floating on top of the blades of grass that carpeted the space between the two houses. He was starting to understand Gene Kelly and the famous scene from the movie 'Singing in the Rain'.

Fred walked in the 'people' door of the garage and carefully checked the door to the house. It was unlocked, just as Julie said it would be. He turned the knob and pushed it open. There was a night light on in the laundry/mud room. Freckles was standing at the door, waiting to see if the entrant was friend or foe. Fred leaned over and scratched Freckles behind his ears and told him quietly he was a good boy. Freckles took the praise and then turned to go back to Cory's room.

Fred got half way down the hall when he saw June come out of her bedroom. He stopped, he didn't want to startle her so he said, "Hi June," and then thought immediately afterward how stupid that sounded.

"Is that you Fred?"

"Yes."

"Okay. I thought I heard something."

"Just me."

"I'm going back to bed."

"Good night."

"Good night."

Fred got to Mason's room and shut the door. He almost made it in without waking up anyone. Of course Freckles didn't count. He was supposed to wake up and be on alert, but he was hoping he wouldn't wake Bill or June. He got undressed and climbed into the bed that was his second choice tonight.

"So, June, that's the deal. We need another NP and you are the closest one to it. I've looked at your records and discussed it with our student aid counselor. The courses you still need are all on line. We'll pay the tuition and expenses and we'll pay you a small stipend while you complete your studies." John Franklin had been making an inspection of the St. Agnes Clinic in Helen. As the head of the rural clinic program, he would visit each one periodically. This stop in Helen had the added duty of checking in with the Helen

Clinic's Administrator of record, currently on baby leave.

June was still skeptical. "What's the catch, John? We've been good friends for some time now. This is too good a deal. There has to be a catch."

"No catch, June. We want you back. We know as things stand now, you might not come back. John leaned back in his chair, he looked to June like a professor about to go off his lesson plan. "You know the shortages we have for medical professionals in this state. We attract who we can and promote the rest from within. You are still being carried as the Administrator for the Helen Clinic, but I can't get away with that much longer. Jonas is still being carried as 'acting temporary administrator'. He either wants to get back to Sioux Falls or move to Helen. He's fine with it either way, he just wants a permanent situation."

"I can understand that," June agreed

"So, here's my thinking. We keep you as resident NP in Helen, bring on an LPN as an assistant and we can take Helen off the rotation." John leaned forward for emphasis, "June, you will still be the administrator. You will work Monday, Tuesday and Wednesday. The specialists will still rotate in on Thursdays, so you won't need to be there. For that we'll pay for your schooling, like I told you, and give you an increase in salary once you're certified."

"So, I stay in Helen? No rotation?" She knew John Franklin had something up his sleeve. He mentioned it on July Fourth. This was an amazing offer. She would work about eighteen hours a week and earn full time money. Plus they would pay for her to complete her Nurse Practitioner training and certification.

"Under normal circumstances you will stay in the Helen Clinic. We will lock in our Helen personal. With an NP and an LPN, plus Carol at reception and appointments of course, the Helen clinic will able to operate without rotating PA's or physicians."

"That would make us different from the others," June said.

"That is the model I'm trying to build throughout the system. Something that looks like an old time country doctor's office, but with all the backing of the St. Agnes Medical

Group's assets and facilities. Eventually, I want all the clinics to be set up in a similar fashion."

"What do you need me to do?" June asked.

"Well, first, say yes. Second we'll assign a counselor from our HR department to help you get the courses you need. This is a new program for St. Agnes, We call it 'Up and In'. We stole a counselor away from the South Dakota State University system and set her up in an office in the Sioux Falls headquarters. She knows the medical programs SDSU has to offer at the Brooking Campus. She knows the people there as well. Once you get started, she will monitor your progress and help you avoid the pitfalls. She was the one who told me you could do this and do it in under a year and a half."

"I didn't think that was possible." June shook her head.

"Frances says it is."

"Do you have her full name and phone number, I'd like to talk to her."

"I have better than that." John reached into his shirt pocket. "Here's her card. She's expecting you to call."

June looked at the card. She stayed still. She didn't want to give away anything. This was incredible. The offer was too good to turn down, but she had to be sure of it and she had to talk to Bill. "John, I can't commit to this today."

"I know that," John Franklin nodded. "You call Francis Alden and talk to her."

"I need to talk to Bill about this too."

"That goes without saying." John reached into his pocket again. He read what was on the screen of his phone and pushed some buttons in return, "I've got to get going, June. They have a break at the clinic and I want to get the quarterly controlled substance inventory done."

June stood up, "You gave me a lot to think about John."

"No more than when we hired you, I think." He walked to the door leading to the garage. "Give the baby a kiss for me."

"I'll do that." June smiled and closed the door behind him. She turned around and leaned against the door. What to do? This was a sweetheart deal if it was the way John Franklin described it. In a year and half Mason would be almost two. That would be easier. Plus it was only part time. Eighteen hours a week, that was doable, wasn't it? It was one day less

159

than she had been working before, and for more money. She needed to call this Frances Alden and talk to her. She wanted to have all the information at the ready when she talked to Bill. He would balk, but if she presented it right, he would go along.

* * *

"Good morning Fred Weber," Henry Woodson called from the big round table. "What brings you out this early morning?"

"Good morning to you Mr. Mayor," Fred said. He walked over and pulled up a chair. "Just getting some air. Can I join the Round Table this morning?"

"Well, I'm not so sure," Wendell said with a laugh. "Have you changed your voting registration yet?"

"I intend to. As soon as I have a permanent address," Fred answered the lighthearted challenge.

"Then that's good enough for us," Henry said.

Darla came out through the double saloon style doors from the café's kitchen. "Here's trouble." She walked over with a coffee pot, placed a mug in front of Fred and poured. "Don't tell me you're giving up the Navy to join this crew."

"A fine group," Fred said. "I'm only an apprentice seeking full membership."

"And a BS artist too. You'll fit right in," Darla added, "I have blueberry muffins hot from the oven, anyone interested?"

"I'd like one please," Fred answered.

"I'm in," Wendell replied."

"Not for me, Darla," The man across the table answered.

"I'll take one to go, if I may," Bob Meyers added.

"Henry just nodded in the affirmative. "Thank you, Darla"

"My name is Fred too," the man across the table reached out. "Fred Hansen."

"Fred Weber, nice to meet you."

"Fred has a farm north of town. He's busy in the summer, obviously, and doesn't get here in the mornings much," Wendell said.

"Well, I've got to get going," Bob Meyers said. "That

160

mail isn't going to deliver itself. When you're ready, Fred, stop by the Post Office, Beverly will fix you up with a change of address."

"Thanks."

"So, I hear you're going to move into Stewart Godfrey's place," Henry said.

"You're ahead of me, Mr. Mayor," Fred countered. "I'm not sure if my brother has set up a deal yet or not. You see, I don't want to buy the place outright. I'm looking to rent for a time. If it turns out that this rural lifestyle isn't for me. I want to keep my baggage light."

"I was talking to Stewart last night. The way he was talking, it sounded liked it was a done deal."

"I guess I need to talk with my brother." The men around the table laughed.

"Let me tell you something about a small town, Fred." Henry looked over at the man on his right, "The stereotype is true. News gets around fast, but we're not busybodies. You can have as much privacy or as little as you want. Tell us you want to be left alone and that's what will happen. Join in community events and become engaged and you'll be welcomed with open arms. Your choice."

"Well, I'm not moving out here to become a hermit."

"Glad to hear it." Wendell said. "Your brother's a good man, helped me sell my mother's house in Kent. If you're cut from the same cloth, the town will be richer for it."

Darla walked up with the muffins. "Don't go tellin' him that already, it'll go right to his head."

"Just like this muffin is going to my stomach," Wendell replied after the snickering ebbed.

"Have you met Mike Finney?" Fred asked. "He's retired Navy too, I think."

"I went by his place yesterday. I wanted him to look at a car I'm buying. Good sort, seems to know his stuff."

"He got me out of a real jam this spring," Fred added. "My four wheel drive tractor kept quitting in the field. I would have to wait about ten minutes before it would start again. I called Helen Implement, but you know how busy they get. They told me it would be at least a week before they could look at it. So I called Mike. He came out. He found a sensor telling the computer that the engine was overheating. So the computer was shutting the engine down. Once the sensor cooled down a bit, it would be fine. Mike used a jumper wire to go around the sensor so I could finish planting. He told me that it was a safety sensor to protect the engine and now I would have to watch temperature gauge more carefully because now it could really overheat and ruin the engine."

"Did you ever get the sensor replaced?"

"Mike got one and put it in before I started the next morning. The thing's been fine ever since."

"I won't take my car to anyone else," Darla said. "I have almost three hundred thousand miles on my Buick and Mike says it's still good for some more. I'll keep it until he says scrap it."

"I tried him once with one of my tractors," Wendell said. "I wanted to swap engines. Mike said it was too big a job for one man and turned me down flat."

"A smart man knows when to say no," Henry said with a bit of a flourish.

"Then from what I've seen at the town meetings, Henry, you must be a genius," Darla said as she walked away.

Fred had the morning to himself. Bill was going to work in Kent, June had an early meeting with her old boss from the Helen clinic. Julie was busy writing and talking to her bosses. He wasn't sure what to do. He thought about asking Jessie and Cory if they wanted to go to the zoo, but changed his mind. Not that they wouldn't have a good time, he wasn't sure if he wanted them in close quarters all day. They were great kids and he cared for them, but they were still kids and he wasn't used to them.

He drove around town for a bit, then onto the highway. He wasn't quite sure where he was going, but it didn't matter. He had things to think about. After a few minutes he turned around. He went back to the place Julie showed him. He parked the car and got out. He walked over to the bank that looked down on the small brook and sat down. He had a lot on his mind. His whole life was about to change. This visit had told him just how much. No more shipboard life, no more twelve hour days. No more deployments. That part he would

162

enjoy. The other part concerned him. No routine, no standardization. No pecking order in social gatherings. He had been Navy all his adult life. He didn't know how he was going to adjust. He was looking forward to the change but at the same time he was a bit anxious at the magnitude of it. Even small things would be changing. No uniforms for instance. He would have to decide what to wear everyday.

At least finances were not a factor. Years as a single man and being conservative with his cash had allowed him to put aside a good sized nest egg. He was going to get a retirement check from the Navy each month. That would pay for all his living expenses if he was frugal. No, money was not an issue.

It was the unknown; what job was out there for him? He was a spook. There was no equivalent job outside the NSA for his trade. ELINT (Electronic Intelligence) was not a word people around here knew. Nobody was going to hire him for electronic surveillance. He had to do something else. He wanted to do something else, but what?

He had thought if he came out here to Helen and stayed with his brother, things like a job would fall into place. It hadn't. Maybe he should just start writing. It worked for Julie.

Julie... that was further complication. He had intended to settle down with his new life and new job (whatever that was) before starting a social life. That was his intent, then Julie stepped into his life. Bumped into his life was more like it. He saw in her everything he liked about a woman. She was bright, quick witted and intelligent, not to mention easy on the eyes. She was mature and level headed. She was her own woman, yet she let him be a man. He could move in with her tomorrow and be comfortable, but that would never do, for too many reasons; Julie's reputation in this tiny Bible Belt town being the first and foremost.

As he sat there he watched a doe and two fawns walk across the corn field on the other side of the brook. They were in no hurry. Fred didn't move. He watched as they walked down to the brook for a drink. They were only about thirty feet away. He wanted to get a picture but he knew reaching for his phone would spook them, so he sat perfectly still. He turned his mind off and just enjoyed the show nature was providing. The deer wandered off into the waste high corn again and disappeared into a distant grove of trees.

Fred could finally move. He stood up. Things hadn't changed in his life in the last few minutes, but he was less anxious about it some how. He understood why this was Julie's happy place.

**

> She was sure he was the one, the man she was meant to spend the rest of her life with, but how could she tell him. Her heart pounded every time he held her, she wanted so badly to take him to her bed. She was afraid. If they slept together would it be over?
>
> He was leaving soon. He said he would be back, but would he? This could just be a fling for him. After all, he told her he had never been serious with any woman. Was she just another girl, another conquest?
>
> She could go with him. Maybe she could follow. No, that was asking too much, or was it? What is the price of love?

"Oh, crap!" Julie said to herself. She pushed her chair back away from the keyboard. "This just isn't working!"

Julie took the thumb drive containing her latest book and put it in her purse. She quickly dressed and poured the rest of her coffee from the pot to the thermos. She took it, along with her folding chaise lounge chair, and put in her car. She walked back inside for her purse and laptop. She decided she needed a better place to write, so it was off to her 'happy place'.

Fred's phone rang with the ring-tone that told him it was his Leading Petty Officer, the equivalent of a shop foreman. "This is Chief Weber," he answered officially.

"Chief, this is Petty Officer Nelson."

"What's up Anne?"

"You have a letter here from the NSA."

164

"The NSA?"

"Yes Chief," Nelson said. "I thought you should know."

"Thanks Anne, put it in with the rest of my mail, please."

"You don't want me to forward it?"

"No thanks."

"Don't you want to know what they want?"

"I know what they want."

"Okay Chief." Anne paused, "How's your leave going?"

"I think I'm going to like it here."

"You're going to stay out there in nowhere's-land?" Anne sounded disbelieving. "Doesn't it get cold?"

"I've stood on an ice bound deck in the North Atlantic in January; I've been in the Bearing Sea during a winter gale; I understand cold. This can't be like that."

"How about people? Does anybody live there?"

"The town is about three hundred." Now Fred was starting to have fun.

"Three hundred?" Anne now sounded surprised. "I'm from Staten Island, Chief. We put more people than that on a ferry boat. What will you do? Is there any work?"

"You should see the place. There are help wanted signs all over."

"All over where? The corn fields?"

Fred laughed. He was starting to see something he had not noticed before. His underling was a snob. "Look, put that letter with my other personal mail. I'll look at it when I get back," Fred said bringing the conversation to a close.

"Sure thing Chief."

"See you the end of the month."

"I've got a note here, they want Smitty's transfer evaluation by the first."

"You write it. You're in the spaces with him every day."

"Chief, you know I'm no good at writing evals. Especially for someone like Smitty. You know him. He's a nice guy and all, but professionally, he's mediocre at best."

"Those are the hardest ones to write, Anne. If you're going to make a good Chief, you're going to have to know how to do it. Write it and I'll look at it when I get back."

"You won't be back in time."

"Just write the eval, I'll handle the time line."

165

"Okay Chief," Anne said. "Enjoy the rest of your leave."

"I intend to. Goodbye."

"Bye."

Fred dialed another number. "USS Kauffman Quarter Deck, Petty Officer of the Watch, Emberg speaking. This is not a secure line. How can I help you Sir, or Ma'am?"

Even though he had only been away a week, the official phone greeting sounded out of the ordinary to him. He recovered quickly, "Emberg, this is Chief Weber. Is Senior Chief Holman on board?"

"No, Chief, I saw him depart a few minutes ago. Can I take a message for him?"

"He left the ship?"

"Yes, Chief. I watched him and the First Lieutenant take the duty truck."

"Thanks, I'll try his cell phone."

"Have a good day Chief."

"Bye," Fred ended the call and selected another number.

"Freddy!" The phone answered. "How's your leave going?"

"Great Sam," Fred answered. "Look, I just got a call from Petty Officer Nelson. She has a note that admin wants Smitty's transfer eval by the end of the month. I want to push that a week. I want to be back in the spaces to chop it."

"No problem, Fred," the phone answered, "I'll take care of it."

"See you at the end of the month."

"Not if I see you first," Sam jibed. "Hey, we working folks are busy, you need anything else?"

"No, Nelson has everything under control."

"How about a retirement ceremony?"

"I'll work on that when I get back."

"You got it."

"Okay, Bye"

"Out." Came the reply and the phone went dead.

Chapter Fourteen

Jessie had been running, running away from Jeremy Finney. He was holding a baseball bat and running after her. But it wasn't a baseball bat; she knew what it was. She was running and running…

Jessie sat straight up in bed. She looked around. Reality slowly overcame the dream. She threw off the covers. She was soaked in sweat. She put her two feet on the floor and stood up. The fan on her dresser was on low. She walked over to it and turned it on high. She stood in front of the cool, man made, breeze for a full minute. She was still shaken by the nightmare. She had to get beyond this somehow. She couldn't wake up like this every morning.

She picked up her phone, eight forty six. Too early to text Mickie. She thought about breakfast, but her stomach wasn't up to it yet. She decided to take a shower and wash the dream away.

In the shower, Jessie thought about the incident again. Jeremy had said. "I'm only doing what you want me to do." She hadn't understood it. At the time she didn't want to understand. But now she did. If Mary Bayer had told him she was a slut, then he did what he thought she wanted. Mary Bayer had not only ruined any chance she could have with Jeremy, but she had ruined any chance she had with anybody!

Except Frank.

Frank said he would stand up for her. Frank said they would destroy the rumor and Mary Bayer with it. She couldn't see how. She hoped Frank had a plan. They had to make Mary Bayer out to be the liar she was. That was the only way her reputation could be saved, but they couldn't tell anyone what Jeremy did. If that got out it would be the end. Period.

Julie turned the corner onto the drive. She cleared the last of the trees and saw the red Charger parked by the brook. Two emotions ran through her simultaneously. Her heart jumped at the sight of Fred as he turned to see her drive up, but her mind said her plans to get away from the writers block Fred caused had just been ruined.

167

Fred turned as he heard the sound of tires on gravel. It was Julie's car. He stood up and walked over. "Good morning!" he smiled.

Irritation won over desire and Julie said, "What are you doing here?"

"I needed a place to sit and think. This seemed to be a good spot." He reached down and opened her car door.

Julie didn't get out. "You know you're trespassing."

"I didn't think the owner would mind," Fred said with a smile.

"Well, she does." Julie snapped.

Fred stepped back from the car. He finally realized that Julie was upset. "I'm sorry. I didn't think I was causing any harm." He turned and walked toward his car.

Julie realized that it was not Fred that was the problem. It was her emotions. He caused her writers block, but not by anything he did. He caused it by just being. She had to say something. "Fred, wait."

Fred stopped. He turned and looked at Julie. This time she got out of the car. "Look, if I've overstepped…."

"Fred stop," Julie interrupted, "this isn't you. It's me."

Now Fred was confused. He was a passenger on a roller coaster of emotions. He didn't know what to say. So he said nothing.

"I've got writers block. I can't seem to get in the groove. I've tried all my tricks. This was my last one."

"And I got in the way," Fred nodded. "I'm sorry. I'll just go."

"It's too late now Fred," Julie said. "I can't work here today."

"I destroyed the vibe?"

"You destroyed the vibe the morning I saw you sitting at June's table," Julie said. "I haven't been able to write a decent word since."

Fred felt the roller coaster cascade over the next hill. "I didn't mean to get in the way of your career." Fred thought about it for a few seconds; he knew what he had to do. "Maybe I should just leave you alone. Give you some space so you can work."

"Maybe you should," Julie answered.

168

Fred turned and walked away. Julie watched as he got in his car and drove out of the glade. She sat there. She started crying. This was the wrong answer. She wanted Fred. She realized that she had fallen in love with him. She wanted him around. She had to work this out. She had to be able to have Fred and her work. She grabbed her phone. The text read, PLZ CM BK.

"I think it's a match made in heaven, Tom." Bill was on the phone. "You love going to auctions. Fred needs a proxy to get the appliances, kitchen things and some furniture from Stewart's sale."

"I don't mind helping your brother out, but why don't you do it?"

"I'm no good at auctions."

"You did all right in Groton."

"That was a house. I was in my element. I don't know how much a chair should sell for, let along a refrigerator."

"Hold on..." Tom said. Bill had called him at work. His job at the Helen Elevator wasn't busy after the wheat harvest but he would still get an occasional truck looking to unload grain. Bill could hear a speaker in the background but not what it said. He heard movement and then a sound like popcorn being poured into an old time air popper. There was more discussion and then another announcement from the speaker. Bill could hear the rustle of Tom picking up his phone. "Bill, I've got to go. I have a load of moldy corn and I have to reject it. I know the guy who brought it in and I know there's going to be an argument. Call me tonight."

"Sure thing," Bill said. Then added, "Good luck."

"Thanks," Tom said, and the phone went dead.

Bill let the Fred problem go. He turned his attention back to Huber Realty. He had three resumes on his desk. He was hoping one would be a good fit for Teresa Beseler. Serena had narrowed the applicants down to the three. She had asked Bill to review them and form an opinion. Although she worked for him as office manager, he often found himself following her orders. Not that he minded, she was an excellent office manager. It took a special person to handle real estate professionals. The profession tended to attract independent thinkers and doers. She had often referred to her job as herding cats.

Bill also knew that copies of these same resumes were being reviewed by his partner, Laura Huber, surviving wife of the founder, Jack Huber. He presumed another set had been faxed to Teresa.

He read all three. Any of them could do the job. Since Bill took over, Huber Realty had become a powerhouse in eastern South Dakota. They were the hobby farm kings. More than half of all small farm properties were going through them now. Their reputation for attracting out of state clients and higher selling prices was spreading. Huber Realty was a growing success and people wanted to be a part of that growth.

Bill put down the third resume and pushed the call button on the old time intercom. "Mrs. Townsend?"

"Yes, Mr. Weber?"

"I'd like to see you please."

"Yes, Mr. Weber."

It was fifteen seconds before Serena walked into Bill's office. "Yes, Mr. Weber?"

"These three applicants, have you talked to them?"

"I've talked to Mr. Welch on the phone. Ms. Kimball and Mr. Taylor personally delivered their applications."

"And yet, Mr. Welch is still under consideration. Why is that?"

"Mr. Welsh is currently working in Williston, North Dakota. With the oil boom he's working fifteen hours a day, seven days a week."

"So, why does he want to come here?"

Serena smiled, "Because he's working fifteen hours a day, seven days a week."

Bill chuckled. "I understand."

"I kept his name in the hat because he made a better impression on the phone than many of the other applicants did in person."

Bill brought up another concern, "If he's working in North Dakota, does he have a South Dakota shingle?"

"His family is in Watertown. He only went north to take advantage of the insanity that is a boomtown. His license in

170

South Dakota is current."

"If he's working those kind of hours, when can we see him?"

"He's taking a long weekend next week to visit his family."

"Okay, let's talk with the other two in the mean time and get together with Mr. Welsh while he's home."

Jessie was ready for the pool, but not ready for what it might bring. She was terrified with what the kids would say. Frank said he could fix it. She wasn't sure anyone could. She picked up her phone. The text to Mickie read:

R U RDY
N
WN
SN
K

Jessie put down her phone again. She knew she couldn't go to the pool without the support of both Mickie and Frank. To get there first would be a disaster.

Frank had texted her that he would be there at one. She wouldn't even think about getting there before he did. Mickie wasn't ready. She couldn't walk over alone. She would wait.

Though Jessie heard the door bell, it didn't register. She was still thinking about her ruined life. Nobody could salvage the wreck that Mary had made.

"Jessie, Frankie's here," her mother called from the kitchen.

Jessie got up and walked out of her room. She got to the kitchen in time to see Frank and his mother, Sarah, being served an iced tea.

"Good morning Aunt Sarah."

"Good morning Jessie. Frankie wanted to walk with you to the pool, so that gave me an excuse to visit your mother and baby Mason."

Jessie nodded. She wasn't really listening. She was looking at Frank. He seemed different somehow. He was taller or maybe his shoulders were wider. She wasn't sure.

"Would you like a glass of iced tea before you go?"

"Okay."

"How about yes please?"

"Yes please," Jessie repeated.

Jessie's mom poured another drink and sat down at the table. This was exactly what Jessie did NOT want to happen. She needed to talk to Frank privately. She did what they used to do last year before the break up. She made up a story that sounded good to adults. Frank would know it for what it was, a ruse. "I got to one hundred ninety thousand on Jumping Giants."

"Really?" Frank played along. "I can't get past one forty."

"It's easy, I'll show you." They got up from the table and walked to Jessie's room. Once inside, she closed the door. "So, what are we going to do?" Jessie asked.

"I have a plan."

"What is it?"

"You have a birth mark on your butt," Frank said.

"I do not!" Jessie was confused.

"You do too," Frank answered. "Listen. You have a birthmark on your right cheek that looks like a heart. I know it because you told me, because I'm your boyfriend. Nobody else knows about it because nobody has seen it."

"I don't understand."

"That's the challenge," Frank said. "Anybody that says they hooked up with you has to prove it by telling me where the birthmark is. They can't, so they're lying."

Jessie started to see the plan. "We have to tell Mickie."

"She can be in on it," Frank said. "She can swear to it."

"How does this get Mary?"

"Simple, when I challenge someone who can't tell me about the birth mark, I'll make them tell that Mary told them about you being a…"

"Shhh!" Jessie pointed to the door.

"You get the idea," Frank continued. "We can show Mary Bayer to be the vicious bitch she is."

Jessie thought about it. It was dangerous. "Will it work?"

"I think so."

Jessie's phone buzzed.

172

RDY
MT US WLK TGTHR
MT WHO
FRNK
K

Mickie's ready. She'll meet us on the way to the pool.

"The problem is not you, Fred. It's me. You're a distraction. A very pleasant one, but still a distraction."

"I'm not sure what I can do about that, other than leave you alone," Fred answered. He had seen the text asking him to come back and had turned around and driven back to the glade.

"That's just it, I don't want you to leave me alone. I like being around you. We have something together, I'm not sure what, but I like the way things are going."

"To be perfectly honest, I like it too," Fred answered. "I had planned to move here and see what my brother was talking about. Like I told you the other night, Bill is the only family I have left. I was pretty sure I wanted to live near him, June and the kids. I'm looking forward to being Uncle Fred." He took her hands and they faced one another. "You are an added bonus. I didn't expect my brother to have a smart, attractive woman living next door.

"But…"

Fred held up his hand. "It seems I've created a problem for you. That's not something I wanted. The only way I can see to fix it is to back off a bit and let you work."

"That's not what I want, Fred," Julie said. "I want you around. I'm simply going to have to work through this."

"How can I help?"

"I don't think you can," Julie said. "It's something I have to figure out for myself."

"How about a motivator?" Fred asked.

"What kind of motivator?"

"Now this might sound conceited, it's not meant to be. I don't think of myself this way, but to make my point I'll have to say it this way."

"What?"

173

"When I have trouble with my troops getting things done I either use a carrot or a stick. I try the carrot first. If that doesn't work I can always go to the stick. Here's what we're going to do. I am not going to see you until you finish another chapter. You have to work and I'm in the way."

"I've already tried that, Fred. It didn't work."

Fred looked away for a moment then said, "There is a process that I learned in the Navy. It isn't taught, it is learned by osmosis. They call it 'compartmentalization'. I call it life in a box."

"I don't understand."

"To explain this I'll tell you about my friend Eddy." Fred led Julie over to the bank where he had been sitting. He indicated that they should sit. Once situated he started his story. "Eddy was married, happily married. They were crazy in love. Because of what he did, he and his wife would only see each other for a few days at a time. Once in a while they would have a whole month together, but never more than that. Then Eddie retired out of the Navy. He got a good job with Electric Boat in Groton, Connecticut. They moved into a nice house and started living large on the two big pay checks plus his retirement."

"I don't see the point," Julie said.

"They were divorced one year later."

"Why?"

"They didn't get along. They fought all the time."

"I thought you said they were crazy about each other," Julie asked as a statement.

"They were," Fred answered. "In fact they still are. They go out all the time."

"Now I'm really confused."

"Life in a box," Fred said. "Eddie and Linda were never together for any length of time. When they were, they were in their 'honeymoon' box'. When Eddie was away, Linda was independent. She had a career, she had friends and a life without Eddie. That was her 'myself by myself' box.

"Eddie, at the same time, had his 'Navy' box. When he was in uniform he was all Navy, all the time. There was no room for a wife. They both had their separate boxes for when they were apart."

"Okay, I can see how that could happen."

"Well, once Eddy got out and went to work for Electric Boat, the boxes clashed. Eddie had his 'work' box and so did Linda. They did alright until the honeymoon box didn't fit anymore. They were both type 'A' personalities. Both wanted to be in control. They tried, but the marriage had failed in six months. They went to counseling and worked at it for another six months hoping to make a box that would hold both of them as a married couple. It didn't work and they finally split up."

"That's a shame," Julie said. "They couldn't work it out?"

"They did work it out," Fred said. "They went back to the boxes that worked. Linda moved back to Virginia Beach and her old job while Eddie stayed at Electric Boat. They spend every three day weekend together, either in Connecticut or in Virginia. Once a year they take a vacation together. Last year it was Tahiti. They're back on their honeymoon."

"That's amazing." Julie got quiet again. After a minute, she asked. "How does that help us?"

"You need to build some boxes."

"I thought boxes were bad. They weren't good for your friends."

"Compartmentalization is a tool, just like a hammer. Use it right and you drive the nail, use it wrong and you hit your thumb. You need a 'writing' box and you need a 'Fred' box. Those two boxes are separate and different. You can only have one open at a time. That means when you're writing, you are writing. You're not thinking about last night or tomorrow. You are thinking about your hero and heroine, not you and me."

"To go with that you have the 'Fred' box. When you're with me, you are not thinking about work. You are not playing scenarios from your books in your mind. We'll write our own story, good or bad, without author Julie sticking her nose in."

"What about you?"

"I know I compartmentalize. I have a 'Navy' box that I'm about to close for good. I need to build another box called 'work' to replace it, but until I know what kind of work that will be, I can't do much with it. "I have a 'Julie' box already. It is a special place. But I'll warn you today, when I go back to the ship, I'll take the 'Julie' box and put it on the shelf."

175

"You mean you'll forget about me?"

"Hardly, you're there in my mind. You're just set aside on the shelf until I have time to open you up again. I can see you, sitting on the shelf. I simply know that the ship is the wrong place to open that box."

Julie started to say something but Fred interrupted, "Hold on - before you say anything, this is not cold, nor is it emotionless. It is a form of mental discipline. If you only open a box when you have the time to enjoy it, then the experience is richer.

"You need to put me in a box and put the box away so you can write. You can do it. You are one of the smartest people I know. You can train yourself to open the writing box and stay there until you reach your preset goal. That's what I suggest you do, and I'm going to help. Please do not call me until you have another chapter done. When you do, I'll take you to supper."

Julie thought about it. She had heard about the concept of compartmentalization. She always thought it was a negative. It had never been explained quite this way. "I'll give it a try."

"Good, now kiss me and get out your laptop. I've got to go."

"Where are you going?"

"Down to Sioux Falls to get a suit."

"I thought we were doing that tomorrow together."

"We can't."

"Why?

"You're working."

Jessie and Frank met Mickie at her corner. As they walked, with Frank in the middle, he explained the plan to Micky. Once through the locker room with their belongings safely put away, the two girls walked out to the pool deck. Frank was waiting by the locker room door and stayed with them as they walked around to the far side.

Jessie could feel eyes burning into her back as she walked. She knew they were all staring at her. She tried to act like she didn't notice. She looked around for Mary Bayer, but she wasn't there.

"I'm going off the high dive, who's with me?" Frank said.

Not wanting to be away from him, Jessie said, "I'm in."

"Not me," Mickie said. "I want to tan for a while."

Jessie followed Frank to the tall ladder that led to the regulation three meter high board. Frank reached the top and ran to the end. He made one bounce and went off into the air. Jessie followed with a practiced swan dive. Once they were in the water, Jessie felt less conspicuous. She still thought people were watching her, but they could no longer stare at her body. She decided to stay in the deep end.

Frank swam to the side and jumped out, "I'm going again, You coming?"

"No, I'll stay here and watch."

Frank climbed out of the pool and walked toward the ladder. He saw three boys walk up. Jeremy Finney was one of them, Glenn Carr was another. Bobby Stacks was the third. Bobby nodded at Jessie, "You tapping that?"

"What?" Frank was ready. He looked surprised. "No. She's not that way."

"She was with me," Bobby said.

"Me too," Jeremy said. "We hooked up at the lake just the other day."

"So, you've all been with her?"

"Sure," Bobby said. "Don't tell me you haven't."

"You're lying," Frank said.

"You calling me a liar?" Stacks said.

"To your face and I can prove it."

"How?"

Frank smiled. "Jessie has a birthmark. If you have seen her naked, you know where it is and what it looks like. I know because she told me. If you don't know, you're a liar."

Bobby Stacks just stood there.

"How about you?" He looked at Jeremy.

"It was dark." Jeremy answered.

Frank looked at Jeremy in disbelief, "It was dark when we went to the lake the other day? Come on Jeremy, tell the truth."

Frank turned to Glenn, "How about you? You going to tell the truth?"

Glenn Carr shrugged. "I have never even been on a date with her."

"Jeremy?"

Jeremy said "Oh go fu…"

That's when the roundhouse hit him and ended the sentence. "If you go spreading rumors about my girlfriend again I'll give you that and more."

"I didn't start it," Jeremy said. The punch set him back about five feet. He knew he was in the wrong so he didn't retaliate.

"Who did?"

"Mary Bayer."

"That figures," Frank nodded. "Sounds to me like the pot's trying to call the kettle black."

"You mean…?" Glenn took the bait.

"I'm not saying anything." Frank looked at each one of them in the eye, "But for someone to spread a rumor like that, she must have some experience. You know what I mean?"

The three boys nodded in unison. They understood exactly what Frank meant. They turned and walked away.

Frank jumped back in the water and swam to Jessie. "They won't bother you again," he said.

"What did you tell them?"

"Just what I said I would. I called them on the lie and twisted it back on Mary Bayer."

"How?"

"Never mind how. Just remember you have a heart shaped birthmark on your right butt."

"What happens when we get back to school? I have to change for phys-ed Mary will see I don't have a birth mark."

"That's over a month away. It will be ancient history by then. Mary will be known as a liar and maybe a slut herself. Even if she notices, she won't be believed."

"Francis Ogden, you have got to be one of the smartest men I have ever known."

"And don't forget it," Frank replied then they both laughed.

The laughter got a glare from the other side of the pool. "Look at them," Jeremy said, "they're laughing at us."

"If they are, we deserve it," Bobby said.

"I'll never listen to Mary again," Glenn agreed.

"I wonder if Frank is right?" Jeremy asked no one in

178

particular.

"You mean if Mary is really the one who..." Bobby started.

"That's exactly what I mean." Jeremy answered. A young man's attention, like electricity, once again seeking the path of least resistance.

Chapter Fifteen

"I don't know how to thank you Tom." Fred and Tom Ogden were walking up the driveway to Stewart Godfrey's house. Bill had spoken to Tom and Tom had agreed to be the proxy bidder for Fred. That was as long as Fred's brother, Bill, was there too.

"I don't mind. I was going to come to this sale anyway," Tom smiled. "Getting your brother to come along is a bonus."

"He doesn't like auctions?"

"He never got the bug."

"You mean it's addicting?"

"I'll never admit that in public." Tom smiled again. "It's been hard for Bill and me to get away since Mason was born." Tom Ogden and Bill Weber had known each other as acquaintances when they both lived on the I-95 corridor between Philadelphia and Baltimore. In fact, it was Tom that introduced Bill to small town living in South Dakota. Tom had called Bill to sell his Fairview house after moving into his grandfather's house outside of Helen two years ago. In the process of selling Tom's east coast house, he and Bill had become good friends. The friendship only grew when Bill and family moved to Helen last year.

"I'm not sure how the whole thing works. I've seen auctions. But never an auction for personal property," Fred said.

"It's pretty simple really. Stewart will set back or move out what he wants to keep and then the family will set everything else out for the sale. The auctioneer will have flatbed trailers delivered ahead of the sale. Family and friends will load them up. On auction day we'll go from trailer to trailer and they'll auction off each item or box of items. Once that's done they'll move to the furniture and larger items."

"Okay, I get it." Fred answered. "So I guess I'd better walk through the place with you.

"This is the best way to furnish a house, Fred. I only wish I had known about these auctions before moving all my things out here. After the moving van left and I crunched some numbers, I realized I had paid more to move furniture and appliances than I would have spent replacing them here."

"That's amazing." Fred said.

"Here's how it works, Tom continued. "We get anything you need to set up your household at this sale if the bids stay low enough. Don't be too picky at first. You bid on the furniture, appliances and kitchen gadgets. Once you have a base, you and I go to other auctions and replace the things you have with better things. Plus we add the things you don't have. You can do the whole job, with nice clean appliances and furniture for less than a thousand dollars if you have the time and the patience."

"You mean I can fill the house with quality furniture and appliances, plus all the things I need for a household, for less than a thousand dollars?" Fred's tone was disbelieving.

"Yup," Tom said, "we start today. If there's a couch, we bid on it. If he leaves the dining room table we bid on that. Same for the refrigerator, stove and the like. Later on, when we go to other auctions, if you see something better, you buy it and replace what you have.

"What do I do with the old stuff?" Fred asked. "Take it to the dump?"

Tom put his hand over his heart feigning a heart attack, "Perish the thought! You trying to break the cycle?"

"I beg your pardon?"

"We take the things you don't want anymore down to Cantor and Lonnie Nicks."

"Who's Lonnie Nicks?"

"He runs a weekly consignment auction house."

"So we sell it again?"

"We sell it again," Tom affirmed.

"Well, I don't know what my job is going to be, but I think I found my new hobby," Fred said.

"Welcome to the club." Tom laughed as he knocked on the door. "Let's look around. We'll see what you need to get started and I'll give you an idea as to what we can expect to pay for it."

"I'll have to figure that out," Fred said. "How to pay for it, I mean."

"That's why I'm bringing Bill. He can write the check and you can pay him."

181

"Works for me if it will work for him," Fred said.

"He's the one who suggested it."

"You have reached the desk of Francis Alden, I am either not in my office, or in conference. Please leave a message and I'll return you're call as quickly as possible." ….Beeep

"Ms. Alden, this is June Weber. I talked to John Franklin this morning and he gave me your card. When you have a moment, could you please give me a call? I am very much interested in what John had to say. My contact numbers are in the system. Thank you." June hung up the phone. Mason chose that moment to let her know he was awake and in need of some kind of attention. She knew instinctively what needed to be done for her newest family member. Time for his afternoon feeding and once that was done, it would be time for his bath.

Half way through the bath the house phone rang. June let it go to message. She didn't want to stop the bath to talk shop with a counselor. After she got the baby dried, diapered and dressed, she put Mason in his swing and listened to the message. "June this is Sarah. Call me. Something is going on with Frankie and Jessie. I just learned that Frankie hit Jeremy Finney at the pool. It was over Jessie somehow, but I can't get any more out of him."

June called Sarah. She got her voicemail. After the 'beep' June said. "I guess we're playing phone tag. I'll try your cell phone."

This time Sarah answered. "Hi June. I'm on my way to the pool to get Frankie. What did Jessie say?"

"She's not home from the pool yet. I'll text her and see if she'll tell me what this is about."

"Good luck."

"I'll call you right back."

"Okay," Sarah said. "Bye."

June took out her cell phone and sent:

R U OK
Y
FRNK OK
Y

WHT HPND
L8TR
HM SN
K

June called Sarah, "Hi, what did you find out?"

"I texted Jessie and asked if she and Frankie were all right. She said yes. I asked her to come home," June replied.

"Maybe I'll know more when I pick up Frankie."

"Let me know what you find out."

Frank looked at Jessie. "Well, it's out. My mom knows I hit Jeremy. She's on her way to pick me up."

"I know. My mom wants me home too."

"What do we tell them?"

"We can't tell them my secret. I'll never get out of the house again."

Frank pressed, "I have to say something."

"You can tell them Jeremy was calling me names and you stood up for me."

"Okay," Frank agreed. "I hope it works."

"It has to work."

Mickie walked up. She had been talking to Glenn Carr. "Oh, you two have stirred up a hornet's nest. Glenn texted Mary and called her a liar. She called him stupid for believing her. Now he won't even talk to her. He told me that he thinks Mary started the rumors to get you away from Jeremy."

"She did," Jessie said.

"Bobby asked me about your birth mark." Mickie added. "I told him it was none of his business."

"Good," Frank said. "This is turning out just how we wanted. The whole thing is back on Mary Bayer."

Jessie fluttered her eyes and leaned into Frank's shoulder, "My hero…" She said jokingly and the three of them laughed.

Jeremy stood at the other side of the pool watching them. He was still angry. He was mad at himself for being taken in by Mary's lie, he was mad at Mary for lying, and he was mad at Frank for slugging him. He was upset with the whole situation. He had been made to look like a pervert. He had nowhere to go and nothing to do. Maybe he could join the

Navy like his dad and get out of town, but he wouldn't be eighteen for two more years. No, all he could do was let the whole ugly situation die.

Glenn Carr walked up to Jeremy. "Mary told me she lied."

"I didn't like her before, now I hate her," Jeremy said.

"We need to find a way to get even." Glenn said.

Jeremy nodded, "Yeah, but it'll have to be good."

Julie sat at her desk. The glade and the talk with Fred brought some control back to her life. Fred was right. She could 'put him in a box' for a time. At least long enough to get her editor off her back.

Her editor did not control her output. On the other hand, the publisher wanted a new release in time for the Christmas travel season. They were pushing. Julie didn't like deadlines, but she did like advance payments. In order to keep them flowing, she had to write.

She pulled up her chair close to her desk. She had three storylines going. She decided to go back to the story set in the Spanish Civil War in 1938.

> Alonzo burst through the door, his clothes torn from the explosion. "Rachael! Rachael? Are you in here?"
>
> He heard a pounding from under him and a muffled "Down here!"
>
> "How do I get to you?"
>
> "The stairs are in back, but be careful."
>
> Alonzo pushed aside the debris and moved to the back of the old farmhouse. He crawled over the bookcase that had fallen in his path and finally found the door to the cellar. He made his way through what was left of the kitchen. He struggled with the cast iron stove that had been pushed in front of the door by the explosion. He had to pull with all his strength. His muscles quivered with the strain. "I'm almost there!" He heard no reply.

Rachael saw the light from the opening door. "Be careful, I don't think those steps are attached anymore."

Alonzo put some weight on the first step and it held. Then the second. It felt sound. He moved quickly down the remaining steps. He looked at Rachael. Even with torn and bloody clothes, she was the most beautiful woman he had ever seen. "You're bleeding." He tore a off piece of his shirt and moved to her.

"It's nothing," Rachael said.

Alonzo looked at Rachael. She still had on the habit of her order. It was torn and tattered. A symbol of her broken commitment. He started at the top of her head and let his eyes rest on her breasts for a moment then down to her belly. The belly that now held his child. His eyes moved further down and it was only then he noticed her left foot was pointing in the wrong direction. "You have broken your ankle."

"That's better," Julie said to herself. "This 'life in a box' thing is doable." She continued typing.

"I know. I can't move my foot."

"We have to splint it. I have to get you out of here. Franco's army has taken over the town."

"Alonzo, no. You must go. If they find you they will shoot you as a spy."

"I will not leave you. I will die here protecting you or we will leave together."

"You must not. They will not harm me. I'm a nurse and they need me."

"You are a nurse with a broken leg. They will shoot you like a horse, after they have their way with you. Here," he reached over and picked up a piece of board. "We'll

185

splint your leg and I'll carry you out."

Julie's phone rang. She knew the ring-tone. "Good morning Martha."

"Hi Julie! How's that new man in your life?"

"He's in a box on the shelf."

"He's what?"

Julie couldn't help but smile at her editor's confusion. "Fred has taught me about compartmentalization. I can do what he calls, "Life in a Box." He said he would not talk to me again until I caught up on my writing. I had to mentally put him in a box and put the box away until my work was done."

"And how's that working?"

"Just listen, then you tell me."

Jessie walked into the house via the garage door. She stopped at the laundry basket to deposit her wet towel. She heard Mason laughing and splashing in the kitchen sink. She wondered if she could get by unnoticed. She almost made it through the kitchen and to the safety of her bedroom when Freckles jumped on her and started licking her face. He had surprised her so she said, "Freckles stop," and giggled.

June turned, still keeping both hands on the baby. "Good, you're home."

Jessie didn't know how to answer so she said, "Yes." She turned to put some distance between her mother and herself but the dreaded sentence came before she could get away.

"We need to talk," June said.

"Now?" Jessie answered.

"No, go get out of that wet suit and once you're dressed, we'll talk. I want to know what happened today."

"I need a shower."

"Okay," June agreed, "but we *are* going to talk.

Jessie turned and walked away. She had avoided probing questions for at least the next half hour.

"Hi June, what's news?" Bill answered his cell phone with a smile. He knew by the ring tone it was his wife.

"Trouble in paradise, I think."

"What's going on?" Bill got serious. "Is everything all

right?"

"I don't know yet. Seems Frankie punched Jeremy Finney at the pool earlier."

"What was that about?"

"We don't know yet."

"What does Jessie say? Bill asked, "Was she there? Did she see it?"

"Jessie was there," June answered. "I think it was about her. She just got home and is in the shower. I'll see what I can find out when she is dressed."

"Would you like me to come home?"

"I don't think so. Whatever happened, happened. It's over now."

"Well I hope so."

"Let me talk to Jessie. This is only an info call. I'll fill you in as I find out more."

"All right June, but take notes. I'm having trouble keeping up with our daughter's social life."

"This is just the beginning," June chuckled.

"God help us. We're the parents of a teenager." Bill laughed.

"I'll call you when I know more."

"Please do that. Use my cell. I'm on the road this afternoon."

"Got another showing?"

"No, another listing."

"Break a leg."

"See ya." Bill chuckled and hung up the phone. He continued driving down the gravel county road that lead to the Harlow property. He was excited about this one. It was much like the property he had just sold near Groton. The house was less than twenty years old and the buildings were all in great condition. Christine Harlow was a widow. She had lost her husband the year before. Her sons had taken over the farm and were also taking care of her.

Bill pulled into the long driveway and parked near the garage. He knew better than to go to the front door. He walked to the garage and through the open door. He pushed the door bell button next to the door leading to the house. He heard "I'll be right there."

It was almost a minute before the door opened. Bill saw a short thin woman walking with a cane. He pegged her age in the seventies. He was short by ten years. "Good afternoon Mr. Weber. You're right on time."

"Thank you, Mrs. Harlow, but please call me Bill." The age and cultural background of Christine Harlow led him to use Mrs. rather than Ms.

"Only if you call me Christine."

"Done."

"Would you like a cup of coffee?"

"That isn't necessary."

"I have it fresh made."

"Well then, certainly, thanks."

Christine slowly led Bill to the kitchen. She got down two cups and placed them on the table. She pointed to a chair, Bill understood and sat. Once the coffee and pound cake was set, Christine sat down. "Now, where would you like to start?"

"I'd like to start right here." Bill answered. "The house and property are beautiful."

"Thank you. My sons do most of the hard work. I still mow the lawn and keep my gardens when this hip isn't acting up."

"Do your sons live nearby?"

"Just down the road. Dad gave each of them a quarter out of the east section."

Bill wasn't sure if 'dad' meant her father or her husband. Since it didn't matter, he let it go. "I see. So they take care of the farm?"

"That's right. All told we have nineteen quarters. The two of them work it together."

Bill mentally did the math. It worked out to just under five square miles of land. "It's a wonderful thing that they can work together like that."

"It's how they were taught," Christine said, putting a period on the subject. "So, how do we do this, Bill? I've never been involved in the sale of a property. Do I need Sam and Donald here?"

"They can be here if you feel the need. Are they on the deed for this parcel?"

"No, this is mine, my quarter, I mean. Dad gave it to me

for a wedding present. I hold clear title."

"That makes things easier," Bill said. "Let me tell you how the market works. If you are looking to just sell the house, the appeal will be minimal. The same happens if you want to sell the whole quarter. What we do at Huber Realty is help people like you get the maximum amount of money out of a small part of the quarter. If we can list this house and, say, about fifteen acres or so, you will get top dollar."

"How does that work? Nobody would want a farm that small."

"You're right, no one around here would even consider a property that small and this far out of town. On the other hand you would be surprised at the number of people I have waiting for a property just like this."

"You just contradicted yourself."

"Not really. The people looking for hobby farms are not from here. They come from busier places. The majority are suburban or urban residents. They look at fifteen acres as a large parcel of land. They are either semi retired or working from home. They want the peace and quiet of country living. Huber Realty gives them the opportunity to do what I did. Leave the rat race and get into the country."

At that moment a man walked into the kitchen. He stood tall, very tall. His graying hair was the only thing revealing his age. He was wearing jeans and a blue chambray button up shirt. "Hi Mom, this the realtor?"

"Bill Weber, this is my son, Sam."

Bill stood and put out his hand, "Pleased to meet you, Sam."

Sam pulled his hand out of his work glove. He looked at it quickly, as if to check it for cleanliness. It passed inspection, so he extended it, "Good to meet you, Bill."

Bill was surprised, his own hand was completely engulfed in Sam's grip. Bill knew that Sam was holding back on the handshake. He had the feeling Sam could crush every bone in his hand if he cared to. "Your mother tells me you do the farming."

"That's right, my brother and I. He'll be along shortly."

"Now, Sam, I told you I'd take care of this myself."

"We know mom, we won't get in the way. We're here to

189

answer questions and show Bill around." Sam walked over to the coffee pot, he took a cup down for a cabinet and filled it. "Mom has lived on this quarter since her wedding day. Dad gave her this quarter as a wedding gift. We are selling it with mixed feelings. We don't want to. If we could afford it, we would keep the place ourselves and turn it into a hunting lodge. That would at least keep it in the family."

"We tried to pencil that out and it just doesn't work. It will not generate enough cash to get Mom's money out of it." The voice came from the door. Bill turned and saw a man about five foot six, small in stature.

"This is my other son, Donald."

"Don," the man said and put out a hand half the size of his brother's.

Bill did his best not to show his surprise. "Good to meet you," Bill said formally.

"I told the boys they could just have the place, but they wanted nothing of it."

"That's right," Don said. "We won't have it that way. Dad set this up and we'll do it the way he said."

"Mom is moving down with us," Don said. "We added an addition onto my house. It's an apartment of her own. She'll still be independent, but we can be near if she needs something."

"Most of the time I can take care of myself. There are some days, like today," she held up the cane, "when these old bones rebel."

Jessie walked into the kitchen and then to the refrigerator. Her need for food overcame her desire to avoid her mother. She looked around. She could hear her mother in her bedroom with the baby. Maybe she could make a sandwich and get back to her bedroom before her mother came back. She had just finished the final spread of peanut butter on the P B & J when her mother walked in.

"There you are."

Jessie didn't say anything. She turned and walked to the table.

"You know, you could at least acknowledge my existence," June said.

190

"Sorry."

June pulled out a kitchen chair and sat down next to her daughter. "So… what happened at the pool?"

"Nothing much."

"I heard Frankie had a fight with Jeremy."

"They didn't fight," Jessie answered.

"But Frankie hit Jeremy," June asked as a statement.

"Yes."

"All right."

"Is that all?" Jessie asked, getting her hopes up.

"No, young lady," June said sternly, "stop hedging and tell me what happened."

"Mom…" Jessie said, as only a teenage girl can. "It's not important. Besides it's over already."

"What's over?"

Jessie made a sigh of surrender. "Jeremy was calling me names and Frank stood up to him for me. That's all."

"That's all?" June wasn't convinced. "Why was Jeremy calling you names?"

"Because I won't go out with him again."

"And why is that."

Jessie panicked. She tried to keep her composure but she could tell her mother saw through it. "Because I don't like him anymore."

"Why?"

"Can't we just drop it? It's over."

"No I can't drop it." June was getting irritated. "Did he do something to you?"

"No!" Jessie lied. She had to get away from her mom. She knew she had LIAR posted in big letters on her forehead. "Can't you just leave this alone!" Jessie said and ran from the room.

June called Sarah, "I got mostly nowhere. Near as I can figure out Jeremy Finny was picking on Jessie and Frankie stood up to him."

"I got the same story from Frankie with a bit more detail. Jeremy wouldn't back off so Frankie got in his face. Eventually he punched him."

"Well, I guess I'm glad Frankie was there to stop the

insults, but I'm not so happy that there was fight."

"Frankie insists there wasn't a fight. Jeremy just walked away."

"But why was Jeremy doing it?" June asked. "That's the part that doesn't make sense. It was just a couple days ago Jessie was all gaga over the boy. Now they are calling each other names."

"June, don't you remember those early teen years?" Sarah said. "One week you are in love and can't live without a boy and the next week you hate him and hope to never see him again."

June chuckled. She did remember. She remembered a boy named David, not Dave, David. She knew he was 'The One', she just knew it. Then they started school and he sat behind her. He turned out to be a real jerk. He wouldn't leave her alone in class. He kept tugging her hair and tickling her neck. She hated him by the end of the first week. "Yes, I guess I do remember those days."

"I don't think we'll find out what the whole thing was about. I think we need to let it go and let them sort it out themselves."

"But what if this Finney boy tried something with Jessie?"

"You know Mike Finney, you know Sandy. Do you think they would tolerate any kind of bad behavior on the part of Jeremy?"

"No, I don't. And for that matter, I've seen Jeremy in the clinic. He is always polite and respectful." June made a decision. "All right, Sarah, I'll let it go, for now. As long as she is with Frankie, I'm comfortable."

Chapter Sixteen

Tom and Sarah had invited Fred along with Bill and June Weber to the weekly supper that had grown into tradition between the two families. Sarah had initially hoped that Fred would hit it off with her sister, Ruth. She backed off on the idea when June told her about Julie.

Tom had almost completed his antique pick up truck restoration. He needed to put another coat of polyurethane on the cherry wood slats for the bed. That was the reason the three men wound up in the shop after supper. "You know, Fred, you can leave the Charger here in my barn until you get back," Tom Ogden offered.

"That won't be necessary. I made arrangements with Stewart to leave the car in the garage there once the auction is done."

"Suit yourself," Tom replied. "Park it here and I'll move it over later."

Fred thought about it. "You know, that's silly. If you don't mind it here, we'll just leave it here."

"Fine by me, it's a big barn, it won't be in the way," Tom replied. "When are you going back to Norfolk?"

"I've got about a week yet. I took three weeks leave. I'm half way through it."

"Seems like you just got here," Tom said.

"Not to me," Bill jibed. "I want my office back."

"You have your office," Fred returned the barb. "All you have to do is climb over the baby crib."

"Wonderful," Bill answered.

"What year is this truck?" Fred asked.

"Fifty three."

"It's beautiful."

"Thanks. I wanted to keep it as original as I could. The engine was in good shape. I didn't even rebuild it. It doesn't smoke or use oil."

"That's amazing."

Tom turned to Bill. "You know Oscar Platt," he asked as a statement.

"Sure, he lives south of town with his dad."

"Well Oscar's dad, Emit, used to own a service station in town. He really knows these old pickups. I invited the two of them over for supper and Emit helped me get the shift linkage right again."

Fred saw an opening, "How's the transmission?"

"When I had the engine and trans out, Emit took a look at it. He said it was hardly worn at all. I changed the gear lube and stuffed it back in once the paint was done."

"You told me it was running when the farmer put it away," Bill said. "I guess you were lucky."

"You can say that again. Other than some light rust and some body work, this thing has been an easy restoration."

"Is this your first?"

"By myself, yes," Tom answered. "When I was young I helped my grandfather restore a 1918 Oliver."

"Oliver?" Fred asked. "I don't know that car."

"Oliver is a tractor," Tom said.

"No wonder I hadn't heard of it."

"It looks beautiful, Tom," Bill said. "I thought you were going to chrome the metal slats between the wood in the bed."

"I was, but when everything else worked out original, I decided to keep them to original, too."

"Well, it looks great," Fred said. "Now, what do you do with it?"

"There is the Antique Power Show on the State Fair grounds in Huron and the July Fourth parade. Plus there are a few car shows around."

"So you're going to show off," Bill said with a smile.

"Why not?" Tom laughed. "What's ego for if not to be stroked."

Jessie was in Frank's room. Unlike other visits they weren't involved in a video game. They were sitting on the floor using the bed as a backrest. The video game controllers were in their laps but the game held second place to the conversation. "So now what do we do?"

"Nothing."

"Nothing! Frank, we have to make sure."

"It's over. When Mickie told us that Mary admitted to Glenn she lied, it was over that minute."

"I'm not sure."

"It is."

"So, what's next?" Jessie asked.

Frank leaned over and kissed her. Gently at first, then with more passion. Jessie felt her body heat up. She returned the kiss, giving as much as she got. She started to get lost in a world that contained only them when Frank pulled back. "That's what's next."

Jessie didn't talk. She leaned in and kissed him again, this time even harder. She thought Jeremy's kiss was the best she would ever experience. She was wrong. Frank was a master. She wanted to crawl inside him and stay there forever.

Frank pulled away and quickly picked up the game controller. Jessie was about to ask why when the bedroom door opened. "Jessie," Sarah said, "your dad and Uncle Fred are ready to go."

Jessie only had a half a second to regain her composure. She hoped she looked normal. "Thanks Aunt Sarah."

As Sarah walked away, Jessie giggled, "That was close. I didn't hear her coming."

"I did. I have mom radar."

Frank stood up and turned to pull Jessie up but she had stood up on her own. "We have to be more careful."

Frank nodded, "You're right. If we don't, we'll never be left alone again."

Bill was awake early. It was Saturday and he had a list of things to get done. Since it was early, he decided to go to the Café for the daily morning coffee round table. He quickly threw on a pair of jeans, a Mount Rushmore tee shirt and boat shoes.

When he got to the Helen House, he noticed his brother's car already there. He had not noticed that it was gone from in front of the house. He told himself he had to get more observant, especially since he had a teenager at home. Bill walked into the Café and proceeded to take a seat at the big round table. "Good morning."

The table was filled with several people. His brother had taken the seat with his back to the corner. The mayor had his usual spot. Next to him was Bob Meyer. April Kline was next

195

and last was Wendell Olsen. "Good morning to you, Bill," Mayor Henry Woodson answered for the table. "I'm glad you came out today. Saves me a trip later."

"You wanted to talk to me?"

"Actually, I did," Henry said. "What have you decided about the County Commission?"

Bill felt put on the spot. "I haven't really made up my mind yet. With the expansion of Huber Realty and the new baby, I'm not sure if the timing is right."

"Let me get you off the hook," Henry said. "April came to me the other day and said she would like the job. I told her we had offered the position to you and I had to talk to you about it."

Bill felt disappointed and relieved at the same time. He looked over at April Kline, "I will be happy to step aside and let you run."

"Thanks, Bill," April said. "This is something I've wanted to do for a while. I'm in the opposite position, the timing is just right for me."

"That's settled, we will have a meeting next week and put your name in to replace Jake Samuelsson."

"How's he doing?" April asked. "I haven't seen him at the bank."

"I was out there the other day," Wendell said. "He's all right. The treatments take a lot out of him. The good news is the doctors are telling him it's working. The tumor is shrinking."

"So, he'll make it then?"

"It looks good."

"Fred, when are you due back?" Wendell asked.

"To the ship?"

"No, back in Helen."

"I should be here by the end of September," Fred answered.

"Got any plans for work yet?"

"Not really," Fred answered.

"Want a harvest job?" Wendell smiled as he asked.

"I'm no farmer. What would you like me to do?"

"I need a grain cart driver for the harvest."

"What does that entail?" Fred asked.

Wendell explained, "We run the two combines in the field. They're doing the actual harvesting. The grain cart picks up the grain from the combines and takes it to the semi trailer. With a grain cart in the field, the combines don't have to stop what they're doing to go unload their hoppers. You pull up next to the combine with the grain cart and they unload into the cart. Then you drive the cart to the truck and load it for transport to the farm or the elevator."

"That might be fun. I've never done anything like that."

"Then I have your commitment?"

Fred looked to his brother, saw the unspoken signal and answered, "If you're willing to train a rookie, I'm willing to learn."

"Good," Wendell nodded, "I think we'll be going the first week in October, maybe earlier."

"I'd better hurry back then."

"If the Navy will let you," Bill said.

"If everything goes according to plan, I will be done with the Navy on September fifth. At least that's how I have it figured. I have to get that verified with the people in Personnel, but I shouldn't be off more than a day or two either way."

"You don't know the day your hitch is over?" Henry asked. "When I was in the Air Force, I knew my exact out date."

"Oh, I know the exact date of my contract," Fred said taking a sip of coffee, "it's the other variables. How much leave I have left is one variable, the house hunting and transit time that will be allowed is another. Plus there is always some other unseen variable in the works to throw off the retirement ceremony. It might move a day forward or back so as to not conflict with mission requirements. Most of these things are not set in stone yet."

"Not to mention a sudden stop loss order," Henry said. "I saw it happen to Al Stillwell's brother. He got delayed six months."

"I don't see that happening," Fred brushed off the idea. "I'll be working on the rest of it as soon as I get back to the ship. Wendell, if you give me your phone number I'll keep you in the loop. I should know my exact departure date within

197

a week of the time I get back."

"Seven one six three is the house number," Wendell replied.

"That's eight two nine," Bill said. Then added "Every house and business phone in Helen starts with eight two nine."

"So I'm told."

"The cell is two one eight and the same number," Wendell continued, "seven one six three."

Fred punched the numbers into his phone. "Got it."

"If you get delayed, let me know as soon as you can so I can try to find someone else."

"Good luck with that," Bob Meyer said as he stood up. He turned to Fred. "Finding people to work during the harvest is nearly impossible, Fred. Wendell was the first to ask. I'll bet you get four more offers before you leave."

"Maybe I should have held out…" Fred smiled.

"That was why I asked for a commitment." Wendell smiled back.

"Well, I'd better get to the Post Office. See you around."

"Around the mail route you mean," Henry answered the statement with the well used punch line.

"June Weber? This is Francis Alden from St. Agnes Human Relations."

"Good morning Ms. Alden, this is June."

"Good morning to you as well. Do have a few minutes to visit?"

"Yes, in fact you couldn't have picked a better time. You're working on a Saturday?"

"I had some loose ends to clear up. I was in the office and I thought I'd try to touch base with you. Saturday mornings are normally quiet."

"I would think so," June agreed.

"Let's get to work then. I have been looking over your experience and qualifications and I agree with Mr. Franklin. With the classes you have already taken, you can transition to Nurse Practitioner without too much effort. I think I can develop a program that will put you in place in about fourteen months."

"John told me about the "country doctor" feel for the

clinic. I think that's a wonderful idea."

"I'm not sure of those details. What I do know is this. You are already well along in the process. With the proper course of study and some on site training, we can have you certified in just over one year. If you will let me, I will lay out a course of study for you to review."

"I am certainly interested."

"It will be mostly distance learning but we will occasionally want you to come to Sioux Falls or Aberdeen for progress and hands on assessments. St Agnes works closely with the SDSU Brooking campus and the school of nursing. In fact I was hired for just that purpose. As one of the two major employers of medical students in South Dakota, the State University system tries to stay sensitive to our needs."

"I would like to see what you have in mind. Please know that I am not absolutely committed to this until I know all the details and have a chance to discuss it with my husband. I have a new baby in the house and that will take much of my time. If you build too aggressive a schedule, it will simply frustrate both of us."

"I understand. Mr. Franklin told me about your new baby. I'm sure we can work out a schedule that will give you the time you need with him and your family."

"That sounds great."

"Do you still have access to your St. Agnes email?"

"I haven't tried it in a while. Would you like me to check?"

"If you can."

"I'll do it right now." June picked up her cell phone. After a few seconds she said, "Yes, I can still get in."

"Good. I'll send you the package as soon as I put it together. It should be some time Monday afternoon. Look it over and then we'll go over it together and make any changes we need."

"I look forward to seeing it."

"All right then, I'll expect to hear from you within the next few days."

June nodded at the phone. "Good enough."

"Good bye then."

"Good bye."

June put down the phone. She checked and the baby was still sleeping. There was no sound coming from Jessie's room and she knew Cory was down the street with Jeffrey.

The house was quiet. It gave her time to think. The offer was the deal of a lifetime. When she was new to nursing and only had her LPN certificate, she was the medical assistant at a one man office. Dr. Simons was an old school family doctor. He refused to join the larger medical groups until the rising malpractice insurance rates left him no choice. June loved working in the small office. She saw first hand the need for a personal relationship between a doctor and the patient. If John Franklin wanted to try to mimic that kind of service at the St. Agnes Clinic in Helen, she wanted to be a part of it.

On the down side, she also was enjoying her status as stay at home mom. She was nearby when her kids needed her. Mason was only two months old. She wanted to be there for the first step, the first word, even the first tooth. Sometimes she wished she could clone herself. She was divided between the profession she loved and the family she cherished. She knew this was a decision not to be made lightly.

June picked up the phone again. She wanted to talk this out with someone. Sarah came to mind. Her opinion would be valuable.

"Hi June."

"Sarah, are you busy?"

"I won't be in about three minutes. Why, is something wrong?'

"No, actually something is very right, and that's what's wrong."

"I'm confused."

"I know, so am I." June realized she was only adding to the confusion.

"Okay, I've got a knife in my hand and a cake half iced. Let me finish and I'll call you back."

"Sure. Talk to you soon."

"Two minutes."

"Okay, bye"

"See ya."

It was almost two minutes to the second when Sarah called back. "Okay, what's this good thing that has you so upset?"

"I just got off the phone with the counselor at St. Agnes. It looks like I can be a Nurse Practitioner in just over a year. Once that's done, John Franklin says I'll be the primary care giver at the Helen Clinic. No rotations."

"That's fantastic June!"

"Better still, they are building the program so I can do distance learning from home. Almost all of it will be on line."

"Unbelievable!"

"John Franklin says they will pay me to go to school."

"June, that's terrific!" Sarah hesitated, "So, what's wrong?"

"I like being home," June said. "I like not working and being here for the kids. I like being a mom."

"I understand," Sarah said. "So, that's the problem."

"In a nutshell." June nodded at the phone.

"When do you have to decide?"

"They're sending me a package. It will outline the course of study and goals. I get to look it over before I commit."

"Well, June, you know I like being home. I know you do, too. Do you need the money?"

"No, Bill's doing great."

"I know you like working at the clinic. I know the people in town like you working at the clinic. If you go back will it be full time?"

"No I would work about eighteen hours a week," June said. "The trouble is the course of study. If it's too aggressive, I won't have time to be a mom."

"Let's worry about that when you get the package."

June nodded at the phone again. "Good idea. I don't have to decide today, I haven't even talked to Bill about it. Thanks Sarah."

"For what?"

June chuckled, "For helping me avoid a decision."

Sarah laughed in turn, "Anytime."

Fred knew the ring tone. He picked up his phone. "How's my favorite author today?"

Julie was surprised at the question, "Are you alone?"

"Of course I am, I'm in my car." Fred was a bit bothered

by the challenge. "I wouldn't have answered that way if I was around anyone."

"Okay, I'm sorry. I guess I'm a bit paranoid."

Fred smiled, not that she could see. "I forgive you. What's up?"

"Your favorite author is done with her chapters and wants to go to lunch."

"Any place in particular?"

"I think I'd like to go to the Past Times."

"That place in Watertown with the great coffee?'

"That's the one."

"You're on. I'll be right there."

"Where are you now?"

"Just around the corner."

"Give me fifteen minutes. I didn't know you would be ready that quickly."

"You got it." Fred pulled up in front of his brother's house. He had a few minutes so he decided to put on a better shirt and maybe some Dockers. His phone rang again, this time with the 'Anchor's Away' ring tone. He knew who that was too. It was the official ship's phone number. "This is Chief Weber," he answered.

"Chief Weber, this is the XO. Where are you?"

"South Dakota, Commander" Fred used the informal term Commander even though the Executive Officer's rank was one grade below, Lieutenant Commander.

"South Dakota?"

"Yes Sir."

"How soon can you get back?"

"I'm not due back for another eight days, Sir."

"I didn't ask that Chief."

"I suppose I could leave this afternoon," Fred answered. "If the flights align, I could be there by morning muster. What's the rush?"

"This is not a secure line, Chief, I won't discuss it. Suffice it to say we need you back here."

"Are you officially canceling my leave, Sir?"

"I can get the Skipper to do just that if you balk me."

"No Sir, I'll be on the next flight out of Huron. I'm not balking you at all. If you cancel my leave and I have to return to duty early, I may get the airline to give me a refund or not charge me to change dates."

"Chief Weber, consider your leave canceled effective now. I'll have an e-mail sent to you confirming that. Get back to the ship as quickly as you can."

"I'm on my way, Sir."

"Report to me as soon as you get aboard."

"Yes, Sir," Fred said and ended the conversation. Rather than call, he walked over to Julie's house and shouted in the kitchen door.

Julie called back, "You're too early. My hair's still wet."

"I've been recalled to the ship."

"What? Wait." It took less than twenty seconds for Julie to come around the corner and into view. She had on cut off jeans, a white tee shirt and a towel around her head. Fred had not seen anything more beautiful in all his world travels. "What did you say?"

"My leave has been canceled and I have to get back to the ship as quickly as possible."

"What happened?"

"They didn't tell me."

"They didn't tell you?" Julie repeated as a question. "They want you to drop everything, end your vacation early and go running back the yo ship without telling you why?"

"Welcome to the Navy," Fred shrugged. "It's an official order. My leave is canceled and I need to get back ASAP."

Julie recovered. She didn't understand the ways of the Navy but she knew Fred did. If he said he had to go, then he had to go. "When are you leaving?"

"I'm going to look at the flight schedules now. I need to book the next flight out of Huron. Once I'm in either Minneapolis or Denver, I can get back to Norfolk."

"This is going to cost you a fortune," Julie said.

"I'm going to try to get the airline to work with me. Maybe they'll forgive the schedule change."

"Good luck with that," Julie said. "Use my laptop, the screen's bigger. The password is Alonzogreen32."

"With an 's'?"

"With a 'z'," Julie said. "I'm going to dry my hair."

Fred looked up the Huron Airport and checked the flights

out. He realized that he was already too late for the last flight. He checked Watertown and found a flight to Minneapolis he could manage. "I have to get back next door. I need to get Bill to drive me to Watertown."

"I'll do it," Julie answered. "When is the flight?"

"Four ten."

"We'll have to hurry."

"I'd better go pack."

"You need help?"

"No, I don't have much. It'll take me ten minutes."

"All right," Julie said. "I'll be ready."

Fred walked over and pulled her close. "This is not the way I wanted this afternoon to go."

Julie responded by melting against him making her meaning more than clear. "Not what I had planned either."

Chapter Seventeen

It was only a sense of duty and twenty plus years of Navy training that pulled Fred away from Julie and back to his brother's house. No one was around. He had his bags packed in a matter of minutes. He loaded his luggage into his car and walked back to get Julie. She met him at the door. The cutoff jeans and tee shirt had been replaced with shorts and a short sleeve button up top. Her hair was dry and no longer sporting a towel. "Did you tell June and the kids?"

"Nobody's home," Fred said. "Will you drive? I need to make some phone calls as we go."

"Sure," Julie walked toward her car.

"I have my bags in the Charger, we can use it."

"Okay," Julie changed direction.

Fred held the driver's door for Julie than walked around to the passenger side. Once he got in, Julie started the Charger. The car jumped forward as she pulled out. "Sorry, it has more power than my Cobalt."

"Do you mind if I make some phone calls?"

"Not at all," Julie replied, "that's why you asked me to drive."

"Thanks." Fred took out his phone. The first call was to his brother.

"Hey Fred, what's cookin'?"

"Jet fuel."

"Jet fuel?"

"My leave has been canceled. I'm on my way back to Norfolk."

"What happened.?"

"I don't know. They won't tell me over an open phone line."

"I've been listening to the news, there's nothing going on, other than the usual, I mean."

"It could be anything, but when you get a call from the Executive Officer telling you to get back to the ship ASAP, you don't ask, you just get."

"You mean just jump, don't ask how high?"

"Something like that," Fred said, then shifted gears.

"Look, this puts me in a bind."

"You need a lift to the airport?"

"No, Julie is driving me. I need help with some loose ends. The car I'm in is one of them. I'm going to call Marty and tell him what happened. Hopefully he'll work with me on the car."

"I'm sure he will. If he needs something tell him to call me." Bill answered.

"Okay. Here's another thing, June and the kids weren't home. Can you tell them what's going on?"

"Sure, as little as I know."

"You know what I know."

"I know," Bill chuckled at his own play on words. "What else?"

"I didn't get the chance to set up an account at the Farmer's Bank and Trust. I was going to use that account to buy the car and pay Stewart. I left a check made out to you for fifteen thousand dollars. I hid it under the breadbox in the kitchen. Don't do anything with it until I tell you. I have to transfer some money around. Once that's done put it in the bank for me."

"All right, I can be your agent, but I'll need a Power of Attorney."

"Thank you brother," Fred said and meant it.

"Where's the car?"

"With me. Julie's driving it."

"I'll take care of it. You want it left at Tom's?"

"If that's not too much trouble," Fred said. "Or you could just leave it in the street in front of your house."

"I'll take it to Tom's. What else?"

"Hug the kids for me. They won't understand, but tell them the Navy needed me back."

"All right."

"I'll call you as other things come up. Right now I've got to call the Navy travel office and get this ticket switched."

"Okay, call me when you get to Norfolk if you can."

"I will." Fred put down the phone. He turned to Julie, "That's done."

"You're not going to call June?"

"I'll call her from Minneapolis or Atlanta," Fred

answered. "Bill will give her the word, and that's enough for now."

"What's next?"

"Marty, and this car." Fred opened the glove box. He found the rental contract and Marty's number.

"Used Cars… Marty."

"Marty, Fred Weber."

"How ya doin' Fred?"

"I'm doing fine, but the Navy just threw me a curve ball. They canceled my leave and I'm on my way back to the ship."

"We got a war on or something?"

"Not that I know of. Look, Marty, I'm going to keep this car. Bill will have a check for you in the next few days. Is that all right with you?"

"That's fine. I can stop the clock on the rental contract as soon as I see your brother, but I'm going to need some signatures."

"I understand," Fred said. "I'm sending Bill a limited Power of Attorney as soon as I have the chance. He is doing some other things for me, too."

"No problem. Get Bill to call me and we'll work it out."

"Thanks Marty."

"Sure thing, sailor. Enjoy the car."

"I already am."

"Good enough then. Tell Bill to call me."

"Will do, bye."

"Safe journey."

"Thanks." Fred hung up. "That was the easy one," he said to Julie.

"What's next?"

"The airlines."

"How do you do that?"

"I booked the flight originally through the Navy Travel Office in Norfolk. I'm going to call them and see if they can help me change the ticket or at least get me my money back on the return leg I'm not using." While he was talking, he was manipulating his phone. "Looks like the office is closed on weekends, go figure."

"What will you do now?"

"I sent them an emergency message. We'll see what that

207

does. In the mean time I'll just buy a ticket."

"That's going to cost you a fortune."

"It is part of the job. When you go on leave or liberty, you are responsible to get back. If you are recalled, like I was, they don't care how or how much it costs, you just get back."

"It doesn't seem fair."

"I'm the one who came to South Dakota," Fred said. "If they had sent me, it would be up to them to get me home. Since I did this myself, the responsibility is all mine."

Julie let it drop. She still thought Fred should be compensated for the travel, but she wasn't the head of the Navy. "Do we have time for a quick bite to eat?"

Fred looked at the clock on the dash, "Let's go to the airport and get the tickets I need. Then we'll see how much time we have."

"Okay."

"So he just left?" June asked her husband after hearing the news.

"I don't think he had much of a choice," Bill answered.

"Well, he could have at least said goodbye to the kids."

"I don't think he had the time. He called me on the way to the airport."

"What's the crisis?"

"He didn't know."

"He didn't know?" June repeated as a question.

"You know how the government is with secrets. They wouldn't tell him over the phone."

"They want him back but they won't tell him why?"

"That's about it." Bill shrugged at the phone.

"Where are you?"

"I'm driving back from Tom's. How about you?"

"I'm still in Kent."

"Okay," Bill replied. "Fred left a check at the house. I want to get it and put it in my wallet."

"Why did he leave us a check?"

"Not for us," Bill explained. "He left the money to buy the Charger and to pay Stewart the deposit and rent. He asked me to put it in the bank for him and act as his agent."

"What can I do?"

"I don't think anything for right now. Explain to Jessie why he left suddenly."

"How can I do that when I don't understand it myself?"

"If you want to wait until we all get home, I'll try to explain it."

"That might be better."

"All right. We'll do it that way."

"Yes, sir, I can book that for you."

"Great," Fred said. "How about the refund on the other ticket?"

"You bought a non refundable fare, sir."

"I understand that, but I am under Navy orders to return today."

"You can contact our customer relations department, perhaps they can work out something, I can't do anything from this terminal."

"Okay, thanks. Let's get this done and I'll argue with the customer relations people when I get back."

"I'll be happy too." After about a minute the agent on the phone said, "Everything is all set Mr. Weber. You can print your boarding pass when you get to the airport."

"Thank you."

"Thank you and thank you for booking with Alliance Air."

Fred put down his phone. It was warm from being held. Like his brother, he didn't like ear pieces. He used them enough at work and tried not to when he was away. "I think that covers everything," Fred said.

"Just in time," Julie said as she turned onto Airport Drive. She drove up the right side of the lollypop shaped road and stopped in front of the terminal. "Your destination, sir."

"Thank you driver" Fred continued the game. "If you will park I'll tend to the bags."

"Yes sir," Julie said.

Fred got out of the car and pulled his two bags from the back seat. He closed the door and walked into the terminal. Once inside he found the electronic check in kiosk and printed his ticket information and boarding passes. He checked in his luggage and looked at the time. He had about an hour and a

209

half before departure time. He checked with the person who took his large bag. She said, since his luggage was here, he had about an hour before they would call the flight and start the security screening. He turned to find Julie and saw her walking in the door. He walked up to her still holding his carry on bag. "We have an hour."

"Okay," Julie said. "I don't think that's enough time for the Past Times Cafe."

"I think you're right. There was a restaurant down the road a bit. Maybe we should get something there."

"Good idea." Julie turned and walked back toward the door. She slowed just enough that Fred could get ahead and open the door for her. It was starting to become a habit. She giggled at the thought that if he had not opened the door she might have walked into it.

When they got to the car she turned toward the passenger door. "Why don't you drive?" Fred said.

"All right." Julie changed direction. Fred followed and opened the driver's door. Once he closed it he walked around to the passenger side and got in. Julie was not sure of the whole situation. Fred always drove, that is until today. She understood why he wanted her to drive to the airport, but not now. But how to bring it up? "You tired of driving?"

"Say again?"

She could feel Fred slipping away from her. His voice was getting more official and terse. She had to have him for the next hour. The Navy might have a claim on him, but this hour was hers. "Put that box away," She said firmly. "You'll have plenty of time to play with it in the plane. Right now I want you in my box."

Fred looked at her and laughed. "Is that what you meant to say?"

Julie replayed the last sentence in her mind and laughed. "Doctor Freud would say so. What I meant was that you are starting to switch to your Navy box and it's not time yet. I have this hour and I want it just for me. Can you do that?"

Fred put his hand on her hand, "I can and will."

"Good. Now where did you see this place?"

"Up ahead on the left. See the sign?"

"The Wheel Inn?"

210

"That's it."

Julie pulled in and parked in the gravel parking lot in front of an older but well kept building. They walked in and saw a large U shaped counter with several men sitting, eating and drinking coffee. Fred looked and saw a table on the far side that offered a bit of privacy. He led Julie to that table, not knowing that his final meal on the way to the airport was in the same restaurant and at the same table his bother Bill had chosen for their first meal coming from the airport almost a year and half before. "I don't know what the situation is on the ship but it has to be serious to want me back." He pointed to the television in the corner. The channel was on CNN. "I don't see anything going on that would cause a mass recall, so it has to have something to do with the ship."

"I thought we weren't going to talk about the Navy," Julie said.

"I'm not," Fred smiled. "I'm talking about us."

"How?"

"If there is something on a national scale they can delay my retirement and hold me on active duty. If it is the ship, then I will be done at the end of my contract."

The waitress came by and gave them menus. "I'm Maggie, welcome to the Wheel Inn. The special today is a roast pork open face sandwich with mashed potatoes and gravy. You can have a garden salad or corn. Two coffees?"

"Yes, thank you Maggie," Fred replied. As Maggie walked away Fred said, "That special sounds good to me. It should be fast."

"Okay, I'll have that too."

Maggie returned with the coffee and they both ordered the special with the salad. Once Maggie left again they didn't say a word. They just sat looking at one another across that table. Time stood still for them or so it seemed. They didn't need words. They were speaking and communicating just fine without them. The trance was broken when Maggie came back with two small salads and a dressing server. Fred picked up his cup, "To Julie… the reason I want to hurry back."

Julie smiled and picked up her cup, "To your new home in Helen, South Dakota."

"Here's your sandwiches," Maggie said, placing a plate in

211

front of each of them.

"Thank you," Fred answered for them both.

"This is not exactly the meal I had in mind for your departure day," Julie said. I had a whole scenario played out in my head for our last day."

"This is plenty good enough. The food is good and company is the best I could ask for."

"Thanks." She reached across the table. "I'll miss you."

"I certainly hope so," Fred said lightly. "I would hate for that missing to only be one way."

"What about life in a box?" Julie asked.

"The boxes aren't air tight. You will be on my mind, believe me."

"I'll bet you won't even remember my name once you cross the gangplank or what ever it is you call it."

"I'll remember, and I'll remember why I'm in a hurry to get back."

Julie changed the subject, "Would you like me to do anything with the house?"

"Like what?'

"Oh, I don't know, put the dishes and pot and pans away that Tom will get at the sale, help arrange the furniture, things like that."

"That's nice of you."

"Just being neighborly," Julie smiled.

"Here's an idea," Fred said. "Come to the retirement."

"In Virginia?"

"If you can. That is if you're not up against a deadline or whatever you call it," Fred repeated the phrase.

"I'll have to work it out but I think I could do it. We could drive back together."

"You want to ride across the country in a ratty old pick up truck?"

"Why not?" Julie giggled. She was starting to relish the idea. "My great-great grandparents did it in a Conestoga wagon."

Fred chuckled. He was also playing out the scenario in his head. It played well. "Let's see how this works out."

"It might be fun."

"It might be a disaster. "That truck hasn't been more than

ten miles from the Norfolk naval base in ten years. I'll have to make sure it is up to the trip."

"We could fly back together."

"There's that too." Fred made a decision. "Okay, this is official. If you can make it, please come to my retirement ceremony."

"I'll do my best to work it out."

"Good enough." Fred looked up at the wall clock, "We have to get going."

He took the check and placed it half under his plate with cash for the meals and a generous tip.

They stood as one and walked to the door. "You might as well drive again, the seat is adjusted for you and it's only a mile or so."

Julie stood as she watched the plane taxi and move out of sight. She stood there until she saw it roar down the runway and climb away from her. She turned slowly and walked to the car. When she climbed in she could still smell a hint of Fred's cologne. She decided to drive with the windows up to keep the smell in the car.

It took the normal amount of time for Julie to get home. It only seemed longer. She felt like she was driving on roads made from molasses. Everything moved slower. The speedometer read seventy but it felt like thirty. She knew better than to go faster; that would just get her a ticket. She tried the radio, but that didn't help. Even the songs seemed longer.

Julie parked the car in front of her next door neighbor's house and walked into the garage. She knocked on June's door and opened it. "June?" She shouted quietly so as not to wake a sleeping baby, "are you here?"

June walked to the mud room door, "Come on in," she said quietly. "Mason's sleeping," she cautioned.

Julie followed June into the kitchen. She sat at the table, in the chair indicated by her host. "I brought in the keys from Fred's car."

"You could have left them. Bill and I will take it out to Tom's later. June poured water into the coffee maker. "Did he tell you why he had to go so suddenly?"

"He doesn't know. All they told him was his leave was canceled and to get back to the ship by morning."

"You think it was something we did? Maybe the kids got to him."

"June, he had to go. He didn't want to. I was with him. He wanted to stay. He is looking forward to being here permanently. That was the Navy, not us."

"You're sure?"

"I am absolutely sure," Julie said emphatically. "He had to go, he didn't want to."

"That's a relief. I was concerned we had pushed him out."

"Quite the opposite, he is more excited about living here now than when he first flew in."

"I think you might have something to do with that."

"I think so too. He asked me to fly in for his retirement ceremony."

"Really?" June looked at her good friend and neighbor. "This is getting serious."

"I hope so."

Fred Weber crossed the Quarterdeck after paying the proper and official respects to the flag and the man on watch. He was told again the Executive Officer wanted to see him as soon as he was aboard.

Not quite complying literally with that order, his first stop was the CPO (Chief Petty Officer) berthing compartment, known by tradition as the Goat Locker. He didn't quite make it. His LPO (Leading Petty Officer) met him at the door. "Chief! Am I glad you're back."

"What's going on, Anne?"

"It was a fire, Chief."

"A fire?"

"A bad one. The spaces are a wreck. The equipment is badly damaged, but that's not the worst of it. The fire destroyed logs and records. We don't have proper documentation on the classified material."

This was big, bigger than he thought. It was a major catastrophe that could effect the whole fleet. He knew he would have to certify the destruction of classified material, but without the proper documentation the responsibility would fall on him, his LPO and his Lieutenant. If one piece of classified material found its way to the normal trash, it could compromise the entire fleet. "How is the space secured?"

"The Master At Arms has a watch posted. No one is allowed in that does not work there and no one is allowed in alone. DC (Damage Control) is working on securing the door and setting a new cipher lock. There's no power down there so the mag-lock is not working."

"What about during the fire? Who had access?"

"That's just it, once the fire was under control the doors were wide open. DC was in and out many times. Nobody was checking for clearances or security."

"That's trouble. I'd better get to the XO."

"Okay Chief."

Chief Weber, now fully entrenched in his 'Navy box', changed into a working jumpsuit and headed for the Executive Officer's office. He did not expect to find him there, but he did expect to find the Admin Chief, Chad Nester would know where the XO was.

"Welcome back Chief," The ship's senior Yeoman said with a smirk as he looked up.

"And a fine Navy welcome it is, Chief," Fred replied in the same style.

"I guess you're here for the briefing?" Chief Nester pointed to the conference room door.

Fred hadn't heard about a briefing, he recovered quickly. "If I'm invited."

"How long have you been aboard?"

Fred looked at the clock on the wall, "About eight minutes."

Chad's eyebrows went up, "You know what happened?"

"I saw Petty Officer Nelson in the passageway when I came aboard. She filled me in. I haven't been down there yet."

"Your spaces took the most damage. I'm sure the XO will want you in on the briefing."

"The Quarterdeck Watch told me the XO wanted to see me as soon as I checked aboard."

"Through that door, Chief," Chad said. "Mind the Lions."

"Thanks," Fred said, referring to the warning. He walked over to the closed door of the conference room and knocked in the official manner, three times.

"Enter!" was heard from the other side of the door. He opened it and walked in. The Damage Control Officer was standing at the head of the table. "Oh, Chief Weber, I'm glad you're here. Please have a seat."

Fred moved to the table. He chose a place next to a fellow Chief and good friend. He took out his small green pocket notebook from the vest pocket of his coveralls, along with a pen. Using a "wheel book" was old school. He learned it early in his career and saw no reason to change. That pocket sized notebook was his "flash drive" memory for all things Navy.

It seemed that he had arrived just in time to get the meat of the meeting and miss the opening boilerplate. He listened carefully to the full damage report. It was serious. He knew he was facing a major challenge. The ship was in good condition. The damage was superficial from a structural point of view. That had to be verified with the shipyard engineers, but he knew the DC Chief. If Alex said the ship was fine, than the ship was fine.

The damage was to the equipment in the burned spaces and to the electrical power circuits that fed them. The electrical power had been "tagged out" and would not be reset until all the debris was cleared and repairs were made. Temporary lighting and power using long cords were being rigged as the meeting occurred.

The Executive Officer looked at Chief Weber, "Welcome back from leave, Chief. Have you been to your shops yet?"

"No, Sir, I was told you wanted to see me soonest, so I came right up here."

"I understand. I won't bother you with any specific questions for now. We'll talk again once you review the damage. In the mean time, what are your initial thoughts?"

"If protocols were followed we should be able to get this done in a reasonable time. My two concerns are safety and security. I want to make sure my crew is safe. Also, we absolutely need to ensure the security of the classified data that was out at the time of the fire. I will be leaving here to go take a look around. I'll know more once I look at things myself and talk a bit more with my LPO."

"Very well," the Exec said officially. "I've talked to the

yard and they are looking at adding a re-wire to the contract."

"We can do that ourselves, Sir," the Damage Control Chief said. "I'd rather it be done right than let these yard birds fu… foul it up."

"We'll make that decision when we have full access to the spaces." The XO looked around. "Any further questions or discussions?" The room was silent as an answer. "Then let's get to work."

Chapter Eighteen

"Used Cars, Marty."

"Marty, Bill Weber."

"Bill!" Marty responded like he just found a long lost friend. "You heard from your brother?"

"I got his Power of Attorney this morning."

"That's great news. I'll start the paperwork for the Charger. It will need your signature."

"I'll head over there this afternoon. I want to talk to a prospect about a listing."

"Something over my way? That's a stretch for you isn't it?"

"It would be if it were just a house. There are plenty of good realtors in Watertown. With the housing shortage in town, you folks don't need my kind of service. I'm looking at a farm near Castlewood. It is a typical arrangement for me. The kids are running the place and they want their mother to move to assisted living in town."

"Watertown realtors don't want it?"

"I want it," Bill said. "Huber Realty can get twice to three times the money in most cases, sometimes even more."

"I've heard you say that before; I can't figure out how," Marty said. "What do you do? Salt the ground with gold before a showing?"

Bill laughed. "Marty, what I have to offer is what I know. I know there are people in other parts of the country that are tired of the congestion and the high taxes. I advertise to them. You'll never see a hobby farm advertised by Huber Realty in South Dakota. At the same time, I'm the only South Dakota realtor advertising in the Marietta Daily Journal."

"The what?"

"The Marietta Daily Journal. Marietta is a suburb of Atlanta."

"I'm not sure I follow, but that doesn't matter. I'm here to sell cars and you're there to sell property. What time do you think you'll be by?"

"I'll stop on the way to Castlewood. Say about two?"

"I'll have everything ready. If you can, I'd like two

checks. One for the rental and the other for the car. My wife keeps the books. Sales and Rentals are two different accounts. I like to keep her happy."

"No problem, see you this afternoon."

"Okay - later."

The first thing Fred noticed was the smell. It was not his first shipboard fire. At least this time no one had been trapped and killed. The smell hit him twenty feet from the door. The passageway reeked of burned paper and melted plastic from equipment and electrical wiring. There was a hint of an odor from the mold that was already starting to grow inside the books and manuals. The door was open and there was a watch posted. "Chief, I'd say good morning, but…"

"Nobody was hurt or killed, Stan, so it is a good morning."

Chief Weber turned to his senior operator. "Give me the full rundown."

"It started during the mid watch. Petty Officer Kirtland was on watch. He told me later he thought he heard something like a firecracker. He said it sounded like it had come from the compartment on the other side of the bulkhead. Since he was on watch, he couldn't leave to check it out. Later in the watch he smelled smoke and reported it. When the fire alarm went off, he secured the compartment and activated the Halon bomb."

"Okay, so far so good."

"The fire team was here and waited for the heat in the compartment to subside. I guess they didn't wait long enough. When they opened the compartment, the fire flashed and engulfed the space. That's when they hit it with the hose."

"And that's when we lost control of the secure spaces?"

"Yes, Chief."

"All right, let's go inside and take a look. We'll see how bad it is."

The room was a mess. The walls were black from soot, the floors were still sticky with residue of water and some unidentifiable goo. There was a 500 watt Halogen work light in the center of the room. It flooded the space with a garish white light that had no corresponding color in the natural world. The light was bright, too bright. It made the shadows look unusually dark. The room looked like someone had adjusted the contrast too high. "If this was not a secure space it would be easy," Petty Officer Nelson said as she looked around. "Get a working party, and a bunch of shovels and send everything to the recycling center."

"We can't do that. Every scrap of paper has to be checked."

"I understand, Chief. I'm glad you got back right away. I didn't want to start without you here," Anne Nelson said candidly.

"You could have handled it Anne. You know your job."

"Not good enough for the Chief's board, though," she said with a hint of bitterness in her voice.

"It was your first time up before the promotion board Anne. It's very rare these days for someone to make Chief the first time up."

"I know, it's just that…"

At that moment Lieutenant (Junior Grade) Davis appeared at the door. He cleared his throat and lowered his voice half an octave. "Chief, from this moment forward everything in this space is to be considered classified."

"Already done, Lieutenant. Petty Officer Nelson made sure of that as soon as the DC party was out. The MAA has had a watch here since."

Chief Weber was used to young officers. He knew from experience just how to work with them. He would encourage, push and prod a bit to try to make good leaders of them. Most of the time it worked. LTJG Davis was no special case. He had been in the Navy for just over two years and had just recently been promoted from Ensign. He had been Chief Weber's 'boss' for the past ten months.

"We need to find a way to get that door secured, Chief."

"I'll take care of it, sir."

"Good," Davis nodded. "If you need me I'll be in the wardroom."

Fred knew his Lieutenant wanted to help, but he also knew the man would not put on coveralls and get dirty with the rest of the crew. He had to keep him out of the way. "There is one thing, sir."

"What is it Chief."

"While I'm sorting through the debris, can you review the instructions on handling damaged classified material? We could also use a secure space to sort this stuff out, sir. Can you see what you can find?"

"Of course, Chief," Davis said. "You carry on. I'll look into the instructions."

"Thank you, Sir."

Once the Lieutenant walked away Anne Nelson smiled and looked at her Chief. "You might as well have asked him to find two gallons of military bearing grease."

"It will keep him busy and let him feel important," Fred answered.

"And it will keep him out of our hair," Anne agreed.

"Exactly." Fred looked at his next in line, "Look, I need to run an errand. You gather up the crew and we'll meet on the mess deck in fifteen minutes."

"Okay Chief." They walked out together, receiving a nod from the bored junior sailor standing watch at the door.

"You were right, Frank. Look over there. Mary is sitting all alone," Mickie said. They were in the deep end of the pool holding on to the sides.

"It almost makes me feel sorry for her," Jessie said. Then added, "Almost."

"She did it to herself," Frank said firmly.

"Look, there goes Bobby Kline," Mickie said as they watched Bobby walk up to Mary. He stood over her and said something. She replied and he said something else.

Mary got up and shouted, "That's not true! You're a LIAR!" and ran from the pool to the locker room.

"Looks like she can't take what she gives," Frank said with a smile. This had worked out just like he wanted. He had Jeremy Finney out of the picture and Jessie Weber back in his life. The icing on the cake was turning Mary's lies back on her.

Frank saw Bobby walking their way. He didn't want to get involved with any more rumors. He looked at the two girls, "Race you to the other side."

"Go!" Jessie said and pushed off the wall.

Frank tried just hard enough to make sure he lost. When he got to the other side he put one arm on each side of Jessie and moved in to kiss her.

"Oh, why don't you guys get a room!" Mickie said and swam away.

Frank was undeterred. He moved closer to his conquest. Jessie dodged the kiss and put her head on his shoulder. Frank moved in tight. He could feel the heat of her body through the water. She molded herself into him as he held her close.

"Hey Frank!" the voice broke the spell and he pulled back to see Candy Parks walking in.

"Hey Candy," Frank said.

"Hey Jessie."

"Hey Candy. What are you doing here?"

"Even a farm girl likes to swim and cool off sometimes," Candy said as she sat down on the edge of the pool.

"You won't cool off like that," Frank said. "You need to get wet!" He grabbed her arm and pulled her into the water.

When she surfaced she looked at Frank. "Frankie Ogden, you are such a child!"

"Just trying to help," Frank smiled.

"Jessie, I'm glad you're here. You know Blaze, the gelding we board," Candy asked as a statement.

"Sure I know Blaze, he's a beautiful horse."

"He's for sale."

"Really?"

"The Traver's are moving to the Twin Cities and they can't take him."

"Why not?" Frank asked.

"I don't know, but they can't."

"So they want to sell him?" Jessie asked.

"That's what my dad told me. I thought of you. You have always wanted a horse."

"I do want a horse. I don't know if my mom and dad will go for it. I'll have to talk to them. Do you know how much they want?"

"I think they're taking offers."

"I'll talk to my parents."

"I hope you can talk them into it. We could go riding together."

"That would be great." Jessie was already picturing the whole thing in her mind; riding with Candy, learning how to barrel race, performing in horse shows. This was a dream come true.

"I'm going to have my license next month. You could ride with me from school and we could go to the stables together," Frank added. He just managed to get Jessie away from Jeremy Finney; he wasn't about to get shut out by horseflesh.

"You're right!" Jessie beamed, "that's perfect." She jumped up and spun to sit on the edge of the pool then stood up "I'm going home to talk to my mom."

Frank looked at her as she walked away. He had a feeling that maybe Blaze would win after all. He got out of the pool and walked into the locker room. He knew he could change and be at the exit door of the girls locker room before Jessie. He hurried anyway. He wanted to walk home with her. He wanted to make sure she had room for a horse and a boyfriend.

***

"Thanks for the use of the sawzall, Alex." Fred looked at the red metal box on the counter. He opened it and made sure there were blades in the storage compartment.

"Sure thing Fred, no problem. Just don't cut into any of my bulkheads," the Damage Control Chief said.

"I don't intend to."

"Just what is it you do intend to do?" the DC Chief asked. It was said he was a bit overprotective of 'his' ship. The opinion was correct.

"I want to cut off the bottom two inches of the door that leads from my shops to the passageway. That way we can have extension cords run underneath into the spaces and still keep the door locked.

"What about ventilation?" Alex asked. "Medical will never let you work in an enclosed space without ventilation."

"I thought of that. How about a floor dryer type blower? If it gets stuffy we can push air under the door. That is until you get the vents open and moving air again."

"That fancy cipher door lock of yours needs power. How

223

you gonna do that?"

"Nelson asked supply for a mechanical cipher lock. They said they'd get us one this morning."

"Don't go trying to install it yourself. No telling how you spooks would screw that up. I'll send one of my kids to do it. In fact," Alex took the saw off the counter, "I think I'll handle the cutting of the door too."

Now Fred had what he wanted. "I'd like to get that done soonest so we can secure the Master At Arms security watch."

"I'll have one of my kids there before you get back."

"Thanks, Alex, don't know what I'd do without you," Fred said with a bit of tongue in cheek.

"Probably cut a hole in the side of my ship," Alex traded barb for barb.

Fred smiled and nodded his goodbye. He walked down to the mess deck and found his whole team waiting. Walking over to the large urn, he poured himself a cup of coffee then moved back to where his people were assembled and sat down. "This is a mess. It's going to be a lot of work for the next few days but we'll see it through. I'm moving everyone onto days starting now. Both shifts will work together. This is the important part. Nothing, and I mean nothing, will be removed from our spaces until it is certified as unclassified by myself or Petty Officer Nelson. I want to start two piles. One pile will be for things we know are classified and another pile that may be classified."

"What about things that are not classified, Chief?" a crewmember asked.

"You will not be making that determination. Any thing you think is not classified goes in the may be classified pile until Nelson or I see it. I can't stress how important this is. Things get mixed together in an emergency, so we have to sort page by page."

"Yes Chief."

"The first thing that needs to be done is inventorying the safe. I'll do that with Lieutenant Davis. I've made arrangements with the communications Chief to store the undamaged material in the Comm Center. We'll do that first. Once we have the inventory from inside the safe reconciled, we will know better what was adrift when the fire started.

"Chief," Petty Officer Kirtland said, "the check out log was on the table next to the safe."

"It's not there now," Anne Nelson said. The irritating tone in her voice indicated her disapproval. The check out log was supposed to be kept inside the locked safe when it wasn't being used. Some of the hands had become complacent and had not been putting it away and leaving the safe open during their watch.

"I know," Kirkland said looking at the floor. "I always thought the computer log was the primary and the hard log was the back up."

"Now you know it's the other way around," Anne said.

"Actually they both back up each other," Fred said. "We don't have either now, what we do have is the inventory that is contained in the safe."

"But that won't show what was out," Kirkland said.

"By subtraction it will," Chief Weber said. "We can inventory the safe and we will know what was out by what is not in."

Kirkland brightened as the understanding of the statement hit him. "Yes… it will."

"That doesn't get you off the hook," Anne said. And the young sailor shrunk down in his seat again.

"All right. This is a job that has to be done by us. So let's get started." Chief Weber looked to his senior technician, "Nelson, I'm going to get the Lieutenant, you get the troops moving. Be ready to have two people transport the classified material to the Comm Center."

"Okay Chief," Anne Nelson nodded. She turned to the eight other people at the table, "Let's get started."

Fred walked out as head of the parade. He turned left as the rest turned right. He walked down to the CPO spaces and got another cup of coffee. The coffee in the CPO Mess tasted better than coffee in the crew's mess. He knew it was the same stuff, but it still tasted better from the drip pot rather than the urn. His office was severely damaged, not from the fire, but from the fire fighters. He decided he would use this space temporarily. He picked up the interphone and called the wardroom. Lieutenant Davis answered the phone.

"Lieutenant, Chief Weber. If you have some time I'd like

to inventory the classified document safe. I've made arrangements for the material to be secured in the Comm Center."

"Very well, Chief. I'll be right down."

I don't know, Jessie." June sensed that this was going to be one of 'those' conversations. She turned from the kitchen counter and moved to sit with her daughter at the table. "Owning a horse is a lot of responsibility. They need daily care."

"I know, but we have that figured out. Frank is getting his driver's license in a few weeks and I can ride with him to the stables."

"How would you get home?" June asked.

"Frank said he would bring me."

June was about to mention that Frank didn't have a car when she realized she was already losing the argument. It was not transportation, it was owning a horse that was the problem. Jessie already deflected the primary objection and was working her on the smaller issues. She took a mental step back. "Jessie, you and your brother don't even take care of Freckles. I do the feeding and your dad does the picking up in the back yard. How are you going to take care of a horse?"

"A horse is different."

"You're right it's different. It is much more work."

"I can do it, I'm almost fourteen."

"Almost is quite a stretch. I don't think it's practical. A horse will take all of your time. You'll have no time for anything else at school. I thought you wanted to try out for cheerleading?"

"I do. I can do both."

"I don't believe you can." June could read the build up of frustration in her daughter's face. She had to stop and defuse this conversation before it blew up. "Look, this is not a conversation we can have alone. Your dad needs to be in on this too. After all, someone has to pay for the horse and for the board. Let's put this whole thing on hold until after supper."

Jessie thought about it. She was hoping she could get one of her parents on her side before they sat down together. She couldn't work Mom, so now she had to work her dad. Mom had said after supper. That gave her time to talk to Dad alone. "Okay."

"I'm making chocolate chip cookies, you want to help?"

Jessie didn't want to help, but she didn't want to do anything to alienate her mom, so she agreed. They worked together, June read the instructions from the chip package and Jessie mixed the ingredients. Once the first batch was in the oven, she escaped to her room.

Mickie was sympathetic to her plight, they texted back and forth, playing out different ways to bring Jessie's dad onto her side. She knew if Dad would go for it, Mom would back off. She also knew if dad saw how much Mom was against the idea, she had no chance of winning her father over. She had to get her father's attention before Mom did.

In a desperate move she called her dad's cell phone. He answered right away. "Hi peanut! What's cookin'?"

"I have some great news!" Jessie said, using her most excited voice.

"If it's about the horse, I already know about it. Your mother said we will sit down and talk about it after supper."

Jessie was surprised, it seemed that her mother got to Dad first. "That's not fair!"

"What's not fair?"

"You already know her side and you don't know mine."

"I didn't know there were any sides. Your mother called me and told me that there is a horse for sale at the Parks farm. She said you wanted to sit down with us after supper and talk about the possibility of getting it."

Jessie panicked. She had had spoken too soon. Her mom had not mentioned her feelings about the horse. Jessie, on the other hand had just done it for her. She had to think and think fast. What could she say. "Mom said we had to all discuss it together, but I thought I could talk to you first."

"Trying to work the room?" Bill asked.

"What?"

"Nothing," Bill chuckled. "I'll be home by five thirty. Your mom told me that she would have supper on the table at six. Let's schedule our meeting for seven after the dishes are done."

"So we can all discuss this together?" Jessie smelled a set

227

up.

"That's right. We're a family, that's what we do," Bill affirmed. "What we also do is accept the agreement the family chooses."

"That's not fair!"

"What's not fair. We are going to talk about it and then decide what's best. What's not fair about that?"

"You have two votes and I only have one."

"Nobody's voting. We will talk and come to an agreement. Now, if you want me to have an informed opinion on you getting a horse I have to make some calls. I need to know what this costs. Do you know how much they want for the horse?"

Jessie saw a glimmer of hope. If Dad was looking into costs, then he wasn't rejecting the idea out right. "Candy says they are taking offers."

"That doesn't help," Bill said. "I'll call around and see what horses sell for. We'll talk about this after supper tonight, all right?"

"Okay Daddy," Jessie said in her cutest little girl voice. "I'll wait for tonight."

Bill knew he wasn't going to let Jessie get a horse. He and June had discussed it several times during the year they had been in Helen. Jessie saw the glamor of the horse shows and the barrel racing. She saw the long rides along the wide right of ways and down the country roads. She didn't see the mucking out of the stalls, the constant care and visits from the vet and farrier. She was not nearly old enough to be responsible for a horse.

Yet, to be fair, he would call around and find out what horse flesh sold for and what the monthly maintenance would be like. When they met later, he would have his facts ready. Unfortunately, Bill was still under the delusion that an argument, based on facts and logic, would satisfy a teenage girl. He looked at his phone and selected the listing for his partner at Huber Realty.

Laura Huber, partner and surviving wife and founder of Huber Realty answered on the third ring, "Hi Bill."

"Good afternoon Laura, do you have a minute to talk?"

"I will, give me about twenty seconds." Bill could hear the phone rustling. He knew she had placed it in her pocket. It wasn't quite twenty seconds, it was more like thirty when he heard. "That puts me three strokes ahead." The rustling got louder. "Okay, Bill," Laura said. "What can I do for you?"

"I need an expert on horses."

"What kind of expert?"

"Jessie is all gaga over a gelding that is for sale. The owner is taking offers, I have no clue about the horse market."

"You're thinking about getting Jessie get a horse?"

"Actually I'm looking for reasons not to get a horse. I'm hoping it is too much money."

"How old is the horse?"

"I don't know."

"Where is it?"

"At the Parks Stables near Helen."

"I know a man in Basford Corners who deals in horses. I can talk to him. He'll give you an idea of the costs."

"Costs?"

"Costs," Laura repeated. "It goes along the lines of a free puppy. There's no such thing. You have the monthly board and feed etc. Bobby can go look at it and give you an idea of the animal's value and the expenses you'll face."

"I hate to ask anyone to go out of the way just to provide me ammunition to say no."

"Bobby won't mind. He's in the business. He may just buy the thing himself and solve your problem."

"I should be so lucky," Bill chuckled. He changed the subject. "I could hear through the phone you're winning. Anybody I know?"

"Sure. I'm here with the Kent City Council. I'm trying to talk them into a new trailer park ordnance."

"Actually she's just taking us to the cleaners!" a voice Bill knew as familiar shouted toward the phone.

Bill laughed. "Tell Oscar he can afford it." Bill switched back, "Thanks Laura. I'll look forward to hearing from your friend Bobby."

"Robert Luts Sales," Laura told him the official name.

"I'll watch for the call. Thanks."

229

Chapter Nineteen

"You know, Chief, this safe will have to be re-certified to house classified material."

"I'm aware of that, Sir." Chief Weber agreed. "It's one of the two reasons we are inventorying and removing the material."

"What's the other one?"

"I want to see what's here. Once we know what is here we will know what was adrift during the fire."

"I see," the Lieutenant said. "Where is the check out log?"

"The check out log was destroyed in the fire," Chief Weber answered without giving any further detail.

Herman Davis had learned, that when working with Chief Weber, not to ask questions if he didn't want to know the answer. There was a reason the log was destroyed, but if he found out that a violation had occurred, he would have to act. He knew his Chief. He knew if his Chief wanted an official response to a violation, he would be informed. He also knew his Chief would not hang him out to dry. "We will have to work without it."

"Yes Sir," Fred agreed.

"How can we account for the validity of the safe's inventory?"

"The watch had just changed an hour before. The safe inventory was completed at that time, sir. That's noted here in the inventory log," Fred pointed. "Our electronic log for the door cipher lock will show that the space was secured and no one entered or left between the inventory and the fire. That means anything not in the safe right now was out. But that also means nothing left here prior to the fire. Petty Officer Kirkland hit the Halon fire suppression system and secured the door behind him. All the material had to be here."

"That makes sense," the Lieutenant agreed, "but you are going to have to write that up as convincingly as you just told me. The JAG investigation will be all over this security breech. You were on leave, Chief. They'll be after my neck."

"I'll write up the brief and get it to you later today."

"Very well." Lieutenant Davis picked up the inventory

log, "I'll read it off, you check it."

"Yes, sir."

Bill Weber looked at his phone. The caller ID read Luts Sales. He answered, "Good afternoon, this is Bill Weber."

"Mr. Weber? This is Bobby Luts. Laura Huber called and told me you are interested in buying a horse and needed an appraisal."

"Good afternoon Mr. Luts. She was close. I have a thirteen year old daughter who is interested in me buying a horse."

"I understand," Bobby chuckled. "If it were not for teenage girls I might not have a business. Where is the horse?"

"It is at the Parks Stables, near Helen."

"I know Brad Parks, Bill. He runs a good outfit. If the horse is there, it's been well taken care of."

"That's good to know." Bill shifted the conversation, "Bobby, I want you to understand, I do not want to get this horse."

"You don't want the horse?"

"No."

"Then why are you talking to me?"

"I'm looking for reasons not to get this horse that I can present to my daughter. I know they are time consuming, more than she might think. I'm half hoping I can't afford it. How much do horses sell for in South Dakota?"

"That's like asking how much cars sell for in South Dakota," Bobby replied. "How old is the horse you are trying not to buy?"

"I don't know. All Jessie told me was that it was a gelding."

"I see." There was a pause. "Bill, let me call Brad Parks and see about the horse. Once I know more about the animal, I can start forming an estimate of its value."

"That would be great," Bill answered. "Thank you."

"Don't thank me yet. I think every teenage farm girl should have a horse."

"Jessie's no farm girl. We moved here a year ago from the east coast. We have a house in Helen now."

"In Helen?"

"That's right."

"So you won't be boarding the horse yourself." Bobby asked as a statement.

"No, I would most likely leave it right where it is."

"I see. Well that's a horse of a different color - sorry inside joke."

"I don't mind a bit of stable humor," Bill fired back. "You see my problem. Jeooie would have to be at the stable almost every day. She would have no time for anything else."

"I'm afraid you are right. She might be too young. If she was fifteen and driving, I would argue the point. But right now, Bill, with not being able to board the horse at home, it might be too much for a thirteen year old girl."

"That's what I'm thinking."

"Let me do this. I'll talk with Brad Parks, find out about the horse and I'll also ask about board and feed costs."

"Thanks, Bobby." Bill meant it. "I wouldn't even know the right questions to ask."

"That's why you have me," Bobby said with a chuckle. "I'll do some homework and get back to you in a bit."

"Great, thank you. Good bye"

"See Ya."

"Fred, I'm not too excited about you folks working in this enclosed space," Chief Hospital Corpsman James McNiel said standing at the door looking into the water soaked, soot laden room. "I can almost hear the black mold growing in this mess."

"I think I have an answer that will allow you to sign off, Jim." Fred nodded to a young sailor arriving with a Sawzall. "This Petty officer is going to cut the bottom two inches off the door."

"That's not enough. The ventilation system is secured in this space. You'll have no airflow."

"How about if we have a squirrel cage fan outside blowing air under the door?"

"One of those floor drier fans?"

"Exactly." Fred nodded, then added, "It's only temporary until DC gets the ventilation back on line."

Chief James McNiel had a nervous habit of stroking the

beard he didn't have when he was trying to make a decision. "Make that cut three inches high and I'll sign off on it."

"Thanks Jim."

"I want to be able to check the air in here every four hours."

"No problem. As long as your Corpsmen have the proper security clearance, they can check as often as they like."

"Now you're being unreasonable, Chief. You know my people don't have the kind of clearances required for these spaces."

"I know," Fred smiled. "Here's what we'll do. Your corpsman can come to the door, we'll take the sniffer inside and get the sample and bring it back out. Then you can have it tested. Will that work?"

"That'll work but it's stupid. If my Corpsman can see you taking a sample than they can see everything else."

"Yup," Fred agreed.

"I'll never understand you spooks. Okay, do it your way, but don't close that door until you have the bottom cut and the fan set up."

"You got it."

Bill hung up from Bobby just as he pulled into Marty's parking lot. He found Marty in his office talking with a customer. Marty made eye contact and held up his hand indicating he would be about five more minutes. Bill decided to walk around outside to give Marty and the young couple some privacy. He looked at other big SUV's on the lot. Marty had a two year old Suburban that was slightly larger than his Escalade. He also had an Expedition. Bill found himself being drawn to a Buick Enclave. He liked the lines and the look of the car. What he didn't like was the stigma of the Buick name. When he lived back east, only old people drove Buicks. He decided he couldn't get past that so he walked back to the Expedition. The thing was larger then his Escalade, it was almost too large.

He didn't notice Marty walking up behind him. "Use that old wreck of a Caddy for a trade and I can get you into that Enclave for a song."

Bill turned. "No thanks. I'm not old enough to drive a

233

Buick."

"That Enclave ain't no old man's car, Bill. Drive it around and you'll see what I mean. You're going down to Castlewood from here? Take that Enclave and you'll gladly trade that Caddy truck of yours when you get back."

"That's tempting, Marty, but that's not why I'm here."

"I know, but you think about it for a bit while we tend to your brother's car." He pointed toward his office, "I've got Fred's paperwork ready, let's go inside."

Bill and Marty quickly went through the required paperwork. As Marty had requested, Bill wrote two checks; one for the car rental and the other for the purchase price. Marty gave Bill the title for the Charger and they walked out together. "You know, when we sell a car, we wash it before delivery."

"That's going to be hard to do. It's parked in a friend's barn."

"I figure I owe you a car wash just the same." Marty hesitated, he made it look like he was thinking. "I've got an idea, you leave that Caddy with me and take the Enclave to your appointment. When you get back I'll have the Escalade clean as a whistle."

"You don't miss a trick, do you Marty?"

"I try not to." Marty chuckled, then got serious, "Look, Bill, I know you and I know what you like. I know you'll like that Enclave if I can just get you to drive it. So, humor me, take the Enclave to Castlewood and let me wash your Caddy."

"All right." Bill gave in to the pressure. "Let me just get some things that I'll need."

"You got a deal," Marty said.

"Not yet we don't," Bill retorted.

After gathering his briefcase and other essentials from the Escalade, Bill climbed in and started the Enclave. As he pulled out into traffic he noticed the car had a better response than his Cadillac SUV. The handling seemed crisper, "grippier" he thought. As he left Watertown and drove down the highway toward his Castlewood appointment, he noticed the car was quieter too. The streamlined design seemed to reduce the wind noise. He had to admit, it was nice, but, it was still a Buick.

"I've got the download on the cipher lock, Chief. It says just what Kirkland said. The door was not opened from change of watch until he opened it for the fire."

"Thanks, Anne," Chief Weber answered. "Now that it's confirmed, I can get to the report."

"What are we going to do about the check out log violation?" Weber's senior watch stander asked. "We can't just let it go."

"We could," Fred answered. "I'm sure he will never make that mistake again."

"But it was just laziness that caused it. The procedure is to put the check out log back in the safe and lock it. I know what he did, he left the safe open and when he had to evacuate, he simply slammed the safe shut and left the check out log on the desk. He didn't follow procedure."

"And if we make big deal about it, it will cost him a stripe at the very least. At the extreme end it could cost him prison time. Do you want to see that?"

"Well, no Chief, but…"

"But nothing. If this gets to the Captain by official channels I'll have little control over it. It could go to the max. The Skipper could throw the book at him just to save his own neck. I'd like to avoid that."

"I understated, but what do we do?'

"To start with, every job that requires getting filthy is his. Make sure he knows that he is paying for his mistake. I will also talk to him about volunteering to clean some of the ship's voids. He is, until further notice, our go to guy on all working parties and crap jobs. Once I'm gone, you can decide when to slack off'.

"So we'll work the laziness out of him?"

"We'll try," Fred agreed. "At the very least, he'll realize that laziness can be painful."

"So, how are you going to get your dad to go for it?" Mickie asked. They were sitting on Mickie's bed, each with a controller in her hand. The game went on while they double tasked.

"I don't know," Jessie answered, her thumbs moving at light speed. "He said we would all talk about it after supper. I know mom isn't for it, but I can still work on Dad before supper."

"How are you going to get to the stable every day?"

"Frank said he'd drive me and take me home," Jessie said. "He's taking care of it."

"Are you still going to go out with Frank?"

"Sure, he saved me from a life of hell because of that rumor."

"But he turned on you last year, remember. Just when you thought you had a good thing he took someone else to the dance."

"He apologized for that."

"Really…" Mickie said skeptically.

"No, really, he did. He told me it was the biggest mistake of his life."

"You should do the same thing to him. Show him how it feels."

"I can't," Jessie said.

"Why not?"

"Because I like him and I don't want to hurt him."

"Watch that clown, he has the scepter." Mickie said, and they turned their attention back to the game.

It was a full ten minutes before either one talked again. This time it was Jessie that started, "I think my dad will let me get the horse if I tell him I don't want to go out for cheerleading."

"What does that have to do with it?"

"He thinks having to take care of a horse and cheerleading is too much," Jessie explained. "If I tell him that I only want the horse, then maybe he'll go for it."

"But you wanted to play in the band, too," Mickie pointed out.

"I can't be in the band and be a cheerleader. So that's already over."

"What about cooking club? You said you would go with me to that." Mickie was realizing that her best friend having a horse would push her aside. Now she had to try to get her off the idea.

"I forgot about cooking club," Jessie admitted. "I guess I won't be able to do it."

236

"You promised."

"I didn't promise, I just said." Jessie was getting defensive.

Mickie put the game on pause. "Okay." She took a deep breath. "Let's look at this whole thing. If you have a horse, you have to be there every day to take care of it. You have to let it know you are the owner and give it a chance to get to know you. That takes a lot of time. You won't be able to do anything else. You'll smell like horses all the time like Mary does."

"Mary smells like horses because she never takes a bath," Jessie fired back.

"You might be right, but only a cowboy would like a girl that stinks of horse all the time."

"Now you're being stupid."

"No, I'm not." Mickie turned and looked Jessie in the eye for emphasis. "What about Frank?"

"What about Frank? I'll see him every day. He's going to drive me to the stable and bring me home."

"What's he going to do while you're out riding? Sit in the car?"

"I don't know. I hadn't thought of that, but I know he'll wait for me."

"Until he gets bored with a girlfriend who is in love with a horse."

"What do you mean?"

Mickie saw she had the advantage, she moved in. "Frank doesn't have a horse. I have a feeling he doesn't even like horses that much. He likes you and you like horses. That's okay. But soon enough he's going to get bored sitting around a stable waiting for you to finish playing with your horse. He'll find someone else."

"He wouldn't!"

"He will." Mickie pressed home. "My mom says they're all alike, when they get bored, they bolt."

"That's Not True!"

"It is and you know it." Mickie drove home the point. "If you want to keep Frank, you have to at least wait a while before getting a horse. You can't have both, not now. Maybe when you have a car and can get back and forth yourself…"

"That's almost two years away!" Jessie was trying to cling to any hope, but she knew Mickie was right.

"It might work then," Mickie said. "You could still have Frank without having to drag him to the stables each day. "And," she paused for emphasis, "it will give you two years to talk Frank into getting a horse too."

"I hadn't thought of that. If Frank had a horse it would solve everything."

"There you are." Mickie smiled, mission accomplished.

"So, what do you think?" Marty met Bill as he pulled up in front of the used car dealer's showroom.

"You're right, it's a great car."

"Let's go inside and talk some numbers. You can drive it home today." He turned toward the office door.

"Not so fast Marty." Bill held his ground.

"This is the perfect car for you, Bill. It's great for work and for family."

"I agree, almost."

Marty didn't say anything. He didn't want to leave an opening.

Bill filled the void. "It's a Buick."

"Buicks are fine automobiles, on par with your Cadillac," Marty replied. Then he added, "Look, it's quieter, easier to handle and gets better gas mileage. I know you like the lines, you should take it home for the night and show June."

"Marty, it's a Buick," Bill repeated. "June would laugh me right out of the driveway."

"So that's your only argument?"

"That's it."

Marty was quiet for a moment which made Bill nervous. Whenever that happened he knew Marty thought he had the advantage. "I got something in the works that might just trip your trigger."

Bill took the bait. "What is that?"

"I got a two year old Caddy SRX comin' in next week. They are the same body style. The one I got comin' in is a real doll. Only twenty two thousand miles. It's owned by the mother of my accountant."

"Why are they selling it?"

238

"He doesn't want her driving anymore," Marty said. "I'm telling ya, this is a great car. It's been garage kept and has never been out in the snow. You trade that Escalade and I can put you in it for just over pocket change."

Bill saw the hook, he dodged it, at least for now. "I'll tell you what, Marty, you get that car and I'll look at it."

"It's a deal."

Bill laughed, "I hate it when you say that."

"Have a good one," Marty said with a soft laugh.

"You too," Bill replied automatically. On the way back through Kent he stopped in the office to drop off the listing agreement he had and to make arrangements for the virtual tour. It was a good property, the kind that was perfectly suited for Bill's realty office. Eighteen acres with a house, a barn and a machine shed. The local realtor told the owner it would never sell over sixty thousand because it was too far out from any town. Bill looked at the property and saw it quite differently. The farm was within forty five minutes of two major towns. Watertown to the north and Brookings to the south. Brookings was a college town and had all the excitement that came with a youthful population. His clients were mostly from out of state. They would find the distance and rural setting a plus rather than a minus.

Walking out of the office door, he looked at his Escalade. He kept it in good condition but it had lost it's 'new' look. He needed to keep a look of success as a matter of advertising. Presentation was everything, he reminded himself. If he looked poor, his client wouldn't respect his opinion. Buying that almost new SRX from Marty is a business investment, not a car. Now all he had to do was convince June. Not today, he had some time to warm her to the idea. He called before leaving town and was asked to bring home two loaves of bread and a gallon of milk.

Bill's phone played the tune that meant he had a generic phone call. He looked at the screen and saw it was Bobby Luts. "Good afternoon, this is Bill Weber," he answered officially.

"Bill, good afternoon. Bobby Luts. Did I understand you did not want that gelding?"

"That's right, why? Is there something wrong with it?"

"It's no longer for sale."

"That's actually good news."

"I had a chance to go by Brad Park's place this afternoon. I had business down that way. He told me an offer had been accepted on the animal."

"Good, that means I can kick this can down the road for a while longer. Just to satisfy my curiosity what does it cost to board a horse?"

"That's another 'how high is up' type question. The board runs from as low as two hundred to four hundred a month. Brad is right in the middle with a rate between two fifty and three hundred depending on how much the owner contributes to the work."

"Three hundred," Bill repeated. "Thanks, Bobby, for looking into this for me."

"Just remember me when you're ready to buy."

"I'll do that."

"Have a good day then."

"You too," Bill said, then put the phone away. He was thinking about the parting comment, 'Just remember me when you're ready to buy.' It came so natural to Bobby. How many times had he wanted to say something similar to someone who was house shopping. It always felt like it was pushy, yet when Bobby did it, it seemed natural. He had to think about that.

Bill looked down at the dash, the 'Service Engine Soon' light was on. He didn't remember that being on before. The last time that happened it was an oxygen sensor. He called Mike Finney and told him about it.

"How is the car running?"

"It seems okay."

"All right," Mike answered, "bring it by and I'll check the code."

Bill pulled into the driveway after a stop at Mike's Garage. The code was for a sensor. Mike said the car was drivable but the sensor should be changed to keep the engine running efficiently. Bill accepted his opinion but still thought the engine felt rough when he pulled it into the garage.

The door to the mudroom opened and Freckles bounded out to greet his senior owner. The dog had bonded with Cory but was always happy to greet Bill at the car. Bill opened the door and said "Down!" to remind the dog not to jump. Then he bent over, "How you doin' fella? You take care of my family today?"

Freckles answered with a head rub and a wagging tail.

Bill grabbed his briefcase, the bread and the milk, along with a bouquet of flowers and walked toward the door leading into the house. He knew June was nearby, because she had let Freckles out. He opened the door, "June?"

"In the kitchen."

Bill saw his wife's back was turned. He had left his briefcase in the mud / laundry room and placed the milk and bread on the kitchen table. Then he walked over and held the flowers in front of his wife.

"Aren't they pretty." she said as she took them. She turned around and kissed her husband hello. "What's the occasion?"

"Nothing special, I saw them in the grocery store. It was an impulse buy."

"Was there a line at the store?"

"No, why?

"It took you a while to get home."

"I had to stop at Mike's," Bill explained. "The Escalade is acting up again."

"What happened?"

"Another sensor went out."

"Another sensor?" June sensed something more than a sensor was wrong, but wasn't quite sure what her husband was up to - yet.

"This time it was the MAP sensor."

"For the GPS?"

"No, something to do with the fuel and the air pressure. Mike explained it, but it was over my head. It has to do with engine efficiency, he said."

"Did he change it?"

"No, he has to order one," Bill said.

"Is it expensive?"

"About eighty dollars, plus his labor."

"That's not bad."

Bill let it go for now. "Where's Jessie?"

241

"I think she's with Mickie."

"That's odd. I thought I knew my daughter. I figured she'd be here trying to butter me up before our conversation tonight."

"Speaking of that conversation, what are we going to do? I don't want her getting a horse," June said as she trimmed and arranged the flowers.

"Neither do I," Bill agreed. "It's moot anyway. At least for now. The horse she wanted has been sold."

"Already? How do you know?"

"Laura Huber knows a horse broker, she gave me his number. He looked into it for me and found the horse had already been sold."

"Well that makes it easier."

"I know," Bill conceded. "This horse thing had a good chance to build up to a battle royal; now it can just be a generic conversation. If she ever gets home."

"She'll be home by six thirty. I told her not to miss supper."

Bill stood up, "I'm going to get a shower."

"Okay."

Bill arrived back in the kitchen just in time to help Cory reach the things he needed to set the table. "Here you go," Bill said as he handed the dishes to his seven year old 'mini me'.

Cory took the plates to the table and placed one in front of each chair. "The swing at Jeffery's broke today."

"Broke? How?" June remembered last year when one of the steel swings had hit Cory on the head and opened a gash. It was right after they had moved to Helen.

"We were swinging together, trying to see who could get higher and the bars left the ground. Jeffrey's mom stopped us and said we couldn't use it anymore."

"Maybe they can fix it," Bill said.

"Jeffrey's mom called it a time bomb," Cory added. "We're not allowed to go on it."

"Here are the glasses," Bill said. He was thinking maybe he should look into a new play set for his son. He didn't mention it out loud.

The door from the garage to the mud room opened and

closed. Jessie walked into the kitchen. "Hi peanut," Bill said, "how was your day?"

"Fine," she answered and kept walking through the kitchen and toward her bedroom.

Bill was even more confused. Normally when she wanted something, she would be all over him. Something wasn't right. He decided to find out. "Hold on Jessie."

"What?"

"Are you okay?"

"I'm fine, Dad." Jessie stood there looking at her father. "Why?"

"I thought you wanted to talk," Bill said.

"It doesn't matter now."

"So, you know they sold the horse."

Jessie's eyes got wide, "They did?"

"I heard today that the horse was already sold."

Jessie stood there silent for about four seconds. "That's okay, I don't want a horse right now anyway."

"You don't?" June jumped in. "Earlier today you wanted nothing else."

"I know, but I thought about it." Jessie's phone buzzed. She looked at it. "Can I go?"

"Sure, but supper is almost ready."

"Okay." Jessie turned and walked toward her room.

Bill stood there looking at the spot where his daughter had been standing. After about three seconds he turned to June, "Do you have any idea what just happened?"

June laughed, "Not a clue."

"I guess we're not getting a horse."

"Guess not."

Chapter Twenty

"I'm sorry Chief Weber, our banquet rooms are booked for that afternoon. Have you tried the Officer's Club?"

"I'd sooner use the local bagnio," Chief Weber said to the Enlisted Club manager.

"The local what?"

"Never mind," Fred said with a chuckle. He wasn't about to tell the nice young voice at the other end of the conversation that a bagnio was another word for bordello. "The 'O' Club will not do."

"How about the golf course? They have a party room."

"That might work. Thanks."

"Anytime Chief. Good luck with your retirement."

"Thanks again, bye."

"Good bye to you."

There was a loud three knocks on the passageway door. Rather then hollering 'Enter!' Chief Weber stood and opened the door. He saw one of 'his' men standing there. "What is it?"

"Mr. Davis would like to see you in your office, Chief."

"He sent you?"

"Yes Chief."

Wondering why his Lieutenant didn't call, he put away the notes on his retirement ceremony and after party. He looked at the young man standing there nervously. He smiled, "Lead on Petty Officer Kirkland!"

Fred Weber followed Kirkland to the work spaces. When they arrived there, the young sailor stepped aside to allow his Chief to enter first. Fred entered the almost empty room that had once been filled with the tools of his trade. On the other side of the room was a small cubicle known as the Chief's office. He walked in and found Lieutenant Davis sitting at an old beat up desk. He looked up as Fred entered the room. "Chief, where did you get this desk?"

"Property Salvage," Fred answered.

"This desk is not authorized for secure spaces. It hasn't been certified," the Lieutenant said with authority.

"I'm aware of that, Sir."

"So why is it in here?"

"So you don't have to sit on the floor, Sir."

"I.. Ah…."

"Mr. Davis, since we have removed the debris, and all the classified material from our safes are now being stored in Communications, this is hardly a secure space. None the less, if you look at the instructions for office furniture, you will see I have complied with them to the letter. That included removing the lock mechanism from the desk drawers," he pointed.

"You know supply is ordering new furniture for this space."

"I'm aware of that, sir. I'm also aware of how long that might take. I'd like to have this shop up and running as soon as the new paint dries and power is restored. I don't want to wait for Navy supply and its slowly grinding wheels."

"Chief, there are corners that shouldn't be cut."

"Yessir," Fred used the common slang, "but putting some salvaged tables and chairs in here to use as work stations will get us going again, at least for the sake of training. I think we're within the margin of safety. Security will be maintained even if log books are kept on used furniture."

The twenty four and half year old Lieutenant Junior Grade looked at his forty one year old Chief Petty Officer, nodded and said in his official half octave lower voice, "Make it so, Chief."

Chief Weber just as seriously answered "Aye Aye Sir."

With that, Herman Davis turned and left the area, leaving a wake of self importance behind.

"Chief, George and I are going to see to the last of the property disposal. Do you want to come along?"

"Anne, you are the Leading Petty Officer. If I had to continually look over your shoulder, you would not be my Leading Petty Officer. You go ahead and finish up over there, I've seen that place enough."

"Okay Chief."

"Once you're done, turn the troops loose for the day."

Anne smiled, "You got it!" then she stopped, "What about Kirkland?"

"He can stay and finish prepping these bulkheads for

paint."

Just as Anne was walking out, DCC (Damage Control Chief) Alex Broden walked up to the door. He was with EMC (Electrician's Mate Chief) Howard Tuthill. Alex held the door from closing. "Permission to enter?" he asked formally.

"Sure, Alex, come in. There's nothing classified left in here. It's an open space, for now."

"Good, because Howard and I want to get to work."

"You're going to do the rewire?"

"My shop is," Howard answered.

"How'd you pull that off. I thought the yardbirds would get the contract."

"It's the word contract that did the trick. The Yard wanted to make an assessment and then present their findings to the yard staff so they could work out a contract and work order. Then they would put the repair on the schedule."

"Sounds like it could take months," Fred nodded.

"Weeks at least," Alex agreed.

"We talked to the XO. Harold simply explained to him that the damage was wiring and he had a whole shop of people at his disposal who were trained to do wiring. We told him we would handle the job and have the spaces up and running before the yard could even begin to wipe their butt with their assessment." He used air quotes on the word "assessment".

"He bought it?"

"The Skipper did, at least to a point. He wants our evaluation on the work needed and the time involved."

"That's why we're here," Alex said.

"Well, don't let me get in your way. I have the fans blowing to dry things out the rest of the way. We'll be painting in here tomorrow, but I gave the kids liberty for the rest of the day. All but Petty Officer Kirkland here," Fred pointed. "He was gracious enough to volunteer to stay and finish the paint prep and taping. He'll stay out of your way and you can have full run of the place."

"You're making this too easy," Howard said.

"I aim to please."

"Kirkland, this space is still listed as a secure space. That means one of us has to be here as an escort. You continue to do what needs to be done here to get ready for tomorrow.

Once these two Chiefs are done in here, you can secure too."

"Okay Chief."

Fred left the ship and drove over to the golf course. He had never seen their banquet room so he decided to take a look for himself. Norfolk was one of the Navy's oldest facilities still in operation; it was a mix of old and new. He wanted to make sure the room was not some relic from the past. He also wanted to stop by the Navy lodge, the on-base motel, and book a room for Julie.

The dates and times for his official retirement ceremony had been set. He was ready to get this part of his life done and move to the next. All that was left was to turn over the job to his relief and march through the ceremonial bullets to civilian life.

Vacation Bible School was something Bill and June had insisted on. Jessie resisted but eventually gave in. The Helen United Church had held its VBS early the previous year so the Weber kids had missed it. This year because of scheduling conflicts the church board had decided on August for the week long event. Though it was the first VBS for Jessie, it was not as traumatic as the first day of public school. She knew everyone and everyone knew her. She was still the new kid from back east, but she was accepted as a part of the community.

She walked together with Mickie, just as they did for the normal school year. Jessie kept watching the road leading to the church. "What are you looking for?"

"Frank's mom's car."

"You going to meet Frank?" Mickie asked.

"I want to see him before we have to go in," Jessie replied.

"I'll meet you in the classroom," Mickie said.

"Don't you like Frank anymore?"

"He's your boyfriend, I want one for me."

"Who?"

"Cody Bockler."

"Cody Bockler?"

"He's cute and I like him."

Jessie shrugged, "All right, see you inside." Jessie walked

to the front parking lot.

June pulled up in her minivan about a block behind Cory. After a long conversation between parents and children they had decided that Jeffery and Cory could walk together to the Vacation Bible School. Since it was the first day, June wanted to make sure they didn't get side tracked along the way. She was no longer concerned for her son's safety, not in Helen. It was more curiosity. She wanted to see the route they took and how long it took them.

The route was fairly direct. They only had to walk two and half blocks to the church and there was little to distract them. They arrived with plenty of time to spare. June turned and drove back to the house. Bill was still at home. She figured there was an even chance that Bill was either busy getting dressed or playing with the baby.

June had a lot to think about. She had an appointment at one that afternoon in Aberdeen to meet her education counselor. Frances Alden would be in the St. Agnes's Aberdeen HR office this week. Francis and June had been talking and working out details over the phone. Now it was time to finalize the learning schedule. They both decided meeting in person was long overdue.

June had to get back home and relieve Bill so he could get to work. Then she had to get herself and baby Mason dressed, take Mason to Sarah Ogden's and drive the hour plus to Aberdeen. It was going to be tight.

She noticed on the last turn the car was trying to pull to the right. She stopped, then started again. It was, in fact, pulling. "No, I can't have car trouble today," she said to the windshield. As she drove the last block she realized it was getting worse. She pulled into her driveway and walked into the house to find her husband sitting at the kitchen table holding Mason's bottle. Mason, oblivious to his mother's arrival, continued working on his snack. "Bill, there's something wrong with my car."

"What's it doing?"

"It was okay when I left here, but on the way back it started pulling to the right."

"I'll take a look, but we'll most likely have to call Mike."

248

"I have that appointment with Francis Aldon at one today. I barely have time as it is."

"June, it's only eight o'clock."

Rather than trying to explain to her husband why taking care of Mason, giving him a bath and getting him ready to go to Sarah's plus getting a shower and getting ready herself would take most of her morning, she simple said, "Can you look at it, please."

Bill didn't understand her frustration. Rather than push the issue, it was easier to go look at the car. "Sure."

"I'll take the bottle."

Bill got up and handed the bottle to June. Mason was in mid suckle when the bottle disappeared from his mouth. He started to screw up his face and let out a cry of protest when June brought it back to position. All was right in baby Mason's world once again.

It was under a minute when Bill walked back into the room. "You have a flat tire on the front right."

"That would explain it," June said.

"I'll change it and put on the spare."

"I don't want to go all the way up to Aberdeen without a spare tire."

"I'll drop the flat at Mike's to fix or replace it on my way out. You go by there on your way out of town and let him put it back on"

"Thanks, Bill." The delay at Mike's would only be ten minutes or so. She could live with that.

Bill, as the dutiful husband, changed the tire and put the flat in his Escalade. Once done, he returned to the house for a change from work clothes to going to work clothes. June in the meantime had finished feeding Mason. She had him in the kitchen sink for his bath. She had to hurry, she needed to get Mason dried and dressed, then work on herself.

"Hello neighbor!" came the call from the garage door.

"Hi Julie, come in please."

Julie walked through the laundry room from the garage and into the kitchen. "Good morning."

"Good morning to you. What's cookin'?"

"I got a text from Fred. He made reservations for me at the Navy Lodge on the base at Norfolk."

"When is the ceremony?"

"Three in the afternoon on the eighth of September," Julie answered. "Fred made airline reservations for me for the seventh and booked the motel room for the seventh and the eighth."

"So, you're flying home on the ninth?" June asked.

"Actually, Fred has this old pick up truck that he wants to bring back. He figures it would come in handy here. We're driving it back."

"That sounds like fun," June said.

"I think so too. We'll have three to four days to really get to know one another."

"That could be good or bad."

"Better to know now…" Julie agreed.

While they had been talking, June had finished drying and dressing baby Mason. "I have to get ready," she hinted. "I have an appointment with my education counselor in Aberdeen today."

"I'll get out of your way," Julie replied. "I just came by to tell you the news."

"I wish we could take the whole family, but that would be a fortune."

"I know," Julie agreed. "I'm sure Fred understands."

"If you're there, he won't even notice we're not," June said with a grin.

"I'm not so sure of that, but I'll do my best to distract him." With that Julie turned toward the door. She took about four steps and turned, "Are you taking Mason? Want me to watch him?"

"Thanks, but Sarah volunteered."

"Do the kids know to stop in and see me when they get home?"

"I told them I would be out and you are in charge," June answered.

"Good enough then. See ya." And she was out the door before June could reply.

"So, how did it go with the horse?" Laura Huber asked. They were sitting at the table in the conference room that once had been the kitchen of the old Craftsman style house. Jack

Huber, founder of Huber Realty had removed the Stove, and large refrigerator. He left some of the cabinets, and replaced the big kitchen sink and counter top with a smaller sink and added a dorm room refrigerator. The room was reminiscent of a kitchen, yet still worked as a meeting place. There was a more formal conference room in what had once been the dining room, but Jack had felt that some people were more comfortable in this more relaxed setting. He had been right.

"The horse was sold before we got to discuss it," Bill replied.

"I'm sure Jessie was disappointed," Laura Huber said.

"That's the funny part. By the time I got home she was completely off the idea. I don't know what happened. At one in the afternoon it was all she could do to keep her skin on. To hear it from her, having a horse was a matter of life or death. By the time I got home at six, it wasn't even on the radar."

Laura chuckled. "There's only one thing that can get a young girl's mind off a horse that quickly. That's a boy. Is there a new boy in her life?"

"Not that I know of." Bill shook his head. "How can you tell? They hardly ever see one another. They're texting or gaming with each other, but they don't talk anymore. How can I tell who is a boyfriend and who is a friend who happens to be a boy?"

"I don't envy you, Bill," Laura smiled and said, "I think it was easier when my kids grew up. They were outside more than they were in."

Bill had this dream in his mind of playing basketball with his son. He thought about watching him get better at the game and eventually beating his father. It seemed the electronic age had taken that dream away. "You know I put up the basketball hoop over the garage for Cory. He never uses it. I try to get him out to play but I can't get him away from one screen or another. Now that he has his own phone, I hardly ever have a one on one conversation."

"It is a different world, Bill."

"You are all too right, and I'm not too sure a better one." Bill agreed then added, "When I caught Cory texting his sister telling her supper was ready. I almost lost it. She was only a few steps down the hall."

251

Laura changed the subject. "I see you aquired the listing on the Castlewood house."

"I did, and I have a family in mind for it. They live in Boulder, Colorado, right in the city. They want to get away from the crowds."

"It's pretty flat out here for mountain people," Laura said. "Have they been here?"

I talked to Beverly Winters about that just last week. It seems her husband was caught in a mudslide last spring when all the storms went through the area. The slide pushed his car right off the road and down a hill. They actually think flatland is a plus. Paul Winters has hunted here for the past ten years during Pheasant Season. They are looking for fifteen acres with some woods, not too far from a major town. This property is less than thirty minutes from Watertown and forty five minutes from Brookings. It has a good sized shelter belt on the north side. Once I have the virtual tour done, I'll contact them."

"How about your brother?" Laura asked. "When will he be here?"

"In about three weeks. I'm going to Stewart Godfrey's auction this weekend to try to get the appliances and other things he might need."

"What is he bringing?"

"Nothing much. It turns out he has little in the way of personal possessions."

"He never had a house?"

"He spent most of his time on a ship. The few times he did have an apartment, he rented it furnished. He has a small storage unit there in Virginia. He plans on renting a u-haul trailer and bringing everything out with him."

"Well, you bring him by once he's settled."

"I'll make sure of it."

Laura left for her office, Bill topped off his coffee cup and did the same.

"It's good to see you again, Fred." James Lynch stood up when Fred walked into the Goatlocker.

"Welcome aboard Jimmy. I've been wondering when you'd show up. Ready to relieve me?" Fred asked.

"From what I've been told, there's not much to relieve."

"You're right. I guess you heard about the fire," Fred asked as a statement.

"I saw the message traffic. I'm glad it happened now as you were going into the yard for overhaul, rather than when you were going back on line."

"You and me both. The shop was going to get a refit anyway, this just sped the process along some."

"Hell of a way to clear a shop for a refit."

"We didn't have much choice. The damage to the equipment was extensive. You checked aboard yet?"

"Only as far as the quarterdeck," Jimmy answered. "I need to do the rest of the run around."

"Well, let me know when you're ready and I'll take you to admin and pick up the check in sheet."

"Good enough," Jimmy nodded, "I guess I'm ready now."

Fred started to fill in Chief Lynch. He knew him from a tour they did together about five years back. The CT community was not very big. In the twenty plus career span, a person got to know most of the others in this highly specialized field. James Lynch was still a "Boot Chief". He had been selected and promoted the year before. Moving into the position of division Chief was the next natural step in Lynch's career.

Jimmy Lynch was young, almost six years younger than Fred. He had climbed the enlisted ranks at a rocket pace. Fred knew him to be a charger. It would be good for 'his' troops to be under the leadership of Jim Lynch. One of the most important sub-missions of a Chief is to bring up leadership and teach others how to fill your position. He knew Lynch understood this. Under Chief Lynch, his CT crew would grow in professionalism and in rank.

Both men walked together to the Ship's Administration office. Chief Chad Nester was there to meet them. "Chad," Fred said with a smile, "I'd like you to meet my relief, CTTC James Lynch."

"Jimmy!" Chad said with a larger smile, "I was wondering when you'd show up. How the heck are ya?"

"I'm doing great Chad. How's Molly?"

"She's doing great. We bought a house here in town and

253

I'm looking forward to being home most nights while the ship is laid up. You'll have to come by for supper."

"I'll bring Jan."

"She's here?"

"When I got my orders, she managed to get a transfer to Virginia Beach. She'll be the assistant GM at the Hilton Oceanfront Hotel."

"Well," Fred interrupted, "I see I don't need to introduce you two."

"Chad and I go way back." Jimmy turned to Fred, "He was my sea daddy on my first cruise."

"And in spite of that, we became friends," Chad added

"Actually our wives did," Jimmy chuckled, "we just kind of followed along."

"Look, I'll let you two old friends get reacquainted. I've got some things to do."

"Just so you know, I got the flag box to the Master Chief."

"Thanks Chad," Fred answered. The flag box is a container to hold the flag presented at the time of retirement. It also contained a brass plaque listing the service dates and duty assignments of the recipient. This was normally given as a gift from the fellow Chief's in the retiree's command. "That's where I was heading. I need to talk to the CMC (Command Master Chief) about some of the details in the retirement ceremony."

"I'll catch up with you later, Fred," Jimmy answered.

As Fred left the office he heard Jimmy's next sentence, "So, what ever happened to Crazy Charlie Sample?" He didn't hear the reply.

Chapter Twenty One

Military ceremonies, like career retirement ceremonies, are set in stone from time immemorial. There are few things that can be changed without raising an eyebrow. Fred looked at the canned ceremony and decided he didn't need to change much of it. He shifted the order of a couple of the guest speakers and left the other details with his Command Master Chief. He double checked the flag box just to make sure the dates and commands were right, and then left the ship. He wanted to run one more errand before introducing his crew to their new Chief.

The Navy Exchange in Norfolk is one of the largest department stores on Navy soil. It was built to serve tens of thousands of sailors. Now in the days of the leaner military, the aisles almost looked deserted.

Fred walked up to the jewelry counter. He wanted something to give to Julie when she arrived. He looked at gold earrings that said 'Navy Wife' and laughed. Even if his relationship got that far, he could never see Julie wearing something like that. He settled for a heart pendant. The heart was an 18 ct. gold outline with a hint of a yin yang type curve running through the center, there were two small diamonds, one set on each side.

His Navy life was almost over. Now that his relief was aboard and about to take charge, he would have little to do in these last two plus weeks. He thought about asking Julie to come out early, but that wouldn't be fair to her. He did at least have to show up for work every day and that would leave her sitting in a motel room with nothing to do.

He had things of his own to get done. He asked a motor head friend to go over his truck and look for flaws. His friend had provided a list. Most of the things he could do himself. Buying new tires was among them. He would do that later in the week, along with the oil change.

He was excited to see Julie again. Buying the pendant reminded him how much he missed her. He pulled his phone out of his pocket and selected the number.

"Hi Fred!" Julie answered.

Fred could hear the smile in her voice. "Good morning. How's my favorite author?"

"Struggling," Julie said, her voice still cheerful. "I am having trouble keeping a sailor friend of mine contained in his box. He keeps wanting to come out and distract me."

Fred misunderstood. "You want me to hang up?"

"No," Julie said quickly, "you have it wrong. This call is exactly what I needed to put my thoughts of you back in the box. We can talk for a bit and then I can get back to work."

"All right. As long as I'm not keeping you from anything."

"Not a problem. Alonzo will have to keep his shirt on a bit longer."

"Alonzo?"

"The hero in my latest book."

"Does he get the girl?" Fred started kidding around.

"Several times," Julie giggled.

"Should I be jealous?"

This time Julie laughed. "No, Rachael is not me."

"Well, that's okay then."

Julie changed the subject. "I see you sent me a one way ticket."

"I decided to keep the pick up truck. I'm hoping your offer to ride back with me still stands."

"Why wouldn't it?"

"Well, it is a pretty ugly truck. Maybe you'll be embarrassed."

"I'm never ashamed of practical," Julie said.

That sentence took Fred back for a second. He was fairly sure he was moving past desire and attraction to something deeper. Julie's answer only served to strengthen that feeling. He almost said 'That's why I love you,' but choked it back. Instead he said, "You're one of the most practical people I have ever met."

Julie detected the hesitation in Fred's answer. She had a feeling she knew what he wanted to say. When he didn't say it, she decided to let him squirm a bit. "I'm not sure that's a compliment."

Again, Fred hesitated. "You are not only practical, but you're a real person. No pretenses. That is what attracted me

256

to you in the first place." Fred was back in the game.

"I don't like phonies either." Julie let him off the hook. "So, we'll drive the pick up truck back to Helen?"

"Sure, we'll take a week or so if you want. If you need to get back in a hurry I can do it in two days."

"I think I'll have time. I'll have this story finished by then." She hesitated, "that is if I can keep that sailor in the box on my bookshelf quiet."

"I'll have a talk with him."

"You do that."

Fred got serious, "You know, I miss this."

"Miss what?"

"The time we talk together. I'm really looking forward to the drive back."

"To the drive home," Julie corrected. "I like our chats too."

"Can I call you tomorrow?"

"You can call me anytime."

"All right then. I'll call tomorrow afternoon."

"Call my cell phone, I'll be at the Stewart Godfrey auction."

"Is that tomorrow?"

"Sure is. I want to make sure your brother bids on the right things."

"I put Tom Ogden in charge as my proxy."

"That's good." Julie nodded even though it wasn't a video call. "Tom is an auction hound. He'll know what to get and what to let go."

"Text me after the auction. I'll wait and call you then."

"Okay," Julie said. "In the mean time don't go fooling around with any dockside floozies."

"I'll make sure of it. I'll be too busy keeping a country girl I know contained in the box on the shelf."

Julie laughed. "See ya."

"Good bye."

"Hi Tom, what's cookin?" Even though the text read 'wireless caller', Bill Weber knew the number displayed on his phone.

"What time should I pick you up in the morning?"

"You're picking me up?"

"Sure, we're going to the auction together, aren't we?"

"Sure we are. But I didn't know I needed a ride. It's only a block and a half away. Tomorrow is supposed to be nice. I thought I'd walk."

"Walk?" Tom asked. "How are you going to get your stuff home?"

"What stuff?"

"Bill," Tom said, feigning frustration, "sometimes I think you just got here yesterday. We're going to an auction sale. There are things that are being sold. You may want something. If you do, where will you put it?"

"I don't intend to buy anything," Bill replied. "I'm going to get things my brother needs."

"That's why I'm going. You're going to write the check," Tom corrected. "But back to my point, what if you see something there you can use yourself?"

"I'll put it in your truck."

"Good answer," Tom said. "Now, when should I pick you up?"

Bill gave up. "Why don't we meet at ten? We can have coffee and then head over to the auction."

"How about I pick you up at nine thirty and we head straight for the auction?"

"They won't start until eleven. Why do you want to be there that early?"

"I want the time to look around."

"That's an hour and a half."

"That's right."

Bill really didn't want to stand around for an hour and half just to stand around all afternoon for the auction. He made a decision. "Look, Tom, like you said, I'm there to write the check. You go ahead without me and I'll meet you at Stewart's house at about ten thirty."

"Suit yourself."

It is common practice in the Midwest to hold a household auction for a person who is downsizing. That was the case for Stewart Godfrey. He had moved in with his son in Kent and needed to sell off the remaining contents of his Helen home.

The people of Helen were more than happy to oblige. The addicted auction hunters and the professional pickers started gathering around nine. Some looked over the offering and chose to leave, hoping for better picking at another sale. Stewart had a bit of everything, so most stayed behind.

Tom Ogden was not the first to arrive, but he was in the first ten. He started his methodical search for gems. He rooted through the boxes that had been placed on tables and trailers across the front of the house. He looked at the furniture and appliances carefully. He knew Fred would need several of these items. He wanted to check them for quality, age and cleanliness.

"Hey, Tom."

He recognized the voice. He turned to find Julie standing behind him. "Hi Julie. I didn't think you went to auctions."

"I normally don't, but I told Fred I'd look things over and see if I could get some basics for him."

"That's why I'm here."

"I know, he told me yesterday."

"Well, let's look together."

"Okay," Julie agreed. "Where's Bill?"

"Probably still asleep," Tom quipped. "I called him last night and told him I was getting an early start. He begged off and said he would be here around ten thirty."

"That doesn't give him much time."

Tom raised his finger, "He doesn't need time, he has us."

"Good point."

***

Lieutenant Junior Grade Herman Davis said, "Enter!" in a loud voice in reply to the standard Navy three knocks on his office door.

Chiefs Weber and Lynch walked in. "Lieutenant," Fred Weber started, this is my relief, Chief James Lynch."

The Lieutenant didn't stand. "Welcome aboard Lynch."

"Thank you, Sir."

"If you'll excuse me, I'm going to muster the troops to meet their new Chief. How much time would you like Lieutenant?"

"For now, just a few minutes, Chief. I'll have a real briefing from Chief Lynch after he meets his crew."

"I still need to go over the school schedule with you, Sir. Can we meet later?"

"Chief Lynch and I will take care of that," LTJG Davis replied. "I'm sure you have other things to do."

"Yes, sir," Fred said. He turned and walked out of the office and closed the door behind him. Somehow it had a sound of permanence. It bothered him to be pushed out the door so quickly, but at the same time, it was the right thing to do. Let the new guy take over and run things while the 'old guy' is still around to answer questions. There had been no formal ceremony, but he knew that he had just been dismissed. He went back to the CPO lounge for a cup of coffee.

It was about twenty minutes later when the two Chiefs walked into the freshly painted and recently re-powered and re-ventilated work spaces they now jointly controlled. "I want to introduce Chief Lynch. He's my relief," Fred said to his crew. "Chief, this is your LPO (Leading Petty Officer), CTT1 Anne Nelson."

Chief Lynch reached over and shook her hand, "Petty Officer Nelson."

"Welcome aboard, Chief," Nelson replied. She then in turn, from senior to junior, introduced the rest of the crew.

"I'm glad to know you and glad to be here," Chief Lynch said. "Chief Weber and I have made arrangements over at the school for training while the ship is in refit. I'll go over the schedule with Nelson later today. As the day goes along, I'll want to talk with each of you. I want us to get to know one another."

"In the mean time," Fred interrupted, "let me show you your office space."

"Good enough," Jimmy Lynch agreed and followed Fred to his cubicle. Once inside, he looked around at the empty room, he noted the ancient metal desk and two straight back armless chairs. "I like what you've done with the place."

"They're doing a spread on it in 'Shipboard Living'," Fred continued the joke. "It'll be out in the next issue."

"You got everything set for your retirement?"

"Most of it. The CMC (Command Master Chief) is taking care of the nuts and bolts."

"Well, let me know if I can help in any way," Lynch said.

"In other words 'Get out of my spaces and let me take over.'"

"Something like that. I've been through the service records and training jackets of the crew. They look on paper to be a good bunch of kids."

"They are."

"I want to talk to each one individually and get a gut feeling for them. After that, I'll want to talk to you about any problem children we might have."

"We'll do that in the Goat Locker."

"Of course."

"I'll get out of your way. The sooner I'm gone, the sooner the shop will take on your flavor."

"I'll meet up with you later. How about evening chow?"

"All right," Fred said with a smile and a handshake.

Making a joke of the formality of a change of command, Jimmy Lynch said, "I relieve you, Chief."

"And I stand relieved," Fred answered in turn. With that Fred turn around in the fashion of a military about face, and left the shop.

Bill walked up on Tom and Julie. "Well, what do you think?"

"The appliances are in good shape; if they go cheap enough they'll work for Fred," Tom answered.

"I looked at the kitchen stuff, it's clean. We'll bid on that too," Julie added.

"How about the furniture?"

"Some good, some bad. If it goes cheap enough, we'll buy it. I'm not too worried. There are two other sales before Fred gets here. What we don't get here I can get for him somewhere else."

The loudspeaker near the garage door made a clicking noise then said, "All right, ladies and gentlemen. We're going to get started in about ten minutes. We use a number system for bidding, so if you don't have one, please sign up for one in the garage."

261

"Do you have a number?" Tom asked Bill.

"I told you, I don't intend to buy anything," Bill replied.

"It doesn't hurt to have a number, just in case you see something,"

"Okay, you win. I'll go get a number." He turned to Julie, "I don't know why I keep him as a friend. He's really pushy."

"Who said we were friends?" Tom fired back.

Julie stood there and looked at them. Then she realized that the whole act was for her benefit and laughed. "Now children, stop bickering."

"He started it," Bill said with a chuckle. "I'm going to get a number."

"Good idea, wish I had thought of it," Tom said. "How about some coffee too?"

Bill walked up to the table where the daughter of the auctioneer was taking signups. "Good morning."

"Good morning to you. You'll be number sixty one. Fill out the bottom of the card and tear it on the dotted line. Give that part back to me and keep the top for bidding."

"How many times have you said that today?" Bill asked.

"Well, you are number sixty one." She smiled. "I'd bet around fifty."

"I don't go to many auctions, is this a good turnout?"

"When I hand out card number one hundred one, it will be a good turnout."

"You think you will?"

"Most likely."

Bill took his bid card and moved to the table that held the pastries and coffee. It was 'manned' by the Ladies Fellowship of the Helen United Church. "Good morning Agnes" Bill greeted his children's principal.

"Hi Bill. How about a coffee?"

"I want three."

"You must be thirsty."

"Something like that," Bill replied. "Actually, I'm the gopher today. Tom Ogden and Julie Sorenson are buying things for my brother Fred. He is renting this house from Stewart. I'm here in a supporting role."

"I see. I had heard your brother was moving into town. Does he have any children?" the school administrator asked.

"Fred is single, he never married."

"That's too bad. We always like new kids in school." Agnes passed him three cups with lids. "That'll be seventy five cents."

Bill handed her a one dollar bill, "Keep the change."

"Thanks, Bill."

The loudspeaker clicked again. Bill figured out it was the switch on the auctioneer's microphone making the scratchy clicking noise.

"Okay. We'll get going in just a few minutes. Just so you know the house is not for sale and will be closed to the public today. We have a porta-potty on a trailer behind the garage for your convenience. We will start on the trailers on the east side of the house and work our way around. My son is on the first trailer, so gather around and we'll get things going shortly. Don't forget the ladies who have a lunch prepared in the garage."

As Bill walked up to his two friends, Tom noted how he was carefully keeping the three cups trapped in his two hands. "What," he asked, "no donuts?"

Bill held his hands so each of them could rescue a cup. He made a motion pointing to Tom's waist line and said, "I don't think you need any more."

Julie got things back to the business at hand. "Where are we going to put the things we buy for Fred?"

"I have the keys. I'll unlock the kitchen door. We can move the small stuff in there. Once the auction is over, Tom and I can move any of the big stuff and put it in place inside the house."

"That works for me."

"What did you think of the appliances, Tom?"

"They're doable. They are older, but not in bad shape."

"I like some of the furniture, but not all of it," Julie said. "The kitchen table is nice but what Stewart left of the living room furniture is not the greatest."

"Not to worry, there is another sale tomorrow afternoon over in Foster City." Tom was looking at Julie. "I looked at the sale bill on line and the furniture looks to be nice. You can go along with us if you'd like."

"Us?" Bill asked.

"Us." Tom repeated, "He's your brother."

"Wonderful."

Click, "Okay folks, let's get started. My name is Edgar Howard, I am the auctioneer today. Cary is my son. Together we'll sell the items on the trailers and then go onto the larger things on the side of the house. What'cha got first Cary?"

"A box of wool blankets."

"Okay, who's got the first bid on the wool blankets? Do I hear thirty? Thirty? Okay twenty-five, who's got twenty five? Now thirty, thirty five, now fifty, I got fifty who's got seventy five, seventy five…"

"I'll bet that goes over a hundred," Tom said.

"For a box of blankets?" Bill was surprised.

"Those are antique one hundred percent wool blankets. See that couple over by the tree?"

"You mean the blonde standing next to the bald fat guy?"

"That's them. Vick and Daryl. They show up at a lot of auctions. They're pickers. They want them, but so does that guy wearing the red Huron, SD hat. He has a collectables and oddities store."

"Vick and Daryl? Which one's which?"

"Vickie goes by Vick."

"Who's going to win?"

"The guy with the hat. He can get more for them in his store than they can get selling them on line. Watch, they're already above their profit margin. They're just bidding him up now."

"Does he know that?"

"Sure he does."

"Why would they do that?"

"To set the tone for the sale," Tom answered. "He'll get the message and back away from the things they bid on or he'll retaliate and bid them up on the next one. It can be fun to watch."

"… sold one hundred thirty dollars to number seven." The auctioneer completed his chant.

The man with the red Huron hat moved forward and grabbed the box. "See?" Tom pointed. "He paid top dollar for those."

"So, he'll lose money?"

"No, I looked at that box. There are four blankets and they're in good shape. He'll get fifty a piece for them in his store. But if Vick and Darryl had not been here, he might have walked away with that box for ten bucks."

Bill nodded in understanding. "So, I figure they don't like one another."

"Not a bit."

The auction continued with Tom pointing out the interactions of the people at the sale. Julie, using Tom's bidding number, bought a box of kitchen gadgets for two dollars. Tom bid on and won the countertop microwave. Bill started hauling the winnings to the back door and placing them in the kitchen of what was to be his brother's new home.

"What about the lawn mower?" Julie asked.

"That thing looks pretty tired," Bill answered. "He'd be better off getting a rebuilt one from Henry."

"If they don't start it, we'll let the lawnmower go," Tom agreed, "but I think we should bid on the yard tools."

"I think so too," Bill said. "Don't want my kid brother letting the place get shabby."

Tom nodded and played along, "Wouldn't reflect good on the family."

"You two are tough," Julie said. "I can't imagine what you're like when you don't like somebody."

"There they go again," Tom pointed.

"There who go?" Bill asked.

"Vick and Daryl."

"Where? I don't see them?" Julie added.

"Daryl is at the head of the trailer and Vick is right behind the auctioneer. They are after something and don't want anyone else to know. They have almost indiscernible signals they use. Daryl will raise his eyebrow just a hint and Vick will put the bid with the auctioneer. Watch."

Julie and Bill watched intently. To Bill it looked like Daryl just stood there. Then he saw it. There was a slight facial movement, almost a hint of a wink. To many, it would simply look like a facial tic. Bill picked it up for what it was, a signal. When Daryl made the tic movement, Vick would say something under her breath to the auctioneer. The auctioneer would increment the bid. This continued for several bids until the others gave up. Once the auctioneer said, "Sold, number sixteen." Daryl moved in the pick up the box.

As Daryl walked by Tom, Tom asked him what he was after.

Daryl smiled, "Give me a minute and I'll show you," and kept walking. He returned under a minute later with something in his hand. "Want to hear the ball game?" It was an original six transistor radio made by General Electric.

"I didn't see that," Tom said.

"It was there, someone had switched it into a box of Tupperware but I put it back." Daryl nodded to the guy in the red hat. "He's going to be really surprised to find out he just paid fifteen dollars for worthless Tupperware.

"So he thinks he got one over on you?" Julie asked.

"He thinks he got one over on everyone."

"This is Julie Sorenson, she lives here in Helen."

"Good to meet you Julie. Here comes my wife, Vick."

"Hi Tom. You catch that action?"

"I did. Nice score."

"Daryl wanted the radio, but he didn't notice the paperweight."

"What about the paperweight?" Daryl asked his wife.

"It's Tiffany. I'll put it on Ebay starting at thirty dollars, it'll go for much more."

"How do you know it's Tiffany?" Julie asked.

"I had one like it last year," Vick explained. "A lurker on Ebay told me where to find the mark. This one has it too."

"So, both of you were after a different thing in the same box?" Bill asked.

Vick nodded, "It happens a lot. We have different interests. Daryl only likes to sell what he calls 'man stuff.' I'll sell anything."

"They're moving to the appliances," Tom pointed. "We've got to go."

"Nice to meet you," Daryl said.

"Nice to meet you too." Julie added.

As they followed the auctioneer around to the side of the house. Julie wondered out loud. "I'm curious, how somebody gets started in this kind of thing."

"Vick told me once, something about her daughters

266

wedding plans that had gone bad."

"Wedding plans?" Bill had caught up after taking another box into the house. "Who has wedding plans?"

Chapter Twenty Two

"So, what kind of tires are you looking for?"

"I'm moving to South Dakota when I retire next month, I need something with grip."

"South Dakota?" the clerk answered, "I guess you do!"

"What do you have that's good in mud and snow?"

"Cooper makes a great mud and snow tire. The Discoverer series comes in several levels of aggressiveness."

"I want the best you've got for snow."

"I've got the Discover M plus S for mud and snow." The clerk was using two fingers to punch in information into his computer. "That's your Chevy pick up outside, isn't it?"

"That's right. You need the tire size?"

"I know it. Let me see if we have any here. There's not much of a demand for that kind of aggressive tire here in Virginia Beach. We keep a good sand tire on hand but not..." his voice trailed off.

Fred didn't say anything. He really did want to get this job done today. If this store didn't have them, he would look on his phone for another. He was only loyal to this place because he'd bought tires here before.

"I have two here and two in our Hampton store. Let me make a quick phone call. Our regional manager is over there and coming here next. If I can catch him, he can bring them over."

"How long will that take?" Fred asked.

"Let me find out." The clerk walked into a glass enclosed office and picked up the phone. It was less than a minute before he came out. "Some days I have perfect timing. The regional manager was just about to leave. He'll bring the other two tires with him. We'll get you set up and he'll be here by the time the crew is ready for them."

"What kind of price are you talking?"

"Well, this time it's a case of getting what you pay for." The clerk was punching buttons and clicking the mouse. After a short time he reached under the counter and pulled out a sheet of paper. "Here's the quote. If you want to take the old tires with you, we can knock off twenty bucks for the disposal fee. Of course, there's the balancing, but I threw in the new valve stems."

The kid was good. "You got a deal. I'll take the old tires with me. I can get rid of them on the base."

"That's right, they collect them to make artificial reefs, don't they?"

"It's a test project being run by a private nonprofit group. The Navy is letting them use some old hangar space to build the reef units."

"Beats throwing them in the landfill." The clerk came around the counter, "Let's get you started. Bay two is open."

Fred's phone told him he had a new text. He looked, "auction done".

He replied, "call u soon".

Fred climbed into his old pick up and drove it to the open bay entrance. The clerk was at the far end directing him in and held up his hand when he wanted him to stop.

"Please put it in park and leave the keys in the ignition," the clerk instructed.

Fred complied, he got out and left the keys. The clerk indicated he should follow him back to the showroom. Which he did, dutifully. Once the clerk was talking to another customer, Fred walked back outside. The steamy air of the Virginia summer hit him full force. It didn't matter, he wanted a little privacy and outdoors was the only place to get it. He called Julie's land line number.

"Hey Fred!" Julie's voice sounded excited. "I was hoping you would call back right away."

"How did we do?"

"Tom is a wonder at these sales. I learned a lot from him. He got the microwave, the refrigerator, the stove and most of the good furniture. I got the things he missed; kitchen gadgets, linens and things like that. Your brother got you the yard tools."

"That's amazing."

"Tom knows about an auction tomorrow afternoon in a nearby town. He's taking us to look at the furniture."

"Us?"

"Bill and myself."

"Sounds like you're getting the auction bug."

Julie giggled, "Not really. I wouldn't be going if it weren't to help you get set up."

"Well, first, thank you for helping," Fred said. "What else will I need?"

"You have one whole bedroom that has nothing. I didn't know if you wanted a guest room or a den. Tom got the bigger dresser but stopped bidding on the smaller one. He said it went too high. You don't have a bed yet."

"I think I want to buy that new."

"Probably a good idea," Julie agreed.

"You'll also have to decide how to decorate. We didn't get any art for the walls."

"I hadn't even thought about that. I've never decorated a house or apartment. I always rented them furnished and didn't pay much attention."

"I'll help."

"I would like that."

"Mr. Weber? Can you come into the bay for a moment? My mechanic has something to show you."

"I'll be right there," he said to the clerk. Then back to the phone, "Look, Julie, I'm getting new tires for the truck. I'm at the tire store and they want to up-sell me something. I've got to go. Can I call later?"

"Sure, anytime."

"Okay - bye."

"See ya."

Fred walked into the service bay. His truck was six feet in the air. "What'd you find?"

"As part of our inspection we noticed the front brakes are getting near the end of their service life. We wanted to point it out."

Fred took advantage of the invitation to walk under his truck. He looked at the front brakes. He already knew they were worn. It was on his list. Replacing the brake pads was an easy job. He intended to do it himself. He looked at what the clerk was showing him. "I see, how about the rear?"

"We don't normally pull the rear drums unless we are doing a brake job."

"Brake job?" Fred thought, "Snow job is more like it." He didn't say anything like that out loud. He just took advantage of the situation. "Can we look please? Since the truck is already up and the wheels are off."

The mechanic made a sound expressing his displeasure, lowered the truck half way and removed the brake drums. "They're about half worn."

"Thanks. I'll let them go for now. As to the front, I'll do them myself. Thanks."

"Whatever you say, Mr. Weber, but those front brakes are the most vital when it comes to an emergency stop. We highly recommend a professional ASC certified mechanic do the work."

"In other words, you."

The clerk sidestepped the challenge, "Well, if not us, someone with our experience and knowledge."

"I'll take that under advisement," Fred said.

The clerk wasn't quite ready to give up, "We have a special this week. Eighty nine dollars plus tax."

"Do you resurface the rotors?"

"Of course." The clerk smiled, he thought he had set the hook.

"And if you find the rotors are too worn and can no longer be machined, do you replace them?"

"Of course." The clerk hesitated then added, "The cost of the rotors would be additional."

"I would expect nothing less," Fred said.

"There would be no labor charge to replace the rotors, since we had to remove the old ones for inspection and machining."

"I see," Fred was playing with him now.

"So, we should move forward on the brakes?"

"No, I don't think so." Fred let the kid down gently. He had tried. "I'm in a bit of a hurry today."

"All right, but I would see to it soon. Can I make an appointment for next week?"

"Things are busy on the ship right now. Let me get back to you," Fred said.

Just as the clerk was ready to try another pitch, the phone at the desk rang allowing Fred to get away from this young world class salesman. He stepped outside and called Tom Ogden.

"This is Tom."

"Tom, Fred Weber. I just heard from Julie. Sounds like you did all right."

"I got you the basics, Fred. Your brother and I just moved the stove and refrigerator back inside and now we're moving the boxes to the center of the rooms."

"Why?"

"Stewart wants to get the place painted before you move in."

"Tell him that's not necessary."

"Tell your brother. He's the one who's got me shoving things around."

"Is he there?"

"Here…" Fred heard muffled voices.

"Hi Fred. How's it going?" Bill asked.

"Things are shaping up here. We'll be on the road the morning of the ninth."

"Great. The whole town is looking forward to you moving in."

"I can't imagine that." He changed the subject, "Look, Bill, tell Mr. Godfrey he doesn't need to paint the place. I can do that when I get there."

"It's too late. He already has it contracted. The church youth group is doing it."

"That's a frightening thought. I know what kind of mess young sailors make when they paint. I can imagine what happens when a bunch of teenagers do it."

"You'd be surprised," Bill said with confidence. "They're very neat. It looks professional when they're done."

"I'll take your word for it," Fred said. "Thank Tom for me and thank you for the help."

"No problem, I'll take my agent's commission out of the account when we're done."

Fred laughed. "Commission? How about I treat your family to supper at the Helen House."

Bill chuckled. "I'll hold you to that."

"Good." Fred looked over to see his truck rolling out of the service bay. "Look, my truck's done. I've got to go."

"Stay in touch, brother," Bill said.

"Will do," Fred answered and put the phone away.

Fred paid the bill and drove back to the ship. He may not have a job there anymore, but he still lived there.

Jessie wasn't sure what had happened. She texted Frank and didn't get an answer. She tried again later and still got nothing. In desperation she called his number. It went straight to voice mail. She tried email next but still got nothing back. Something was very wrong.

Her phone buzzed, she looked, it was Mickie,

HME
Y
POL
N
Y
BZY
WHT
CNT GT FRNK
Y
DN
TN GO TO POL
N
Y
2 CLD
WLK T SKOL
Y
PK DSKS
K
5 MN UR HS
K

Jessie put the phone down. She was upset that she couldn't find Frank. But this was the week before school and she did want to claim her desk. She met Mickie outside her front door and they walked together toward the school. This continued the ritual that had started last year when Jessie was the 'new kid'. Mickie had helped her then and they had become best friends.

"Where's Frank?" Mickie asked.

"I don't know. He won't answer texts. I even called and

e-mailed and got nothing. You think he's mad at me?"

"You do anything to make him mad?"

"I don't think so."

"Then maybe his phone is dead."

"He never lets it go dead."

"Maybe he did this time."

Jessie changed the subject. "What do you know about our teacher?"

"I don't know anything. She's new."

"Nobody knows her?"

"I talked to Cody. He says she's from Aberdeen."

"Is she moving here?"

"She did already. She lives north of town."

"But what does Cody say she's like?"

"He doesn't know. He just knows his dad has been out there fixing the plumbing."

"Maybe we'll meet her at the school."

"Maybe," Mickie repeated, "but that could be good or bad."

"That's true."

"Hey author lady! How's it going?"

"Hi Fred. What's going on?"

"Well I just finished the last major job on the truck. It has new brakes and new oil. Next stop is to get a topper for the bed in the back. I want something I can lock."

"Sounds like a good idea," Julie agreed. "Are you getting excited?"

"Excited to see you," Fred answered correctly.

"Well, it won't be long now. We have the State Fair next weekend and then I'll get packing."

"I'm sorry I'm going to miss the Fair. Bill told me about it last year. It sounds like a slice of Middle America."

"I suppose it is," Julie agreed. "I'm going to support a friend of mine. She is a romance novel writer too, but she's been 'outed'. She's going to be the featured author on Saturday. I want to go see her."

"Thinking of revealing your secret?"

"Not really. The stuff I write is too racy."

"I've read four of your books so far, Margaret. They turn

274

heads but they don't make this old sailor blush."

"Fred!" Julie almost shouted, "How do you know my pen name?"

"I've spent enough time around you and in your writing den to figure it out."

"Please keep it a secret."

"The Navy has trusted me to keep their secrets for the past twenty years, it's a habit now." Fred reassured Julie, "Not to worry, your secrets are safe with me."

"Secrets?" Julie asked. "You know more than one?"

"I can't say."

"Why not?"

"It's a secret," Fred smiled at his phone.

"Fred!" Julie laughed "You're incorrigible."

"I hope so."

"What do your shipmates think about you reading romance novels?"

"It turns out that my next in line is a fan of yours. She had one in the shop so I picked it up."

"I'll have to bring her an autographed copy."

"She'll love that, and, because I trained her, she'll keep your secret too."

"I don't think it will be a problem on a ship in Norfolk, Virginia. Just as long as she doesn't follow you to Helen, South Dakota."

"Not much chance of that," Fred replied, "She's a city girl. She thinks corn comes from a can."

Julie changed the subject, "So, the truck is ready?"

"Almost," Fred answered, "Like I said, I want a topper for the pick up bed. I'll do that later today."

"I'm looking forward to the drive home with you."

"I can't think of a better way to start the rest of my life."

"I'll bet you say that to all the girls."

"Only the pretty ones."

Julie laughed. "I've got to get back to work. Alonzo is hanging on a rope outside Abigail's window."

"What happened to Rachael?'

"You'll have to read the book."

Now it was Fred's turn to laugh. "I'll call you later."

"See ya."

"Here is our classroom," Mickie pointed.

"I see it," Jessie said absentmindedly. She was sending another text to Frank.

"Let's go in," Mickie said. Jessie didn't comment, she simply followed.

The classroom was on the second floor. Since the first floor was half buried, it was considered the basement level. The rooms in this 'second' floor all started with the number one. The eighth grade class was in room 108. Unlike last year's seventh grade room, the windows of this room looked toward town instead of across the fields. The trees in front of the school blocked any view. So, choosing desks had nothing to do with looking out the windows.

"The desks are in a circle again," Jessie commented.

"Actually it's more like a 'U'," Mickie replied.

"Just like last year," Jessie agreed.

"There are eleven of them," Mickie commented.

"There are only ten kids in the class," Jessie said. "Unless somebody new is coming in that we don't know about."

"We would know," Mickie said assuredly.

"It used to happen back east, one morning a new kid would be there and nobody knew ahead of time. Maybe that's happening here."

"Has anybody moved into town this summer?" Mickie asked in a tone that Jessie understood to be condescending.

"Well, no but…"

"Has anyone moved onto a farm nearby?"

Jessie had to let her friend run down, "No."

"Has there been anybody new at the pool?"

"There was that kid from Portland," Jessie said.

"He was visiting, he said so."

"Okay. So there's nobody new that we know about."

"Right," Mickie agreed, "so there's nobody new."

"So why eleven desks?"

"I don't know."

"Where do you want to sit?" Jessie asked.

"How about at the bottom?"

"Okay, just as long as I'm not stuck sitting next to Mary Bayer."

"Well, we could do it this way," Mickie pointed to the top of the 'U', "you could sit on the end and I could sit next to you and that way you can't get stuck sitting next to Mary Bayer."

"What if you get stuck with her?"

"I won't mind, I can make her squirm."

"I like that," Jessie agreed, "let's do it."

"That's settled," Mickie said with finality.

"How do we claim them?"

Mickie reached into her purse. She pulled out two three by five cards. "I got these from my mom. We'll write our names on them and tape them on the desks."

"What if somebody moves them?"

"They wouldn't dare," Mickie said firmly. "They know the rules and first is first."

"Well, we'll find out tomorrow," Jessie answered.

"We'll be sure we get in first. That way we'll have our places claimed."

"Okay," Jessie answered absentmindedly. She was texting Frank again.

"I still think we should go to the pool. It's the last day."

"It's too cold," Jessie said. She looked at her phone again, "Why doesn't he text me?" she said in frustration.

"Will you forget about Frank for a while? It's the last day of summer. Let's do something."

"Like what?"

"We need to finish level five of Golden Dragon Cubes."

"Okay," Jessie shrugged, "we'll go to your house."

"Okay."

"What do you mean you broke it?" Sarah was looking at her forlorn son.

"I was mowing the lawn when I noticed it wasn't in my pocket. I looked around and found it. I think I mowed over it, it's smashed."

"Frankie, that's a one hundred fifty dollar phone!" Sarah said.

"I didn't mean to do it. It must have fell out of my pocket when I ducked under the trees."

"Must have fallen…" Sarah corrected.

"Then you understand how it can happen. Anyway, it's

277

insured." Frank started to relax. He had broken two other phones this past year. He had been warned about this one. If he lost or broke it he would go without for a month before getting a new one.

"I was not agreeing with you, Frankie, I was correcting your English," Sarah said. "Let me see the phone." Frank handed it to her. It had a slice through the display screen and the whole phone was slightly bent. "I guess it doesn't work." She stated the obvious.

"I need to get a new one," Frank also stated the obvious.

"You know what we agreed." Sarah looked at her son.

"But Mom, I can't wait a whole month! There's school starting tomorrow and the State Fair. You wouldn't want me to be without a phone at the fair."

"I know our agreement, it was made by the three of us. In order to break it, we all have to agree. Your dad and I will discuss it and talk to you about it tonight."

"But how am I going to communicate? I'm all the way out here and my friends are in town."

"Use the land line phone."

Frank looked at his mother like she suggested two soup cans and a length of string. "You can't text on that!"

"No, but you can talk on it."

"Mom," Frank said in his most serious voice, "School starts tomorrow. I have to have a phone to download my homework."

"The school issues you a tablet, you can get your homework on that."

"But what if I have a question? I can't text on a tablet."

"Frank, if you do not stop right now I'll get you a basic phone, no text and no internet." Sarah was starting to lose patience "I said the three of us will take it up after supper."

"Don't you see? That's too late to go to the store and get a new phone. School starts tomorrow and I NEED a phone." Frank took a breath, he knew he was pushing, but this was vital. "Can't you call Dad and discuss it now?"

Sarah knew her older son. He would not continue to challenge if it wasn't very important to him. She gave in, "Okay, I'll call your father and see what he says."

"Thanks mom," Frank said, "I wouldn't ask if it wasn't

important".

"Well, don't hang around, let me talk to your father in private. Go finish the lawn."

"Okay." Frank turned and left the room. It was only moments later that Sarah heard the riding mower start again.

"Tom, Frankie ran over his phone with the lawn mower. He's in a panic because school starts tomorrow."

"How did he manage to mow his phone?" Tom asked. It had been a slow day at the elevator. The incoming trucks were sporadic. He only had four in the past hour. He had time to talk.

"He said it must have fallen out of his pocket when he ducked to get under the trees. He thinks he hit it on the next pass."

"This will be the third phone this year," Tom said.

"I know."

"Didn't we decide that he would have to go without for a month this time?"

"Well, we did, but with tomorrow starting the first day of school he says he really needs his phone. I told him he would have to wait, but he wanted me to call you and ask you to reconsider." Sarah took a deep breath. "Tom, I know Frankie, he understands consequences. If it were not the first day of school tomorrow, I don't think he would have said anything. But he did, when I reminded him of our agreement he continued to push. I think this is really important to him."

Tom was quiet for a moment, "He needs to know a contract is a contract. Circumstances don't change what was agreed upon." Tom could see where this was going, Sarah was close to letting her son off the hook, but if she did, what would he learn? He had to think of a solution that still taught a lesson but did not traumatize his soon to be fifteen year old son.

"Can't we let it go for a week?" Sarah asked.

"No, I don't think we can." Tom had the answer. "Here's what we'll do. Go with Frankie and get the new phone. Once you have it, put it in your purse. He can use it when he goes to school and for thirty minutes after he gets home. That will let him use it for homework. Then he gives it to us and we keep it. We also keep it on weekends."

"For the month?"

"Right."

"That'll work Tom." Sarah nodded at the phone, "I'll go tell him."

"Get ready for a fight."

"There won't be a fight. He knows he was warned."

"Alright, but if you need back up, have him call me."

"He won't."

"There's a truck coming in, I have to go."

"Okay, I love you."

"Love you too." Tom put down the handset. He knew the driver pulling in under the probe. Since he had time, he pushed the button and said, "Good afternoon Fred. How's the Hansen family today?"

"We'd be doing better if these soybeans were worth more money. You know they're right. A farmer buys everything he needs for the field at retail and then sells his crops at wholesale."

"And he pays the shipping both ways," Tom repeated the often said lament. "You have a contract on them?'

"Yup."

"Okay, let me pull a sample."

Tom used the joystick on the control panel to manipulate the probe arm and suck about a half gallon of soybeans from three points, front middle and back of Fred's semi trailer. He made a quick check for obvious deficiencies and finding none he walked back to his control panel. He pushed the intercom button, "Slot two, Fred." Telling the driver where to unload. He then made a more thorough inspection looking for moisture content, foreign material and other detriments. All these factors would affect the final value of the load.

Chapter Twenty Three

For the last several years the South Dakota State Fair was held over the Labor Day weekend. This year Julie's author friend, Marie, had been Monday's featured author in the Fine Arts Building. Julie had gone to the fair to support her friend and ended up sitting with her for the afternoon. The book signing and presentation ended at four o'clock. They finished the day with a great supper at the Hangar Restaurant. It was fine dining, with a view of the Huron airport runway. While they were there, only one plane landed. Once Julie checked the room for people she knew, they talked shop. They were both romance novel writers, but because of the high demand for what they wrote, there was no competition between them. They were colleagues, not rivals.

"In three days I'll be back here again," Julie said.

"That's right, you're flying east to see your sailor friend."

"He's more than a friend."

"I figured that. How did you meet?"

"He's the brother of my next door neighbor. I'm flying out to attend his Navy retirement ceremony and then we'll drive back together."

The waiter arrived with the wine. Once he poured and moved away, the conversation continued.

"He's moving to South Dakota?" Marie asked.

"He's moving to Helen, South Dakota." Julie's tone was not unlike a teenager who had been invited to the prom by the coolest kid.

"I guess you're serious about this one."

"More than serious, I think."

"Well good luck to you. I've had three husbands and I'm single again, so I won't try to give you advice."

"That's good, because I wouldn't take it." They both laughed.

Marie looked at the menu again, "You say the Prime Rib is good?"

"It was the last time I was here. I would order the smaller portion though. They run large."

"Thanks, I will."

The waiter took their main course orders and brought the shrimp cocktail they had ordered with the wine.

During the meal the conversation wandered from books they had either written or read to romances they were living or had lived. Once the last of the carrot cake was consumed, the conversation came back to Julie and Fred. "Once he gets settled," Marie said, "why don't you come out to visit me West River. I have a nice cabin in the Black Hills that I use as a get away. It has two bedrooms and a deck with a view that goes on forever. I do some of my best writing there."

"I think we will. That should be fun."

"Give me a call," Marie said as she stood.

"Okay." They parted at the restaurant door, each heading to her own car.

The day had finally arrived. Julie's travel day started at four a.m.. As much as she tried, she couldn't sleep the night before. Her mind would not turn off. It was playing and replaying the trip. She was looking forward to holding Fred in her arms and melting into his chest. She finally gave up and got out of bed. The clock read two a.m.. Everything was packed, but she went through it again.

June had volunteered to take her to the airport. The flight was scheduled to depart before seven a.m.; they arrived with time to spare. They hugged each other goodbye and Julie turned to walk into the small terminal. June returned to her car and drove out of the parking lot.

Julie went through the security procedures and boarded the small twin turboprop 19 seat aircraft. It didn't take long. There were only two other passengers. She had two more stops before landing in Norfolk. The travel would take the whole day. Fred had built in time for delays into the travel itinerary. Julie had agreed, it was better to sit for an hour or two at an airport with a confirmed seat than it was to arrive late and have to wait for a standby seat to open on a later flight. It was Huron to Minneapolis, to Charlotte NC, then to Norfolk International Airport in Virginia. She was scheduled to arrive about fifteen hours after she left Helen.

Julie was excited. She missed Fred. She had come to the realization that she was fully and completely in love with him.

She wanted nothing else for her life than to have him as part of it. She wanted him to know that, but she couldn't push. She might drive him away. She wasn't sure if she could live in the same little town with him, and not have him as part of her life.

Was he "the one"? If there was even such a thing, she was convinced he was it. She had to have him and keep him.

Julie jumped when the little plane's wheels hit the runway. She had dozed off. She hadn't realized she was falling asleep, but they were in Minneapolis and taxiing to the terminal. She found her way to the United concourse and found her departing gate. It would be about ninety minutes before they called for boarding. She had her friend Marie's newest book. She sat by the big glass windows near the gate and started reading.

Bill and June had a simple rule that they had established at the beginning of their marriage. Neither of them would make a major purchase without first discussing it with the other. Bill often wondered if the divorce rate would be a little lower if more newlywed couples had made the same promise. Bill was going to be late to the office, but he had to finish talking to June about the Cadillac SRX Crossover Marty had. "I looked at it and it's a very nice car. I think it's time I upgraded."

"What's wrong with your Escalade?"

"Nothing really, other than it's getting dated. I can get the Crossover SRX that Marty has for my car and five thousand."

"Five thousand dollars?" June loudly repeated.

Bill continued. "Look June, a realtor needs to look successful in order to list properties. If he looks poor, nobody will trust him with the sale."

June smiled a smile that indicated her disbelief. "Wow, that's a real rationalization, Bill."

"No, it's true." Bill continued to state his case, "For a real estate business to be successful, it has to look successful."

"And that includes the car you drive?" June was laughing inside. She knew Bill wanted the new car. She had no problem with it. She just wanted him to admit *he* wanted it for himself, not the office.

"Of course it includes the car you drive," Bill replied.

"Imagine you are selling this house, you call a realtor and this guy shows up with a beat up old car. Would you trust him with your biggest investment?"

"But you don't have a beat up old car. You have a car that is in great shape."

"But it's old. It doesn't have presence anymore."

"Presence?"

"Sure, it doesn't impress anymore. Here's another thing, the SRX will get about ten miles to the gallon better gas mileage. If you do the math, the thing will pay for itself in under twenty thousand miles."

"The office pays for your travel expenses. So, why don't you get the office to buy it?"

"Because I'm using my personal property as a down payment. That would be co-mingling."

"All right. You can sell your Escalade outright and then get the office to buy you a new Cadillac."

"I don't want to burden the office with that kind of expense."

"You want to own the car?"

"I think I should. I'm the one who's going to be driving it."

"You bought the Escalade through your office back east."

"I was the sole owner of Weber Realty. Here, I have a partner."

June got tired of playing the game. "Oh, come on, Bill," June looked at her husband, "give me a break. Like your brother says, 'stop trying to blow smoke up my butt'. Just tell me you want the car."

"I want the car," Bill said.

"Good, go get it. You spend a good deal of time in your car. If you want it, get it."

"I'm picking it up this afternoon."

"You knew I would go along?"

"Of course."

"Well, Chief, that's it," Chad Nester said. "All the paperwork is done. You check out on terminal leave day after tomorrow and kiss the Navy good bye."

"Thanks for all your help, Chad."

"That's what I do." Chad smiled. "Your lady friend is coming in today, right?"

"She's due to arrive just before seven this evening."

"Where are you staying?"

"I got a couple rooms at the Navy Lodge."

"A couple rooms?" Chad grinned, "You must be seriously in love."

Fred smiled, "I guess I am."

"Well, things are on track for tomorrow afternoon. Master Chief has everything lined up for the ceremony. The weather guessers say it will be nice so we'll set up out on the Helo Deck. If they're wrong, we'll move it indoors to the hangar."

"I checked the weather too," Fred said. "Eighty nine, partly cloudy with a breeze off the water to cool things. I couldn't ask for better."

"We aim to please." Chad smiled.

"I have one more stop to make."

"Down to the shop?" Chad asked.

"That's right. I won't have time to say a proper good by tomorrow."

"Probably not."

Fred left the ship's Admin office. He didn't notice Chad moving over to the phone.

Fred made a side trip up to the deck. Looking at his watch and comparing it with the itinerary he had in his head, he figured Julie would be in Minneapolis. He called.

"Hey sailor."

"Hey yourself," Fred replied. "You in the Minneapolis airport?"

"Sure am, everything's right on schedule. I checked with the desk and they anticipate no delays with boarding."

Fred nodded at the phone. "So that would put you in Charlotte on time."

"Looks like it," Julie answered. "I'll try to call you or leave a text if anything changes."

"Great. I'm doing last minute goodbyes. I'll try to call you when you get to Charlotte."

"Okay, Fred. See you soon."

"I'm waiting with baited breath."

"Oh Fred Weber," Julie used the voice of a southern bell,

"you say the nicest things."

Fred chuckled. "Bye."

"See ya."

Fred put the phone back in his pocket. He went down into the bowels of what would soon no longer be "his" ship. He proceeded to what was already no longer "his" shop. He punched in the code to enter the space and walked in. He saw a flash of movement from behind the door, a large trash can was being dumped over his head. He ducked, expecting to get very wet and very cold. It didn't happen. He opened his eyes and saw confetti falling around him. "I expected to be wet."

"We couldn't do that, Chief," Anne Nelson explained. "Not with all our new equipment in here. Chief Lynch gave us this idea."

"It's not even mine. It's what they did to me when I left my last command."

"It has the same effect, but doesn't kill computers," Kirkland said.

Fred didn't ask how they knew he was about to enter the shop. There are very few things on a small ship that can be kept secret. He made a mental note to thank Chad for his part in the conspiracy. "I wanted to take a minute to thank you for all the hard work you did making these spaces into a work place again. I have a gift certificate here for Harry's Bar-B-Que, it should cover a nice lunch for all of you."

"Thanks Chief, we have a gift for you too," Anne said and handed him a flat box.

Fred opened it and found a heavy mahogany plaque with a brass plate that read:

To Chief Weber on the occasion of his retirement.
Fair Winds and Following Seas
From the CT Crew of the USS Kaufman

"This is great," Fred said. He was doing his best not to get emotional - he was losing. "This will take center stage on my 'I love me' wall. Thanks."

"We are also taking you to lunch at the Enlisted Club," Nelson said. "I reserved a table."

"All right, what time should I be there?"

"We'll secure the spaces for chow at eleven thirty," Chief Lynch said.

"Great, I'll be there."

Chief Lynch looked to his leading Petty Officer, "In the mean time, let's get the shop cleaned up and start on installing this new equipment."

"Right Chief," Anne said.

Taking his cue, Fred said, "See you at the E club," and left the shop for the last time.

He walked into the CPO mess and poured a cup of coffee. He looked at the plaque again. This time it hit him. This is over, really over. He had been in the Navy since he was a teenager. It was all he knew as an adult. Now it was done. No more sea time, no more ships at all. It was as if, all of a sudden, the bottom of his life had been jerked out from under him. He had no idea what kind of job he would go to next. He didn't know anything about civilian life. How did people work together without uniforms telling them the order of leadership? What was he going to do? He had skills, but those skills had to do with intelligence gathering and little else. He was a trained leader, but a leader should know the product. He had his degree, but he had only wanted it to ease the way for promotion. So, here he was, no job, no future, no ship, no Navy. He had a home to go to, but not much else. He wasn't even sure if he would stay in Helen.

The only thing firm in his future was Julie. She was something he could reach out to and hold. She could be the stabilizer in what he realized was an unsettled future. Julie was going to be his kingpost, his pivot point to use in the transition. He was thinking about marriage, but he wasn't sure. He needed to be sure. The changes in his life were already major and he didn't want to add any more stress to the mix. He would wait. Maybe in six months or so he could look at marriage, but not today. By then, there were even odds that he would be back onboard a ship as a company tech rep and not have any place for a wife and family. Maybe...

Fred went back to his quarters one last time. He needed to 'pack his seabag'. It took him less than twenty minutes to pack his uniforms, his civilian clothes, hygiene and small personal items. Crew's on Navy ships had little space for personal items. Even as a Chief Petty Officer, he couldn't keep much on board. It is why he kept a small storage locker out in town.

He thought about what he carried to the truck, "twenty years ago I carried a seabag onto my first ship, today I'm not carrying out much more." Though he put it in the back, his meager possessions would have fit in the passenger seat of his pickup truck.

Prior to packing he had thought about wearing his uniform to the airport, but changed his mind. Julie was not part of that life, she was part of the new life. The one without uniforms.

"Good morning ladies and gentleman, we will begin normal boarding of flight 453 to Charlotte, North Carolina in a few minutes. We ask those with special needs to hobble up to the jet way at this time."

Julie woke with a start. She had fallen asleep again. She replayed in her mind what she thought she heard and giggled to herself. She knew that couldn't possibly have been right. She stood up, she wanted to make sure she stayed awake. The lack of sleep from the night before was catching up to her. Other than these two short naps, she had not really slept in over thirty six hours.

There was a coffee stand down the concourse but she didn't want to leave the gate. She walked over and looked out at the tarmac. It looked to her like every other airport she had been in. She saw tractors, trucks and baggage trains moving about in some sort of dance. Occasionally a plane would taxi by. She watched as the airliner in the next gate was being pushed back. Then it was time for her to board. It was only when she was aboard did she realize that Fred had paid for first class seating.

"Marty, Bill Weber. You ready for me?"
"Ready as I'm gonna be. I have all the paperwork here."
"I'm on my way."
"Good enough."
Bill realized that Marty had hung up. He walked to the front office, "Mrs. Townsend, I'll be out of the office the rest of the day."

"You going to get your new car?"

"That's right. Then I'm going to the Castlewood property to check some measurements."

"I can send Phillip if you'd like."

"No, I'll be right near there. My client wants a few dimensions we didn't have in the listing. I know what she's looking for. I'll take care of it."

"All right, Mr. Weber," Serena Townsend answered. "Have a nice afternoon."

"It's always nice when you're picking up a new car."

"I suppose it is," Serena agreed. The phone rang and she turned "Good afternoon. Huber Realty. This is Serena, how may I help you today? ... Let me see if he is in, Mr. Cleveland. May I put you on hold for just a moment? ... Thank you."

"Is that for me?" Bill asked.

"Mr. Gange," Serena answered.

"Okay, see you in the morning."

"Good afternoon Mr. Weber."

As Bill walked out the door he heard Serena call John Gange on the intercom. Business would continue without him the rest of the day.

"Hi Fred, I have good news and bad news."

"What's the good news?"

"I'm in Charlotte."

"And the bad."

"There's a two hour delay for weather," Julie told Fred. "The ride in here was rough. We bounced all over the place."

"Are you all right?"

"Sure, but when I got to the gate for the flight to Norfolk, I was told there would be a one to two hour delay in boarding."

"One to two hours isn't a high price to keep you safe," Fred said.

"I was talking to one of the passengers. He travels this route all the time. He told me the plane is coming in from Dallas and since it isn't here yet it will be a least two hours."

"Do you believe him?"

"Why would he lie?"

"Some people will say anything to catch the eye of a pretty girl."

"Fred, you're funny."

"Just watch him; if invites you to the bar for a drink, he's up to no good."

Julie smiled a smile that Fred could hear but not see. "Don't worry, I'm sticking with tea until I'm on the ground in Norfolk."

"I'll see you then. You'll be able to find me easily. I'll be the one wearing the big smile."

"Not as big as mine. Bye for now."

"See ya," Fred said, using Julie's normal goodbye.

Chief Weber walked back to the table, but he didn't sit down. He had said his good byes. After a final round of handshakes, he left the Enlisted Club and drove to the U-Haul lot. He had a trailer on reserve.

Once at the storage unit, it didn't take long to load his worldly possessions into the trailer. His entire life fit in a pickup truck and a four by eight U-Haul trailer. The storage unit contained souvenirs and momentous from previous commands and deployments. It had his, now obsolete, stereo component system including eighty pound mega speakers. He had a twenty three inch picture tube television and one fully restored extra plush high backed StratoLounger recliner originally built in nineteen seventy. Once it was loaded, he pulled the trailer to the back of the compound and parked it. It would stay there until they were ready to drive to Helen.

The time seemed to drag. He walked into the office and told them the unit was open and that he had the trailer parked out back. They thanked him for his business.

Now what to do? He drove to the Navy Lodge and got the key cards for both rooms. He inspected them looking to give the better one to Julie. They were the identical mirror image of one another. He put his suitcase on the stand intended for that purpose. He had picked up his Dress White Uniform at the cleaners on the way over. Not to let anything happen by chance, he had checked on it at the cleaners yesterday. He simply chose to leave it where it would be safe. He took the time now to place the collar devices, ribbons and Surface Warfare Insignia in place. He looked over the Dress White

Uniform one more time with the eye of an inspector, it passed. He hung it on the bar provided.

He looked at his watch. It was still four hours before Julie's scheduled arrival time.

Fred thought for minute, then drove to the Navy Exchange Flower shop and bought a bouquet of pink roses and baby's breath to put in Julie's room. He had the girl at the shop arrange the roses in a vase he had purchased inside the store. The vase was cheap clear glass, but he intended to leave it in the room anyway. He just needed something to hold the flowers and the water.

He looked at his watch. That used up a whole thirty five minutes.

Fred had been right. The man had asked Julie if she would like to join him for a drink. She declined. A few minutes later she saw the same man hitting on another woman seated at the gate.

Her phone played a jingle. She took it out and looked at the number. She knew the ring tone, but habit made her look. "Hi June."

"How are you? Better yet where are you?"

"I'm in Charlotte, North Carolina."

"So you're right on time?"

"So far, but now they are saying there will be a delay."

"How long?" June asked.

"One or two hours. Something about the weather."

"Well better to be safe."

"That's what Fred said."

"Call when you get to Norfolk, please. I want to know you're okay."

"I will."

"Good," June said. Then almost absent mindedly, "Bye."

"See ya."

It normally took under twenty minutes to drive from the Naval Base to the airport. Fred knew that, but he left an hour early just in case the rush hour traffic was worse than usual. It turned out the traffic was minimal. He got to the airport forty five minutes before the scheduled arrival time for Julie's flight. He found a monitor and noted that Julie's flight was about an hour behind that schedule. He didn't want to sit in a bar, so he went to the USO lounge. They had fresh coffee and comfortable chairs. He struck up a conversation with a man in a CPO uniform. As often happened, they started comparing notes. They had been on two of the same ships, but at different times. That led to the usual swapping of sea stories.

"You fly in uniform?" Fred asked.

"Always," the fellow Chief replied. "It seems to get you a bit of preferential treatment."

"I guess it would."

"Wasn't always that way. My father did a four year hitch just after Viet Nam. He would never wear a uniform off base. They called him a baby killer. Once he even got spit on."

"I had heard about that," Fred said. "I'm certainly glad that era is over."

"Now, when I travel, I always wear my dress blues. It seems to grease the skids a bit. So where you going next?"

"I'm retiring tomorrow."

"Well... Congratulations!"

"Thanks."

"I was thinking about it. I decided to wait for the E-8 board to get out. I'm glad I did. I got selected for Senior Chief and decided to stay around for a little while longer."

"Looks like congratulations goes both ways."

"I'm not going to set a very good example if I miss my flight." he stood up. "Good to meet you Fred."

"You too, Dave. If you ever get to South Dakota, look me up."

"Don't hold your breath. I spent one summer in Antarctica. I've had enough of the cold. It's Key West for me when I quit."

"To each his own." Fred watched the man leave. For the first time that day, time had moved along quickly. He looked at the clock on the wall. Only twenty minutes more. He walked out to the terminal proper. He stopped short of the security area. He went as far as he could legally go and picked a spot where he could see people walking down the concourse and waited. Every time a cluster of people would walk through exiting from an arriving aircraft, he would watch carefully for

Julie. He had placed himself so he could see everyone as they passed. However, with each passing group of travelers he started to second guess. He wondered if he had missed her after all. The last time he checked the monitor the arrival time was seven fifteen. His phone said it was seven twenty. He watched as another cluster pf passengers walked by. Another five minutes passed. Each minute felt like an hour. He continued his vigil, all the time holding his phone in his hand, wondering if he should call.

Chapter Twenty Four

Then he saw her. His heart skipped a beat and, for a moment, he forgot to breathe. He couldn't help smiling. It was all he could do to keep from jumping and waving.

Julie had seen Fred before he saw her. She was watching the intensity on his face as he looked over the crowd. Then their eyes met and the intensity on his face turned to excitement. Her world exploded around her. Her heart was trying to escape her chest. She smiled and sent a small wave. She got back a smile that was warm and inviting.

They were fifty feet apart when the world went into slow motion. It took Julie what felt like hours to close the gap between them. Once they met, she held him close. She felt Fred return the embrace with gentle strength. She made a mental vow to never let go of him again.

After what must have been close to a minute, but felt like a second, Fred pulled back and looked at her with serious eyes. He smiled and said, "Have we met?"

That broke the tension and Julie laughed out loud. "No, I always pick up sailors at airports."

"How was the flight?" he asked as they turned to start their trek to the baggage claim area.

"It was bumpy going into and out of Charlotte but the rest was fine. I didn't know you bought first class tickets. I had never flown first class."

"You deserve nothing less," Fred said. Then added, "Besides, I had to make up for the third class seating on the trip back to Helen."

"I'm looking forward to the trip since I will have a first class driver."

"A Chief driver, I was promoted from First Class five years ago," Fred said. Not having been around the Navy, Julie missed the joke.

They arrived at the baggage pick up and checked the monitor, They walked over to carousel number three just in time to see the thing start up. Julie found her luggage. Fred gallantly pulled it from the oval shaped conveyor. They turned and walked through the automatic doors into the humid

Virginia evening air. "I'll bet you're hungry," he said.

"Actually, I am."

"Do you like seafood?"

"Sure."

"Then I have the perfect place; it's downtown. They serve the finest swordfish steak on three continents."

"You're on."

"There's the truck."

"That's not ugly, Fred," Julie lied.

"Come on, I know ugly when I see it; just like I know beauty." He reached over and pulled her to his side. They walked the rest of the way with his arm around her waist.

Fred put her luggage into the back of the pick up truck and locked the rear hatch of the topper. He then escorted her to the passenger side and opened the door. "Your chariot madam," he said sweeping his arm and feigning a slight bow.

"Thank you, kind Sir." Julie got in and slid to the middle.

Fred walked around to the driver's side and got in. He didn't start the truck right away; he leaned over and kissed her. She responded in kind.

It might have been hours, it might have been days. In actuality it was about ninety seconds when they pulled apart. Fred's voice sounded throaty when he said, "We'd better get some food."

Julie caught her breath and regained some of her composure. "Good idea."

Fred started the truck. It purred softly in the parking garage stall as if waiting for the next command. Fred didn't move, instead he opened the glove box door and pulled out a small box. Julie's heart leaped. Was he going to... "I bought you a welcome present. I was going to wait until we got to dinner, but I want you to wear it when we get there. He opened the box and showed Julie the heart pendant.

Julie was relieved, disappointed and elated at the same time. "Oh Fred, it's beautiful."

"Let me put it on you," he said. Julie turned sideways on the bench seat of the pick up truck and held her hair out of the way. She felt Fred's hands gently touch the back of her neck and it gave her chills. "Okay, good."

Julie turned around and looked down at the pendant "I

love it."

"I love you," Fred said, knowing he truly meant it.

Julie was taken in the moment. It was all so natural. She leaned in and kissed him again. This time there was a feeling of genuine warmth and caring as much as there was a passion and a yearning. "I love you too," Julie said as they pulled apart. "I knew it the day you left."

"I thought I knew it, then I saw you walking down from the plane and I was sure." Fred put the truck in reverse. "We'd better get moving or we'll be late for dinner."

"You have reservations?'

"No, but the place closes early." Fred drove the fifteen minutes to a downtown restaurant. He pulled up in front and looked at the valet. "I don't have the heart," he said and drove into the parking lot. Fred found a spot just opening near the front door and pulled in. After he got out, Julie slid over and got out with him on his side. They walked together, her arm in his, to the entrance.

The inside of the restaurant was decorated to look like outdoor seating on a wharf. The room was long and narrow. There were murals on both sides depicting fishing boats and sailing ships. Fred guided Julie to the hostess stand. They were greeted by a woman in her fifties who led them to a table about half way back. "That's Casey, she and her husband own the place. He used to fish but he lost most of the use of his left hand in a fishing accident. Doesn't stop him from being a great chef."

Julie just nodded; she was taking in the decor. She saw the nets hanging from the ceiling and the glass ball floats being used as shades for the lighting. The place was both bright and dark at the same time. It would work for a business lunch or for the intimate dinner Fred had in mind. It all depended on where one sat.

"So," he said after ordering a bottle of wine, "you're finished with Alonzo and Rachael?"

"I'm finished with Rachael, Alonso will surface again. He's like a bad penny."

"Like me I guess."

"Not at all like you, at least I hope not. He's a horn dog, jumping from bed to bed. It's only his good looks and smooth talking ways that lets him get away with it."

The meal was ordered and consumed quickly with an urgency that was lurking just below the surface. They decided against desert or an after dinner drink. They elected instead to head directly to the Navy Lodge.

Fred led Julie to her room then pointed out that his was right next door through the adjoining door. He carried her luggage in and placed the bags on the floor. Once the door clicked shut behind them they embraced again. This time there was nothing holding them back, they were alone and there was nothing else in the world. They moved as if by nature to the bed and slowly melted into it. They both knew where this was going and neither saw any reason to stop it. Julie looked up at Fred, her blouse was already half off as was his shirt. "Fred?"

"Yes."

"You don't need that adjoining room. Why don't you cancel it?"

"I'll cancel it in the morning, I'm busy right now," and he leaned in again.

Jean Phelman loved this time of year. The air was warm and fresh. The weatherman had predicted a perfect day. The sun would shine and the high would be eighty six degrees. The predawn air was pegged at sixty two. It was the perfect temperature for a brisk walk to work. She held a part time job at the Quick Stop. She left the house and set a quick pace up the street toward the highway. As she got near the Stewart Godfrey house she saw what looked like a light on inside. She knew Stewart had moved to De Smet to be with his son, and Fred Weber wasn't in town yet. So the light behind the curtains was a curiosity. It was not even six in the morning, so there shouldn't be any workman around yet. As she got closer she saw the curtains roar into flames. "It's a fire!" she shouted to no one. She grabbed her phone and called 911. When the dispatcher answered she blurted out "I'm Jean Phelman, the Godfrey house is on fire!"

"The Godfrey house?" The dispatcher answered. "Do you have the address?"

"I … Uh… Oh, never mind." She put the phone back in her purse and ran the one and a half blocks to Henry

Woodson's house. She banged on the door, "Mayor! The Godfrey house is on fire! I don't have Bob's number and the 911 is useless!"

Henry was awake and had started coffee in the kitchen when he heard the front door bell and the heavy banging. He couldn't understand what the voice was saying but he did understand the urgency. He ran to the door and opened it. "What's going on Jean?"

"Stewart Geoffrey's house is on fire!"

"Okay, I'll call Bob Houser and trigger the alarm."

"There's nobody living there," Jean said.

"I know. Look, stay away from the place. There will be a lot of activity and I don't want you hurt. I've got to get to the firehouse."

Bob Houser was pulled from a dream where he had his wife alone on a deserted south sea island. They had everything they needed, food, water and each other. They were content....

The alarm sounded. Bob reached over to turn it off and it continued. From his dream state he realized it was the fire alarm, not the clock radio. His house phone rang. He was awake enough now to answer, "This is Bob."

"Bob, we have a house fire."

Bob was in his feet in under a second. The rapid movement woke his wife. "What is it Bob?"

"Which house?"

"Stewart Godfrey's."

"I'm on my way, Henry. Don't hold the truck. As soon as you have enough people get it rolling."

"You got it."

The 911 dispatcher was concerned about the phone call. She saw the number was a Kent county cell number. That didn't help. She called back but there was no answer. Her new software system told her the location of the phone and she called the number for the Fire Chief.

"Hello?" Grace's voice was still groggy.

"This is the nine one one dispatcher in Kent. Is this the home of the Fire Chief?"

"Yes it is."

"I had a call a few minutes ago that said something about a house fire."

"We know about it, Bob is on his way."

"I'll note that the fire house is responding. Thank you."

"You're welcome."

Henry arrived at the fire house just as the large overhead doors opened. The primary truck was already running and there were three people climbing into their fire gear. Henry ran to his locker and started gearing up. He heard the truck's engine rev up and drive out of the station. He would get on the second truck.

"We waiting for Bob?" Carl Sands asked from the driver's seat of the second truck.

"No, we'll take his equipment with us," Henry replied. "He has to come in from home." Henry didn't get the chance to ask Carl how he got here so quickly, since he lived farther out than Bob. The question came into his mind and out again before it took any root.

"Okay, I'll get it." Carl jumped down and ran to the Fire Chief's locker.

It was two and half blocks from the fire station to the Stewart Godfrey house. The first truck was there in four minutes. The second arrived six minutes later. The entire volunteer unit, including the Chief was on scene in less than fifteen. Despite their rapid arrival, the house was fully engulfed in flames. "We're not going to save it," Bob said. "Let's work on keeping it contained. Move the four wheel drive to the back alley. Pick up the hydrant on Liberty Street on the way."

Paul and his brother Wesley were the last to arrive. "Sorry Chief. For some reason the ambulance didn't want to start. We got Mike out of bed and he got it going."

"It's all right now?"

"The battery was low, he said keep it running and it will be fine."

"Hopefully we won't need it."

"Amen," Wesley answered.

"Chief, the back of the house just caved in," the radio chirped.

Bob Houser pushed the talk button, "Watch the sparks."

"The rear garage took most of them. It's soaked down

299

pretty good."

"Don't trust it." Bob picked up his phone. He called the Kent Fire Chief. "Larry, Bob Houser, I got a house fire here that could get away from me, can you send an engine my way?"

"You want the whole unit?"

"No, not yet."

"I'll send number three and six men. I'll put the rest on standby."

"Thanks Larry."

"Twenty minutes."

"Chief! The tree!"

Bob looked up to see the fire race up the large cottonwood tree in the front yard. That took the fire higher than the house. Forgetting about the phone call he mechanically hung up and put the phone away. "Get two hoses on that! Knock down those flames. Once that's done we can go back to keeping this in check."

The tree was quickly doused and the volunteer crew continued soaking the surrounding buildings.

Bill heard the phone ringing. He worked it into his dream about selling the capital building. It finally woke him. He opened his eyes. It was dark. He looked at the time, five fifteen. "Who would be calling at this hour?"

"Must be a wrong number, Bill. Let it go to message," June mumbled from her side of the bed.

He followed her suggestion and just as he started to drift off, the ringing started again. He reached over to the phone on the night stand, "Hello?"

"Bill? Mike Finney."

"Mike, do you know what time it is?"

"I know. Look, I wanted you to know. The firemen are at Stewart Godfrey's house. It's on fire."

"What!" Bill pulled himself out of bed and was standing.

"I can see the flames from here, Bill. I'll bet it's going to be a total loss."

"All my brother's stuff is in there!"

"That's why I called."

Bill started to think rationally, the cobwebs had cleared.

"Thanks Mike. I'll get dressed and go over there. Maybe it's not as bad as you think. Thanks for calling."

June was out of bed, "What's wrong?"

"Fred's house is on fire."

"Fred's house?"

"Stewart's house."

"How bad is it?"

"I don't know, I have to get dressed and get over there."

June walked to the window. "I can see the reflection of emergency lights but the window isn't at the right angle. Give me a minute and I'll go with you."

"I'll leave a note for the kids," Bill said.

"They won't wake up, but you're right," June agreed.

"If they do, I want them to know where we went," Bill said.

"And to stay away," June added. "Wait a minute, I can't take Mason. You go ahead."

It took less than three minutes for Bill to get into his Cadillac and drive out of the garage. He didn't get far. The road was blocked at the corner. Bill turned the car around and tried approaching from the other direction. This time he got within five houses of the inferno. He got out and walked toward the house. The sky was getting brighter with the dawn, but the flames were brighter still. Bill saw that there would be nothing left of the house or the contents. He stood with several other watchers and said nothing. He was thinking he needed to find another house for his brother. This one was finished. He was also glad that there were not a lot of Fred's things inside. All of it had been auction purchases. He had only spent about six hundred dollars of Fred's money

He looked at his phone. Five thirty five. That would make it six thirty five on the east coast. Too early. He would call after the ceremony. There was no sense ruining his day. The house would still be gone. He turned and headed back for home.

To the good fortune of the town of Helen, as the Godfrey house continued to burn it folded itself into the basement. The truck arrived from Kent and didn't even pull a hose. It was only forty five minutes from the time of the first alarm. The

301

fire was fully contained inside the basement walls and the hoses were now trained on the remaining cinders. It would be several hours before Bob Houser would declare the fire out and secure the sight.

"How's it going Bob?" Roger Grant was standing next to him.

"Oh, Sheriff," he replied. "I didn't see you standing there."

"I didn't mean to sneak up."

"We've got this. I'm sending the Kent engine home."

"Good. Any idea how it started?"

"The house wasn't occupied. The owner moved out last month and the new renter isn't in town yet."

"So it wasn't careless smoking," the Sheriff said. "Electrical?"

"Who's to know? I'll call the state fire marshal, but I doubt he'll find anything in the ashes."

"Anybody have a grudge?"

"No, Stewart was everyone's friend and Fred Weber hasn't been here long enough to make friends, let alone enemies."

"All right."

"I'll send you my report."

"Good. I'll get the one from the fire marshal too. That should do it. Got time for breakfast?"

"I won't be going anywhere for a while. I want to make sure we don't have a re-flash."

"I doubt that. It looks to me like you're turning that basement into a swimming pool."

"Better that than to lose the town."

"You bet," the Sheriff said. "I'll get out of your way."

"See Ya," Bob said and turned back to the smoldering hole. He walked over and took the lead on one of the hoses.

"Good morning." Fred was laying on his side looking across the king size bed at Julie. She had just opened her eyes.

"Good morning," she said with a smile. "Have you been awake long?"

"About half an hour."

"What have you been doing"?"

302

"Watching you sleep."

"Watching me sleep? Why?"

"Because I had never seen you asleep before. You looked so peaceful I didn't want to disturb you."

"You watching me sleep will never be a disturbance," Julie said. It was so natural. She felt like this was the way it was supposed to be. She didn't want the sensation to end. He reached across and put his right hand behind her head, they moved together.

"Are you going to call Fred?" June asked as she got Mason's bottle ready.

"Not right now."

"He should know. It was going to be his home."

"I thought of that, but this is a big day for him. I don't want to spoil it. Tonight is soon enough."

"You're very thoughtful, Bill."

"Thanks."

"We'd better wake up the kids, it's still a school day."

"I'll do it."

Bill felt his phone vibrate, he looked at the screen. It showed a number he didn't know and 'wireless caller' for a description. "This is Bill Weber," he told the phone.

"Bill, Stewart Godfrey. I guess you heard about the house."

"Yes I did Stewart. I'm so sorry."

"Nothing to be sorry about. I'm just glad your brother wasn't in it yet."

"Me too," Bill agreed.

"Look, I just got off the phone with Bobby Houser. He said the house is a total loss."

"I was over there, it didn't look like anything could be salvaged."

"That's what I'm calling about. The house was insured. I hadn't changed the policy yet so the contents were, too. Anything you got from my auction will be covered as contents. In fact anything Fred had in there is covered. Just make me a list for my insurance man."

"That's good news for Fred. I'll do that."

"Good. Looks like you'll be out the sale. I'm not going to

303

rebuild. There's no reason to. I'll hire the basement filled and that will be that."

"That's probably the best answer Stewart." Bill replied. "The sooner the hole is filled in the better."

"My son knows a man here that has fill dirt. As soon as I can get an all clear from the Fire Marshal, I'll get it done. Tell your brother I'm sorry."

"I'll pass it along. Thanks."

"You bet, we'll see ya."

"Good bye, Stewart." Bill pushed the end button on his phone.

"Stewart Godfrey?" June asked walking back into the kitchen.

"He called to tell me his insurance would cover all of Fred's purchases."

"That was nice of him."

"That solves one problem; a small one. I still have the big one."

"What's that?'" June asked.

"I need to find another place for Fred. I can't think of any place in town."

"Neither can I," June replied. Then added, "What about Oscar Richland? Maybe he has something coming up."

"It's worth a shot," Bill agreed. "I think we could still get the lot and have a house moved in."

"That's another thought," June agreed.

"If we don't get up and get a shower we're going to be late for your own ceremony," Julie said.

"You're right," Fred agreed. "We also need breakfast." Fred bounded out of the king sized bed and cracked the curtains. "It looks to be a beautiful day."

Julie stood up. She was looking at the curtains, "I'm looking forward to seeing the view."

"I like the view just fine right now," Fred grinned.

"Get that idea out of your head, or you'll get a cold shower."

"Aye Aye Captain," Fred said and turned from the curtains. He walked over to the adjoining door and into the other room to find some clothes. "We can both shower at the

304

same time."

"You seem to have developed a one track mind Mr. Weber. Besides, I don't think there's room for that," Julie responded.

"We have two showers."

Julie laughed at her misunderstanding. "That's right, we do."

Julie's phone played her generic ring tone tune. She looked. It was Beverly Smith. "Hi Bev, what's cookin'?"

Julie was surprised when Beverly laughed. "That's funny. You're taking this well."

"Taking what well?"

"You don't know?"

"Know what?"

"Stewart's house burned down this morning."

"What?"

"I thought Bill would have told you by now."

"Bill hasn't called." Julie walked through the adjoining doors to the room next door. She saw Fred's wavy shadow through the rippled shower door.

"That's strange," Beverly said.

"So, tell me what happened."

Fred stepped from the shower. Julie was there to hand him a towel. "That's service," he said.

"Fred, Stewart Godfrey's house burned down this morning."

Fred stopped drying. "That's not funny."

"No, it isn't," Julie agreed. "I just got a call from a friend of mine in Helen. She said it's gone."

"It must be some kind of joke, Bill would have called."

"Maybe you'd better call him."

"Let me get dry first."

"I'm going to go get my shower." Julie turned and went back to the other room.

"Okay." Fred finished the dry cycle grabbed a robe and his phone. He called his brother.

"Hi Fred, today's the big day!"

Fred wasted no time on pleasantries. "What's this I hear about Stewart's house?"

305

"I was going to wait until after your ceremony. The house is gone."

"Gone?"

"Gone, right to the ground. The firemen couldn't save it. The only thing left is the garage out back."

Speaking of garages, was my car there?"

"No, that's still in Tom's barn."

"Well, that's good anyway."

"Stewart called me this morning. He told me your possessions are covered by the insurance."

"Not much there to cover, but thank him. It was a nice gesture."

"I'll start working on finding you another place."

"All right. I have an idea, too. I'll call you later. Don't forget to watch the Ceremony. My guys are setting the whole thing up to stream on the ship's web site."

"Don't worry, we'll be watching."

"Call you later."

"See Ya," Bill said.

"Who was that?" June asked.

"Fred," Bill answered. "He knows about the house."

"How?"

"I don't know. I should have known better than to try to keep it a secret. I guess someone called Julie."

"What's he going to do?"

"I don't know," Bill shrugged. "He said he was working on something. Maybe he's not moving here after all."

Chapter Twenty Five

Julie opened the door to her shower and found Fred standing there holding a towel. "Turn about's fair play," he smiled.

"I guess it is." She took the towel. "Look Fred, I've been thinking; you don't have to get a house. You can just move in with me."

"That would never do," Fred said. "What would the neighbors think?"

Julie giggled, "They're your family."

"Seriously, in a small town like Helen, people would talk. I don't want to put you in that position."

"Let them talk, I love you."

"I love you too. That's why I won't do it your way."

"Well, what's your way?"

"I've never done this before." He bent down on one knee and took her hand, "Julie Sorenson, will you marry me?"

"Fred! I'm naked!"

"You can say yes when you're naked."

"Yes!"

Bill had his laptop connected to the television in the living room. The whole family had gathered to watch the live feed of Fred's retirement ceremony. The camera was on but was left unmanned pointing to the guest seating. "Look," Bill said, "there they are."

"Where?" Jessie asked.

"Walking in from the left."

"That's a pretty dress," June said.

"Look at all the white," Bill commented. "It looks like a convention of ice cream men."

"Bill," June chastised.

"Where's Uncle Fred?" Cory asked.

"Right there in the front, stupid," Jessie replied.

"Jessie!"

"Sorry."

The camera moved to the podium, "Good afternoon ladies and gentlemen. Please rise for the parading of the Colors and the National Anthem."

Cory stood up. "You don't have to stand up, stu..." Jessie ended her sentence abruptly.

"I can if I want," Cory replied.

The ceremony went on without a hitch. Several people made small speeches. There were some final awards to present, and then Fred made his parting speech. After a bit more of pomp and circumstance, Fred walked through the ceremonial bullets and sideboys as the Boson piped him ashore. He then walked back to the beginning and took Julie from the arm of an escort and walked through again.

"That concludes our ceremony. Chief Weber has invited all who wish to attend a reception at the golf course clubhouse. Commander, you may dismiss the crew."

It was about two hours later that Bill heard from his brother, "Bill, Fred. Stop looking for a house. I have it all figured out."

Bill knew his brother, he was either very happy or slightly drunk. He was, in fact, both.

"You have it figured out? You're not coming back?"

"Of course we're coming back. It will just be a few weeks later than we originally planned. Julie and I have decided to take a side trip on the drive home."

"A side trip?" Bill was confused. "Where are you going?"

"Well, I've always wanted to see the Hoover Dam and we're thinking Vegas."

"Vegas? That's one long side step."

"I know, but it's important. You see, there's this Little White Wedding Chapel there we want to visit."

Thanks For Reading

The Fred Weber Story
A Flyover County Novel

Please go to www.flyovercounty.com/ and leave a comment.

You can also go to Flyover County on Facebook and tell me
what you think.
I would love your feedback

Follow Flyover County on Twitter.

Other Books by Richard Skorupski

FLYOVER COUNTY
Available on Amazon

Coming Soon

The Tom Ogden Story

The Frank Stanbauer Story

Justin and Natalie

ACKNOWLEDGMENTS

I would like to thank the following people for their help in writing and editing this book.

Cheryl Skorupski - Ideas and review - The ultimate Muse.

Julie Rutushny - Encouragement and editing - Thanks for your support.

Lillie Bucholz – For her support and proof reading.

Charleen Hofer - and her "Perfect Eye" - for helping with proofreading the final draft.

And one final thank you to the people of Rural South Dakota who have welcomed us city dwellers into their homeland.

COVER BY: Cheryl Skorupski

ABOUT THE AUTHOR

Richard grew up in what is considered by some to be a medium sized town in Central New Jersey, in an area almost equally distant from New York and Philadelphia. He left home for a career the Navy and stayed away for twenty one years before retiring in 1993.

He returned from the Navy to buy the house where he grew up. Ten years later he moved to South Dakota and retired again.

Using money from his writing, on-line sales and his Navy pension, he lives on a hobby farm with his wife Cheryl and enjoys the peace and quiet that comes with rural living.

Made in the USA
Charleston, SC
07 July 2015